I0661321

Visions in Smoke

Heir to the Firstborn, Volume 5

Elizabeth Schechter

Published by Elizabeth Schechter, 2022.

Visions in Smoke

Published by Raven's Wing Books

Previously published as **Heir to the Firstborn: The Crossroads** (Elizabeth Schechter, 2021)

Editor: Michael Schechter
Cover design by GetCovers

Raven's Wing Books

ravens-wing-books.com
ISBN: 978-1-952598-48-7

Table of Contents

What a long, strange trip this has been! And it's not over yet.

Thank you for taking it with me. All of you.

Chapter One

The eastern sky was still streaked with golds and pinks when Treesi came out onto the part of the Palace wall that Jehan called the Water Walk. To the west, out over the sea, the sky was deep indigo blue, and she could still pick out a few stray stars that were behaving like errant children trying to stay up past their bedtimes. She tugged her shawl tighter around her shoulders and started along the walk to the overlook. From the Water Walk, she could see the entire harbor, and far out to sea. It was, according to Jehan, the best place to watch the ships coming into the harbor.

Except there had been no ships coming into the harbor in days. No ships...and no canoes.

Jehan was at the overlook already, leaning his elbows on the wall, staring out over the water.

"You're not sleeping, are you?" Treesi asked as she joined him. She looked down at the water, but already knew what she'd see – the same ships and canoes she'd seen the night before.

"Memfis makes sure I sleep," Jehan answered without looking away from the sea. "And he's already warned me that he's putting me to bed early tonight, so we're ready to ride out early."

"We're really going to leave without them," Treesi murmured. It wasn't a question. They couldn't delay the Progress anymore, not without risking Aria giving birth somewhere en route.

Jehan sighed. "We don't have much choice."

"I know," Treesi said. "It's just...where *are* they? They should be back by now!"

Jehan nodded and looked at her. "I know," he said. "They'll come back. Tomorrow, or the next day. They'll just miss us. And Aleia and Othi, they'll catch up to us in Terraces."

Treesi swallowed, looking out at the sky that was starting to turn a brighter blue, at the sea that looked somehow as smooth as a mirror. "Keep saying that?" she said without turning. "If you keep saying it, maybe it will come true."

"Why do you think I said it?" Jehan stood up, putting one arm around her shoulders. "Come on, sweetheart. Let's go and find some breakfast. We still have work to do. How's Owyn?"

"He was still asleep when I left," Treesi answered, letting Jehan steer her away from the wall. "But he was nervous enough that he had trouble falling asleep. What's so terrible about the Smoke Dancer testing?"

"I haven't any idea," Jehan admitted. "Memfis won't tell me. All he's told me about today is that I should stay close to the room where Meris does the testing, just in case." He snorted as he stepped forward to open the door for Treesi. "Which is why I think every healer in the Palace will be waiting outside that door."

Treesi nodded. "I don't think you'd be able to get Alanar away from the door with a harnessed team of plow horses."

Jehan chuckled, closing the door and starting down the stairs. "How is he?"

"Possibly more nervous than Owyn, enough that he's lost all ability to hide it," Treesi answered. "I don't think he slept at all. He was in the sitting room when I left, and he's snappish. Not knowing what's going to happen only makes it worse. And having him this nervous is only going to make it worse for Owyn when he wakes up." She ran her hand down the railing and followed Jehan down the stairs. "Is there anything you can do?"

"Well, it's too early in the day to take him and get him drunk," Jehan answered. "Maybe I'll borrow the basket of kittens from the kitchen and pour them on him."

"He'd love it until they started to make him sneeze," Treesi said.

"Didn't know that he got cat-sick." Jehan stopped on the landing and waited until she caught up to him. "You really don't think he'll leave the doors?"

"I doubt it."

Jehan nodded slowly. Then he smiled. "I know. Let's take a walk."

"Where?"

"The practice yards."

They headed down more stairs, and out into the Palace courtyard. It was already busy, full of people running this way and that, doing the million little jobs that kept the Palace running. They'd added people to the staff, and Treesi didn't recognize half of the faces.

"By the time we come back, I'm not going to know anyone!" she complained as she followed Jehan around the Palace and through the healer's garden. "There are so many new people."

"The Palace needs all of them," Jehan said, holding open the gate. She followed him out of the garden, and they walked around the wall to the practice yards. She could hear Karse shouting instructions, and the clash of metal on metal as the guards drilled. She looked around, and caught sight of Del. He'd been up with her every morning for days, but when she went to the Water Walk, he came here to practice his archery, and to learn falling stars from Skela. At the moment, Del was on the archery range, holding a crossbow, and as Treesi watched, he raised it and fired, and the quarrel pierced the center of the target with a heavy thump.

"He's gotten very good at that," Jehan said.

"Aria says that it's part of the Air sense. Having extra awareness of balance helps with aim," Treesi said. "She told me when she tried to teach me how to use her javelins."

Jehan smiled. "And are you any good?"

"Not at all." Treesi laughed. "I'm not allowed to use them anymore. I'll stay with my blowgun."

Jehan chuckled. "Where's Karse?" he asked, looking around. "I hear him...there he is." He waved.

Treesi looked and saw Karse waving at them, then coming toward them. The Guard Captain had lost weight over the past two weeks, enough that he was starting to look gaunt. And he hadn't yet lost his habit of looking to his left when he needed to make a decision.

As far as they knew, Trey was alive. But the last time Owyn had danced, he'd spent six hours in trance and frightened all of them to the point that Meris had forbidden him to dance again until after he was properly tested. Which meant that they had to wait until he was strong enough to do so.

Which brought Treesi right back to today.

"Jehan," Karse said, coming up and catching Jehan's hand. "What are you doing up this early?"

"We were on the Water Walk," Jehan said. "Still no signs. And I need your help."

Karse frowned. "Doing what?"

"Distracting Alanar," Jehan answered. He looked around. "You know, we're leaving the Palace tomorrow. I think Alanar needs to drill with his staff fighting. Don't you?"

"Why are we distracting Alanar?" Karse asked.

"Because Meris is testing Owyn this morning," Treesi answered. "And it's scaring the piss out of Alanar."

"Oh," Karse murmured. "Well, do you honestly think we can get him out here?"

"Jehan, maybe having him come out to fight isn't a good idea," Treesi said. "He didn't sleep. His patience is already frayed. It might not be safe."

"I won't let anyone hurt him—" Karse started.

Treesi shook her head. "It's not Alanar I'm worried about," she said. "It's the guards you put against him. Alanar has a temper." She looked up at Jehan. "Did we warn you about his temper?"

Jehan looked thoughtful. "I don't think...wait. Wait. Breaking Teva's arms?"

"I wasn't in Terraces yet," Treesi said. "Marik told me about it. But yes. He was angry at Teva because a practical joke went badly and Malani got hurt. And he broke both of Teva's arms."

Karse whistled. "Right. Let's not get him angry, then." He glanced at Jehan. "Drunk?"

"It's too early," Jehan answered. "Thought of that, though. And if I send him to sleep, he'll never forgive me."

Treesi turned when someone touched her arm. She smiled when she saw it was Del.

"How was practice?" she asked.

"*It's going to rain, and that means Skela's bones hurt. No falling stars today,*" Del signed. "*Which is good, because I'm tired of hitting myself with the practice stars. What are you talking about?*"

"Alanar," Treesi answered. "He didn't sleep because he's worried about Owyn, and you know how nervous Owyn is about today. When he sees how Alanar is reacting, he'll be even worse."

Del frowned slightly. Then he nodded. "*Can I help?*"

"You have an idea?" Jehan asked. "One that doesn't involve alcohol, kittens or sex?"

Del snorted. "*My ideas never involve sex,*" he signed. "*And...maybe? I'm not sure he'll say yes.*"

"Care to tell us?" Jehan asked.

Del shook his head, then looked at Treesi. "*Where is he?*"

"Last I saw, in the suite," Treesi answered. "He was waiting for Owyn to wake up."

"*Is anyone else there? Are Aria and Aven still asleep?*"

Treesi frowned. "I think so. They were when I came out. But Aven's been getting up early to swim because of his hip, so he might be up and out by now."

Del nodded. "*I'll go see if I can distract Alanar.*" He walked back toward the Palace.

Karse watched him go, then turned to Jehan and Treesi. "Any idea what that was about?" he asked.

"None," Jehan answered. "But I trust Del."

Karse nodded. "Yeah. He'll do something. Jehan, do you know if Owyn will be able to do anything after today?" He looked from Jehan to her, and the hope in his eyes was almost painful. "Treesi, do you know?"

"Neither of us know what's involved in the testing," Jehan said gently. "Or if Owyn is going to be able to keep making contact with Milon."

"He'll keep trying," Karse said. "I know him. He'll burn himself to ash trying. And I don't want that. But..." He looked to his left, then flinched and closed his eyes. Treesi reached out and took his hand, and he shivered.

"Come walk with me," she said softly. "Take a moment."

"Yeah," Karse mumbled, his voice thick. "Yeah, all right." He looked down at the ground, then at Jehan. "Keep an eye on them, will you? They know what to do. Just...make sure they don't cut their feet off or anything."

Jehan nodded. "I'll handle it. Go."

Treesi tugged on Karse's hand, leading him back toward the healer's garden. There were benches tucked away inside the fenced area, and she brought him to one and drew him down to sit with her. She started massaging his left hand, kneading the callouses and the ridges that marked where he'd broken bones.

"Tell me about Trey," she said, focusing all her attention on Karse.

"You know about him," Karse said. "Owyn's told you about him."

"I want to hear about him from you," Treesi insisted. "Tell me about him."

Karse shrugged, looking down at the hand she was massaging. "Can you tell I broke that one?"

"I can feel where the bones healed," Treesi answered. "And you're not answering me."

"Trey," Karse murmured. "Known him...nearly four years now. Memfis introduced me to him when he'd just gotten away from Fandor." He took a deep breath. "You know about Fandor? About Trey being one of his brothel boys?"

"I know enough," Treesi answered. "You don't have to tell me the details. I can wait for Trey to tell me if he wants me to know."

Karse nodded. "Trey was a year under his majority. Fandor could have claimed him under guardian rights, and we knew that would mean he'd end up dead. So to keep him safe, we kept Trey hidden in Memfis' forge for a full year. I'd see him sometimes, when I went in to visit with Mem and Owyn. And we'd talk, sometimes. I think I'm the reason he got it into his head that he wanted to be a guard." He smiled. "He told me the night we got married that he'd been in love with me since about halfway through that year. And I never noticed, not once. Took me until the beginning of last winter to see what I had in front of me." He snorted. "We were dealing with someone selling doctored paradise flower. You know that one?"

"I know paradise flower," Treesi answered. "We use it in healing, when we can't use healing trance for some reason. It's safer than dreamflower." She pointed. "It's growing right over there."

Karse coughed. "Really? Are you keeping an eye on it so no one makes off with it?"

"Do we have to?" Treesi asked. "Paradise flower is harmless. As a lotion, it isn't strong enough to do more than relax someone's muscles, and if you make tea from it, you fall asleep before you can drink too much."

"That's normal paradise flower," Karse said. "Not doctored."

"Doctored how?"

Karse took a deep breath and blew it out. "If you soak paradise flower leaves in alcohol, you get a tincture, right?"

Treesi nodded. "That's right. That's how we make the lotion. The tincture gets mixed into melted beeswax and a neutral oil."

"Yeah, but some smart person down in Forge figured out that if you boil off the alcohol, you get concentrated paradise flower oil. And if you soak more paradise flower in the concentrated oil for a few weeks, then dry the leaves and use them like pipeweed, it's hallucinogenic and very addictive. They call it diceweed. Addicts are called diceheads."

Treesi stopped massaging his hand. "It's what? Really? That's horrible!"

Karse nodded. "Surprised you didn't know that. But it might not have made it up to Terraces. They'll have it now, I warrant. With all the refugees? They'll have had someone bring it in." He rubbed his forehead with his free hand. "So, we had someone bring it into Forge. Someone smart. Someone who knew how to hide from us. We finally found them working out of a warehouse off Tannery. My men and I went in to put a stop to it." He paused, and Treesi felt his hand shake in hers. "There were guards. We were expecting that. We weren't expecting them to be as well armed as they were, or as good. They were too good. They...most of the time, we went in after drunks and addicts, their guards are hopped up on the shit, and their weapons are trash. These group? Fuck if I know where they got the weapons, but they were quality. And they were all sober. We were damn near wiped out. And Trey...well, he took a knife meant for me." He stopped again, ran his finger diagonally from his left shoulder to his right hip. "He's got a scar from here to here. Lost a lot of blood. Meris took him in, took care of him while he was healing. We don't have healers like you in Forge. We didn't, I mean. When there was a Forge. Our healers are your healing assistants. So Trey was laid up for the entire winter...when you and Aria got to Forge, he'd only been back on duty maybe a month. Just in time to get people evacuated."

"I remember that scar. I saw it when Jassic shot him in Terraces. Jehan said he'd ask about it."

Karse nodded. "He did. He never told you?"

"No. I had no idea," Treesi murmured. "I couldn't even tell when I met him. He didn't move like he was hurt. And he was...so cheerful."

"He is. He's cheerful even when there's nothing to laugh at." Karse smiled. "I told him that the only thing that stops him from being the happiest man I have ever met is that he makes me happier." His hand shook violently as he shuddered. "I can't lose him. I can't. I wasted so much time not seeing him. Not realizing what I had. I can't—" His breath caught, and Treesi twisted on the bench so she could wrap her arms around him as he crumpled.

"We'll find him," she crooned into his short hair. "We will find him." She looked up, then gently tugged on him. "Come with me. Let's go where it's private."

Karse stumbled to his feet and let her lead him by the hand through the door that led into the healing center. It was quiet inside, and Treesi led Karse into one of the examination rooms. She led Karse to sit down, then went back and closed all the doors.

"We can stay here as long as you need. As long as you want," she said as she closed the examination room door. She sat down next to him, and took his hand, resting her other hand on his thigh. "And I'm here for whatever you need."

He nodded. Then she felt his heartrate spike. He stared at her. "*Whatever* I need?" he repeated. "Treesi—"

"If that is what you need, Karse," she said gently. "I'm a Healer. It's part of what we do."

"But...Treesi, I'm married." He tapped the bracelet on his left wrist. "Fire tribe, we don't take this lightly. We don't marry like this. Not unless it's really, really serious." He ran his fingers over the bracelet. "I'm married. And you...I'm not even sure what you are, other than a Companion."

Treesi started massaging Karse's hand again. "What I am is a Healer. Does this hand bother you when it's cold?"

"Not much. When I get older, it probably will, but I..." He stopped and shook his head. "No. Thank you, but no. I'm not...I'm not replacing my Trey with you. And...and what about Othi? He's my friend." He blinked. "Honestly, he's dizzy over you, girl!"

"I know," Treesi said. "And I'm worried about him. He should have been back by now." She paused, dragging her attention back to Karse. "And that's not what I meant. I'm not looking to replace Trey in your heart or in your life. You're in pain, and I want to help you. Help you manage the pain until he comes back to you." She paused. "Oh. I'm an idiot. You're all Fire, aren't you? I thought you were born in the Palace, but you're all Fire?"

"Yeah. Born here. But grew up mostly in Forge. I think I was five when everything happened, and my mother took me to Forge." Karse nodded slowly. "Yeah, that's about right. What does that have to do with it?"

"It means I should have remembered what the Fire tribe thinks of Healers. Healers the way we are in Earth," Treesi answered. "By your tribal laws, Earth Healers are whores—"

"Now, I never said that!"

Treesi smiled. "You didn't, but I've read your laws. Well, had them read to me. It was part of my training, because we know that there was a healing center in Forge once, and that there might be one again. The healers who might be stationed there needed to know. Now, despite what Fire thinks of us, Earth Healers occasionally work horizontally. Because sometimes, the best way to start easing emotional pain or stress is by release. And the easiest release is sex." She smoothed the skin of his palm with her thumbs. "Sometimes it helps."

Karse frowned. "And sometimes it just makes things complicated." He took a deep breath. "I understand now. I think I knew that, once. But it's been a long time since I last thought about it. It never was an issue in Terraces, and you caught me by surprise. So...thank you, for offering. But until my husband is back and safe, I'm sleeping alone. I'm not sure how he'd react, so I'm not doing anything like what you're offering." He looked at Treesi and smiled. "I do appreciate you offering."

"Even though I made a mess of it?" Treesi asked. "I'm not usually that inept. I promise."

"I didn't think you were," Karse answered. "And let me tell you. If you had given me that opening two years ago? I'd have had you on your back in a minute, and don't think I wouldn't!"

Treesi giggled. "Well, that's a relief."

Karse took her hand, raised it to his lips, and kissed her wrist, right over the pulse. "I do mean it, Treesi," he said as he lowered her hand. "Thank you. I'm feeling less raw. So maybe the shock helped."

"That wasn't what I was planning," Treesi said.

"I didn't think so." Karse stood up, letting her hand go. "Come on. I need to get back to my trainees before they mutiny. Or get lazy." He led the way back out into the garden. As he held open the gate, he asked, "Speaking of plans, what do you think Del is planning?"

"I honestly don't know," Treesi answered. "He has good ideas, though. I think whatever it is, it'll help.

Chapter Two

This was a horrible idea.

Del stood outside the suite door and closed his eyes. Somewhere between the practice yards and here, he'd started worrying that this would only make things worse. That it would make Alanar angry. That he'd go to Steward, and Del's secret would be out.

But he had to do something. He'd told the others he would. And this...well, Alanar himself had given Del the opening. He just needed to take it.

And maybe it would help them both.

He let himself into the suite, and smiled when he saw Alanar sitting in one of the overstuffed chairs, his long legs stretched out and crossed at the ankle. His eyes were closed, but Del could tell he wasn't asleep. He whistled softly, and Alanar smiled.

"Good morning, Del," he said. "Owyn is still asleep. Aven went out to swim. You just missed him. And I'm not sure where Aria is. Possibly still asleep."

Del nodded, then grimaced. He let out a long breath, then took Alanar's hand, tugging on it. Alanar arched a brow.

"You want me to come with you?" he asked, and stood up. "Where are we going?"

Del tugged Alanar's hand and led him across the suite and through the door marked with the Air sigil. When he closed the door behind them, Alanar folded his arms over his chest.

"Why are we in your room?" he asked.

Del licked his lips and took Alanar's hand again, bringing him over to a chair. He looked around his sitting room. It was comfortable, even though he rarely spent a lot of time here during the day. He had a pair of comfortable chairs, and a low table. There were shelves that held his books and keepsakes. His blue-green tea bowls were displayed on one shelf, with Captain standing between them. It was a nice room. A safe room. He was safe here. And Alanar was safe. He could do this. He clasped his hands behind his back and closed his eyes.

"Ah..." he slowly said, trying to enunciate clearly. "Ah...ned...hep."

Alanar sat up straight. "I thought we weren't doing this?"

"Wan...try." Del took a shaking breath. This was harder than he'd thought it would be. Harder, and more terrifying. He was sweating, shivering like he had the ague. He wanted to run, to hide, to cry.

"Del," Alanar breathed, and stood up. He held his arms open. "Come here, love."

Del fled into his arms, burying his face in Alanar's chest. Alanar hugged him tightly, smoothing his hair with one hand.

"Oh, Del," he murmured. "Del, are you sure you're ready for this?"

Del nodded, his cheek scraping against Alanar's shirt.

"I want you to understand what you're getting yourself into, Del," Alanar said softly, his breath ruffling Del's hair. "It's going to take a lot of time, and a lot of work. I'm not sure we'd be able to keep it secret on the Progress." He rubbed one hand up and down Del's back. "But we could wait. It could wait until we get back from the Progress. And that will let you think about it. Be absolutely sure." His hands went still. "This is upsetting you so much, and we're just talking about it. I don't want to upset you anymore."

Del nodded again. Then he turned, hearing Owyn's voice out in the sitting room.

"Allie?"

Alanar tensed. "He's awake. I need to get him to eat something. Come help me?" He let go of Del and stepped back. "Del, I will absolutely help you with this, if that is what you truly want. But I want to know that you truly want it." He frowned slightly. "Come and tell Owyn. Try not to speak to him in his mind. He needs to stay balanced for his test."

Del took Alanar's hand and led him back out of the room. Owyn was standing near the table, and turned to them as they came out.

"There you are!" he said, smiling. "What were you doing?"

Del looked up at Alanar, then signed to Owyn, "*I was asking Alanar to help me learn to talk again. And I had to talk to him to ask.*"

Owyn's eyes widened. "You *asked* him?"

"He did," Alanar said. "And I'll tell you what I told him. I want to be absolutely certain this is what he truly wants. Because just asking upset him. So we'll make it very clear how much work is involved, and what the exercises entail. And then we're going to wait until after the Progress."

Owyn went over and tugged the bell-rope to call for breakfast. "Why so long?" he asked as he turned back.

"*Because I don't want anyone knowing I'm doing it,*" Del signed. "*I don't want my father knowing I'm doing it, because then he'll know I was keeping it from him. And how will I keep it secret on the Progress?*"

Owyn nodded. "Makes sense. Allie, have you eaten?"

"Not yet, no. And I'm sure Del could eat again." Alanar tugged Del into a one-armed embrace. "How was practice?"

"Just archery today," Del signed. *"It's going to rain, so Skela's bones hurt."*

Alanar nodded when Owyn translated. "Maybe later we can go down to the canoe and see if I can help ease the pain," he said. "Once the testing is over."

Del could feel Alanar growing more tense, so he raised his hands. *"How will I know what the exercises are? Are there books?"*

Owyn studied Del, then translated. Then he added, "Allie, maybe after breakfast you can take Del down to the library?" he suggested. "You can tell him what to look for, and he can take those books on the Progress."

Alanar nodded. "This afternoon," he said. "After you're done...." His voice trailed off, and he turned to Del, a quizzical expression on his face. "Del? Were you trying to distract me?"

Owyn groaned. "And I just fucked it up, didn't I?"

Del sighed. *"Yes, and sort of no,"* he signed, and Owyn translated. *"Yes, I was trying to distract Alanar. And I do want to try, and see if I can learn more. I may not talk to anyone but you, but I want to try."* He shivered, and Alanar hugged him closer. *"It seemed like a good idea when I thought of it. A better idea than getting you drunk."*

Owyn laughed. "Whose idea was it to get him drunk?"

"Jehan. And Karse. They both thought of it."

Owyn translated, and Alanar burst out laughing. "Have neither of them ever noticed that I don't drink to excess?" he asked. "It completely destroys my sense of where I am. I can get lost in an empty room. I have gotten lost in an empty room."

"Who is getting drunk? And at this hour of the morning?"

Del couldn't see Aria until she came past Alanar. She went first to Owyn to kiss him good morning, then came over to him and Alanar. "Who is getting drunk?"

"Apparently, there's an idea being bandied around by Jehan and Karse to get me drunk, so I won't worry about Owyn and his test," Alanar answered.

Aria laughed. "They mean well, I'm certain."

Alanar nodded. "They do. So I won't be angry at them. Annoyed, but not angry."

Aria stepped closer and kissed Del on the cheek. "Were you practicing this morning?" she asked as she sat down at the table. Del pulled out of Alanar's embrace and caught his hand, bringing him to join her.

"*Archery today,*" he signed as he sat down next to Aria. "*No dancing. It will rain today. I need to practice when we travel, though.*"

She nodded. "That's a good plan. Now, are you packed?" she asked. When Del nodded, she looked across the table at Owyn and Alanar. "Are all of you packed?"

"I think so," Owyn answered. He sat down next to Alanar and leaned over to kiss his husband. "I'll look again later, make sure I didn't miss anything." He frowned, looking at the door. "I'm not sure what I should eat."

"Well, are you likely to purge?" Alanar asked. "If you are, then you want a lighter meal."

Owyn shrugged. "Not sure, Allie. I didn't the last time, but I'm different now." He closed his eyes. "Del, if you're trying not to be in my head, it's not working. I can hear you thinking about what you're going to sign, right before you do it."

"I asked him to try not to," Alanar admitted. "I didn't want there to be any added stress on you today."

"Thank you, Allie. I'm fine. A little nervous, but fine. Honestly, I think you're worse than I am. I can feel you."

Alanar grimaced. "Maybe I shouldn't be outside the door, then. I'll be a distraction."

Someone knocked, and a servant came into the suite. Behind him was Lexi, who bowed formally, then smiled.

"Good morning," she said. "Shall I bring breakfast, and for how many?"

"I am not certain when Aven or Treesi will be back," Aria said. "Should we have something up for them, or let them ask when they come in?"

"*At this hour, Aven will probably eat with the cousins,*" Del signed. "*But Treesi may be back soon. She was with Jehan and Karse at the practice yard.*"

Aria nodded, then turned back to Lexi. "Bring for everyone, please. Aven may eat with his family, but he may not."

"Very good," Lexi said with a nod. "I'll have everything brought up right away." She paused on her way to the door, then turned back to the table. "Aria, will you have time after breakfast to go over our instructions for while you're gone? Since Steward seems to be so intent on going with you. Mother only knows why — we might as well paint a target on his back!" Owyn snorted, and Lexi blushed. "I apologize," she said. "That was uncalled for."

"No, that was very much called for," Owyn grumbled. "You're right. But there's not a lot of choice. He has to go with us, right?"

"He does," Aria agreed. "He has to be seen by the people. They have to hear from his own lips that the Usurper is no more, that his name has been forgotten. They have to see that Steward is true to me, and they have to see him by my side."

"Yeah, so that no one gets all notional and tries to rise up in his name," Owyn added. "We'll just need to make sure he's got like...half a dozen bodyguards around him at all times—"

Del leaned his elbows on the table and rested his chin on one upraised hand. There was something wrong with Owyn's logic, but he wasn't certain what. His stomach growled, loud enough that Alanar laughed.

"Well, I think that's a clear enough signal," Lexi said with a smile. "I've lingered long enough. I'll go see about your breakfast." She bowed again and left the suite, closing the door behind her.

Aria laced her fingers together and rested them on the table. "We can't assign him a half a dozen guards, no matter how much we want him to stay safe," she said. "It will look as if he's under coercion, or is a prisoner. One guard, perhaps. But that would be true of all of us. Each of us should have a guard when we leave the others. No one should go anywhere alone. But a half dozen guards? No, that's excessive."

Del nodded and sat up. "*And he won't stand for it. Not even if you order him to.*"

Aria sighed. "I'm sorry, I missed the first part. I wasn't looking."

"He says Steward won't stand for that many guards, even if you tell him to." Owyn answered. He nodded. "Del's right." He rubbed one hand over his face.

"Owyn, what can we expect from today?" Aria asked softly. "Knowing something — anything!— will help all of us, I think."

"He won't tell you," Alanar grumbled. "He won't tell me anything."

"I can't tell you!" Owyn protested. "You can't know what happens once that door closes. Not until it's your turn, Aria." He took a deep breath. "And Allie? I want you outside the door. You won't be a distraction. Unless you completely panic, so don't do that, all right?"

Alanar took Owyn's hand, kissing his fingers. "I will try very hard not to panic. But what can you tell us about what will happen leading up to the door closing?"

Owyn looked startled. "I...yeah, I suppose I can talk about that. Granna says they'll come and get me. I'll go down to the room where we're doing this just like this." He gestured to himself, the plain shirt and trousers he was wearing. "Nothing fancy. When we get there, Mem will meet us, and he'll challenge me—"

"Challenge you?" Aria interrupted.

"Yeah, it's part of the ritual," Owyn answered. "You'll see that part. Once I answer the challenge, he'll let me in. And then the door closes and that's all you get to know."

"*Do you bring your smoke blades with you?*" Del signed.

Owyn shook his head. "No. Mem took them, and I won't get them back until I pass the testing." He tugged his hand out of Alanar's, then folded his hands on the table. "I really don't know what to expect. No one has ever done this before. Retesting, I mean. Granna says there's never been a need to retest anyone. So it might just be going through the motions." He paused. "And I'm getting too close to telling you stuff I'm not supposed to tell you, so I'm going to stop talking now."

The door opened, and Treesi came inside, followed by Aven and Jehan.

"Good morning!" Treesi called. "Have you eaten yet?"

"Not yet," Aria answered. "Lexi will be bringing breakfast up soon." She tipped her head back as Aven came to lean down over her, touching his forehead to hers. Then he kissed her and straightened, wincing as he leaned on his walking stick.

"I hunted with Melody, and ate with the cousins," he said. "But I could eat again." He turned to share breath with Del, then kissed him on the cheek before limping around the table to Owyn and Alanar. Once he'd greeted them, he came back to take his usual chair on Aria's other side. Treesi followed him around the table, kissing everyone good morning.

"Owyn, how are you this morning?" she asked as she reached him.

"Calmer than I expected," Owyn answered. He tipped his head back to kiss Treesi, and as she sat down, he looked over at Jehan. "So, you're getting my husband drunk? Without telling me?"

"No, we decided that it's too early for that," Jehan answered. "Del, you told them that?"

"*They figured out I was trying to distract Alanar.*" Del answered. "*Alanar thought it was funny that you and Karse thought of the same thing.*"

"Jehan, I don't drink to excess," Alanar added. "One glass of wine, maybe two. That's my limit." He smiled. "But thank you for trying to take care of me. Even if it means you'd have had to nurse me through being completely lost until I was sober."

"Come and sit, Jehan," Aria said. "Have breakfast with us."

A few minutes later, Lexi led a parade of servants into the suite, carrying trays laden with covered bowls and platters, pitchers and teapots, and plates, bowls and cutlery. They loaded the table and the sideboard, and Lexi nodded her approval as the last cover was whisked away to reveal the fragrant rice-and-fish dish underneath.

"Very good," she murmured. "Now, you all prefer to serve yourselves, so I'll leave you to it."

"Thank you, Lexi," Aria said. "We will ring if we need anything."

Lexi bowed and led the servants out, and Aven stood up, picking up an empty plate.

"Who wants what?" he asked.

They ate, and talked about the Progress. Del looked around the suite.

"*I'm getting tired of settling in and then having to leave again,*" he signed.

"I think we all are," Aven agreed. "We're comfortable here. But we have to do this. Even if it wasn't required, we'd still need to go. We need to be seen."

"And we need to see," Aria added. "We need to see what's out there."

Del nodded. "*It will be nice to get back to Terraces, though. I miss Rhexa and Pirit.*" He glanced over at the door. "*And I think I'm not the only one who missed Rhexa.*"

Aria looked amused. "Del, are you gossiping?" Her smile widened. "Is it very good gossip?"

Del grinned. "*Fa has been sending a lot of letters out with Destria on the regular message runs to Terraces. A new letter every run.*" He looked at the door again. "*He's started carving again. He hasn't done that since Mama died.*"

"Carving," Owyn repeated. "You mean like Captain?"

Del nodded. "*He would carve little figures, and give them to Mama. They made her laugh. The last time he touched his carving tools was when he tried to make a new soldier for me.*" He smiled. "*I think he's making a present for Rhexa.*"

Alanar laughed. "Owyn, you said it, didn't you?"

"What, that at some point Steward might ask Auntie Rhexa for something more than a night?" Owyn nodded. "Yeah, I did. And if it happens, I'd have absolutely no objections." He paused. "Except that Steward might end up moving to Terraces. Because I can't see Auntie Rhexa moving here. She and Lexi would be like two cats in a box."

Del sat up. "*You think he'd leave?*" he signed, and saw Owyn wince. "*Oh. Sorry. Did I shout?*"

"Just a little, love," Owyn answered. "Still echoes when you do that. And I don't know. And I don't think we should worry about it, either. Whatever happens, happens." He looked down at his plate. "Jehan, can I have some more of that rice? It's really good. I need to learn how to make that."

"Ask Lexi," Jehan said. "She'll give you the recipe. And you may have a little more, but only because there's fish and eggs in it."

Owyn started to reach for the serving bowl, only to stop when someone knocked on the door. When the door opened, Afansa was in the corridor.

"Owyn," she said. "It's time."

Chapter Three

The corridor they wanted was right off the main entryway, which was empty when they reached it. That alone was odd — there were always people in the entryway, servants and guards and visitors passing in front of the ornate double doors that led into the Hall. But now, there was no one, except for a single person standing before the door at the end of the corridor. Owyn knew it was Memfis, even though he couldn't see his adoptive father's face. No one else in the Palace would have the right arm of their shirt pinned up to their shoulder so it wouldn't hang loose. Memfis was dressed head to toe in gray, and wore a gray veil that obscured his face.

"What is he wearing?" Aven whispered.

"He is the Smoke," Owyn whispered back. "It's part of it." He turned to face them. "This is where I leave you. I'll see you on the other side." He forced a smile. "I'll be all right. You don't need to worry about me."

"You realize that saying that only makes me worry more?" Alanar asked. He pulled Owyn close. "I wish I knew what you were going to be doing. I wish you could tell us." Owyn felt him shiver. "I wish I understood."

"I'm sorry, Allie," Owyn whispered. He hugged his husband tightly, then stretched up to kiss him. "Does it help if I tell you that the last time I did this, it took under an hour?"

"No," Alanar answered. "Because the first time you danced in the caves in Terraces, it took about three-quarters of an hour. This last time, it took you six hours to wake up."

Owyn grimaced. "Sorry. I thought it might help. I just...I just keep making it worse." He hugged Alanar more tightly. "I...I don't have to. I can...I can just not do it."

"No," Alanar said. "No, you have to. We need to know how to control the heart visions before they kill you." He shivered again. "I...I'm not helping at all. Maybe I should have let them get me drunk. Or knock me out. Or...or something." He laughed, sounding strained. "I love you. I'm scared—"

"I know," Owyn said. "I know. I love you, too. And I told you my new waking vision. You're stuck with me for a long time yet." He tugged out of Alanar's arms, looking around. "Aven, would you—" He paused, looked up at Alanar. "I don't need four healers here. Jehan can stay. You and Treesi, you take Alanar back to the suite. You take care of him."

Alanar looked shocked. "You...I...what?"

Aven rested his hand on Alanar's shoulder. "Only if he agrees, Mouse."

Owyn smiled and nodded, then tugged Alanar down so he could whisper in his ear. "Let them take you back to the suite. Let them take care of you. And let them help you."

"Take care of me?" Alanar asked.

Owyn laced his fingers into Alanar's short hair, tugging gently. It was enough to make Alanar shudder, and Owyn smiled. "Yes, take care of you."

Alanar snorted. "I thought you wanted to be there to watch when that happened," he whispered back.

"I'm patient," Owyn laughed. "Really patient. We won't have a chance to do that again until we're back. So go do it now, and you can tell me about it later. Bedtime stories."

Alanar laughed again. It had a wet sound to it, almost like a sob. "Bedtime stories," he said with a nod. He kissed Owyn, hard enough that their teeth clicked together. "You had better be awake for them."

"I'll do my best," Owyn promised. "Fishie?"

"We'll take care of him, Mouse," Aven said. He kissed Owyn, then took Alanar's hand. "Come on. Let's see if I learned anything."

Treesi threw herself at Owyn and hugged him tightly, then kissed him. "You be careful," she warned. "Or...or I'll turn your ears around."

"Turn my..." Owyn burst out laughing. "What kind of a threat is that?"

She made a face at him. "I'm horrible at threatening anyone. I'll come up with something better later." She kissed him again, then let him go and went to take Alanar's other hand. Together, Aven and Treesi led Alanar down the corridor and away. Once his husband was gone, Owyn sagged.

"Well, now that I don't have to keep the brave front up anymore," he said softly. "Right. I'm going. I'll be done when I'm done."

Aria held her hands out to him. He took them, and let her pull him into a tight embrace. For the second time, he hesitated. Did he really need to do this? He was already a Smoke Dancer. He didn't have to test again.

But he was more than a Smoke Dancer now, wasn't he? What, he wasn't sure. Maybe this would tell them.

Alanar was right. He had to do this. He had to know.

"Don't you worry about me," he said softly. "There's nothing to this, really. You'll see."

"In a year or two, it will be my turn," Aria replied. "And will you be the one who stands at the door as the Smoke?"

He smiled. "If you want me there. I'd be honored."

She kissed him, gently at first, then with more heat, and he pulled her tighter to him, holding her closer, breathing her in. She drew back slightly, resting her forehead against his, breathing with him the way she would with Aven. "That's not the only place I want you."

Owyn chuckled. "I'd be honored," he answered, and she giggled. "But perhaps not tonight. I'm not sure what state I'll be in, and Alanar is going to want to be sure I came through safely."

Aria stepped back, nodding. "I understand." She looked past him, at the door, and the figure standing there. She nodded. "Go on. Does...does one wish a Smoke Dancer good hunting or good dancing?"

Owyn laughed. "I don't know. We'll ask Granna later." He kissed her again, then turned to where Del was standing. "Thanks, for trying to distract him."

Aria blinked and turned to Del. "How were you trying to do that?"

"*I asked his help with some research,*" Del signed.

In Owyn's mind, he heard Del growl in annoyance, and realized his mistake. He reached out and rested his hand on Del's shoulder, tugging him closer for a quick hug.

"Sorry," he whispered. "But thank you."

Del snorted. He nodded and kissed Owyn on the cheek, then stepped back and took Aria's hand. Owyn smiled at them, then turned back toward the door and the Smoke. He closed his eyes, took a deep breath, and walked forward. He knew what to expect.

As he approached, Memfis shifted, barring the way. "Who seeks the Smoke?"

The first time Owyn had done this, he had been nervous enough that he nearly forgot his name. Now, he had an entirely new name, which he once again nearly forgot. "Owyn," he stammered. "Owyn Jaxis, son of Huris of the Smoke. Son of Dyneh. Son of

Memfis of the Smoke. I've come to claim what the Smoke holds and hides. I have come to claim the Smoke for myself."

The figure tipped his head to the side, and Owyn could almost picture Memfis smiling at him.

"The Smoke will not be claimed by force," he answered. "The Smoke chooses to claim only those who are strong enough to bear it." He stepped out of the way, and opened the door to reveal billows of smoke inside the room. "Enter, and see if the Smoke will claim you."

Owyn bowed, then walked forward. The last time had been in a cave that had smelled of hot iron, sulfur, brimstone and something that he never really could explain. This time, he couldn't identify the incense that had filled the room with scented clouds, but the smell was close. Close enough. He stepped inside, hearing the door closing behind him, plunging the room into near darkness. The only light came from a brazier in the middle of the room. In the dim glow, he could see the veiled figure seated on the other side. He walked forward, and went to one knee in front of the brazier.

His smoke blades were on the floor in front of him. When he'd done this at the beginning of his training, there had been no blades — he hadn't yet earned them. What were they doing here? It took all of his will not to reach down and pick them up. He bit his lip, took a deep breath of the heavy, scented air, and looked up at the veiled figure.

"I am Owyn Jaxis, and I come to speak to the Smoke," he said.

"The Smoke listens."

It was Meris' voice...but it wasn't. She was the Lady of the Smoke. Owyn shivered, even though the room was warm.

"I have seen things that were not," Owyn said. "And I have seen things that will be. The Smoke calls me."

"Then you must listen," the Lady of the Smoke answered. "What does the Smoke say? Where lies your end?"

Owyn smiled. "I will die old," he answered. "In my own bed. In my own time, and with my loved ones with me." All at once, he realized that Alanar hadn't been in that vision. Would Alanar die first? He swallowed. "The Smoke knows I have died already," he added. "I died, and was reborn."

"The Smoke knows," the Lady agreed. "And now we must see what the Smoke says. Come closer to the brazier and sit."

Owyn shifted, moving his smoke blades to the side and sitting cross-legged on the floor on one side of the brazier, watching as the Lady threw a handful of something onto the coals. It hissed, and gave off another billow of fragrant smoke. This wasn't what had happened the last time. He had no idea what was going to happen now.

"You have danced the Smoke."

Owyn nodded. "I have. I was named a Smoke Dancer already. And after I died and was reborn, I danced again, and saw my new end. I am a Smoke Dancer still."

The Lady held her hand out over the brazier. "Take my hand. We will seek the truth in the Smoke together."

Owyn coughed. "I—" He swallowed. If he objected, they were done. There were no second chances when the Smoke called. He reached out and took the Lady's hand, feeling the rising heat from the coals against his skin.

"Breathe, Owyn Jaxis. As you were taught."

Owyn closed his eyes and took his first deep breath.

His skin tingled.

His second deep breath.

Every hair stood on end.

He took his third deep breath, and fell through the floor and into darkness and smoke. He could still feel a hand in his, and he clung to it. The Lady was his anchor. If he lost her, he'd never find his way back.

He heard laughter, and headed toward the sound, bringing the Lady with him.

"*I was wondering when you'd come again.*"

Owyn would have smiled if he'd had a face. "*Hello, Milon. How are you?*"

"*Glad to touch your mind, my boy,*" Milon said. "*And, to answer your question, hungry, cold and worried. They took Trey out quite a while ago, and I don't know why. I can't hear anything.*" He paused. "*We've stopped, and we're not in the cart anymore. I'm not sure where we are. Some kind of a cellar, I think. The walls are damp and cold. Trey says that there is an air vent, but it is up too high for him to reach. I...*" He paused again. "*I...are you...is there someone with you?*"

"*I'm being retested,*" Owyn answered. "*Did Trey tell you I died, and that Aven brought me back?*"

"*Yes,*" Milon said. "*Funny, that. I'm told I did the same.*"

"*You what?*" Owyn squeaked, and felt a surge from the Lady.

Clearly, Milon felt it, too. "*Owyn...who is with you?*" he asked slowly. "*I...no. No, it can't be. They told me she died!*"

Then, Owyn heard another voice. "*My darling. I thought I'd lost you. Oh, my darling boy.*"

"*Grandmother—*" Milon's mental presence shattered, and Owyn knew he was alone in the dark with the Lady.

"*Come back,*" the Lady said. "*Come back and let me look into you. Let me see the truth in the heart of your world.*"

Owyn turned back to the Lady, and felt her mind meet his. Felt her warmth, the depth of her love for him. Had this been what Milon had felt? He could understand why he'd lost his control and fallen out of their connection.

No, he needed to focus. He drew himself back, basking in the Lady's warmth.

"*The paths of your heart are like thoroughfares,*" she murmured. "*And the threads that bind you to your loves are like cables. It's no wonder that you're so open to their minds. Your barriers are as clear as glass."* She paused, then laughed. *"Nerris, who loved with his whole being, and who knew the heart of the world as he knew the palm of his own hand."*

"What's that?" Owyn asked. *"Sounds like a verse."*

"It is," the Lady answered. *"It is, and I'd forgotten it. Come back now, my Owyn. We've been here long enough."*

Owyn started to follow, and felt a tug. The tug turned to a pull, and the pull to a jerk that pulled his hand free, dragging him away from the Lady and into the darkness.

He opened his eyes to green — dozens of shades of green, more than he ever knew existed, painting the grass and the leaves and the moss on the rocks, and even the buds of flowers not yet open. He rolled onto his knees and looked around. This wasn't a vision. This was real. And it was nowhere he knew. He slowly got to his feet.

"Owyn."

He turned, and saw a woman sitting on a rock. He blinked — he'd just looked at that rock, and there had not been a woman sitting there. She seemed familiar. Older than Rhexa, younger than Meris. She reminded him a little of Aleia.

"I...hello?" he said slowly. "Where are we? And...ah...do...do I know you?"

She smiled, and her smile was full of warmth and love and laughter, and her eyes were the bluest he had ever seen. And all at once he realized who she was. Who she had to be, to have pulled him out of the Smoke like this.

He dropped to his knees and ducked his head. "Mother. I'm sorry. I didn't know—"

Her laughter was like bells. "There's no reason you should have known, my son. It's been a very long time since I last spoke to any of my children like this." She paused. "You're very quick. You are very much like him, you know."

"Like...who?" Owyn looked up. "Who am I like?"

"Nerris. Your distant father." She held one hand out. "Come closer, my son. I won't hurt you."

"Didn't even think that for a minute. Never even crossed my mind. But I bet you knew that," Owyn said. He got up and moved closer, sitting tailor-fashion at the Mother's feet. He took her offered hand, and felt warmth racing up his arm. He sighed and closed his eyes. "What are you doing, though?"

"Resettling your new gifts," she answered. "You are unbalanced, which is why it's hurting you to see so deeply. That was not what I intended, and I'm making it right."

"Oh," Owyn murmured. "Thank you. And...you did that? Why?" He tried to think, but the warmth was making him relaxed and sleepy. Could he sleep here? No, Owyn. Focus. "Jehan said you changed us. All of us. You made me have heart visions, and you made Aven a level five healer."

"I did change you," she answered. "But at the same time, I did not. You had the potential. You all did. I honed it."

"You refined it," Owyn said, opening his eyes as the warmth faded. "I think I told that to Jehan once. That you were refining us, like burning the impurities out of ore."

She laughed. "Yes, you've said that before. You are correct. I had hoped that I would not need to act thus. I thought that perhaps one of my chosen might be able to succeed without intercession. But this has become too urgent." She paused, then shook her head. "I did not act on my chosen daughter Yana, and I failed her. I cannot fail my chosen daughter Aria, or the Companions who walk with her. We no longer have the luxury of time."

"What?" Owyn asked. "Why?"

"Because Adavar has lost patience." the Mother answered. "He began to wake when our daughter Tirine died. He is awake now, and not pleased. If nothing is done, if the Firstborn falls, or his Heir, then Adavar will rise."

Owyn frowned, then remembered Aven saying something. "Father Adavar rolling in His sleep," he murmured. "That's what the Water tribe calls a quake. Aven said we don't want Him to wake. And...and Mem said He was close to it. Close to waking." He swallowed. "He's awake already? What...what happens if He does rise?"

"He is awake. And watching. And if He rises, then everything ends," the Mother answered, her voice barely a whisper.

"Everything ends?" Owyn repeated

The Mother nodded. "There," she said as she let go of his hand. "You shouldn't feel as much of a strain when you use your gifts now. It will still drain you, but not as much."

"I...thank you. I mean...thank you for making it so I don't fall on my face every time I dance. But what do you mean everything ends?" He frowned. "Aleia thinks that Aven getting tortured triggered the storm, and me dying triggered the Smoking Mountain blowing up and destroying Forge. If Aria or Milon dies, everything blows up?"

The Mother nodded. "They must be protected."

Owyn smiled. "We're doing that. With Aria, anyway. And we're going to find Milon. Trey will take care of him until we find them both."

The Mother met his eyes. "Trey can no longer protect him. We no longer have the luxury of time, Owyn."

"Trey can't?" Owyn looked down at his hands, his mind racing. Trey was alive. He was sure of that. But... "I...can't *you* stop her? Risha, I mean. Can't you...do something?"

She shook her head. "Risha has turned her face from me. She is no longer one of my children. Which means I no longer have power over her."

"That..." Owyn frowned. "That seems like a big problem. If you don't mind me saying that."

She smiled ruefully. "It has never been one before. Hopefully, it will not be again. Now, I must send you back, before your grandmother grows too worried. She fears that she lost you in the Smoke."

"May I ask you a question, before you send me back?" Owyn asked. He folded his hands in his lap. "I...I was wondering. My parents. My real parents. I don't remember them at all. I have a lot of people telling me what they think Dyneh and Huris would think of me, but...you'd know, wouldn't you? They went back to you."

The Mother smiled. She leaned forward and kissed Owyn on the forehead. "Your mother and father love you very much, Owyn Jaxis."

Owyn blinked. "They do? I...but—"

"They do. And one day, you'll meet them. I promise you that. But for now, it's time to go back." She reached out and touched his forehead, right between his brows. "You will not remember our conversation. Not now."

"But—"

"Soon, Owyn. You will remember soon. Now, go back."

Owyn gasped and opened his eyes, seeing Meris sitting on the floor next to him, looking down at him. She smiled wearily. "There you are," she said. "I thought I'd lost you. How do you feel?"

"I..." Owyn sat up slowly and looked around. There was a lamp burning, and the drapes were open, filling the room with light. The windows were open, too, and the smoke from the brazier was clearing. "No, I'm all right." He turned to Meris. "I feel fine. Did I pass?"

Meris laughed. "You did, indeed. And I have a better idea of what is happening to you now. I'd forgotten that old verse. Now, I need to find it again." She patted him on the knee. "Help an old woman off the floor, and we'll go tell everyone you're perfectly fine."

Chapter Four

A ria looked up as the door to the meeting room opened, reaching out to touch Del's shoulder. He jerked, and she realized that he must have fallen asleep sitting on the floor next to her. He'd insisted that she sit down, bringing a chair out of one of the other meeting rooms. Then he'd sat down next to her and leaned his head against her leg. To keep her from getting back up to pace, she assumed. She hadn't expected him to fall asleep. Now he scrambled up to his knees, blinking furiously. Across from them, Jehan and Memfis both straightened, intent on the opening door.

Owyn came out, his smoke blades cradled in his left arm, and with Meris on his right. He looked at them, then grinned.

"Well, I...sorry, I decided to be boring today."

Memfis coughed. "Be boring? Did...Meris, did it not work?"

Meris patted Owyn's arm. "It worked beautifully. Our Owyn will be just fine. Whatever it was that unbalanced him so badly seems to have resolved itself in the testing. Now, I will need to do some research, see if I can find the original text to *The First Companions*. Do you know if there's a copy in the library here?"

Del started signing, and Owyn smiled. "Del says there are three. And one of them is kept in a locked case. Steward says it's old enough that it may be the original, and no one handles it without gloves on." He shook his head. "I want to see that. I didn't know books could be that old."

"We'll see it later, my darling," Meris said, patting his arm again. "Now, go see to your Heir." She looked around. "And your husband. Where's Alanar?"

"I sent him off with Aven and Treesi, because he was close enough to panicking that we were worried he'd tip me over the edge," Owyn answered. "So I should go see what they're up to."

"And eat something. You should eat something," Aria added. "Come, and we'll go find them, and see what there is to eat. And we'll let them know you're safe and well." She held her hand out, and Owyn left Meris' side and came to her. He ignored her outstretched hand, handing his blades to Del before pulling Aria into a tight embrace. She wrapped her arms around his neck and closed her eyes, relief washing over her. He was safe. He was whole. And he was still hers.

"What happened in there?" Jehan asked. "I know you said he's fine, and I can tell he's nowhere near as off-balance as he was when he went in. I don't even need to touch him to tell that. What did you do? What did the testing do?"

Meris shook her head and laughed gently. "Jehan, you know I can't tell you that."

"Even if I swear to treat it with healer confidentiality?" Jehan asked. "This might help someone else."

"There's no one else like our Owyn," Meris said.

"No," Aria agreed. "There is no one else like my Owyn."

DEL HELD OWYN'S HAND all the way back to the suite. He also carried Owyn's blades, because Aria refused to relinquish Owyn's other hand.

"You know, I have no idea what kind of mischief they're going to be up to in there," Owyn said as they reached the suite. "Maybe we should let them be? Go down to the kitchens for a bite, come back later?"

"Aren't you curious?" Aria asked. "I am."

Owyn looked at her, and laughed. "You just want to watch."

Aria blushed. "And what harm is there in that?"

Owyn turned to look at Del. "Will this be uncomfortable for you?"

Del shrugged one shoulder. "*I don't know. If it is, I can go to my room.*"

Owyn nodded. "All right. Then let's go see."

Aria opened the door, and they entered the empty sitting room. Owyn looked around, then shook his head. "Aven's room, or mine, or Treesi's?"

"Probably yours," Aria answered. "Especially if there is mischief." She looked at Owyn. "What sort of mischief, do you think?"

"No idea," Owyn admitted. He let Del's hand go, and turned to him to take the smoke blades. "I know what Allie likes, and I know how curious he is. So I'm thinking that pretty much anything Aven thinks of will be fine by him. Especially since I can't think of what Aven might know that Allie doesn't."

The door marked with the Fire sigil opened, and Treesi peered out, then burst out laughing. "I told you I heard him!" she called over her shoulder. The door closed; when it opened again and she came out, she was tying the sash of a dressing gown. She glanced at Del, and he realized why she'd bothered.

Del smiled. "*You don't have to cover up because of me,*" he signed. "*I'm getting used to it.*"

"I don't need to make you uncomfortable, either," Treesi answered. "I got it, didn't I?" When Del nodded, she laughed. "I'm getting better at this!" She looked over her shoulder, then grinned. "Want to see? Aven has interesting ideas, and Allie—"

"Likes being watched," Owyn finished. "Del? You're welcome to come look."

Del hesitated. Normally, watching the others didn't appeal to him, but hearing Treesi say that Aven had interesting ideas? He was curious to see what those ideas were. He nodded, so Owyn put his blades down, and Del followed the others into the Fire suite. Owyn went through the bedroom door first, and Del heard him burst out laughing.

"You used every rope we had, didn't you?" he asked.

"What?" Aria followed him inside. "Oh!"

Now, Del was definitely curious. He peered around the door, and stared.

The bed in Owyn and Alanar's room was wide, and had tall posts at all four corners. Aven had used rope to create a web between the posts at the foot of the bed. Woven into that web was Alanar, arms and legs spread wide. Owyn was on the bed, kneeling in front of his husband, a silly grin on his face.

"Like this, do you?" he asked, and reached out to run one hand down Alanar's side. Alanar whimpered and pulled on the ropes, but it was clear he wasn't going to be able to free himself from them.

"This is impressive, Aven," Aria said. She moved over to stand with Aven, who was standing by the far bedpost, a coil of rope in his hand. He had removed his shirt, but was still wearing his kilt, and there was a prominent tenting in the front of it. "Are you not finished?" Aria asked. "Do you need more rope?"

"I wasn't sure," Aven admitted. "I was checking the connections and the knots, making sure it wasn't going to be too tight." He ran one hand down Alanar's outstretched arm, prompting another moan.

Del stepped closer, studying the knots. "*This is like canoe rigging,*" he signed, and heard Aven laugh.

"A little, yes." Aven laid down the rope he was holding. "Del...I'm not even sure what I'm asking. Are you...?"

"*I'm fine,*" Del signed. "*Just...I've never seen anything like this before. This is...isn't this very elaborate? It must have taken a long time.*" Curiosity got the best of him, and reached out and ran his hand down the length of Alanar's spine. Alanar whined, loud enough to startle Del back a step.

"He liked that," Owyn said. "Del, you can touch him again. He liked it."

Del met Owyn's eyes. "*He likes this?*"

Owyn grinned. "A lot. And he really liked you touching him."

"Yes," Alanar groaned. "Yes, please. Just touch."

Treesi cleared her throat. "Maybe...we should let them be?" she suggested. "Aven, we can...go back to my room. Or...or your room?"

"Or mine," Aria offered. She nodded toward the coil of rope. "And bring that."

Aven's brows rose. But he didn't answer. Instead, he moved to press against Alanar's back. "Shall I leave you with them?" he asked. "With Owyn and Del? Wrapped up nicely for them?"

"A present for me? And it isn't even my naming day," Owyn crooned. Then he laughed. "Not that I know when that is."

Aven laughed. He kissed Alanar's shoulder, then stepped back and picked up the coil of rope. "My Heir?"

Aria laughed. She went to the bed and leaned past Alanar to kiss Owyn. She kissed Alanar, then kissed Del. Instead of her usual light kiss on the cheek, she kissed him on the lips.

"If this interests you, my Air, then perhaps we can explore it further," she whispered. She ran her nails down Alanar's spine, making him yelp. Then she left, taking Aven and Treesi with her.

"Well," Owyn murmured. "Del, if anything makes you feel weird, you don't even worry about it. You just go."

"*I'm fine,*" Del repeated, this time in Owyn's mind. "*I...will he like it if I touch him again? Does he want me to do that?*"

Owyn smiled. "Allie, Del wants to know if you want him to touch you."

Alanar shifted in the ropes and Del realized he was pulling against them. Pulling toward Del.

"Yes," he groaned. "Yes, please. Del, please."

Del blinked, his mouth suddenly gone dry as he realized something.

Alanar would never hurt him. Not intentionally. He knew that. But like this?

Alanar *couldn't* hurt him. He couldn't move. Which meant...he was safe.

"*Owyn? Help? What do I do?*"

"Just touch, love. That's all you have to do."

AVEN DROWSED ON THE bed, a beautiful woman on either side of him. Aria seemed to be deeply asleep, but Treesi was awake. He'd have liked to hold them, but Aria had lashed his wrists together and tied them to the headboard.

"Do you wonder what they're doing, across the suite?" Treesi murmured. She started tracing the edges of his chest tattoos with her nails.

"I'm more interested in what we're doing on this side," Aven answered. He looked up at the headboard. "And if you have other plans for me." He tugged on the ropes. "Trees, I forget. Who's supposed to be in the healing center this afternoon? We're not ignoring our duties, are we?"

"Your father took this afternoon," Treesi answered, and rested her head on his chest. "So stop fussing. You'll wake Aria."

Aven sighed and closed his eyes. "Don't tickle," he murmured. "I'd like to have us all in one bed before we leave. I doubt we'll have a chance to do that again before we get back."

Treesi nodded, her hair sliding against his skin. "I'd like that," she answered. "Aven, do you think they're all right?"

Aven blinked. "I...you're not talking about Owyn and Alanar and Del, are you?"

"No," Treesi shifted so that she could look at him. "I'm worried about Othi."

Aven nodded. "Ah. I should have known. Fa told me you've been keeping him company." He took a deep breath. "Trees, I don't know. I'm worried, too. And we're leaving. If they don't catch us in Terraces, we won't know anything until we get back. I don't like that at all." He looked toward Aria. "But we can't wait."

"We cannot," Aria murmured, and raised her head. She stretched up to kiss Aven, then leaned across him to kiss Treesi. "I don't want to stay in ignorance for so long either, but we cannot delay the Progress anymore. We've waited long enough as it is." She smiled. "And we should not delay our preparations any more, as lovely as this is. We have work to do today."

"Oh, does that mean I don't get to stay tied to the bed all day?" Aven asked, grinning. Aria made a face at him, then dragged her nails over his ribs, making him yelp, "No tickling!"

Laughing, Treesi reached up and untied the knots. Once he was freed, Aven stretched and gathered both women to his sides. Aria kissed him again, then pulled away and got out of bed, stretching and flaring her wings wide.

"Aria, how long before you can fly again?" Aven asked. "Once the baby comes?"

"A few weeks," she answered. "Am I obvious? I miss flying."

"You're not obvious, and I miss watching you fly," Aven said. He sat up and stretched again, wincing as his hip spasmed. Next to him, Treesi grimaced.

"I felt that," she said. "We'll work on it again. I really have no idea what you did when we rode out. It shouldn't still hurt like that."

"I'm going to ask Grandmother to look at it when we get to Terraces," Aven said. "Fa said I should." He looked at the door. "Now, are we all curious?"

"We'll go and check on them once we're all ready," Aria said. "Are we bathing together, or going to our own baths?"

They separated to bathe and dress, and met in the sitting room. Without saying anything, Treesi went and knocked on Del's door. When no one answered, she looked at them.

"He must still be with Owyn and Allie," she said. "Do we check on them?"

Aven looked over at the closed door. He nodded. "I'll go."

He let himself into Owyn and Alanar's rooms, walking carefully through to the bedroom door. He could hear nothing from inside. For a moment, he thought about knocking. But Alanar hadn't slept well the night before, and Owyn needed all the sleep he could get. So waking them would do no one any good. He cracked the door open gently and looked inside.

No one had closed the curtains, so sunlight dappled the bed, showing clearly the three curled around each other. Aven smiled and closed the door.

"Are they all right?" Treesi asked as he came back out to the sitting room.

He nodded, leaning on his stick. "They're fine. They're all asleep."

"All of them?" Aria asked. "Does that mean—?"

"I have no idea," Aven answered. "And I'm not going to ask. Nor are you. Del will tell us if he wants us to know." He smiled. "We'll let them sleep."

DEL WOKE UP FEELING squashed and warm and entirely happy. He was lying face down, sprawled over Owyn's chest. Alanar was partially covering them both, his cheek pressed against Del's shoulder. Del closed his eyes, listening to Owyn's heartbeat.

He might not ever want sex for himself, might not ever want someone to do to him what he'd done to Alanar, but making Alanar happy? And making Owyn happy in the process? He'd enjoyed that. Owyn had made sure he'd felt completely safe, completely loved throughout it. And when they realized Del would have left them, Alanar insisted that he stay, that he share their bed. Sharing the bed wasn't new, but somehow, this time it was.

"I can hear you thinking," Owyn whispered, his voice still thick with sleep. "But it's not words. You're almost purring in there."

"I liked that. I liked making you both happy."

Owyn chuckled, running one hand up and down Del's arm, sending tingles of pleasure up and down Del's spine. "You don't have to bring either of us off to make us happy, love. You just have to be here."

"Although bringing me off was very nice," Alanar added, pressing closer against Del's back. He kissed Del's shoulder. "And unexpected. Thank you."

Del smiled. *"Owyn, tell him I said he's welcome. And thank you. Both."*

"He says you're welcome, Allie. And...why are you thanking us, Del?"

Del shook his head. *"I'm not sure. But I think I should be thanking you. For letting me be...me."*

Owyn rolled toward him, pushing Del onto his side so that he was sandwiched between Owyn and Alanar. "You're you," Owyn said. "And you're just fine as you. I don't want to change you. No one here does."

"I'm missing half the conversation," Alanar said.

"Del thanked us for letting him be himself. Which...who else would we want him to be?"

Alanar laughed. "No, I know what he means. He means we don't expect him to change or be anyone other than who he is, and we accept him that way. We don't want him to change so much as a hair." He ran one hand down Del's side. "Am I right?"

Del nodded, then grimaced and opened his mouth. Owyn pressed his finger to Del's lips.

"You don't even have to do that," he said. "You're right, Allie."

"And you were going to talk to tell me that?" Alanar asked. He sighed. "We'll work on it, Del. If you're serious about the exercises, and that wasn't just to try and distract me, I mean."

"I'm serious. I want to try."

"He says he's serious, Allie."

Alanar nodded. "Then once we're ready to get up, we can go to the library and see if there are books there. They might be in the healing library, which may mean taking Jehan into your confidence. He may have to give us access to those books." He launched and ran his hand up and down Del's arm. "But I'm not ready to get up yet." He reached across Del and ran his hand down Owyn's side. "How would you like to help me give Owyn his turn?"

Pressed up against Owyn, Del felt him tense, felt his cock starting to stir. Del looked at him and raised his brows, and Owyn blushed.

"I...I wouldn't mind...if you said yes," he stammered. Del leaned closer to kiss him. Then he looked over his shoulder at Alanar.

"*Ask Allie if we're going to tie you? I don't think I can do the same thing Aven did, but I might be able to come close.*"

Owyn squeaked, "You...you want to do that to me?"

Alanar grinned slowly. "Oh, that does sound like a plan. Is that a yes?" He reached up to touch Del's cheek.

Del nodded, and Alanar smiled. "May I kiss you?"

Del nodded again, shifting around so his back was to Owyn. Alanar leaned in close, his nose brushing against Del's. He smiled, then closed what remained of the distance between them and claimed Del's mouth.

Del was getting used to being kissed. He'd been kissed more times over the past few months that he had over his entire life. And he'd kissed Alanar before. Been kissed by Alanar before. So why was this one different? He wasn't sure.

Maybe he'd figure it out later.

Chapter Five

Aven and Treesi went off to the healing center, and Aria went to her office. There was some last-minute paperwork, and she wanted to spend some time with Lexi and Steward before they left. She tugged on the bell rope, then went to her desk and sat down, lighting the candle underneath the tiny long-handled cauldron of wax that she would need to seal papers she was going to sign. There were two flat boxes on the desk — one for the papers that she needed to look at, the other for papers that Steward needed to take away. At the moment, the box of papers she needed to review was full. She frowned, trying to remember when she'd last gone through them. Surely it had been just yesterday?

No, no, it hadn't. It had been longer. Two days. Maybe three. She'd been avoiding her office, avoiding her work, because she'd been distracted by her worries about Owyn and his test. But he was fine now. And Grandmother Meris said that he'd be better going forward. She reached for the first page, reading through an order allowing the caretakers at the Home farm to make decisions in her absence. She signed it, poured a puddle of hot wax over the signature, and rested the Heir's seal in the wax. Once the wax cooled and the seal was sharp, she put the page into the box for Steward, then reached for the next page.

She'd gone through most of the pages before someone knocked on the door. She looked up from a request that Lexi be granted custody of the Palace fosterlings Bask (boy, age nine,) Trevi (boy, age five), and Ilithi (girl, age three), and called "Come in."

Steward came in, bowed slightly, and took his usual chair. "How was it this morning? Owyn's testing? I'm sorry I couldn't be there. I was busy with wrangling things for tomorrow." He paused. "We are still going, aren't we?"

"We are," Aria confirmed. "And things went well. Grandmother says that whatever it was that was putting Owyn so off-balance has righted itself. He's fine." She held up the page she'd been reading. "Bask, Trevi and Ilithi?"

"Gathi's younger siblings," Steward answered. "Since she's going off with you to train as a healer, Lexi thought it would be best if she took charge of them. Gathi's agreed."

Aria nodded. She signed and sealed the page, putting it into the outgoing box, then adding more wax to the cauldron to melt. "Did Grandmother ask you about the book?" she asked, picking up the next page for her review. The handwriting was crooked and strange — not Lexi's, and not Steward's. "What is this?" she asked.

"Yes, Lady Meris asked about *The First Companions*. I showed the original to her, and then I left her and Memfis in the library with a fair copy. And I don't know." He reached out and took the page. "This isn't my writing."

"It's not Lexi's either," Aria said. He nodded, frowning as he read the page.

"Requisition for...two squadrons to remain at the Palace? Asking for Karse by name?" His frown deepened. "And it's not signed. This handwriting...it looks...well, nothing this sloppy would ever come from my desk. Aria, I'm not sure where this came from. But they were probably hoping you would just sign it without reading it."

Aria frowned. "Karse is supposed to lead my guard on the Progress." She leaned back in her chair, flexing her wings as she rubbed one hand on her stomach, feeling the baby move under her hand. "This was put on my desk sometime over the past two days. Find out where it came from, Steward. And let Karse know."

Steward nodded. He rose, bowed, then turned toward the door, nearly running into Lexi as she came into the office. The housekeeper looked at Steward and immediately said, "Something's wrong. What's wrong?"

"How can you tell?" Aria asked.

Lexi nodded toward Steward. "He has that look. What is it?"

"There was an order on my desk, and the handwriting is nothing that either of us recognize," Aria answered.

Lexi blinked and held her hand out to Steward. "Let me see." She took the page, studied it, then sighed. "Oh, my." She looked up at Steward, then turned to Aria. "May I take this for a moment?"

"Do you know who wrote it?" Steward asked.

Lexi nodded. "I do. And I want to know why. So I'll be back shortly." She smiled slightly. "I don't think any harm was meant." She left, and Steward returned to his chair.

"Do you have any idea?" Aria asked.

"None," Steward answered. He reached out and picked up the pages that Aria had put into the box for him to collect. "What else do you have?"

Aria picked up the last page. Again, it was in handwriting that she didn't recognize, and the paper was old and water stained. She read it, then looked up. "This is a request for aid against raiders, from a coastal village north of here," she said. "How did something like this get buried?"

"I don't know," Steward said. He stood and came around the desk. "Something like this, I'd bring it to you directly. It must have gotten mixed in with household papers. How long ago?"

Aria frowned. "It was on the bottom of the pile. Perhaps two or three days?" She looked up. "Who can we send? And how did this get buried?"

Steward straightened and went to the wall, tugging on the red cord that hung there. "Karse is going to be furious," he murmured. "How did I miss this? How could I have missed this?"

Aria frowned, turning in her chair to look at the map hanging on the wall opposite the windows. She stood up and walked over to the map, running her finger along the jagged line that marked the coast. "Steward, I'm not certain that you did. There's no village marked on the coast," she said. "Not where they say they're located. Unless I'm looking in the wrong place? Where is Jasper Inlet?"

Steward joined her. He studied the map for a moment, then pointed. "That's Jasper Inlet. It's not that far, but it's hard to get to, unless you go by skiff. There's no good road." He frowned. "And no reliable source of fresh water. Jasper is near Turtle Rock." He paused. "There was a fishing village there. Almost entirely Water tribe. They would come south to trade their catches for things they couldn't make themselves. When they stopped coming, the Usurper sent a ship. The village was still there, but there wasn't anyone living there. The reports say that they couldn't tell how long the village had been empty." He paused again. "That was...five years ago, perhaps? And...that's a horrible thought."

Aria licked her lips. "Are you thinking Risha had something to do with it?"

"I am, and not liking it. There were families in that village. Children."

"Skela's grandson vanished," Aria said softly. "He told us that, when Aven asked why he calls Del 'My Del.' He told us that his family canoes ranged to the north."

Steward frowned at the map. "I don't know, Aria. I don't think this request is real."

"Then the question is where did it come from?" Aria went back to her desk and picked up the page. "And how did it get on my desk without you knowing about it?"

Someone knocked, and Karse came in. Behind him was Lexi, leading Danir and Copper.

"You needed me?" Karse asked. "What's wrong?"

"Perhaps nothing, perhaps something," Steward said, taking the page from Aria. "We found this in Aria's papers. But we're not sure where it came from."

"Isn't that always the way?" Karse asked as he took the page. He read it, then looked up. "When did this show up?"

"The best we can guess is two or three days ago," Aria answered. "It was at the bottom of the pile."

"You're not talking about the false orders, are you?" Lexi asked. "Because I know where those came from." She looked down at the boys. "Go ahead."

Danir looked at Copper, then sighed. "That was us," he said. "We...we wanted the Captain to stay."

"What was this?" Karse asked. Lexi held out the false orders, and he looked at the page, then at the boys. He frowned slightly, then sat down and beckoned the boys closer. "All right. You two...you're both training with the guards. You're both going to be very good when you're grown. Tell me why you're risking that. Because if I don't like the answer, you're not training with the guard anymore."

Danir bit his lip and looked at Copper again. Copper swallowed and nodded.

"It's my idea," he said. "So just let it be my fault. Danir told me what to write to make it sound right, but it was my idea."

"And why?" Karse asked again.

Copper took a deep breath, then answered in a rush, "Because if you're not here and she comes back, she's gonna kill us all!"

"Oh, Copper," Aria breathed. Karse just nodded.

"Thought that might have been it," he said. "I'm leaving men behind to guard the Palace while we're gone. You know that, don't you?"

Copper's shoulders drooped. "But they aren't you. Othi's gone, and Trey's gone, and you're going, and..." he said in a low voice. "And...I know Marik and Esai are staying, and they promised to take care of me, but...they're not you."

Karse smiled slightly. "Come here, Copper," he said, holding his hand out. Copper crept closer, his arms wrapped around his chest.

"I—"

"You're not in trouble," Karse said, resting his hand on Copper's shoulder. He gestured for Danir to come closer. "Neither of you is in trouble. I should have thought of this. You were here when Risha attacked. That had to have been terrifying for all of you. I remember how it was for me." Copper looked startled, and Karse nodded. "I was younger than you are now, and I lived here in the Palace when the Usurper came. I know exactly how it felt." He looked up at Lexi. "What I don't know is boys. How do we make this right by them?"

"Can we come with you?" Danir blurted. "We won't be any trouble, and we'll help, and—"

"No!" Lexi gasped. "Absolutely not!"

Karse looked up again. "Why not? I mean...I would think we could use a couple of pages in the Progress? Running errands and helping the camp?"

Danir and Copper both turned to Lexi.

"Mama, please?"

"Mother Lexi, can we? Can we please?"

Lexi rolled her eyes. "You had to say it in front of them," she grumbled at Karse. "Come along. We'll discuss this. I want to talk to your teacher, and to the Senior Healer. Karse, this was your idea—"

"Yes, but we need him for a moment," Aria interrupted. "I..." She stopped and looked at the box. "Copper, was it you or Danir who put that into my papers?"

"That was me," Danir answered.

"There was another page underneath it." She pointed to the paper that Karse still held. "Was that there when you put yours in? Do you remember?"

"The dirty page?" Danir asked. "I put it there, too. One of the new groundskeepers asked me to bring it to you. But you were busy, so I put it with the others." He looked up at Aria. "The writing isn't right for me to read it. Was it something bad?"

"It was...something strange," Aria answered. "Could you show Captain Karse who gave it to you? I'd like to speak to them."

Danir nodded. "I'll see if I can find him."

Karse nodded. "Right. Lexi, let's go discuss these boys and if they deserve to be allowed the privilege of serving the Heir on her Progress. And we'll see if we can't get to the bottom of this." He held up the discolored paper. "Aria, don't worry. I'll take care of it. You focus on getting a good night of sleep. We have an early morning tomorrow."

Aria smiled and looked out the rain-speckled window. "It's hours yet until dark," she said. "I..." She stopped. "Karse, am I seeing sails?"

Karse jumped to his feet and turned to the windows. "I...yes!" He turned, grinning. "They're back! Finally!"

Steward turned and looked at the boys. "Danir, Copper, you both need to run. Fast as you can to the healing center. Senior Healer Jehan and Healer Treesi are there. Tell them that there are sails on the horizon!"

THE CROWD ON THE WATER Walk grew, but Treesi ignored them. She was too busy counting sails.

"That...that's not all of them, is it?" she asked Jehan. He was standing next to her, his eyes shaded with one hand. Memfis and Steward were behind him, and Aria on his far side.

"No," he answered. "That's not all the canoes that sailed out. But we don't know how many are swimming."

Treesi nodded and looked over her shoulder. Aven stood behind her, his hand on her back, his eyes on the horizon.

"How soon do we go down to the beach?" he asked. "When I sent down to Neera, she said she'd wait there."

"We'll give them time to get a little closer," Jehan answered. "Then we'll go join Neera. I wish I still had my glass. It's at the bottom of Forge harbor, and I never thought to replace it."

"We might be able to find one," Memfis said. "Steward?"

"By the time I find one and get back with it, they'll be close enough to count the planks in the decking," Steward answered. He looked up as a large, black bird flew overhead. "But we may not need one. That was Wraith."

Jehan turned and looked around. "Marik?"

"Coming!" Marik called. He came out onto the walk and made his way through the crowd. "Esai is down below. Stairs give her trouble. Wraith said he'd take a look. Want a count of those above the waves, or are we just worried about Aunt Aleia and Othi?"

"How high can Wraith count?" Aria asked.

"I'm not sure," Marik admitted. "I don't really know if he can count over five. Most of the time, anything over that is either 'a lot,' or 'many.' And I'm still not sure if 'a lot' is more or less than 'many.' But he knows Aunt Aleia and Othi."

"Then tell us if he sees them," Treesi said, and turned back to the water. She watched as the shadow hawk circled over the distant canoes, then banked and headed back toward land.

"He says he's seen both of them," Marik called. Treesi shivered, and felt Aven's arms close around her.

"He's back," he whispered. "He's fine."

"He's back," she answered. "I'm not going to say he's fine until I see him myself." She looked up at him. "Can we go down to the canoes now?"

Aven smiled. "Fa, we're going to start down." He stepped back, holding his hand out to Treesi. She took it, and they started toward the stairs. Treesi looked back over her shoulder to see that Aria was following them.

"Memfis says he'll come down when Jehan does," she said. "Steward says he's going to go wake Alanar, in case we need all of the healers."

"He may be in for a surprise," Aven said, glancing back. "Did you warn him?"

"How do you warn someone about that?" Aria asked. "I hope they are awake when he gets there. And that Owyn has eaten something."

Treesi nodded. "Aven, can we hurry?"

"Not easily, no," Aven answered. "Not on stairs."

"Oh." She swallowed. "I'm sorry. That was thoughtless."

"You're forgiven," Aven said. "And I know how you feel." He glanced back at Aria. "I was so tempted to change and swim into Terraces when we came back, but Del wasn't very good with the canoe, and Owyn didn't know how to steer at all. So I had to wait. You don't have to wait for me, Trees. You could go on ahead."

Treesi tightened her grip on his hand. "No. Because if I do go on alone, then I might be tempted to go out and meet him. And I can't swim. So I'm staying with you."

Aven smiled and raised her hand to his lips, kissing her fingers, and they continued down the stairs. At the bottom, Esai was standing outside the door.

"And?" she asked.

"And the canoes are coming in," Aven answered. "Wraith went out, and he saw my mother and Othi. We're going down to the beach."

Esai nodded. She turned and whistled sharply. "Garrity! Come walk with us!"

Garrity had just emerged from the Palace. The man jerked at the sound of his name, and Treesi guessed that he hadn't been paying attention to his surroundings, which seemed to be happening more and more frequently. After Risha's men had dumped the gravely-wounded Garrity at the Palace gates, the healers had fought to save his life. They'd succeeded, but Treesi wasn't entirely certain that they'd managed to save his mind. Garrity hadn't been the same since he'd awakened. Gone was the confident, robust guard with the dry sense of humor, replaced by an easily-startled, frail-looking man who barely spoke at all, and who seemed to be no longer firmly anchored in the real world. He looked at them, and Treesi wasn't certain that he knew who they were. She let go of Aven's hand and walked toward him.

"Garrity?" she called. "Do you know me?"

Garrity squinted at her, then nodded. "Treesi. You're Treesi. I know you. You're a healer."

She smiled and held her hand out. "Will you come and walk with me?"

"Walk where?" Garrity looked around. "Going where?"

"Down to the water," Treesi answered. "We're going to see the canoes come in."

"Canoes." Garrity frowned. He looked around again. "Is Evarra down there? I miss my Vari."

Treesi swallowed hard. They'd told Garrity that Evarra had died from her injuries, but he never seemed to remember for long. "No,

Garrity," she said. "She died, remember? We can go visit her grave later. We can bring her flowers."

Garrity's face fell. "Oh. I knew that. I...you've told me that. I remember now." He looked down. "Walk? Outside the walls?"

"Just down to the water. With Aven and Aria and Esai and me. We're going down to the Water tribe canoes." She offered her hand again. "Come with me, Garrity. It will be good for you to walk."

Garrity stared at her hand, then took it, letting her lead him toward the gates. Aven met them halfway, leaning on his walking stick.

"How are you feeling, Garrity?" he asked as he joined them.

Garrity shrugged. "Nothing hurts. Nothing feels right, but nothing hurts."

Aven nodded. "May I touch you?" Garrity nodded again, and Aven rested his hand on Garrity's shoulder. He nodded after a moment. "You seem to be fine," he said. "Let's walk. We'll go slow."

"Have to go slow," Garrity said. "Don't want to hurt you."

Aven smiled. "I appreciate that, Garrity."

They walked out the gates, and Treesi felt Garrity's hand shake as they reached the road. She squeezed his hand. "It's all right," she murmured. "You're safe with us."

Garrity grimaced, but she could feel his heart starting to beat faster. He looked around, but the lack of anyone around them didn't seem to do much to calm him.

"We're going down to the water," Treesi repeated. "Othi is back. Well, almost back. The canoes are still out in the water."

"Othi?" Garrity brightened. "I like Othi. Vari likes Othi. Did you tell Vari he's back?"

Treesi looked past Garrity to Aven, who sighed. "We'll take Othi to visit her later," he said. "I promise."

Garrity nodded. He smiled. "Evarra likes Othi," he repeated. "She'll like if he brings her flowers." Then he frowned. "Oh. We're bringing her flowers because she's dead." He looked around. "Treesi...I don't want to go down to the water. I don't want to tell him. He'll be upset."

"I'll take you back," Esai said gently. She held her hand out. "Come on, Gar. We'll go back to the yard and walk in the garden."

"Can we pick flowers for Vari?" he asked, taking her hand.

"We'll pick the prettiest ones for her." Esai said as they started back toward the gates.

Treesi wrapped her arms around herself and watched until they disappeared inside the Palace walls. Then she looked at Aven and Aria.

"I don't know what else we can do for him," she said.

"Is there anything that can be done?" Aria asked. "To help his mind heal?"

"I talked to Fa about him. And he thinks that we should send him on to Terraces," Aven said. "Grandmother will know what to do." He held his hand out. "Come on. The canoes will be in soon."

Chapter Six

Steward knocked on the door to the Heir's suite, and when there was no answer, he let himself in. There was no one in the sitting room. Steward stopped to think. Owyn and Alanar might be off in their room, but where was Del? Asleep, maybe? He was walking toward Del's door when he heard a door open behind him.

"Owyn?" Steward said as he turned. "Have you seen—" He stopped.

Del stood in the doorway, naked except for his Air gem. For the first time, Steward saw the Water tattoo on his son's right shoulder, identical to Aven's family tattoo. Del had been adopted by Aven's canoe? Had he known about that?

Del stared at Steward in shock, then disappeared back into the room, slamming the door behind him. Steward heard a raised voice, then Owyn appeared, still tying the sash of a robe around his waist.

"Sorry," he mumbled, sounding not quite awake. "None of us heard you." He scrubbed his hand over his face, and Steward thought he saw red marks on his wrist.

"I..." Steward coughed, feeling his face growing warmer. "I..." He stopped, closed his eyes, and forced his thoughts away from what might have been happening in that room. "Canoes on the horizon. We wanted Alanar to be ready in case the healers are needed."

"Canoes?" Owyn gasped, and burst out laughing. "There's timing! Does Treesi know?"

"She and Aven and Aria went down to the water already," Steward answered. "Jehan and Memfis were going to wait until the canoes were closer."

"Right," Owyn said. "We'll get dressed and come down to the water. Do we have time to fetch something to eat?"

"I'll have the kitchens put something up for you to take with you, so you can eat on the beach while you wait," Steward answered. He looked past Owyn at the closed door. "Owyn, what I saw—"

"Is none of your fucking business," Owyn said, his voice chilly.

"I know that!" Steward protested. The door behind Owyn opened again, and Del and Alanar came out. Alanar was wearing a robe, and Del was wearing the same clothes he'd been wearing when Steward had seen him earlier. He looked at Steward and turned red from the tips of his ears to his collarbone. Steward smiled. "That makes this easier. Del, I'm sorry. I startled you badly. I had no idea—"

"*You caught me by surprise.*" Del smiled slightly. "*And I think I did the same to you.*"

Steward laughed. "You did." He tapped his right shoulder. "I hadn't seen that before. I didn't know you'd been adopted by Aven's canoe. Alanar, did you hear what I told Owyn?"

Alanar shook his head. "No. Am I needed?"

"You may be. There are canoes on the horizon. Treesi, Aven and Aria have already gone down. Jehan and Memfis are going, and I told them I'd fetch you, just in case."

Alanar nodded. "I need to dress. How long do we have? Do we have time to eat?"

"I covered that ground," Owyn said. "Come on. I'll fill you in while we get ready." He started back toward them, then turned and looked at Steward. "Next time?" he said. "Knock harder."

Steward chuckled. "Next time? I'll bring a cowbell."

THE DOOR CLOSED BEHIND Steward, and Owyn sighed.

"That was exciting," Owyn said as he faced Alanar and Del. Del was still flushed, and when Owyn met his eyes, he looked down and away.

"Hey," Owyn said gently. He touched Del's arm, running his hand up Del's sleeve to rest on his shoulder. "Hey, none of that. You didn't do anything wrong."

Del shook his head, and Owyn realized that he wasn't hearing anything from Del.

"Del, why don't you go get a change of clothes, and we'll all bathe together and get ready?" Alanar suggested gently. "And...I don't know if I'll be busy later, but if I am, maybe you could keep Owyn company tonight?"

Del shook his head, gently pulled away from Owyn, and left them, going to his own room and closing the door firmly.

"He's really upset," Alanar murmured. "Owyn, I don't understand why he's upset?"

"I don't know," Owyn answered, looking at the closed door. "He's upset enough that I can't hear him. Which is really weird. I can hear your thoughts buzzing, but not him. I...you go start getting ready. I'll be along in a few minutes. I need to check on him."

Alanar went back to their room, and Owyn crossed the sitting room to Del's door, knocking on it. He waited, and the door opened.

"*You didn't have to wait,*" Del said in his mind.

"Yeah, I did," Owyn answered. "You've had people tromping all over your limits today, and I'm not going to push you. Can I come in, or do you want to be alone?"

Del stepped back and opened the door, letting Owyn in. He closed the door behind Owyn, and went to sit on the couch, picking up a familiar, carved wooden soldier. Owyn moved to sit on the ground at Del's feet.

"You're really upset," he said. "And I'm not sure I understand why. You didn't do anything wrong."

Del frowned. Then he shook his head. "*I'm not sure either. I just...I don't know.*" He turned Captain over in his hands. "*I think I need to think.*"

Owyn nodded. "Understandable. You've done a lot of new things today." He smiled and reached out to touch Del's bare ankle. "We enjoyed having you play with us, Del. Enjoyed it a lot."

Del turned pink. "*I did, too. I made you both happy. I liked that.*" He looked down. "*I didn't know I could like that.*"

Owyn studied Del, then smiled. "You know, I think we're wrong," he said slowly. "You're not upset. You're overwhelmed. You did a lot of new things today. And you enjoyed it, a lot, which I don't think you ever expected to. Not something involving sex. You've just upended a lot of what you thought was true about yourself, and you need to let that all settle. You need to fit all that into your head."

Del looked puzzled for a moment. He cocked his head to the side, gnawing on his lower lip. Then he nodded. "*Maybe?*"

Owyn nodded. "Did I ever tell you what I did when Aria gave me this?" he asked, touching the Fire gem at his throat. When Del shook his head, Owyn smiled. "I panicked. Because they couldn't possibly want me. Nobody ever wanted me. I was a thief and a whore and a slave, and as far as I knew, no one had ever wanted me. I knew I wasn't good enough. Not for the Heir. But...she and Aven insisted. And I had to rework everything I knew about myself. I'm still doing it." He scratched his head, tugging his fingers through his hair. "I need to cut this. I keep saying it and never doing it."

"*Don't,*" Del signed. "*I like the curls.*"

Owyn laughed. "Allie says the same thing. He says I need to let it grow until he finishes growing his out. Did you see his hair before it was cut?"

"*I think so. It was all the way down his back?*"

Owyn nodded. "Yes. Down to his knees. They cut it when he was out of his head. He says it'll grow back, but I miss it." He sighed and shrugged. "Right. You going to come wash up with us, or wash up here?"

"*I'll wash up here,*" Del answered. "*And meet you outside. I need to think, and let things settle.*"

Owyn got to his feet and stepped closer; Del tipped his head back and smiled. He nodded, and Owyn leaned over him and kissed him gently.

"Listen," he said, his forehead touching Del's. "We love you. Even if you never want to do that again, we still love you."

Del closed his eyes. "*I love you, too.*"

Owyn kissed him again and straightened. "Right. Hurry and wash up."

Del nodded again, and stood up. He carried Captain back to the shelf, putting him back in his place. Then he headed into his bedroom. Owyn let himself out, hurrying to get himself ready.

DEL HELD ON TO ALANAR'S hand as he led them out the door to the cliffside path.

"Where are we going?" Owyn called from behind them.

"*The water stairs,*" Del answered. "*It's faster than going out the gates and around.*"

"Stairs?" Owyn repeated. "How many stairs? Allie, do you have trouble with stairs?"

Del stopped. "*I didn't think of that.*"

"I'm fine with stairs," Alanar answered. "So if that's why you stopped, don't stop. How many?"

Del looked at the top of the steps. "*I...never counted. Seventy? Maybe a little more?*"

Owyn translated, and Alanar nodded. "Right. Let's count. Don't distract me."

They made their way down the steps — Del in the lead, with Alanar behind him, and Owyn at the rear. None of them spoke, so the only sounds were the distant waves, and the birds flying overhead. Del could see the canoes, close enough to count individuals on the decks.

Then they reached the bottom step, and Owyn called, "That's the last one, Allie."

"Ninety-seven, and please tell me we don't have to go back up them?" Alanar shook his head. "I kept thinking the next one was going to be the last. But they kept on going!"

"We don't have to go back up them," Owyn said. "We can go around to the gates. Now, let's go. Del?"

Del took Alanar's hand, and led them down the beach and around a rock promontory. On the other side, he could see the docks, and the crowd of people waiting on the beach. He saw wings, and headed for them.

"Slow down, will you?" Alanar said. He tugged Del's hand to pull him back. "I know you're excited, but I have to go slower on sand."

Del looked at him, then at Owyn. Owyn grinned.

"Sand moves," he said. "And it messes with him. If you want to go ahead, we'll catch up."

Del nodded. He stretched up on his toes and kissed Alanar, then kissed Owyn. Then he ran off across the sands.

Aria was standing with Aven, Treesi and Neera. Treesi was staring out at the canoes, and Aven was standing behind her, his hands on her shoulders. Neera glanced over at Del, then smiled at him, holding her hand out.

"Del," she said. "It's good to see you. You're so busy these days, you don't come down to the canoes anymore."

Del took her hand, then kissed her cheek. Her eyes widened, and her face went dusky.

"Well," she murmured. "The things they're teaching you up in the Palace. Maybe I should stop waiting for you to come visit me?"

"You're always welcome," Aven said without looking. Then he looked at Neera. "Oh. Well, I suppose if you were looking for *that* sort of welcome, it would be up to Del."

Del made a rude gesture at Aven, who grinned. He looked past Del, then met his eyes and arched a brow.

"*None of your business,*" Del signed.

Neera looked past Del. "Owyn and Alanar? What are you up to, my Silent Del?"

"*None of your business either, Neera.*"

Neera laughed. "Fine. The Palace business is none of my concern. Right now, my concern is why the War Leader is coming back with half the canoes she left with."

Del coughed, and heard Owyn from behind him. "Half?" A warm hand settled on Del's back. "Neera, can you tell if there are people underwater?"

"I sent hunters out to meet them, but they're not back yet," Neera said. "At this point, they're so close that even if they surfaced and changed, the canoes would be on the beach before they had their voices back."

Del nodded, looking out at the water. He could see Aleia on the canoe closest to them, standing at the lines and guiding it to shore. Othi stood behind her, but there was something odd about the way he was standing. Del tried to puzzle it out, but was distracted by movement to his left. Aven handed his walking stick to Aria and limped down the sand. He stopped long enough to touch his father's arm. Jehan nodded. Then the pair went down to the water, waded out, and dove in. Jehan surfaced almost immediately, swimming with strong strokes toward the canoe. Del could hear Aleia's laughter clearly as it floated over the waves. Then Aven lifted himself out of the water and onto the canoe.

And Othi dove off, disappearing under the waves.

TREESI WATCHED AS OTHI vanished. "Aria," she stammered. "Aria, why did he do that?"

"Perhaps he's coming to shore?" Aria suggested. "He couldn't wait any longer?"

Treesi nodded, feeling her heart thumping in her chest. "Then he'll be here soon."

Out at the canoes, Jehan pulled himself up onto the deck, getting to his feet just as Aven did. Aven went and took the lines from his mother so that Jehan could claim her, pulling her into his arms and kissing her. A cheer rose from the shore, and Treesi heard Owyn explaining to Alanar why people were cheering. She didn't turn until a hand slipped into hers. Then she looked to see Del had joined her. He nodded toward the water and arched a brow.

"I don't know," she said. "But he'll come on shore any minute now. You watch."

The first canoe ran aground, and Aven and Jehan both jumped down to push it up onto the sands. Aleia jumped down, and they walked up the beach toward Aria.

"My Heir," Aleia said. "I'm so glad we didn't miss you."

"You almost did," Aria said. "We're leaving in the morning." She stepped forward to embrace Aleia. "Welcome home."

Aleia laughed and hugged Aria, then stepped back.

"Do you need us, Aleia?" Alanar asked. "All the healers are here."

Aleia shook her head. "No, we're fine. It's been enough time since the last serious battle that our injured have healed already. We've been up and down the coast the past week making sure we found all of her ships." She turned to Treesi. "Treesi," she said. "It's good to see you." She looked back over her shoulder at the water. "Walk with me."

"What?" Treesi looked at the water, then at Aleia. "Why? I...I wanted to be here to wait for Othi." She looked back at the water. "Aleia, what's wrong with Othi?"

Aleia held her hand out. "Walk with me," she repeated.

Treesi let Aleia lead her down toward the water to where Jehan and Aven were waiting.

"Othi is counted among the warriors of our canoe," Aleia said. "But he has never seen real battle. Not until we challenged one of Risha's ships. He killed for the first time, and it's changed him. Now...he's uncertain. He needs time to think."

Aven winced. "I'd wondered why he went deep when I got to the canoe."

"He's uncertain. About me?" Treesi said the words, even though they didn't seem to go together.

"Not you," Aleia answered. "He's questioning himself. He's questioning his tattoos, his place on our canoe, and he's questioning if he's worthy of you." Aleia looked back at the water. "After our last battle, after we brought our dead to the deep, he told me that he was never going to sail as a warrior again. He'll fight if he's called on, but he's not a warrior, and he knows it." She shook her head. "We've talked quite a bit about this. His mother and his grandmother pushed him to become a warrior. They convinced him that being a warrior was his only course. But that's not the course his heart was set on. Now? He's lost. He needs to find his way."

"What course would he have taken?" Aven asked. He looked down at his arm. "Oh. He...he'd have followed the ink and hammer, wouldn't he? But...that's a sacred calling! Why wouldn't Grandmother have let him follow that?"

Aleia sighed. "The same reason she refused to do anything else that she didn't want to do. Pure, unadulterated spite." She looked back at Treesi. "So, that's where Othi is. He'll come back to shore. He'll come back to you. But for now? He needs to think."

"Because deep thinking needs deep water," Treesi said. "You taught me that." She licked her lips and looked out at the waves. "When he comes up, I'll be waiting for him." She walked up the beach until she was just past the high-tide mark, and sat down on the rain-wet sand.

"Trees?" Owyn called. He came down the beach toward them, leading Alanar. "What are you doing?"

"Waiting for Othi," she answered. "When he comes out of the water, I'll be right here. I want him to know that no matter what his course is, that I'll be here for him."

Aven carefully lowered himself to the ground to sit with her. "Do you mind having company?"

She looked at him and smiled. "Not at all."

"Good," Owyn said. He sat down behind her, and Alanar sat with him. Del came over to stretch out on his back on the sand on her other side. She heard the crunch of footsteps on the sand behind her, and looked up to see Aria, Steward, and Memfis. Steward was carrying a basket, which he handed down to Owyn

"There," he said. "That should be enough to share amongst all of you."

"Treesi, will you mind if I do not wait with you?" Aria asked. "If I sit on the sand, someone will have to pick me up and put me to bed, because I will fall asleep. And I have work to do."

"I don't mind," Treesi answered. "And hopefully, we won't be waiting too long. But I'm going to stay here until he comes out of the water."

"Then let's eat," Owyn said, and opened the basket.

The crowd dispersed, and Aleia and Jehan walked up to the Palace so that Aleia could report to Aria. Neera went with them, promising to be back soon. The other Water warriors started working on the canoes, repairing damage, unloading compartments. Treesi ate the stuffed roll that Owyn gave her, then leaned into Aven's arm.

"Tell me about how an artist does this," she said, running her finger over Aven's tattoos. "And why is it sacred?"

"Special tool with sharp points, ink made from the ash of a specific kind of dried seaweed, and a small hammer." Aven said. "It takes hours. I spent a lot of time on my belly while my back was done. Hurts, but in a good way. And it's sacred because the first tattoos were laid into our skin by the Mother's touch. And she taught the first of our artists how to do it, and what the symbols mean." He touched the design on his right shoulder. "They all mean something. The family tattoo is the genealogy of our canoe, and it grows a little every generation. The warrior tattoos are protection and guidance. I don't know all the meanings to all the lines and patterns. You can study them your whole life. Othi is, I think, the only person I know of who isn't sworn to the hammer that knows them, and can do them properly. He did all of mine."

"Because no matter what his ma said, he followed his heart," Owyn murmured. "Is that why you wouldn't let me do it? You said it wouldn't be the same."

"That's why," Aven said.

Owyn nodded. "So how hard will it be for him to stop being a warrior?"

Aven shook his head. "I don't know. I don't know if it's been done before." He took a deep breath and put his arm around Treesi. "We'll find out."

The day dragged on. Alanar and Owyn left when it was time for Alanar to go on duty in the healing center. They were replaced by Neera, who came and sat with them for a time, left, then came back with a gourd that she handed to Treesi.

"Put this on your skin," she said. "You're turning red. Del, you use it, too. You're too pale, the pair of you."

Treesi grimaced. "I always turn red in the sun."

"This will help."

Neera went off to see to her people, and Aven slowly got to his feet as the sun started to sink over the waves. "I need to relieve Alanar," he said. "And I need to make sure Gathi is ready to leave. Are you ready to go back, Trees?" He winced. "Bad thing about sand. I can't use my stick until I get to the road."

"I'm not going anywhere," Treesi answered. "I'm not leaving until he comes to shore. If he doesn't come out by morning, I'll meet you in Terraces. We'll take the cutter."

"You'll go on a ship?" Aven asked.

"I'm not leaving him behind. Not when he needs me." Treesi looked up. "Would you tell Aria that?"

Aven nodded. He leaned down and kissed the top of her head. "I'll tell Aria. And I'll have someone bring you some supper."

It was Steward who came back down the beach, carrying a large basket. He put it down next to Treesi, took a folded blanket off the top, and spread it on the sand.

"The beach can get chilly when the sun goes down, because of the wind," he said. "And the sand is still damp. There's another blanket in the basket, in case it gets too cold." He sat down on the blanket and waited for Treesi and Del to join him before delving into the basket again and taking out plates and covered bowls.

"Steward, you don't have to wait on us," Treesi said.

"I'm not," Steward answered. "I'm having a beachside supper picnic with you. And spending time with you and Del, which none of us have had time to do for the past two weeks." He looked back at the Palace. "And, to be honest, I'm shirking my duties."

Del snorted, signing too fast for Treesi to follow. Whatever he said, it made Steward laugh.

"No, I truly am," he said. "I should be overseeing the last of the packing and making sure the carriages are ready. But it will still be there after I make certain that the pair of you eat." He smiled and passed a plate to Treesi, then filled another for Del. "So, what are you most interested in seeing when we travel?"

They ate and talked as the sky grew darker and the stars came out. Treesi looked out at the waves and sighed.

"He'll come out," Steward said. "He knows you're here, and he loves you." Treesi stared at him, and he smiled. "Trust an old man."

She snorted and looked back at the water. "You're not old."

"I'm old enough that sitting out here in the damp is making my bones ache," Steward said. He slowly got to his feet, picked up the other blanket, and draped it around Treesi's shoulders. "I'll take the basket in and get back to work. Del, are you going to stay with Treesi?"

She turned and looked at Del. "You don't have to. And Owyn and Alanar might be getting worried about you. Go in." He arched a brow at her, and she laughed. "I'm serious. I'm fine by myself. Go in." She kissed his cheek. "Go."

Del smiled. He kissed her gently on the lips, then got up and stepped off the blanket, brushing sand off his trousers. He and Steward walked up the beach toward the Palace, and Treesi turned back to face the water, tugging the blanket a little tighter around her shoulders.

She wasn't sure just when she fell asleep. But the next thing she knew, she was moving, cradled in strong arms. She opened her eyes, saw familiar tattoos, and smiled.

"Othi," she murmured. "I missed you."

"I missed you, too," he said softly. "Let's get you to bed."

She nodded, closing her eyes. "Stay with me?"

He kissed her forehead. "If you want me to."

"Forever?"

She heard his breath catch. "I...if you want me to."

She nodded again. "Forever."

Chapter Seven

Treesi woke up with a lazy heartbeat drumming in her ear. She opened her eyes and smiled, running her fingers over Othi's tattoos.

"I thought I might have dreamed you bringing me up here," she whispered. "You're really here." She raised her head, and giggled. "And you're really asleep." She laid her head back down, cuddling closer. She needed to get up soon. They needed to leave. But Othi was here, and he'd be leaving with them.

Wouldn't he?

There was a soft knock on the door. She raised her head again and looked at Othi, then at the door, which cracked open just far enough that Aven could look in. He saw them, smiled, and closed the door again. It clicked closed, and the sound make Othi jerk. His arm tightened around Treesi, and his breathing and heartrate both increased.

"Shhh," Treesi whispered, smoothing his chest with her open hand. "It's all right. It's just Aven. He was checking on us."

"Treesi?" Othi croaked. He blinked, looked around. "I...that's right. Treesi, what were you doing sleeping on the beach?"

"Waiting for you," Treesi answered. "You needed me, so I was going to wait there until you came out of the water." She rested her hand on his heart. "I wasn't planning on falling asleep."

"I saw you. I spy-hopped and I saw you sitting there with Del and Steward. I thought you were going to give up and go inside after they did," he said. "I didn't think you'd stay out there all night."

"If you needed me to be there all night, I'd have been there all night," Treesi said. She rested her head on his chest. "Othi, I told you. I don't know what we'll have together, but I want to find out."

He took a deep breath, and she giggled as she rose and fell with his chest. But he didn't laugh with her.

"Treesi, I'm not sure what we'll have together anymore. I don't know who I am anymore." He shifted. "I need to sit up. My back aches. How do you sleep like this?"

"I'm used to it." Treesi sat up, let Othi move and sit up to face her. "I can do something about your back. Turn, and I'll make it better."

He made a soft sound, something between a snort and a sob, and turned his back to her. "I don't know if you can make it better."

"I can make your back better," Treesi said, starting to massage his back. "And I can help with the rest."

Othi let his head loll forward. "How does Aven sleep like this?" he asked, and winced.

"Sorry. He doesn't sleep in a bed unless he's sleeping with Aria. He has a salt water pool in his rooms. He hasn't shown you?"

"No," Othi answered. He groaned. "That felt good. Do that again." He sighed as she worked. "Treesi, what did Aunt Aleia tell you?"

"That you don't want to be a warrior anymore," Treesi answered. "And Aven thinks that you might want to be an artist. A tattoo artist. Is there a proper term for that?"

"Not that I can share, no," Othi answered. "And...he's right. It's what I've wanted since I was small. One of my father's brothers was an artist, and I wanted to apprentice with him. But my grandmother said I was to be a warrior, and my sister's right arm.

It was my responsibility to her, to be her strength." He shook his head. "But Neera doesn't need my strength. And I...I can't kill someone. Not again." He twisted, turning to face Treesi. "Treesi, I killed him. I watched the life flow out of him. I watched...I watched his *eyes* die." He swallowed and shook his head. "And I can't do that again."

"Then you don't have to," Treesi said. "Othi, you can be who you need to be. Who you want to be. And I'll be here with you the entire way."

He smiled, a charming, slightly crooked smile. Then he blinked and looked down at himself. "Treesi...do you know...is there a way to remove tattoos?"

"I..." Treesi blinked. "I don't know. I've never done it myself. Alanar might know. Or Jehan. Why?"

He tapped his chest. "Because if I'm not a warrior, I shouldn't have these. An artist, they wear different marks. And you can't remake a warrior's tattoos into anything else. So I need to know if they can be removed. Except for the family tattoo." He frowned. "If Neera lets me keep it."

Treesi coughed. The thought hadn't even occurred to her. "I...why wouldn't she? She loves you, Othi. She'll want to see you happy. And she's already changed so much of what your grandmother did. What's one more thing?" She looked at Othi's tattoos with a healer's eyes. "It would take some time, I think. To bring all the ink to the surface without scarring. We'd have to go slowly. And...and then what?"

Othi took a deep breath. "And...if I sail this course? You wouldn't see me for a year."

Treesi stared at him. "What?"

"If I went to apprentice, it's...isolated. My uncle died in the storm, so I'd have to find a master artist would take me on as an apprentice, even as old as I am. And I'd have to commit to the learning for a full year." He met Treesi's eyes. "Leaving you will be the hardest part of that. And I know you can't come with me. Even if you could come with me, you can't come with me." He sighed.

Treesi swallowed. Then she nodded. "All right. This is what you need to do? I'll be here when you're done."

Othi looked startled. "Really? It's...it's that easy?"

"It's not easy!" Treesi protested. "Letting you go again will be the hardest thing I've ever done. But...it's what you need."

Othi nodded. "It's part of what I need. But I don't have to do it right now. When's the Progress?"

"Today," Treesi answered. "We're supposed to leave today."

Othi blinked, then laughed. "Well, that's timing. What do we need to do?"

Treesi felt relief rush all through her. "You are coming with us?"

Othi reached out and ran his fingers through her hair. "My Treesi. My little Treesi. Did you think I'd stay behind? I can wait to change my course until this is done. I know what I need now. I need the ink and hammer...and you."

Treesi met his eyes, then lunged toward him, throwing her arms around his neck and clinging to him. His arms closed around her. "I love you," he said in her ear. "That I knew. That I never questioned. I knew that one thing was real, even when I didn't know what I was. That's what brought me out of the water." He chuckled. "You know, I got lost twice finding this room."

Treesi burst into laughter. "You're doing better than I am!" she told him. "I always get lost."

"Well, I'm a decent navigator," Othi said. "Not like Aven or Aunt Aleia. I don't have those marks. But I can chart a course."

"Then you'll chart one for us," Treesi said, drawing back so that she could rest her forehead against his, breathing him in. "For now, though, we should go eat. And you should go fetch anything you want to take with you."

They walked hand-in-hand out of the bedroom and across to the door that led out to the main room of the suite. The others were sitting around the table, and they all looked up with Treesi and Othi came out.

"It's good to see you, cousin," Aven said. "Come and sit. There's sea oak."

"Thank you," Othi said. He brought Treesi to the table, held her chair, then sat down next to her. "I...Aria...?"

"You have my permission," Aria said.

Othi laughed. "You don't even know what I was going to ask!"

"You were going to ask if you could marry Treesi? Or otherwise pair with her, since she is not Water and may not wish to build a canoe?"

Othi looked at Treesi, then back at Aria. "All right, you did know what I was going to ask. And—"

"So long as you understand that Treesi is my Earth, and a healer, and has responsibilities that come with both roles," Aria added.

Othi nodded. "I do understand that. Aunt Aleia told me all about that. About marrying an Earthborn healer, and what it means." He looked at Treesi. "She said it was strange, the first time Uncle Jehan went to someone else's bed as a healer. But it's part of who and what he is as a healer. And she had to accept that if she was going to accept him. I can do that."

"And we're all here to help," Owyn added. "No matter what. You're one of us, now. Part of the family." He grinned. "I keep telling them we need our own tattoo. Our own mark, for this family."

Othi looked startled, then thoughtful. "That would be interesting," he said slowly. "This is something you've been talking about?"

Owyn nodded. "Since it was just me and Aven and Aria," he answered. "I suggested it after Aven told us that his grandmother wouldn't let him have his real marks. I offered, because I know how. He told me it wouldn't be the same. Which...yeah, I get it now. I didn't understand it then. But, yeah, we could still do it. Except...Fishie, I'm not sure you have enough empty space left on you to do it."

Laughter rippled around the table, and Othi leaned forward. "You know how to tattoo?"

"It's not the same way you'd do it," Owyn said. "The way I learned it just used needles and ink. Aven says you use a hammer and...something with points?"

Othi grinned. "It's called a comb. I'll show you. I want to know the difference, how you'd do it."

"Sure, we can talk," Owyn said. "I'm curious to know how you do it. But...can you tell me? I mean, Aven said it was sacred. Can you tell me that? I can't tell them things about being a Smoke Dancer, because that's sacred, too. So I get it if you can't tell me much."

Othi leaned forward, resting his arms on the table. "Do you have a design? For the tattoo? Will you show me?"

Owyn grinned. "You don't know how to ride a horse, do you?"

Othi's eyes widened. "I...no. I've seen them, but...no. Why?"

"You'll know by the time the Progress is over," Aven said. "If we can find trousers to fit you."

"If I have to wear those things, I'm not learning," Othi said emphatically, shaking his head. "No."

Aven laughed. "You'll ride in one of the carriages with me."

"And me," Alanar added. "I agree with Othi. He's not wearing trousers, and I'm not wearing boots."

Othi arched a brow. "Boots?"

"I'll explain later," Owyn said. "Since you'll be in the carriage and not on horseback, we can talk on the road. And I can show you my book."

Treesi touched Othi's arm. "You should eat."

Aven pointed. "There's sea oak there, and it's good in the porridge. You can eat the bread and the fruit compote—"

"The what?"

Aven grinned "That soft stuff in the bowl there. It's very good. Oh, and don't eat those." He pointed at a plate of coddled eggs, then passed Othi a bowl of plain hard-boiled eggs. "These eggs are fine."

Othi served himself a bowl of porridge, mixing in sea oak. He helped himself to boiled eggs and bread, then looked around the table. "Why can't I eat those?" he asked, pointing to the coddled eggs.

Treesi nudged his arm. "Those eggs have cheese in them."

"Oh, cheese." Othi nodded and started eating his porridge. "Aunt Aleia told me to watch out for cheese—"

"She warned you?" Aven laughed. "She didn't warn me! Not at all! My first meal on land—"

"I'm still sorry!" Owyn protested. "I didn't mean to try and kill you!"

Aven laughed, then looked at his cousin, who was staring at him. "He gave me cheese. I didn't know—"

"And I did, but I got excited and forgot he wasn't supposed to have it. And I fed him sweet water." Othi winced, and Owyn laughed. "Yup. I fucked all the way up. And down. And back up. And then all the way off, for good measure."

Othi's jaw dropped. He looked at Owyn, then shook his head. "I...I don't think I've heard you swear like that. You didn't, when we were out in the deep. Or did you, and I just missed it?"

"Probably missed it," Alanar said. "Owyn is very sweary." He smiled fondly at Owyn and when he spoke again, his voice had changed. His tones were rounder, his inflections different. "One of these days, Owyn, I should wash your mouth out with soap."

"You and what army?" Owyn growled. Alanar laughed and turned toward him.

"If I get you in the right position, you'll ask me for the soap," he purred, and Owyn turned pink.

"Enough of that," Aria said. "We have to leave, and we cannot wait for the pair of you to crawl back into bed."

Alanar straightened and turned to face her. He smiled. "Oh, I wouldn't be the one crawling."

Owyn stared at him, his face going ashen before he snapped, "Oh, fuck you! And not in the happy, fun way!" He lurched out of his chair, toppling it over. "Allie, I love you," he said. "But I'm not crawling. Not again. Not for nobody." He looked around. "I...I'm going to go...do something."

"What?" Alanar pushed his chair back. "I'm sorry. I was teasing. I didn't mean—" He stood up, held his hand out. "I'm sorry."

"You know what I did to survive," Owyn said, ignoring Alanar's hand. "You *know* that. Why would you think I'd be okay with teasing—"

"Should I leave?" Othi's voice cut through the tension. He looked around the table as everyone turned to face him. "Look, I'm the newcomer here. If this storm needs to happen, I should be somewhere else, so it can happen. You can't do that with me here. I just...Alanar, how'd you do that?"

"Do what?" Alanar asked. His voice, Treesi noticed, was normal, and she realized what had happened just as Othi answered.

"Change your voice," he said. "For a minute there, you sounded right."

Everyone stared at Othi, and no one spoke. Then Owyn breathed, "Oh, fuck." He turned to Alanar. "What's the last thing you remember saying to me before I yelled at you."

Alanar blinked. "I said you were very sweary.... Virrik!" His breath caught, and he grabbed his chair, sitting down hard. "What did he say? Owyn, *what did he say?*"

Owyn picked his chair up and set it back on its feet, then sat down next to Alanar and took his hands. "He said that he needed to wash my mouth out with soap. It sounded like something you'd say, so I played along. You and what army. And when Aria said we didn't have time before we left to crawl back into bed, you said...he said that he wouldn't be the one crawling."

Alanar went impossibly pale, and for a moment, Treesi thought he was going to faint. Then he shook his head. "No," he moaned. "No, I wouldn't...I'd never...Wyn, you *told* me—"

"And I told you before Virrik was in your head," Owyn said softly. "You knew. He didn't. And we haven't discussed it since I came back."

"But I wasn't asleep!" Alanar was starting to look panicked. "I was wide awake! How—" He closed his eyes and shook his head. "He's sputtering."

"What's he saying?" Aven asked.

"It's a cross between groveling and demanding to know what we're talking about."

"I wouldn't mind knowing what we're talking about," Othi said. "And who. Virrik? Virrik from Tersera's canoe? That Virrik?"

Aven turned to look at his cousin. "You knew him?"

Othi looked puzzled, then nodded. "That's right," he said. "You never met my father. Fa was from Tersera's canoe before Mama asked for him. Virrik was a side cousin. I heard Vir was dead, but not much else. Cousin Ketti came and told us. Said the rites were done for him by someone on land—" His eyes widened as Aven raised his hand. "You did them?"

"It's a long story, Othi," Aven said. "And not one to have over the breakfast table. But...Virrik is dead and is somehow also in Alanar's head. And taking liberties that he shouldn't be taking." He glared across the table at Alanar. "If he wasn't inside the body of someone I care about quite a lot, I'd be thrashing him hard enough that we'd see how many times I could get his arse to skip before he sank."

Alanar snorted. "I'm very glad you're taking it into account that no matter what he said, the body is mine and I'm going to need it."

"And...how did Virrik end up in your head?" Othi asked, drawling the words out.

Alanar smiled slightly. "They didn't tell you? I could have sworn someone would have warned you back in Terraces. I'm insane. Completely, irrevocably insane." He cocked his head to one side. "At least, that's what they say."

"Because you have a dead man in your head?" Othi asked. He nodded, slowly. "I can see how that sails. But they're wrong, aren't they?"

Alanar shrugged. "I'm inside it. I can't tell."

Othi nodded again. Then he frowned. "How do you get him out? Can...can healers do that?"

"Healers can't," Aven answered.

"We might need a priest for that," Aria said. "And I do not know if there are any priests at the Temple. There was no one there when I went."

"Something else on the mile-long list of things to make right?" Treesi asked. She looked at Othi. "This is something we don't talk about to outsiders."

Othi nodded. "I can understand why. Does Neera know? All of it, I mean."

Aven frowned slightly. "I...am not certain. I haven't told her."
He looked around. "Who does know?"

Treesi started ticking names off on her fingers. "We all know.
Steward knows, and Jehan and Aleia and Memfis. Lady Meris.
Rhexa. The Healers all know." She frowned. "Karse and Trey. I...I
think that's all? No, wait. Marik and Esai, they know. That's a lot of
people."

"But they are all people who we can trust completely," Aria
said. "I believe I can trust Neera that much, but I do not know if
this is something I would burden her with right before we leave."

Othi nodded. "That makes sense. I need to go down to the
canoes before we leave." He ate the last bite of his porridge, then
stood up. He leaned over to share breath with Treesi, and she
closed her eyes and breathed him in. "I'll be waiting for you in the
courtyard."

Treesi smiled and kissed him. "I'll be down soon."

Chapter Eight

Aven leaned back in his chair after Othi had gone. "Is there anything that needs to be done before we leave?"

Aria frowned. "I need to speak to Karse, and to Aleia. I never had the chance to tell you what we found yesterday." She picked up her teacup and took a sip. "When I went to my office, there were two orders that did not come from Steward. One was a forgery from Copper and Danir. They wanted Karse to stay behind, because they were afraid that there would be no one to protect them if we left and Risha returned."

"Oh, no!" Treesi gasped. "Those poor boys!"

"Karse has assured them that they will be safe. And he's asked permission for them to travel with us as pages," Aria said. "I'm not certain yet if they are. I never heard from Lexi if they were given permission. But there was another order. One that claimed that raiders were attacking a village north of here. But there's no village in the place where they would have had our guards go. At least, not anymore."

"Oh, fuck," Owyn breathed. "Risha. It had to be Risha. What, she wanted more people to kill?"

"*Where did it come from?*" Del signed. "*Who delivered it?*"

"Danir said that he was given it by one of the new groundskeepers, and he was going to show Karse who it was. But I never heard if they were found. Honestly, I doubt they were. I think someone may have come into the Palace just to deliver that letter.

Which is a problem that we need to address. We're none of us safe, nor are our people safe, if Risha can get her people in and out of the Palace at will." Aria finished her tea and set the cup down. "And I want to know why the war party was gone for so long, and what happened while they were gone. They're probably the reason that Risha has taken my father and Trey onto land—"

"Yeah, about that," Owyn interrupted. "I talked to him yesterday, when I was being tested." He folded his hands and rested them on the table. "He says they've stopped. No cart anymore. They're in a cellar of some kind. He says..." He looked over his shoulder, then pitched his voice lower. "This stays between us. He says that they've taken Trey away, and he's worried. And...when I told him I was being retested because I'd died and came back, he said that he was told he did the same thing. Then he realized that Granna was with me, and he fell to pieces and I lost him. They'd told him she was dead."

Treesi stared across the table at Owyn, unable to put two words together. "Oh..." she finally breathed. "Oh, we definitely can't tell Karse that. He's already on a razor's edge over Trey. And...we can't tell Memfis, either. We can't tell them any of that."

Owyn nodded, then asked, "Who do we tell? Jehan? Mamaleia?"

"I...let me think on it," Aria said. "I...I wonder. Owyn, if I gave you a map, would you be able to tell me where they might have gone, given how long it's been since you last talked to my father?"

Owyn frowned. "I...not with any accuracy," he answered. "I mean...there was a cart, so they'd have to stick to roads. We'd have to know where they got off the ship. Where to start the road, and when they came on land. Then...well, I could give you a target area. But it would be a big target. They could be anywhere in there."

"That would be more than we have now," Alanar pointed out. "Can we do this before we leave?"

Aria tapped her lip with one finger, frowning slightly. "No," she finally said. "We need to be on the road. The first riders were supposed to leave at dawn, and if we want to make it to our first camp before dark, we need to leave soon. I'll ask Steward to bring the map from my office. Which means that we cannot have Memfis or Karse in our coach, and I'll need Aleia's report before we're underway."

Owyn nodded. "Then we should get ourselves moving." He stood up and rested his hand on Alanar's shoulder. "Come on, love. Let's go get ready."

"No boots," Alanar grumbled.

"We're bringing them, just in case," Owyn told him. "They're already packed."

"I'm not wearing them," Alanar said, following Owyn into their room. Del smiled and got up as well, going to his room. Aria looked around as the doors closed.

"I'll miss this place. But we'll be back soon enough, and it will be good to see Rhexa and Pirit." She rose from her chair and stretched, her wing flaring wide. "I need to dress to travel. Lexi said something about my travel wardrobe having adjustable waistbands. I hope she's had them made adjustable enough." She ran her fingers over Aven's shoulder. "I may need help with my boots."

Aven tipped his head back and smiled. "I'll be there in a minute."

"Aven, before you go, I wanted to ask you a question, as a healer. Othi asked me something, and I don't know the answer."

Aven nodded. "All right. Your room or mine?"

"Mine, if you don't mind?" Treesi stood up and headed to her room, hearing Aven's uneven step behind her. Inside her sitting room, she turned and waited for Aven to close the door. He leaned on the door, and waited, so she took a deep breath. "How do you remove tattoos?" she asked.

Aven blinked. "I...he wants to know?"

"He says that if he's not going to be a warrior anymore, he shouldn't wear those tattoos, and if he's going to be an artist, they have different marks. So he wants to have his warrior marks removed. I've never heard of how tattoo removal is done. I would think it would take a long time, because we want to do it without scarring. But I don't know how."

Aven nodded slowly. "I...I don't know either. I've never heard of Water tattoos being removed. Not willingly, anyway. And I don't remember anything about it in our studies. But Fa will know. Or Grandmother. And if they don't know, we'll be in Terraces for a few days. We can find the answer in the medical archives."

Treesi smiled. "Thank you." She looked around. "I'm mostly packed. I just need to change."

Aven nodded. "Hurry up. Othi's waiting for you."

THE COURTYARD WAS FULL of people and horses and carriages, and everyone seemed to be moving and shouting and laughing all at once. It was busier than Del had ever seen it, and he lingered near the door, looking for familiar faces. He appeared to be the first one to arrive, and he shifted the strap of his carrybag, feeling more than a little awkward because of the new weight on his arms. After he'd killed the traitor guard, Karse had given him a gift — a dozen slender throwing spikes, and half a dozen throwing knives. He'd drilled Del on how to use them, and told him that he expected Del to wear them at all times when they were on the road. Del wasn't sure what would happen if Karse came to check on him and found that he wasn't wearing them, so he had the spikes in sheaths beneath his sleeves on both arms, and throwing knives in his boots and concealed in his clothes. They didn't make him feel any safer — he just felt self-conscious.

"Good morning, Del."

Del turned and smiled at Jehan and Aleia. "*Good morning,*" he signed, then shifted to catch the strap of his bag as it slipped off his shoulder. He slung the strap over his head and across his chest. "*I think I'm the first one down.*"

Jehan nodded. "A bit chaotic out here. Waiting out of the way is a good idea."

Del smiled. "*I was going to go back in to get away from it. Aleia, Aria said she wanted to talk to you.*"

"Probably questions about the report I was supposed to make yesterday?" Aleia asked. When Del nodded, she smiled. "I thought so. I wrote it up last night. Do you know when she'll be down?" Del shrugged, and Aleia laughed. "I'll give it to her when I see her. So, when did Othi come out of the water?" she asked.

Del shook his head. "*Sometime after I went to bed,*" he signed. "*He was with Treesi at breakfast. And he came out of her room. He went down to the canoes and is supposed to be coming back up to meet us.*"

"Good," Aleia said. "And...oh, there he is."

Del turned and saw Neera coming through the crowd with Othi at her side. Othi had a bundle in one hand, and his hook swords strapped to his back. To Del's surprise, Skela was with them.

"Aunt Aleia," Neera called. "Would you please talk some sense into him? He thinks he's going with you!"

Del blinked and looked at Aleia, who looked confused.

"I thought Othi was coming with us," she said slowly.

"No," Neera said as she reached them. "Not Othi. Grandfather Skela says he's going with you. Tell him he needs to stay behind!"

"Skela?" Jehan looked at the old man. "Why?"

"Because my Del wants to learn to fight, and I can't teach him if he's gone. For all we know, by the time he comes back, I will be seafoam and memory. I am going with him, so I can teach him what he needs." Skela smiled. "And I am going because I have never seen much of this world. I have seen the wonders of the deep, and I have seen this Palace. What is the rest of the world like? And when will I ever have another chance to see it?"

Jehan snorted. "He has a point," he said.

"This isn't a pleasure trip," Aleia countered. "Skela, we have no idea what's waiting for us out there, and you're not a young warrior anymore. You should stay here."

Skela folded his arms over his chest. "And did you tell the same to Lady Meris?" he asked. "I think not. She told me that she was going with you."

Jehan snickered, and Aleia glared at him. He smiled. "He has a point," he repeated. "Aleia, there's no harm in him coming. He can train Del, and Aven wants to learn falling star, too. It'll be good for him to try something new. And it might help."

"And you think he can?" Aleia took a deep breath and shook her head. "Jehan, I think you're fooling yourself. And him. The hip isn't getting better. If anything, it's getting worse, and you need to stop getting his hopes up—"

"I'm right behind you, you know."

Del jerked in shock, turning and seeing Aven standing behind them. Aven had his hook swords in their harness on his back, and was leaning on his walking stick. He was scowling at his parents. Aleia just folded her arms over her chest.

"Tell me I'm wrong," she said.

"You're wrong," Aven snapped. "It was getting better, until I rode out after the guard and tore the hip all up again. I'm starting back at the beginning again, and I am doing everything I can. I'm swimming every morning. And I'm trying to dance every night, starting from the first forms, just like Grandmother Pirit told me before we left Terraces." He looked away, then back at his mother. "It's not helping. Not this time. I'm in pain, every minute of every day. And the best anyone can manage is to make it not hurt as much. It's exhausting, and it's frustrating. I can't walk a straight line. I can't ride. I can't run. I can't be on my feet for any extended period. The change hurts. Swimming hurts. Sometimes even breathing hurts. But it was getting better. And it will get better again, if I can find the right thing." He paused, then shook his head. "And you don't know a fucking thing about it, because you haven't been here. You don't know where I was, and you don't know where I am. I'm starting to wonder if you even know me anymore. Now, excuse me." He limped past them, not looking at either of his parents. Del stole a glance at Aleia, at the shocked look on her face. Then he followed Aven, noticing for the first time that Aven was wearing trousers and boots.

He was dressed for riding.

Del started to trot to catch up with Aven, and heard someone coming up behind him. He looked back to see Othi, and slowed.

"*He's in a bad place, isn't he?*" Othi signed.

Del nodded. Othi looked thoughtful, watching Aven walk away.

"*Let me handle it.*" Othi signed. He smiled. "*I think I know what to do.*" He patted Del on the shoulder and hurried after Aven.

AVEN HEARD THE FAMILIAR footsteps behind him and stopped walking. "Go away, Othi."

"No," Othi said. He dropped his hand on Aven's shoulder. "Come on. Walk with me."

"I need to be here when Aria comes out," Aven said, looking over his shoulder.

"And you're upset. And seeing you upset will get her upset. That's not the way to start a journey. Not this journey. Come walk with me." Othi smiled. "Take a minute to calm down."

Aven took a deep breath and let it out. "All right. Where?"

"Around the back, where the guard drills." Othi nodded his head to the side. "Come on."

Aven fell in next to Othi, walking away from the crowd and back to the quieter, empty areas. They stopped by the bench next to the dancing floor, and Aven sat down. Othi stepped over the low fence and walked around the dancing floor.

"What is this stuff?" he called. "It feels good to walk on."

"Moss. It's like grass, I think. But not really." Aven shook his head. "I'm not sure. Treesi will know."

"I'll ask her." Othi came back to sit on the ground in front of the bench, looking up at Aven. "You never told me what happened," he said, his voice soft. "You told Neera. I know she knows. But she said that if I wanted to know, I had to ask you. And I didn't want to hurt you. I mean, I could see how much it hurt already. And I don't mean the hip. I mean on the inside."

Aven closed his eyes. "You really don't want to know, Othi. I...you don't need to carry this."

"Why not?" Othi asked. When Aven looked at him, he smiled. "Look, I'm bigger than you are. I can help you carry just about anything. Let me help with this."

Aven swallowed and looked away. "It gave Neera nightmares."

"I already have nightmares," Othi said. "This won't be any different."

Aven looked back at him. "You what? What nightmares?"

"Ven, you know I'm walking away from being a warrior. Or don't you?"

"I know that, yes."

"Because I killed some of Risha's men. I didn't know..." Othi stopped. "This was supposed to be about making you feel better."

"So distract me," Aven said. "What happened?"

Othi rested his hand on his knees. "We boarded the ship. One of them. She had five. That one had a weapon that threw fire. Pots of fire, and whatever they hit burned, even underwater—"

"Inferno oil," Aven breathed. "Oh, fuck—"

"That's about what Aunt Aleia said, minus the fuck." Othi sniffed. "You learn that from Owyn? The swearing, I mean."

Aven smiled. "Yeah, I did. All right. That's what happened to the canoes?"

Othi nodded. "We had to stop them before they wiped us all out. So Aunt Aleia sent borers underneath, and I led warriors up onto the deck to stop that weapon." He closed his eyes. "I...don't really know how many people I killed. It was all a blur, until the last one." He stopped again. "Ven, he was younger than me. And I gutted him, and I watched him die. And...that's when I knew I couldn't do it anymore." He looked up and took a deep breath. "I still see him. I still see the light going out of his eyes. He had blue eyes."

Aven took a deep breath. "You really want to know?"

Othi nodded. "I really do. What did she do to you, Ven? Aria said something about breaking the cycle of the change."

"That's what she was trying to do. Risha was trying to break the cycle of the change. She said it would make us human." Aven swallowed. His throat felt tight. His hip ached. "We don't know how many people she killed. We do know she killed Virrik. What she did..." Aven stopped again. "I can still smell that room, Othi. It was...it's in Terraces. Down where the rooms flood when the tides come in. Marik said it was a room the Water tribes who lived there used. But it hadn't been used for a long time. The water in there was stale. I can still smell it. I can still hear the water dripping. But...you remember how I used to be scared of caves?"

Othi nodded. "Yeah."

"Not anymore. Because there's nothing in a cave that's worse than what was in that room." Aven swallowed again, running his sweating hands up and down his thighs. "I woke up chained. Wrists chained, and ankles chained about so far apart." He held his hands wide, and Othi went pale.

"Fuck," Othi breathed.

Aven stared at him, then started laughing. "Got you doing it now!"

Othi didn't laugh. He shook his head. "And you survived that. You said the room flooded. You survived."

Aven rubbed his hand over his face, feeling the swallowed laughter strangling in his chest. "I don't know how," he said. "I don't know how I survived. I was ready to die. I sang my own honor chant, Othi. I thought I was dead. And then I woke up, and Fa was there, and all the others. And I was alive. But..." He gestured to himself. "I was like this. I probably did it to myself, Fa said. I tried to stop the pain and I tried to heal myself. So a large part of this is my fault—"

"None of it is your fault," Othi interrupted. "Don't even say that. If she hadn't done that to you, you'd never have tried to heal yourself. So it's all her. All Risha." He looked up at Aven. "Can I help kill her?"

"I thought you said you were done killing," Aven answered.

"I'll make an exception," Othi said. He looked over his shoulder at the dancing floor. "I don't think I ever saw you dance. You didn't, at the festivals."

"Grandmother wouldn't allow it."

Othi nodded his head toward the floor. "Come on, then. Just you and me." He got to his feet and took his swords off his back. "No one else to see. Come dance with me."

Chapter Nine

Aven slowly got to his feet. "Othi, I'm not sure about this," he said. He reached up and touched the hilt of one of his swords. "I'm not ready to dance—"

Othi arched a brow. "Not ready?" he repeated. "You told Aunt Aleia you're dancing every night—"

"If you can call basic forms dancing," Aven interrupted. "While you were gone, I hurt myself again, and now I'm back to the beginning. I'm trying to—"

"So show me what trying looks like," Othi said. He spread his arms, his blades swinging wide. "You're good, Aunt Aleia says. Show me."

Aven closed his eyes and took a deep breath. He was about to refuse when Othi spoke again.

"Was she right?"

Aven opened his eyes again. "What?"

"Aunt Aleia?" Othi said. "Was she right?" He cocked his head to the side. "She was, wasn't she? You can't."

Aven stared at him, cold and hot and oddly furious, all at the same time. "You have no idea what you're talking about," he stammered. "You haven't been here. You have no idea—"

"So show me!" Othi insisted. "Look, either you can or you can't. But don't lie and say you're trying if you are not really."

"I'm not lying!" Aven growled. He stepped over the low fence, and Othi smirked at him. "You haven't been here—"

"Really, that's your excuse?" Othi shook his head. "Come on, Ven. You said the same thing to your mother. We haven't been here, so that's an excuse for you not to try? You need one of us to be a nursemaid?" He raised his swords. "Fine. I'll play. Come on. I'll even give you the first strike."

Aven turned back toward the fence. "I'm not playing your game, Othi. I need to go meet Aria." He started walking, and saw movement out of the corner of his eye. He reacted before he even recognized the attack, spinning away and pulling both blades free from the harness, blocking Othi's strike, feeling the impact down both arms. "Othi, what are you doing?"

"Proving a point!" Othi snapped, and struck again. He was fast, faster than he should have been for a man his size, and his next blow got through Aven's guard, the flat of his left-hand blade slamming into Aven's right side like a club. Aven staggered, nearly falling, and Othi snorted. "So much for trying."

Aven swallowed, the words hurting worse than the flat of the blade. "I need to go meet Aria," he said softly. "Get out of my way."

Othi just shook his head. "You know, maybe it would be best if you stay here. I'll take care of your women for you, since you can't—"

"WHAT ARE THEY DOING back here?" Owyn asked, following Del as he led them back toward the practice grounds. Treesi and Aria walked on his left, and Alanar on his right. Jehan and Aleia were behind them, and Aleia seemed oddly quiet.

"*I don't know*," Del signed. "*Aven was upset. Othi said he knew what to do. They went this way.*"

"Aven's upset?" Owyn repeated.

"Why was Aven upset," Aria asked. "What happened...Owyn, do you hear that?"

"Sounds like someone's drilling back here?" Owyn suggested. "Is the guard practicing this morning?"

"That's not the guard," Alanar said. "There's not enough noise."

They came around the corner of the building, and Owyn could see the dancing floor. And the two men battling there.

"What the fuck?" Owyn gasped. "What are they doing?"

"Mother of us all," Aleia murmured from behind him. "Jehan, you didn't tell me—"

"I did tell you," Jehan said. "You didn't believe me. Or him. Do you believe him now?"

Owyn didn't turn to ask what they were talking about. He couldn't. Couldn't tear his eyes from the deadly dance on the mossy dancing floor.

He'd seen Aven fight with his hook swords only once. It had been in the Heart of the World, when Fandor had attacked him. But that fight had been nothing like this — in the Heart of the World, Aven had been defending himself against a crazed attacker.

Here, Aven seemed to be the crazed attacker. Othi was holding his own against his cousin, but it looked like it was just barely. There was a look of steely determination on Othi's face, and streaks of blood on his arms and running down his leg. Aven, on the other hand, looked like he was untouched, except for a wide welt across his ribs. He was clearly favoring his left leg and not putting his full weight on it. It made him look as though he was skipping, but it didn't seem to be slowing him down; when Othi tried to attack on that side, Aven drove him back.

"He's bleeding," Treesi gasped. "Othi is bleeding. Aria, make them stop."

Owyn glanced at Aria, who looked dumbstruck. "I've never seen him fight like this," she breathed. "I have seen him practice, but never fight like this." She looked over her shoulder. "Aleia?"

"He's better than he was," Aleia said. "Even with the leg. I wouldn't have thought it possible."

"He's not going to be able to walk when he's done there," Owyn said. "He's going to be in so much pain—"

"Going to be?" Alanar snorted. "He already is. I can feel it from here." He turned his head. "Jehan, can you feel it? Treesi?"

"He needs to stop. He's hurting so much. Make him stop!" Treesi's voice was as shrill as Owyn had ever heard it, and he saw Othi react. Saw him glance to the side. Saw him take his attention off Aven. Treesi saw it, too, and shouted, "Othi, no!"

It was too late — Aven saw the opening and took it, and a heartbeat later, Othi was on his back, his swords in pieces on the ground around him. Aven stood over him, balanced on one foot and breathing hard.

"Was that proof enough?" Aven snapped. "That you're wrong? That I can still fight?"

Othi grinned up at him. "Oh, I never doubted you for a minute. I knew you could still fight," he said. Then he waved his arm toward the group. "And now, so does your mother."

Aven blinked. He turned to look, and the shock at seeing that he and Othi had an audience was clear. He lowered his blades and stepped back.

Onto his left foot.

Owyn heard Alanar's strangled yelp a moment before Aven's face went gray and he dropped like a stone.

Owyn broke into a run, but Jehan was faster, vaulting over the low fence and dropping to his knees next to his son. "Alanar! I need you. Be careful of the fence!"

"Owyn!" Alanar turned. "Help?"

Owyn grabbed Alanar's arm and guided him onto the dancing floor. Then he left his husband and went over to Othi, who was sitting with Treesi by his side.

"You're not hurt?" he asked.

"Not much, no," Othi answered. "And Treesi is taking care of me." He looked past Owyn. "How bad is he?"

"No idea," Owyn answered. He glanced back, then folded his arms over his chest. "So what the fuck was that?" He felt warmth at his shoulder, looked back and saw Aria. Her wings were spread, and Owyn reached back and took her hand, prepared to hold her back.

"Were you trying to die?" Aria snapped. "Because if you had hurt him, I would have killed you myself."

"Me? No!" Othi shook his head. "No, I know him," he said. "I trust him. I know he wouldn't hurt me. Well, not more than scratches, anyway. And I've had worse than this."

"Then what were you doing?"

Othi looked up at her and answered calmly, "He needed to see that he still could. That he could still fight for himself, and for you. And he wasn't going to do that unless I pushed." He rubbed his hands down the front of his kilt. "I can be a stinging cloud better than anyone. Comes from being the little brother. Ask Neera."

"Stinging cloud?" Owyn repeated. "What's that?"

"It's something that lives in the deep," Aleia answered. "It floats on the tides, and the venom makes your skin itch." She folded her arms over her chest and looked at Othi. "Othi, you risked your life. Why?"

Othi got to his feet, putting one arm around Treesi. "Because you told him you thought he was crippled," he answered. His voice was low, and Owyn realized that Aria wasn't the only one who was angry. "And he was ready to believe you. I just proved to him that he wasn't."

"I did not!"

"You did," Jehan said. Aleia turned to face her husband. "You said you didn't think he was going to get any better, and that I was getting his hopes up."

"That's not the same—"

"It is," Aria said. "It is, and how dare you?"

"Aunt Aleia?" Othi added. "You're wrong. Admit it. And when he wakes up, apologize. Because you saw him. You saw him fighting, and you saw him winning."

"More important, you saw him fighting and winning through enough pain that healers could feel it from over there," Jehan said, pointing back the way they'd come. "You saw him beat a bigger opponent through enough pain that he fainted when he put his foot down. So do not tell me that he's not trying, or that he can't do it." Jehan looked back to where Alanar sat on the ground next to Aven. "Leia, he's right. You have no idea of what happened here while you were gone. He injured the hip again to the point where he could not walk, trying to save someone's life. He's a healer to his fingertips, but he's your boy to his fins. He's as stubborn as you are, and for the first day or two, I was worried that he'd crippled himself permanently to try and save a life."

"Jehan, how is he?" Aria asked. "He didn't do permanent damage, did he?"

"No, he didn't. And what he did today may have shown me the mistakes we made in working on his hip after that nightmare ride," Jehan answered. "He's torn everything to shreds. Again. But I know why now. There's a rough spot on the femoral head. Maybe a bone chip. I'm not sure. It's small enough I'll fully admit that I missed it after we worked on the hip after we went after Evarra. That is why he's still been in pain even though he's been doing everything right. It's been acting like sharkskin, aggravating the ligament." He rubbed his hand over his face. "Alanar?"

"I missed it, too," Alanar admitted. "Even though I examine him more frequently than you do. I can feel it now, because you pointed it out. But I missed it before. Pirit will have both our heads for this."

"Probably." Jehan agreed. "And now we have another problem. I'm not sure how we're going to travel. If we're going to make our camp tonight, we need to leave soon. But he'll need to stay in trance at least a few hours while I reconnect the ligaments and do something about that chip. It won't wait for us to get to Terraces."

Othi caught his breath. "I...I didn't know it was that bad!" he stammered. "I didn't know it was going to hurt him that much! I thought...get him out here, get him moving. Get him to see that he can still dance. That he can still fight. That it didn't matter what Al...what anyone said. That he wasn't crippled." He licked his lips. "I'll take him on my canoe? Him and you? That way, he can be comfortable in trance? And I can start apologizing?"

Jehan smiled. "We'll ask him when he wakes—"

That was the moment when Aven gasped, his eyes going wide. He tried to sit up and yelped, and Alanar rested his hand on Aven's chest.

"Easy. Lie still. We're working on the hip."

Aven groaned and flopped back down onto the moss. "How bad is it? How badly did I fuck it up this time?"

"You'll be spending a few hours in trance, Ven," Jehan said. "Othi has volunteered to take us to Shadow Cove on his canoe, so you can be comfortable."

Aven nodded, closing his eyes. "Allie, can you block it?" he asked. "It's hurting badly enough to make my hair ache." Then he gasped and let out a long breath. "Oh, thank you. I...can I sit?" Alanar put his hand behind Aven's back and helped him to sit up. Aven looked across to where Othi was standing with Treesi. "I marked you?" he asked

"A couple of times," Othi said. "Ven, I'm sorry. I didn't know it was going to hurt you this much."

"Explain why, then?"

Othi nodded. "You beat me," he said. "I didn't hold anything back, and you beat me. You shattered my swords." He smiled. "You just proved to everyone who watched us that you are quite probably the best of all the Water warriors." He walked over and held his hand out. "I'm sorry. But you can kick my tail for it once your hip is back to rights, okay?"

Aven snorted. "Why do I have to kick your tail again? I already did it." He reached up and took Othi's hand, letting Othi pull him up off the ground and steady him while he balanced on his right foot. Aven looked around. "Aria—"

"You have nothing to apologize for, my Water," Aria said. "Other than the pain, how do you feel?"

"Other than the pain?" Aven repeated. He looked at Othi, then smiled. "Better. I...Othi, how did you know?"

"Know what?" Othi asked.

"That the worst part was worrying that I wasn't going to be able to protect Aria if I had to." He glanced at Aria. "I wasn't the one to protect you when Hilah tried to take us out of the Palace. Del was the one who stopped the archer."

"And you stopped Hilah," Aria reminded him. "You broke his ribs, remember?"

"He never should have gotten us," Aven replied. "I'm supposed to be better than that."

"What was this?" Aleia asked. "What exactly did happen while we were gone?"

"In a nutshell?" Owyn answered and started ticking things off on his fingers. "Risha left spies who tried to take Aven and Aria out of the Palace, Del killed a man, Aven was poisoned but it was a total accident, Risha lured an entire squadron out and killed most of them and took Trey prisoner, and Aven rode like an absolute fucking madman out to try and save Evarra's life, but she died before he got there." He frowned. "Did I get it all?"

"You left out that you talked to Milon again," Alanar said. "And you were in trance for six hours. And you left out that we found in his journals." He frowned. "Aven, that's the rest of it, isn't it?"

"You found his journals?" Aleia repeated. Before she could say anything else, Othi interrupted.

"Risha has Trey?" he said. "I...I didn't even notice I didn't see him. I thought...I didn't really see anyone. I thought I'd catch up with him on the road." He looked at Aleia. "He wasn't on the ship—"

"Not the ones we sank, no," Aleia answered.

"No, they took him after you drove them back on land. Which, I need to know where that was." Owyn looked at Aven. "After you apologize."

Aleia folded her arms over her chest. "I apologize," she said. "I was wrong."

"Yes, you were," Aven said softly. "Othi, what were you saying about your canoe?"

"I..." Othi stammered. He glanced at Aleia, then looked back at Aven. "I was going to take you and your Fa to Shadow Cove. That way, you can stay in healing trance and be comfortable, and we'll meet everyone else there."

"We could get most of the healing done here, and leave tomorrow," Jehan added. "By canoe, it will only take us a few hours to get to Shadow Cove. We might even be there before them."

Aven frowned, then shook his head. "My place is with my Heir," he said. "I'll manage. And we should go. I'm making us late to leave."

"We're not moving until you tell me what you found in the journals," Aleia said. "Because I'm missing something very important, aren't I?"

"Just a few things, yeah," Owyn muttered. He looked at Aven, then at Del. Then at Aria, who nodded. He turned to Aleia. "Milon's injuries killed his legs—"

"What?" Aleia went pale.

"He can't feel anything below the waist," Owyn answered. "This whole thing? Started out because they were trying to protect him. They were keeping him hidden to heal. Then something changed, and they weren't helping him anymore. They were keeping him locked away, because they couldn't use him anymore. Didn't matter that he was the Firstborn — his legs didn't work. He couldn't walk, so he was broken, so he couldn't possibly be Firstborn anymore. So he was useless to them. They told him you were dead. Then...they told him he was dead. And maybe he was."

"Owyn!" Jehan gasped. "You..."

"Yeah, I didn't tell you that," Owyn said. He dragged his fingers through his hair. "Don't you tell Mem that, okay? It'll upset him. When I talked to him the first time, he told me he didn't have a name anymore. And the last time, yesterday, I told him I was retesting because I died. He thought it was funny, because they told him he died, too. I think that's why they told him he didn't have a name anymore. But, yeah...they stopped helping him because he wasn't getting better." He swallowed and looked at Alanar. "Because he couldn't get better."

"These were healers," Aven said, his voice quiet. "Healers decided that because he couldn't walk, he was useless. Worthless. He was a broken doll that they threw away into a locked room." He frowned. "Maybe it shouldn't surprise me. It's what they do in Terraces to the insane. Lock them up in the green levels. Take care of them, but...they're put away where they won't bother anyone.

That's what they did to Milon. Is that what they'll do to Alanar next? To Del?" He looked at his mother. "To me?"

"Ven—"

"Don't say it won't happen, Fa," Aven interrupted. "It's where this is heading. People like Risha, they already think Water and Air aren't human. It's not a big step to apply the same measure to someone who isn't perfect." He frowned. "How long before they start killing them, rather than waste the time and resources locking them away?"

"Mother of us all," Owyn breathed. "That's sick. That's awful. That's..." He paused. "Oh, fuck. That's already happening. In Forge. I mean, it was happening in Forge. When there was a Forge. They didn't have green levels. They just took people who went insane down to the vents and left them."

"What?" Jehan gasped. "No—"

Owyn nodded. "Yeah, they did. I remember telling Teva. I thought the green levels were better. But..." He paused. "Jehan, when did the green levels start?" he asked. "In Terraces. When did that start? We...we were wondering where the idea that disabled means broken came from. Because Ambaryl thought it, and Nestor. And...I don't know. Maybe Risha. Maybe it's linked? Maybe it's the same?"

Jehan frowned. Then he shook his head. "I...I don't know. We didn't have them when I was training. Not at the main healing complex. Maybe my mother knows. We'll find out when we get to Terraces." He sighed. "Aven, are you sure you want to leave now?"

Aven nodded. "Just help me to the carriage." He looked over at the shards of Othi's swords. "I owe you new blades, Othi."

"Don't worry about it," Othi said. "That was a good end for them, I think. Helping you? That's a good end. And I'm not going to need them anymore. Come on. You can lean on me."

Chapter Ten

"There's a hole in your theory, Aven," Alanar said as they started back to the courtyard. "About the next step being killing the disabled instead of locking them away."

Aven didn't turn to look at Alanar. He was too focused on trying not to scream as he hobbled along next to Othi. Even dampened, the pain was still excruciating. "What?"

"Milon," Alanar answered. "He's still alive. But...I don't know. It doesn't make sense."

"None of this makes sense," Owyn said. "Unless they don't dare kill him because he's Firstborn."

"There you are!" Aven looked up to see Steward coming toward them. "Where did you go? We should be on the road already and what in the Mother's name did you *do*?" He stopped walking and stared at Aven and Othi. "What were you two doing?" he demanded.

Aven looked up at Othi, who grinned. "We were..." Othi started. He stopped. "Aven, what were we doing?"

"Proving a point," Aven finished. "Now, which coach are we in?"

"That's why I was looking for you," Steward said. "How do you want to arrange yourselves? Heir and Companions and...well...spouses? That's seven, and seven will be tight in one coach."

"Especially since you wanted me to work on that map, Aria," Owyn said. "I..." he frowned. Then he shook his head. "I don't know. I don't want to split up. But Aven can't ride. Othi doesn't know how to ride. Allie—"

"Absolutely refuses to put on boots," Alanar grumbled.

"Yeah, that," Owyn continued. "Aria probably shouldn't ride. Treesi?"

"No," Treesi answered. "I don't like it."

"*I'll ride alongside,*" Del signed. "*I don't mind. I like riding, and it's a nice day.*" He looked at Steward. "*Will you ride with me?*"

Steward nodded. "I'll be stuck in a carriage soon enough, so I'll ride today."

"So, in our carriage, it will be me, Aven and Alanar on one side, and Owyn, Othi and Treesi on the other," Aria suggested. "So that Alanar can help Aven be comfortable."

Steward frowned slightly. "You're going to explain to me why. But not now. We need to get on the road. Jehan? Aleia? Memfis, Lady Meris and Afansa are in the second coach. Gathi, Skela and Zarai are in the third coach, as are our two pages—"

"Oh, the boys are coming with us?" Aria asked. Steward nodded.

"Will you be with them, or do you want to ride?" he finished.

"It took me three days after the nightmare ride to be able to walk a straight line. I think I'll be in the coach to start out and build back up to riding all day." Jehan answered. He looked at Aleia. "And there needs to be a long conversation, I think, about what's been missed here."

"Speaking of that," Owyn said. "Can you show me on a map where you drove Risha's ship onto shore? The one she had Milon on?"

Aleia frowned. "She had five ships. We sank two on the deep, and those were searched thoroughly—"

"Before you sank them, I hope?" Owyn interrupted.

Aleia sniffed. "Of course before they sank. Before they sank completely, anyway. And they were searched again under the waves. There were no prisoners. One of them was loaded with inferno oil—"

"Mother of us all," Alanar breathed.

"Those two diverted us enough that when we caught two of the other three ships, Risha wasn't on any of them. Nor were there any prisoners. We scuttled both of them—"

"But you don't know where Risha came on shore. Not exactly, anyway." Owyn frowned. "Approximately?"

"What are you thinking, Mouse?" Aven asked.

"What Aria suggested. That if I have an approximate area, I can see what's around there, and where the roads are," Owyn answered. "It'll be a really big target, but it'll be someplace to look."

"What happened to the fifth ship?" Treesi asked. "You said there were five ships. You only sank four."

"That's what kept us away for so long," Aleia answered. "Finding the last ship. When we did find it, it was south, in Forge harbor. And it had been scuttled, probably by her own men."

Owyn blinked. "Wait...that means they could be anywhere!"

"No, they can't. They took Trey north of here," Aven said. "And you spoke to Milon the next night. Trey was with him already. They had to have gone on shore someplace close to Turtle Rock—"

"And you didn't pass them on the road between the Palace and the standing stones, so they were further north," Jehan added. "Leia, you remember Turtle Rock?"

"Yes, and there's no good harbor near there," Aleia answered. "But there's an inlet, and one of the ships we took was near that—"

"An inlet? Jasper Inlet?" Aria asked.

Aleia blinked. "How did you know?"

"Oh..." Aria turned to Owyn. "I know where your search needs to start."

"Glad one of us does," Owyn said. "Right, let's get going. We've got a long way to go."

They started walking again, heading back to the courtyard. The chaos had calmed somewhat, enough that Aven saw that Gathi was standing outside one of the coaches with Lexi and her younger siblings. Lexi was holding Ilithi, and the two boys were clinging to her skirts.

"You have to promise to mind Mother Lexi," Aven heard Gathi saying. "I'll come visit when I can, and when I come back to stay, I'll be a real healer, like Aven and Treesi and Alanar."

"Lexi is formally adopting Gathi's brothers and sisters," Aria said softly. "So that they won't have to worry now that Gathi is leaving them."

Aven smiled. "That's good. They're sweet children. They need someone to care for them."

"And Ami and Zia adore them," Alanar added. "Bask is just their age, and Ilithi is their favorite doll."

"Steward, it never feels right for me to ask her, but how is she?" Owyn asked. "Lexi. Really, I mean."

Steward frowned. "She's fine, so far as I can tell. She's settled in well to the role of housekeeper, and seems to be thriving. Why?"

"Well, I was worried. I mean, I kind of got her husband killed..."

"We did. It wasn't just you," Alanar corrected. "I was curious about that myself. She doesn't seem to resent either of us, but Denis wouldn't have been out there if it wasn't for us."

"Ah, I see." Steward nodded. "There's no way any of you would have known if neither of them told you. Lexi and Denis didn't have a marriage of affection the way that you and Alanar do, Owyn." He took a deep breath. "You met Nestor. He was Wingless Air. His entire family was. We had quite the small enclave of Wingless Air in the upper level servants here when the Usurper took power. And among that enclave, there were some odd ideas about women and their roles in the Palace. Galia was fine as housekeeper, because she was a widow. Ambaryl...well, clearly Nestor had other reasons for tolerating Ambaryl in a relative position of authority, even though she was unmarried—"

"She probably hung it over his head that she knew the secret, and he needed to let her do whatever the fuck she wanted," Owyn muttered.

Steward nodded. "I've no doubt you're right. Lexi, though...she was a kitchen maid when she found she was pregnant with Danir. Nestor was going to put her out, because she was unmarried and pregnant. She came to the Usurper, and Denis happened to overhear." He smiled. "He was the Usurper's valet at the time, you see. And that one drove Denis to distraction because they never agreed on anything. Denis thought that things ought to be one way, and the Usurper wouldn't do them. Which was why Denis stopped being the Usurper's valet. It made the both of them happier."

"Lexi?" Alanar prompted. Steward chuckled.

"Right. The next thing anyone knew, Denis and Lexi were asking to be married." Steward shook his head. "Their marriage was one of convenience and camouflage. Denis loved the children, but I don't think he sired any of them."

Lexi looked up. "That's none of your concern, Steward," she called.

"You have ears like a hawk, woman," Steward called back.

"Comes from long practice and three children." She shifted Ilithi to her other hip and came over to them. "You were telling them about my arrangement with Denis?"

"Well..." Owyn started. "We were worried. Thought...well...we sort of got your husband killed and all. Thought you might poison our soup one night for revenge."

"Really, Owyn!" Lexi sniffed. "You don't have to be so melodramatic." Then she smiled. "I suppose we should have talked about this before. Denis was a dear friend, yes. But he had absolutely no interest in sharing my bed at all. He volunteered to marry me to protect me from losing my place here."

Aria blinked. "I'm not as familiar with the Wingless as I should be," she said. "I didn't know about this way of thinking. My flock didn't go to the Solstice village often. I thought it was because my grandfather was insular. Now I understand it was because he was trying to protect me and my mother."

Steward nodded. "We'll find out more when we reach the Solstice village. Which we won't, if we don't get moving." He made shooing motions with his hands. "Off to your carriage, all of you. Owyn, Aria asked that I prepare a map for you. It's in your coach."

"Steward, why did the Usurper allow Nestor to do things like that?" Treesi asked as they started walking toward the coach.

Steward frowned. "It's...well...the Firstborn isn't the only dynasty in this Palace. There are servant families that go back nearly as long. Nestor's family was one of those. Everyone was just...accustomed to listening to them, I suppose. They knew the Palace better than anyone, better even than the Firstborn or the Companions who lived here. I think you could argue that the Firstborn ruled Adavar but the stewards ruled the Palace." He paused. "If you believed Nestor and Ankem, they were descended from one of the Firstborn, some seven or eight generations back. Nestor claimed he could trace the lineage, but I don't know that anyone ever saw the proof." He shrugged. "It doesn't matter now. The man is dead, and his line ended with him." He stopped outside the coach. "So Aria and Othi are in the middle. Who sits by which window?"

Othi looked into the coach. "Why am I in the middle?" he asked. "I mean, I understand Aria needing the room for her wings, but me..." He looked at the coach again, then coughed. "Oh, wait. I know. Balance. If I sit near the window, the coach will tip."

Steward nodded. "Exactly."

"But I need to be next to Aven, so I can block the pain," Alanar said. "How—"

"Alanar, can you sit across the coach from Aven?" Othi asked. "You both have long legs—"

Aven and Alanar both started laughing, until Jehan asked, "What's so funny?"

"Healing with my feet?" Alanar gasped.

"You just need to touch him," Jehan pointed out. "Othi is right. Now go get into the coach so we can leave."

"ALL I'M SAYING IS THAT it feels strange!" Alanar protested as the coach started moving. He stretched his legs out in front of him. "This is...it's just strange!"

Aven chuckled, stretching his own legs out and twining them into Alanar's. The pain that had started increasing almost immediately vanished. "It works. I'm not going to complain."

"Good, then you can help me." Owyn unrolled the map that Jehan had left for him. "Where do I start? Where's this inlet?"

Aria took the edge of the map and held it unrolled. "Here," she said, tapping the map. "This is Jasper Inlet."

Owyn nodded, reaching into his bag and taking out a piece of vine charcoal. He marked the inlet, and frowned. "So...this is where they came on land."

"Probably," Othi said. "As far as we could tell, it was the only mooring in that area. The rest was sheer cliffs."

Aria studied the map. "Steward told me that there was no good road to reach the village that was there."

Owyn looked up. "There's a village?"

"It had been dead a long time, it looked like," Othi said. "Ruined houses, old canoes. It looked like a Water village, Aunt Aleia said."

"It was," Aria said.

"I guess that's where the cart came from. Maybe they had it stashed there. After all, who'd go looking?" Owyn nodded. "And how long ago was that?"

Othi frowned slightly. "Call it...ten days maybe?"

Owyn looked up at him. "That isn't right. They've had Trey for two weeks. I need exact numbers, Othi. I need the best numbers you can give me."

Othi nodded and closed his eyes. No one said anything, so the only sound was the steady rhythm of the horses and the squeaking of the wheels.

"Three days after we left. Late in the day. An hour or two before sunset."

"You left three days before the squad was wiped out and Trey was taken," Owyn said. "So you drove them onshore." He frowned down at the map. "On a good road, this kind of coach can go from here to here in a day." He traced a line from the Palace to the ruins of the healing complex. "So, since the road isn't as good over here, I'm guessing that they got this far..." He traced the trail out of Jasper Inlet, and stopped. "Fuck, they must have hit the squad by accident. The trail from Jasper Inlet passes right near Turtle Rock."

"And then where do you think they went?" Aven asked. "From there, where could they go?"

"Well, we know they didn't go south," Owyn said, and ran his finger along the road north, making marks every so often. When the roads branched off, he measured each of them, making more marks. Finally, he looked up.

"I talked to Milon yesterday, and they weren't in the cart anymore. He didn't say how long they'd been stopped, but he said it had been a while. They're in a house, because there's a cellar with an air vent. So...if I were to guess, a while is at least a day or two, three at the outside. And a house? That means a village, right?" He looked around. "That make sense?"

"That does," Aria agreed. "So where do you think?"

"Depending on the road," Owyn answered, and made some circles on the map. "Could be any of these." He held the map level so that everyone could see it.

Aria reached out and tapped one circle in particular. "This is just outside the Solstice village."

Owyn nodded. "I'm trying to decide if she's brazen enough to go there, or too smart to go there. It's either the most likely place for her to go, or the least, and I can't decide which."

"Risha is arrogant," Alanar said. "She thinks she's untouchable, and now...well, she has a hostage that makes her untouchable. No one is going to risk hurting Milon—"

"They don't know he's him," Owyn interjected. "And honestly, who'd believe him? She probably bundled him off like one of the crackpots in the green levels...hey." He leaned over the map. "Is there a healing center up here? Anywhere near any of these spots?"

"I...Fa might know," Aven answered. "Or Grandmother, when we get to Terraces."

"Near the Solstice village?" Alanar asked. "Yes, but it's been empty for years, I think. Even before the purges."

"We'll need to find out for certain. Because if I was Risha, then I'd be telling people that I was transporting crackpots, and no one would look twice at a closed cart with someone inside shouting to be let out." Owyn sat up and wiped charcoal off his fingers, putting the vine back into his bag. "We'll talk about this with Steward, too. He might know."

"Owyn?" Alanar asked. "When you said a coach like this could go so far in a day, what were you measuring by?"

Owyn frowned. "By how far we got when we were trying to get back to Terraces. Why?"

Alanar nodded. "That's what I was afraid of."

"What?" Owyn asked. "What did I miss?"

"Nothing to do with your mapping, love," Alanar answered. "I just...where are we stopping tonight?"

Owyn went pale. "Oh...oh, no. Oh, fuck. You don't think...we can't...he...he wouldn't! Not the same place!"

"Owyn?" Aven asked. "Owyn, if you're going to faint—"

"What is it?" Othi asked.

"A coach can travel so far in a day," Alanar answered. "And when we were trying to get back to Terraces from the Palace when I was so sick, the coach went as far as it could before sunset, then stopped and made camp. And we were attacked that night." He took a deep breath. "We're going as far as we can in a day. Are we going to camp in the same place?"

"If it is the same place, then I'll sleep in the coach tomorrow," Owyn said. "Because I am not sleeping tonight. Not there. I'll keep the guards company."

"You need to sleep, Owyn," Treesi said.

"I will. In the coach tomorrow." He looked down at the map. "I need to update this as we go. I don't need to pay as much attention right now — we've been on the roads between the Palace and the ruins twice. But starting after Smuggler's...sorry. After Shadow Cove, I'll need to ride, so I can pay attention. Need to see if they did anything with the coast road. It was washed out when I was there in the spring."

"Owyn, show me how you navigate on a flat map?" Othi asked. "How do you tell direction?"

"Aven told me a bit about how you navigate at sea," Owyn said. "And it's not really different. Position of the sun and stars and the moon. And it don't matter that we're missing wind and waves, because you have visual landmarks to keep you heading straight. Right?" He looked to the side. "Have I got it?"

Aven nodded at him. Alanar's pain dampening was making him feel sleepy. He closed his eyes and took a deep breath, feeling Aria lace her fingers into his.

If he slept now, then maybe he'd be able to stay up and keep Owyn company tonight.

Chapter Eleven

D el tipped his head back and closed his eyes, letting his mare
follow the entourage. This was one of the better sections of
road on the trip between the Palace and Terraces. It overlooked the
sea on the right, and there were wide, open fields on the left. On a
nice day like today, there was always a cool breeze off the sea, and
he could smell something in bloom. How long had it been since
he'd ridden this road?

"Enjoying yourself?"

He opened his eyes and turned, smiling at his father as he let
the reins fall. "*Yes. It's been a long time since we rode out like this. In
good weather, I mean. The last time we did this, it was in that storm.*"

Steward nodded. "The night everything changed." He looked
around. "For the better, I think. I need to ride down the line. Come
with me, or stay?"

Del looked over at the coach. Aven was at the closest window
and appeared to be asleep. Aria looked out at him, and waved. He
smiled and waved back.

"*I'll stay,*" Del signed. He watched as Steward urged his horse
forward, then reined in so that he was riding alongside the open
window. "*How is Aven?*" he asked Owyn.

Owyn leaned forward so he was visible. "He's asleep," he called.
"I don't want to wake him by yelling. Come around to this side?"

116

Del nodded and turned his horse, circling behind the coach and looking out over the fields as he came around to the landward side of the coach. Owyn smiled at him out the window.

"How does it look out there?" Owyn asked.

"*Quiet,*" Del answered. "*There's no one out here but us, I don't think.*" He looked out at the fields again. There was a broad flush of new green, shockingly bright against the burnt brown grasses. "*Do you see all the green? I don't remember seeing the fields turn green like this before. And I can smell something flowering.*"

"Is that a good thing?" Owyn asked. "Remember, I grew up in a city. We didn't have fields like this."

"*Green is good,*" Del answered. "*Green means that we might have a good planting season because the land is waking up.*" He saw movement, not far in the distance. "*I was wrong. There are people up ahead.*"

"What, farmers?"

"*Maybe. I don't think so, though,*" Del answered. "*I'm going to ride ahead, see if the guards have seen them.*" He tapped his heels against his mare's flanks, and rode up the line of coaches and wagons. He saw his father near the head of the entourage, riding alongside Karse. He joined them, and pointed.

"I saw them," Karse said. "We'll be on them in a few minutes at this rate. What do you think?"

Del blinked, then let his reins fall and signed. "*Farmers, maybe?*"

"He said farmers," Steward said. "I'm not sure. Not the way this road turns. If they're where I think they are, then they're too close to the road for a farm. That's the crossroads there, if I'm not mistaken."

Karse looked around. "Are there any towns along this stretch?"

"None," Steward answered. "Not anymore. At least, none close to the road. There are some a few miles east. But the towns that were supported by the comings and goings of the trade caravans all dried up and fell to dust years ago." He gestured to Karse's saddlebag. "The map I gave you? The marked wells were either towns or guard stations. And now that I'm thinking of them, there's a well around that area. So they might have stopped for water."

"What was there?" Karse asked. "Town or station?"

Steward frowned, then nodded. "That was a waystation, once, for the trade road. That station marked the crossroads for the Earth route to the east, and the Water route along the coast. The waystation has been gone for years, but the well was still good as of last year."

"Seems like a reasonable guess that they stopped for water, then. But we won't be careless," Karse said. He turned and raised his arm, and two of the guards rode up to them. "Wren, Lyka, you two ride on ahead. Take the Heir's banner, and see what's up there," he ordered.

"*That might still scare them,*" Del signed. "*The guards are wearing Palace livery.*"

Steward translated, and Karse nodded. "Can't be helped," he said. "They are Palace guards. But here's hoping the banner will help. They should have heard by now that the Heir is in residence. And maybe even that we're heading out on Progress. They might have come out to see." He looked at Del. "Tell Owyn, will you? That there are people up ahead?"

"*He knows. I told him when I saw them.*"

Karse grinned when Steward translated. "I'll make a guard out of you yet," he said. "And you're armed?"

Del tapped the back of his arm, his fingers thumping on the sheath.

"Good. Stay alert."

They rode on, and Del watched as the group of people grew closer and closer. Men and women. A few children. Handcarts, but no draft animals. He frowned, then reached over to touch his father's arm.

"What?" Steward asked.

"*Go to the other side of the coaches and stay out of sight,*" Del signed. "*We don't want a repeat of the healing center.*"

Steward blinked, then paled. "You're right. And I should have thought of that. I'll go to the far side of Aria's coach, and I'll tell them what's going on."

"*Aven is on that side, and he's asleep.*"

Steward chuckled. "I won't wake him unless it's an emergency." He turned his horse and rode off, and Del rode forward to catch up with Karse, seeing that the people were now much closer. Karse glanced at him, looking surprised.

"Are you sure you want to be up here?" he asked. "We don't know if it'll come to a fight. You should go back and stay under cover." He looked back. "Where's Steward?"

Del raised his hands, then realized that Karse wouldn't understand him. He reached into his bag and took out his tablet. "*We don't want a repeat of the healing center. He's under cover.*"

"Go join him," Karse said. "Especially since I can't be stopping to read what you have to say—"

"Captain!"

"Oh, fuck," Karse murmured, straightening as one of the guards he'd sent on ahead came riding back. "What's the word, Wren?"

"They're camped at the well, Captain. Doesn't seem to be a fighter among them. An older man, some old women, and a bunch of young folks. They're all a bit excited to see the Heir for themselves." He looked back over his shoulder. "One weird thing, though. They're Earthborn, and they said they were sent west to start a new settlement by someone they called the Seer. They said that they were told that the blesséd Mother had come, that she'd bless their settlement, and that she's going to bring everything good back to the world."

Karse glanced at Del, who shrugged. "The blesséd Mother," Karse repeated. "Not Mother of Us All, or any of Her other titles?"

"No, Captain. We didn't talk much, but...I got the feeling they meant Aria."

Karse nodded slowly. "Del, go back and tell the others what he just told us."

Del nodded, turning his horse and riding back the way he'd come. He could see Owyn, who was leaning out the window of the coach.

"*Things have gotten strange,*" Del called silently. He rode past the coach, turned back, and drew up next to the window.

"Strange?" Owyn repeated. "Considering that things are already fucking weird, strange how?"

Del looked ahead. He could see Karse and the people alongside the road. "*The people at the well are Earthborn who have come here to settle and start a new town. They're excited to meet Aria. But they said they were sent from the east by the Seer.*"

"What, a Smoke Dancer?" Owyn leaned further out the window.

"Owyn, tell us what he said," Alanar said.

"That the people up the road are waiting to meet us, because they want to see Aria. And they were sent by a Smoke Dancer."

"*Not a Smoke Dancer,*" Del corrected. "*They said the Seer.*"

"All right. The Seer. Not a Smoke Dancer. But what else is a Smoke Dancer but a seer?"

"And they want to meet me?" Aria asked.

"*Tell Aria they call her the blesséd Mother, who's going to bless their town and bring everything good back to the world.*"

He heard Owyn repeat the words, followed by Aria's voice, "They call me *what?*"

"What?" Aven jerked upright, looking around. "What happened?"

"It's all right," Del heard Othi say. "We're not under attack. Just surprised."

"Surprised by what?"

Del heard a horse coming up behind him, and looked over his shoulder to see his father. "They call Aria blesséd Mother," Steward repeated. "That's...are we sure they're not talking about the Mother?"

"*The guard said he didn't think so. And I've never heard anyone call the Mother by that title.*" Del let his reins fall so that he could sign.

"Del, she's going to run away with you!" Owyn warned. Del laughed and shook his head.

"*She's knee trained, like a warhorse,*" Del signed. "*She won't run.*"

Owyn's brows rose. "Knee trained? Can you teach me that?"

"I will, if you want," Steward offered. "If Del wants to ride in the coach. Lady is a good horse to learn on. She's...well, a lady."

"I don't want Freckles getting jealous," Owyn said.

"About these people," Aria said. "Are we stopping?"

Steward looked down the road, then back at Aria. "Do you want to?"

"Isn't that why we're out here?" Aria asked. "Tell Karse that I wish to meet them. They've clearly been waiting for me. And I am curious about this Seer."

Del nodded and signed, "*I'll ride on and tell Karse. Fa, will you tell the other coaches?*"

"I'll tell them. Go on."

Del nodded and picked up his reins, urging Lady forward. By the time he reached Karse, the Guard captain had dismounted near the well, and was talking to the older man. Del drew Lady to a stop and let his reins fall again, taking his tablet out.

"*Aria wants to meet with them.*" He handed the tablet down to Karse, who read it, then nodded.

"I thought she might say that," Karse said. "A short visit, I think. We've a long way to go."

"You," the man with Karse said, looking up at Del. "The Seer spoke of you, too. You're the Silent One. He called you the Fallen Feather."

Del blinked and looked at Karse, who shook his head slightly.

"Why don't you go see about the others?" Karse suggested. Del nodded and turned Lady back toward the coaches. They came to a stop as he reached them, and Owyn jumped out, helping Aria out. Then he helped Aven. Del dismounted, handed Lady's reins to a guard, and went to meet the others.

"Just us?" Treesi asked as she got out of the coach. "Just the Heir and the Companions?"

"Yes, I think that is what we will do," Aria said. "Othi—?"

"I'll stay here with Alanar," Othi said.

Owyn smiled. "Thank you, Othi."

Del started signing. "*This is really strange. He knows who I am. This Seer called me the Silent one and the Fallen Feather. How could he know?*"

Aria's eyes widened. "Did I understand you correctly? He called you the Fallen Feather?" She looked toward the well. "If the Seer is a Smoke Dancer, then they would know the vision. But not with that much detail, to know you were silent. I need to know more." She started walking, and Del fell in between Treesi and Aria, noting that they'd almost automatically fallen into the same order in which they sat when they were seated in the Hall.

They approached the group at the well, where Del could see that Karse had been joined by Jehan, Aleia, Memfis and Meris. The man who'd known him pointed. "It's her!" he said, sounding excited. "The blesséd Mother, just as the Seer said!"

Aria didn't respond, not until she came to a stop near the well. She looked at the group, who were all watching her intently. Then she smiled. "I am Aria," she said. "Daughter of Milon and Liara, and Heir to the Firstborn. I'm told you were waiting for me?"

One of the older women burst into tears. "It's her!" she sobbed. "It's her, it's her!"

Aria glanced at Aven, and they walked forward together. Aria held her hand out to the woman. "It's me," she said gently. "What's your name?"

The woman took Aria's hand and pressed it to her cheek. "Oh, blesséd Mother! I...I am Narice." She looked up at the older man. "I'm here with my man, to start a new town. To rebuild."

Aria smiled. "That's a good thing. Thank you." She leaned forward and kissed Narice's cheek. "It isn't easy to leave everything you know behind. I know this. What help do you need?"

"Thank you, my lady," the man said. "I'm Torri. Narice is my wife, and Micha, over there, that's our boy. Lissa is his wife, and Rana is her mother." He introduced the others, then nodded. "The Seer said it was time for us to come here and put a town by the well at the crossroads that overlooked the sea. It was time to start rebuilding, because you were here. Our blesséd Mother was here, with her four." He pointed. "The Heart of the Sea. The Twice-born Son of Smoke. The Peace Bringer, and the Silent One, the Fallen Feather."

"Torri, who is this Seer?" Aven asked. "Is he a Smoke Dancer?"

Torri laughed. "No," he answered. "He's full-blood Earth, all the way back to Mother Mika, same as me." He grinned and looked around. "This is the furthest I've ever been from where I sprouted, and that's the truth."

"And what made you decide here?" Owyn asked. "I mean...there's not even a hint of the town that used to be here. I mean...there's a well, so there was a town. Right?" He looked around. "Jehan?"

"There was a waystation here," Jehan answered. "Not a town."

"There will be a town, as soon as we're done. The Seer told us to go west for a full cycle of the moon, and find the well near the crossroads over the sea, where you could see the broken teeth rocks." He pointed. "Go look."

Owyn walked to the far side of the road. "Well, fuck," he called. "They do look like broken teeth."

Del trotted over to join him, and looked down at the water and the row of jagged rocks that did look like teeth. He and Owyn walked back to the group together.

"This is our place now," Torri declared. "We'll build here, and start things anew." He smiled as he looked at Aria. "If you give your blessing, my Lady?"

Aria smiled. "Of course I do," she said. "And my welcome, and my thanks. I look forward to seeing your town when we come back." She looked around. "Steward. Where is Steward?"

"Aria—" Owyn said softly.

"Steward, attend!"

Del went cold, seeing his father come out from the shadow of the coach. His face was pale, but he came forward.

"My Heir?" he said.

"Come and meet Torri," Aria said. "They'll be so close to the Palace. What aid can we offer them?"

Steward swallowed visibly and walked over to stand next to Karse. He bowed slightly. "Torri. I suppose I should call you Headman Torri?"

Torri smiled. "I'd prefer you call me by name," he answered. "If you start calling me Headman, I'll have to call you the Forgotten, and I don't think you'd want that being bandied around. Those who haven't been taught by the Seer, they'll need convincing. But I know you're not the Forgotten One." His eyes widened. "Don't you go falling down now, man. You've got a long road ahead of you."

Del turned to see how pale his father had grown. Steward nodded. "Well, then, Torri," he said in a shaking voice. "It's a pleasure to meet you. You can call me Steward."

Torri stepped forward and held his hand out. "It's a blessing, Steward."

Steward smiled slightly. "Thank you. Yes, it is. I...Aria, if you want to ride on, I'll spend a little time with Torri, find out what they need. Leave me a guard to ride back to the Palace with a message for Lexi, and I'll catch you up in a mile or two." He looked up at the sky. "You'll want to ride on, if you're going to make the camp before dark."

Aria blinked, and Del could see that she'd realized what she'd done. "I thought we'd stay—"

"I'll stay," Jehan said abruptly. "I need to get used to riding again anyway. A mile or two? I can do that. Karse, leave us two guards. One to go back to the Palace, and one to ride escort." He came over and leaned down to say something in Aria's ear. She nodded, and said something in reply that Del couldn't hear.

"Fa—" Aven started, and stopped when Jehan glared at him.

"You're not going near a horse, and don't even think it," Jehan said. "See to Aria, and go let Alanar work on that hip some more."

Aven nodded slowly. "Yes, Fa." He turned back to Torri and smiled. "We'll see you when next we come this way."

Torri nodded. "I look forward to it." He bowed deeply to Aria. "My Lady, blessèd Mother, thank you."

OWYN HELD HIS TONGUE until they were back in the coach and it had started moving again. Then he turned to Aria.

"Really?" he said. "Trying to get us killed on the first day?"

She grimaced. "I spoke without thinking again," she said. "And I realized it too late. You're right. That could have been very bad."

"It could have been another healing center brawl," Aven corrected. "Aria, you need to slow down and think!"

She nodded. "I will apologize to Steward when we see him later." She looked at Aven. "Heart of the Sea, he called you. He knew all of us, even Steward. And he knew you are the Heart. How could the Seer have known that?"

"What's the Heart?" Othi asked. "Or is that something I'm not supposed to ask, because it's Companion stuff?"

"It is Companion stuff," Aria said, smiling. "I will have to ask if it is something I can explain to you."

Othi nodded. "Fair enough," he said. "So who were they?"

"They came to build a town," Treesi answered. "They said they were sent to build a town there, at the crossroads."

"But the Seer isn't a Smoke Dancer," Owyn added. "He's Earth, Torri said. I can't wait to hear what Granna has to say about this."

Chapter Twelve

"An Earthborn seer," Meris murmured. "Memfis and I have been worrying at that like a bone for miles. I've never heard of such a thing. And for him to be so accurate? I can't explain it."

Owyn shifted, crossing his legs and tipping his face up to the sun. They'd stopped for a midday meal and to rest the horses, and he was sitting on the ground at Meris' feet. He smiled as she ran her fingers through his hair.

"I can't get over these curls," she said. "You never let it get long enough to curl before."

"I'm not sure I like it," Owyn admitted. "But Alanar and Del both tell me I'm not allowed to cut it. Allie says I can't cut mine until his grows back out."

Meris chuckled. "When it gets that long, I'll teach you to twist it. When Memfis was your age, he wore his hair in twists."

Owyn looked up at her. "Mem had hair? Long enough to twist?"

Alanar walked over and sat down next to Owyn. "Grandmother," he said. "What can we expect on this Progress? The only places I've been since I was ten are the Palace and the Solstice village to visit my mother's flock."

Meris nodded. "We'll stop at each village and town, and stay. A day for a small village, perhaps two for a larger one. That being said, Steward said that he expected to stay longer than a week in Terraces, but I also think he has an ulterior motive."

Owyn chuckled. "He's been missing Auntie Rhexa."

Meris smiled. "So I gathered from Memfis. The lore says we have to go to Forge, but there's no Forge to go to anymore, so I'm not certain how we'll fulfill that part. In any case, we'll be close enough to see how badly our lands are damaged, but not so close to be unsafe. Once we reach the foothills, we'll turn north, and go north along the Range road until we reach the Solstice village. From there, we'll go to the Temple."

"Are there still passable roads?" Aven asked. He leaned heavily on his walking stick as he came over to join them. "I thought the roads were all fallen to ruin."

"They are and they aren't," Meris answered. "Sit, Aven."

Aven smiled. "If I sit, I'll stiffen up and it will hurt more when I stand. I'm fine, Mother Meris. What do you mean yes and no?"

"The roads are fallen to ruin, as you put it," Meris answered. "But they were built to last, with all the skill of Fire and Earth craftsmen. You saw the roads outside the Palace. They were passable, if a little rough in places."

"The coast road from Shadow to Serenity was washed out when I was there last," Owyn said. "But the inland road was fine."

"People still travel, even though they weren't supposed to," Jehan said as he came to join them.

Aven smiled as he turned to his father. "When did you get here?"

"Just now. Steward is off with Aria, who is apologizing for scaring him out of a year's growth, I think." He sighed. "Speaking of apologies, Aven, go talk to your mother."

Aven blinked and looked around. "Does she want to talk to me?" he asked. "Where is she? I haven't seen her since we stopped."

"I haven't seen her yet, either. I said you should go talk to her," Jehan said. "I didn't say she wanted to talk to you. She's been...." He shook his head. "I don't think she realized that she'd given up on you, Ven. Not until you forced her to see that she had, and how much that hurt you. She's never seen you angry at her before. I think she's afraid she's lost you."

Aven frowned and looked down. "I don't know. She might have. She did give up on me, Fa. She told you that you were getting my hopes up. She had no idea what was happening here, what I was doing. What I'd done and how I'd hurt myself again. She just gave up on me without knowing any of it." He took a deep breath, then let it out. "I...no. Not ready to talk to her. Not yet. I'm still angry." He took another breath. "When I can talk to her without screaming at her, I will. Fair?"

Jehan nodded. "That's fair." He cocked his head to the side. "How is the leg?"

"Besides hurts like fuck?" Aven asked. He shrugged. "Alanar is trying, but every time we hit a rock, it undoes his work. Maybe I should have let Othi take me on his canoe."

"Or not tried to smash his brains all over the dancing floor?" Owyn added. "Because...yeah, that probably wasn't the smartest thing you've done today."

Aven grinned. "That probably wasn't the smartest thing I've done ever."

"Nah, I think riding into a squadron of guards was a whole lot stupider." Owyn frowned. "More stupid? Whichever. Fighting Othi was almost as fuckheaded as nearly getting yourself killed."

Aven chuckled. "Second on my fuckheaded ideas list. Of which there are how many?"

"Three," Owyn answered firmly. "Riding into the squadron, fighting Othi, and leaving us."

Aven looked thoughtful, then nodded. "I can live with having done only three really stupid things in my life."

"You're young," Meris said. "You have time to do even more."

TREESI HEARD THE LAUGHTER behind her and smiled. It was good to hear Aven laugh like that. He was usually in so much pain that it made him short tempered, and when he did laugh, it wasn't the full, merry laugh she was used to from their early days together. This was almost like that. She thought for a moment of going and joining him, of laughing with them. But she had something more important to do. She walked around the rocks and stopped. "Mama Aleia?"

Aleia was sitting in the shadow of the rocks, staring out over the sea. She jerked and looked up when Treesi said her name. "Treesi?"

"I came to see how you were," Treesi said. "May I come sit?"

Aleia looked back out over the water. "You can sit. I may not talk."

"That's fine," Treesi said. She sat down on the ground next to Aleia, looking out at the sparkling blue. "Mama?" she asked. "Is it blue underwater? Is the water blue all the way down?"

Aleia turned toward her and blinked. "No," she answered. "You've seen water in a glass, or in a bowl. It has no color."

"Then why is the sea blue?" Treesi pointed. "It's not the same blue as the sky, so it's not a reflection. Or is it?"

Aleia frowned. "I...no one has ever asked me that before. Aven never asked me that, and he always asked "why" questions. But then...he grew up with the sea as his playground and his nursery. It was there. And the changes in it just...were."

Treesi nodded. "The way I just accept the changing of the leaves, or the way each snowflake is different. They're part of my world, so I never think to question them."

"Each snowflake is different?" Aleia asked. "Truly?"

"You have to look very closely, but yes," Treesi said. She smiled. "You never looked at snowflakes?"

Aleia tipped her head to the side, her brow furrowed. Then she shook her head. "No, I can't say that I did. Out on the deep, in our waters, we never had snow. And when it snowed on the Palace, I stayed inside. I didn't like it." She sniffed. "I still don't like it. I don't like cold."

"The best part about the cold is staying inside and bundling with someone warm," Treesi said. Aleia smiled.

"And that's what I did." Aleia turned and looked at her. "You wanted to know how I am. I am...wondering if I'm truly needed here."

Treesi blinked. "Do you think you aren't?"

"I wonder. I..." she sighed. "I've been away from things too long, from the people I love. From the things I need to know—"

"And leaving will fix that?" Treesi asked. "It sounds like it will only make them worse."

"Oh, I'm making things worse all on my own right now," Aleia said, looking back out to sea. "If I go, I won't make anything worse."

"And if you go, you can't make anything better, either." She waited until Aleia looked back at her. "If you go, you leave an open wound that has no chance to heal. It will fester. By the time we see you again, there might not be anything left to heal."

"There's already nothing there to heal," Aleia murmured.

"You're wrong about that," Treesi said. She reached out and put her arm around Aleia's shoulders. "Aven is angry, but he'll calm down. And then he'll be ready to talk. You need to let him cool. And when he comes to you, and tells you what he needs, you need to help him."

Aleia shivered. "You think he will?"

"I know he will. And you know he will. Once he has a chance to cool his head, that is."

Aleia sniffed. "He has my temper. It runs deep, but when it starts..."

"He'll calm down. And he'll want to talk to you." Treesi hugged Aleia gently. "The question is will you listen?"

Aleia stiffened, looking at Treesi in surprise. "What do you mean, will I listen?"

Treesi didn't look away from her. "Just what I said. Will you listen? You didn't have all the information when you started this morning. You made assumptions, you didn't ask Aven or anyone what was going on, and you said the wrong things based on those assumptions. If you don't want that to happen again, you have to listen to him. He is trying. He's trying so hard, because he's afraid he won't be able to protect Aria and the baby—"

"And he tried to tell me that," Aleia interrupted. "You're right. I didn't listen. I didn't listen to Jehan, who told me all of it, and I didn't listen to Aven. I ignored my own men. I should have listened. And I should have asked." She took a deep breath, then sighed. "Will he want to talk to me now?"

"Not now," Treesi said. "He's in pain, and short tempered. Right now, he's the one who won't listen. Maybe tonight, if he has a chance to swim. He's usually in a better mood after he swims. But I don't know where we're camping tonight, so it might have to wait until we get to Terraces and he can get that hip seen to properly."

Aleia nodded. She looked at Treesi and smiled. "Thank you."

Treesi hugged her with one arm. "You're welcome, Mama. Now, I can tell you who you should go and talk to. Jehan."

"Jehan? Is he back?"

"He just got here, yes. And then maybe Othi. They're both quite vexed with you."

Aleia nodded. "I'll go talk to them."

"And you should come eat. If Aven is just like you, then you need to eat soon or you're going to get cranky." She got to her feet, then held her hand out to Aleia. "Come on."

Aleia smiled and stood up, taking Treesi's hand. "You're very good," she said as they walked out from behind the rocks. "After the

Palace fell, we lived at the main healing complex for most of a year, and I met a lot of healers—"

"That wasn't healing," Treesi interrupted. "That was just talking."

"That was healing," Aleia said. She looked around, and tugged Treesi toward Jehan. "Jehan, didn't you teach your students about mind-healing?"

Jehan looked at them in surprise. "Hello to you, too," he said. He put his arm around Aleia's shoulders and kissed the top of her head. "No, but the only reason I didn't teach them about mind-healing is that they were my students for barely an hour, and I didn't think of it." He turned to Treesi. "Risha didn't cover mind-healing? Even in passing?"

"Risha clearly thought I was an idiot. And she didn't teach me anything she couldn't do herself," Treesi answered, and he snorted.

"All right. Fair. Especially since mind-healing is a slightly different track, and is more advanced." He looked from her to Aleia. "Why?"

"Because Treesi appears to have a talent for it. She reminded me of..." She paused. "What was her name? She stayed with us after Aven was born?"

Jehan smiled. "Miralis? I hadn't thought of her in years."

"Mira! Yes. I think we both would have torn ourselves to bits if it hadn't been for her." She frowned. "Is she still alive, do you think?"

Jehan shook his head. "I don't know. Mother might. We'll find out when we get to Terraces. I'd like to see her again." He looked at Aleia. "Walk with me?"

She took his offered hand, and they walked away together. Treesi watched them go, and heard a heavy footstep coming up behind her.

"Is she feeling better?" Othi asked.

Treesi nodded. "I think so. And she'll feel much better when Aven finally talks with her. Which...now she's willing to wait for that, and not leave." She looked up at him. "She'll be talking to you, too."

Othi arched a brow. "Me? Why me?"

"There need to be apologies to everyone involved. That means you." She reached out and took his hand. "Did you eat?"

"I ate," Othi answered. "Did you?"

"Not yet."

"Come on, Healer Treesi. You need to eat something." Othi tugged her closer, putting his arm around her shoulders, and led her toward the other Companions.

"I'VE AUTHORIZED LEXI to help them however they need," Steward finished. "Torri has good ideas, and plans. Aria, he has drawings, and he says he wasn't the one who drew them. It was this Seer. They're fantastic plans, and the details..." He shook his head. "Torri says that the Seer has never been this far west, has never been to the Palace. But he knew that area as if he'd drawn it standing there. I'm intrigued. I hope we come across them. Whoever they are."

"It is intriguing," Aria agreed. "What will it be, when it's rebuilt?"

"A waystation for traders, to start with. Similar to what was there before. There will be a tavern, and a trading post, and there are expansion plans for farms." Steward shook his head. "It's the sort of long-range plans I'd tried to make, before I knew you were coming."

Aria smiled. "Then they must be very good plans indeed." She took a deep breath. "Steward, I'm sorry—"

"I've already forgiven you, Aria."

"I've gotten so used to having you at my elbow that it feels strange when you are not there," Aria continued. "And I know we want to be careful, but at the same time, I've come to rely on your good sense. Because sometimes, I speak before I think."

"The brashness of youth?" Steward asked, laughing. "I understand. And you'll steady, in time. And I know you'll all protect me from those who think I'm someone I'm not. But at the same time, I don't want to be the cause of trouble." He paused. "More trouble."

Aria nodded. "I'll try to remember to think." She looked around, saw Owyn sitting with Meris, and remembered. "Steward, where are we stopping tonight?"

Steward frowned. "There's a good campsite near the healing center ruins. Why?"

"Is it where Owyn and Alanar would have stopped when they traveled to Terraces, when Alanar was ill?" Aria asked. She looked back at Owyn, listening as his laughter rang out loud. "Because if it is the same place, I think we may want to not camp there."

"What's wrong? What am I missing?" Steward followed her gaze. Then he coughed. "Owyn...oh, I hadn't even thought of that."

"It's not just Owyn," Aria said, keeping her voice low. "I doubt Alanar will be at peace there, either. Owyn has already said that if it's the same site, he will not sleep. Which means Alanar will not sleep. Which might mean that Del will not sleep either."

"I sent the advance riders out an hour ahead of us, so that they'd have camp ready," Steward said. "We might be able to send someone to catch them and have them change the campsite. I'll have someone ride out. Do you have your map?"

"It's in the coach," Aria said. She looked up at Steward. "These chairs are comfortable, but low. Help me up?"

Steward nodded, standing up from one of the tripod stools that had been produced for him and for Aria. He took Aria's hands and helped her to her feet, then tucked her hand into the crook of his arm. "Shall we, my Heir?"

Aria laughed as they walked back to the coach, slowing down as Aven came limping toward them. As he joined them, Steward stepped back and yielded his place at Aria's side. Aven put his arm around Aria's shoulders and hugged her.

"Have you eaten, love?" he asked.

"I have, and I have a packet to eat in the coach in case I get hungry again later. We will not be stopping before we reach the campsite, I'm told."

"There should be similar packets for each of you," Steward said. He looked around. "Where's Del?"

"He ate, and Skela took him off to practice," Aven said. "Karse went with them. Where are we going?"

"To look at the map," Aria answered. "You were asleep, I think, when we talked about where we were camping tonight?"

"No, I was awake for that," Aven said.

"If I send a fast rider out now, we can change where they set up camp," Steward said. "But I want to know where that will be."

"So you need the map," Aven nodded. "Show me how you read it. I'm still learning this."

They unrolled the map, and Steward pointed out where they were, and where they were going.

"If we were pushing through to Terraces on horseback, we'd take this road," he said, tracing a different line that was further west. "It's more direct, but it's not good for coach travel. In the coach, this road is longer, but easier. And this is where it makes the most sense to stop to camp." He tapped the map.

"And that's where Owyn and Alanar were attacked?" Aria asked.

Steward nodded. "Now, we're making good time. So we should be able to make it to a campsite on the far side of the ruins if we don't stop again. And there's no reason we should stop again, except for necessary breaks." He frowned down at the map, then nodded. "I'll need to send a rider. Which means I need Karse. Where did Skela take him and Del?"

Chapter Thirteen

Del let the falling stars slow until they dangled like pendulums from his hands, then turned to look at Skela and Karse.

"Good," Skela said. "Very good. You didn't hit yourself that time." He held his hand out. "Let me have them. You're done for now. Go and wash." He took the practice stars from Del, then turned to Karse. "You wanted to see these up close, you said."

"Yeah." Karse took one from Skela. "I'm always drilling the men when you're out on the dancing floor, so I never really looked at these. And the real ones are sharp, you said? What happens when you hit yourself with those?"

Skela laughed. "You don't," he answered. "You're not entrusted with the barbed stars until you no longer damage yourself with the smooth ones." He started playing with the other star. "The progression is the practice star, the smooth star, then the barbed. You start at the beginning of the exercises whenever you progress to the next stage. And when I was first learning, there were those who never made it past the smooth stars. Barbed stars are for masters."

Del blinked. "*And you can use the barbed stars?*" he signed. "*That means you're a master?*"

Skela nodded. "I was considered such. And I may be the last of my people who dances with the barbed stars." He took the practice star back from Karse, tucking the pair into a bag. "Now go and wash, and then go eat. We will be leaving soon, I think."

Karse pointed. "There's a stream, over there," he said. "I'll walk down with you. The boys were playing over there. I should roust them, too. Those two puppies are probably soaked to the skin."

They walked side-by-side down the gentle slope, hearing the boys shouting in the distance. Del dropped to his knees next to the stream and splashed water on his face, then stripped his sweat-soaked shirt off and held it under the water. He wrung the water out of the shirt, then shook it.

"You're going to put that back on wet?" Karse asked. Then he laughed. "You don't have your tablet, do you?"

Del looked up at him and grinned. He stood up and spread the shirt out over a bush, then signed, "*You could learn these.*"

Karse frowned. Then he grinned. "I could. But I'm slow, 'cause I'm old."

Del laughed. "*You're not old!*" he signed. He picked his shirt up and shook it again, then stopped to listen. The shouting from the other side of the stream had changed tone...

"If you put that on wet, you'll ruin your arm sheaths," Karse pointed out. Then he fell silent, looking across the stream. "You're on alert. What?"

Del tapped his ear and pointed downhill, then tossed his shirt back onto the bush and splashed across the stream when Karse started running.

"Danir!" Karse shouted. "Copper!"

"Captain!" Danir came running toward them.

"Where's Copper?" Karse demanded.

"Down the hill. Come help!" Danir ran back down the hill, with Karse and Del following. Danir led them into a small stand of trees, where Del could see Copper, sitting on his heels. He looked up.

"Captain, I think there's still one of them alive in there," he said. "And I can't reach it."

"One of what?" Karse asked. He walked closer to the boy and stopped. "Oh."

Del came up behind Karse and saw what he was looking at — a dead wolf, an arrow piercing its side.

"She hasn't been dead very long, has she?" Karse murmured, crouching and running his hand over the wolf's ruff. "Poor thing. Looks like she had pups..." Something squeaked, and he raised his head and looked at Copper. "Is that a puppy? You found her litter?"

Copper nodded. "There's only one of them still alive, I think." He pointed to a hollow underneath one of the trees. "Down there."

"Right. Del, come help me. I may not need it, but come help."

Del knelt next to Karse, hearing the squeaking growing louder. Karse put on his gloves, then sprawled flat on his belly and reached into the hollow.

"All right," he crooned. "All right. Come here. It's all right. I've got you!" He rolled onto his back, then sat up, cuddling the wolf pup to his chest.

"How old is it, Captain?" Danir asked. "And...can we keep it?"

Karse examined the growling puppy, chuckling slightly. "Well, you're a fierce one, aren't you?" he said. "He's about a month old, I think. His eyes are open, and he's got some fur coming in." He chuckled again as the puppy attacked his glove. "Teeth, too. He's not weaned yet, though. Not sure how we're going to feed him."

"We can't leave him!" Copper protested. Karse looked up at him.

"Did I say we were going to?" he asked. "Come on. Let's go show him to Jehan, see what he says." He got to his feet, smiling down at the puppy.

"Who shot their mother, Captain?" Copper asked as they started back up the hill. "There's no one around here."

"Wolves will travel for miles to hunt," Karse answered. "She probably got too close to a holding or a farm. It's a good thing we stopped here." They splashed back across the stream, and Del stopped to pick up his shirt.

"There you are!"

Del looked up to see Owyn coming down the slope toward them. "We're starting to pack up, and Skela said you went to wash up and *puppy*!" Owyn's voice spiraled up, higher than Del was used to hearing from him. "Where did you find a puppy?" He came in closer to look at Karse's bundle, laughing as the puppy growled at him. Then the puppy howled. Owyn's jaw dropped. "A wolf puppy?"

"*Someone shot their mother,*" Del answered. "*The boys found him. He's the last survivor of the litter, it looks like.*"

Owyn nodded. "So, we're keeping him? Like the kittens in the kitchen, hm?" he asked, and Copper grinned.

"I think he wants the Captain," Copper said. "Like the kittens wanted Mama Lexi."

"Wanted me?" Karse repeated. He smiled. "Wolf pup recognizes the old wolf? If you say so. Now, I have raised pups before. Dog pups, not wolves. But I'll need your help for one this young."

"We'll help!" Danir said. "What do we need to do?"

"First, we need to find out what we have that he can eat," Karse said. "Like I said, he's not weaned yet. But we may be able to still take care of him."

"Well, let's go find out," Owyn said, and led them back to the coaches.

A basket was emptied and lined with a blanket as a bed for the puppy, and their leaving was delayed as Jehan helped them mix up a gruel to feed the hungry wolf. Karse sat on the ground with the boys on either side of him, letting the puppy lick some of the gruel from his cupped hand.

"This is a big responsibility," he said. "I can't carry him with me. Not yet. When he's used to me, I can start to train him to ride in a saddlebag. But for now, if you're going to help me, you're going to take care of him during the day. You have to keep him warm, and clean, and feed him when I can't. And play with him, but that's the easy part." Both boys laughed, and Karse smiled. "He'll learn to eat from a dish pretty quickly, I think. It's not much different from eating from your hand, and he took to that easy enough. And he'll probably make a huge mess in the basket by the time we reach the campsite. Won't you?" he asked the puppy he was holding. "It's a lot of work and he's counting on you to do it." He looked at the boys. "I'm counting on you to do it. I want you riding in the coach with Jehan, so he can help you for today."

"We'll take care of him, Captain," Copper said.

"Has he got a name yet?" Danir asked.

"Not yet," Karse answered. "He hasn't told me yet." He smiled. "But he will. Now, where's that basket? We need to get on the road."

"IT'S FINE," OWYN ASSURED Del. "I've been inside all morning. You ride in the coach and rest, and I'll spend some time with Freckles."

Del looked as if he wanted to argue. Then he yawned. "*Sorry. Practice wore me out,*" he signed.

"Nothing to be sorry for. Go take a nap."

Del blushed and got into the coach, sitting down next to Aria. Owyn waved, then walked back to where one of the guards was holding Freckles' reins.

"You saddled him for me? Thank you, Keelan."

"They brought him over saddled. Said he's ready for a run," Keelan said. "If you're wanting to give him one."

"Freckles? Run?" Owyn repeated. "You're thinking of some other horse. Not my lazy old Freckles." He walked over to run his hand over Freckles' neck. "He never wants to run. He'll run if I ask him to, but he'd rather eat apples."

"Honestly, do you blame him?" Keelan asked. He laughed. "He's ready for you, Fireborn."

"Thanks," Owyn said. "And Keel? You don't get to call me Fireborn. Not with how long I've known you." Keelan laughed, and Owyn swung up into the saddle and turned Freckles down the road. "You don't really want to run, do you?" he asked, watching Freckles' ears swivel back toward him. Freckles shook his head and kicked his heels up a little, making Owyn laugh. "All right. Maybe you do."

Freckles bucked again, laying his ears back, and Owyn felt a surge of...something. Something wrong.

"Easy," he crooned. "Easy, Freckles. What is it?" He kept talking, kept up the constant patter of nonsense while he dismounted and moved forward, taking Freckles' bridle and gently stroking the horse's nose. "What's wrong?"

"Owyn? Is something wrong?" Jehan called. He must have decided to ride, because he was leading a horse toward Owyn. Aleia was behind him, leading a second horse.

"I'm not sure," Owyn said. "Something's got him upset, and I don't know what. He seems to be calming down a bit, though." He frowned. "He's never tried to throw me before."

Jehan frowned and came closer, resting his hand on Freckles' flank. He closed his eyes slightly, then blinked. "Hold him still. I need to get this saddle off. There's something hurting him."

"Hurting him?" Owyn stammered. He watched as Jehan unbuckled straps and lifted the saddle from Freckles' back. "What's wrong? What is it?"

"Jehan, what's wrong?" Steward guided his horse up to them. "The coaches have started moving out."

Jehan didn't answer. He put the saddle down, lifted the saddle blanket and swore when he saw the blood on Freckles' back. Something shiny fell out of the blanket, and Owyn pointed.

"What was that?" he asked. "What was in the blanket?"

Aleia stopped and picked up what turned out to be something small and metal. "Jehan," she murmured. Jehan swore again, taking the metal piece from Aleia.

"Who saddled Freckles?" he asked.

"One of the grooms, I think," Owyn answered. "Not sure who. Freckles was already saddled when I got there, and Keelan said they brought him out like this. What is that? It looks like...what do you call those things? Ami and Zia play with them. Counting stars. That's it. What's a counting star doing in my saddle blanket?"

"A counting star?" Steward repeated. "That's...I'll go get Karse." He turned his horse, and raced up the road.

"I...Jehan?" Owyn turned back to the healer. "Why is he so upset?"

"Because that's not a counting star," Jehan answered. "It's a caltrop. Someone just tried to kill you."

Owyn stared at him for a moment, trying to understand words that shouldn't be going together like that. "And...and they hurt my Freckles to do it?" he stammered.

"It would look like an accident," Aleia said gently. She took Freckles' reins. "The coaches have stopped. Go ride in the coach, Owyn. Jehan will take care of Freckles."

"No, I want to stay," Owyn protested. "I want to know who hurt my horse. So I can shove that caltrop thing down their throat."

Aleia smiled. "You're more upset over him than you are that someone tried to kill you?"

"It's not like someone trying to kill me is anything new," Owyn replied. "And I don't stay dead. But Freckles don't deserve that. He's a good boy, and he'd never hurt nobody." He ran his hand down Freckles' neck. "And nobody gets to fuck with him." He heard hoof-beats coming up fast, and turned to see Karse and Steward. And behind them, on foot....

"Oh, you didn't tell them," he groaned. "They're coming to check on me?"

Aleia chuckled. "Did you honestly think they wouldn't? The minute they heard?"

Karse threw himself out of his saddle before his big horse had even come to a stop. "A caltrop?" he demanded. "And one of our men put it there?"

"Well, the horse didn't put it there," Jehan answered. He held his hand out, the caltrop sitting on his palm. "Owyn, go let the others know you're fine. I'll take care of Freckles. Best if you don't ride him today, though."

Owyn scowled. "I'm going to shove that thing down someone's throat so hard he'll shit it out. Then I'll shove it down his throat again," he growled. He turned toward the others, and had to smile. His own husband had apparently decided that it was a better choice for his own health to not get between the Heir and her Companion, and had let Aria go first. She was in front, her wings flared wide enough that he could barely see the others behind her.

"I'm fine," he called. He started toward them, glancing back to see that Aleia was keeping Freckles calm while Jehan worked. He turned back to the others. "But someone hurt Freckles."

Aria didn't say anything until she had him in her arms, hugging him tightly. "You're certain you're unhurt?"

"I'm fine," Owyn repeated. Aria let him go, and Alanar was there to take her place. Owyn rested against his chest for a moment before finishing, "What I really am is mad. Freckles didn't do anything. He didn't deserve to be hurt."

"You're more angry about the horse?" Alanar asked.

"Why shouldn't I be?" Owyn asked. "I'm getting used to someone trying to kill me. And, like I told Mamaleia, dying don't stick with me. Freckles didn't do anything to anyone." He looked around at the others. "Look, I'm sorry. You could all be on your way to the camp."

"We're not leaving you behind," Aven said. "We'll make room for you in the coach with us." He looked past Owyn. "Fa, will you catch us up?"

"Wait a minute," Owyn protested. "I want to know who hurt Freckles! Where did Karse go?"

"He and Steward went to talk to the men who were in charge of the horses," Jehan answered. "We'll save what's left for you, Owyn. Not that I expect Karse to leave much." He led Freckles over toward them. "I've healed the slash, but he'll be tender for a few hours. You're not riding him. I'll put him on a leading rein and take care of him myself."

Owyn went over to Freckles, laughing when the horse nudged his chest. "You're going to be fine," he said softly. "Jehan's going to take care of you, and nobody's going to get to take care of you from here on out but me. We'll have a good run tomorrow."

"Go on and get moving," Jehan said. "We'll be right behind you."

JEHAN WAITED UNTIL Aria and her Companions were all inside the coach before going to find Karse and Steward. "Well?"

Karse frowned at him. "Well, what?"

"You were expecting something to happen. I know you were," Jehan said. "The first day?"

"No, that was sooner than I thought anything would happen. And I honestly thought we'd gotten all of Risha's people out of the guard. I mean, all of these guards were ones I'd vouched for personally, or they were from your mother's guards. How could she have gotten them to turn?"

"Why are you just looking at the guard?" Jehan asked. "Owyn said the guard gave him the horse already saddled."

Karse frowned. Then he swore. "Grooms. Did we ever check the grooms? I'll...yeah. I'll know who it was by the time we reach the camp. Go on and catch them up." He looked around. "So, Steward, what's the lore? How fucked are we?"

Steward shook his head as he mounted his horse. "The lore says that the first day of the Progress sets the tone of the entire Progress," he answered. "Which means we're in for a very interesting trip. But I think we all knew that." He clicked his tongue. "Let's go catch them up, Alabaster."

Chapter Fourteen

Owyn ended up back in his original seat, sitting on Aria's left. But because there wasn't enough room for seven people in the coach, he also ended up being a seat — Del was asleep in his lap, his head on Owyn's shoulder, his breath soft against Owyn's skin. His slight weight against Owyn was soothing. And every so often, Aria would touch his arm, or his leg, or she'd take his hand.

"I'm fine," he murmured. "Really, I am."

"I know," she said. "But it is worrying that someone would be so bold as to try this on the day we left the Palace. What does it mean for the rest of the Progress?"

"That we need to be careful," Othi said. "That we need to make sure that we do for ourselves. Anything that we can." He frowned. "Who's going to be cooking for us?"

"Oh," Treesi breathed. "Oh. You don't really think—"

"Aven, I know you know how to flush toxins," Alanar interrupted. "Your father taught me how to do it when you were poisoned. But...did your father ever mention if there was a way to test for poisons or toxins before someone eats them?"

"No!" Aven sat up straighter, wincing as he moved. "Is that something we can do?"

Alanar shook his head. "I don't know. That's why I asked. If it is, then we need to know that. If someone is already trying to kill us, then they won't stop."

"Assuming that Karse doesn't find who did it and turn them inside out," Owyn said. "He said he'd leave something for me, but if he doesn't, I'll be fine with just kicking the corpse." He shifted Del on his lap. "If he sleeps any more, he's not going to sleep tonight." He frowned. "Where are we sleeping tonight?"

Aria ran her nails up his arm, making him shiver. "I spoke to Steward. He was going to send a rider ahead to have the campsite shifted to the far side of the ruins. It will take us a little longer to get there, but you will sleep tonight."

Owyn stared at her. "Aria," he said. "You didn't have to do that!"

She smiled. "Owyn, if something so small as camping a mile further down the road will make you more comfortable, then how could I not do it? For you and for Alanar?"

Owyn looked across the coach to Alanar, who was smiling. "Thank you, Aria."

"Yeah," Owyn said. "I...thank you." He took her hand and kissed her knuckles. "So, we're stopping on the far side of the ruins now. Will there be a place there for Aven to swim? I don't remember." He grinned. "That's where we met...umm...him. The Usurper. And I don't remember a fucking thing about that other than how was I going to keep us from getting killed."

"Garrity thought you were insane," Alanar murmured.

Owyn took a deep breath. "Yeah. He did. Maybe I was." He shook his head. "He ever going to be...I dunno...himself? Ever?"

Alanar shrugged. "I'm not the one to ask. Remember, I'm crackpot insane, too."

"You're not," Treesi protested. "It's different for you."

"Alanar, I have a question," Othi said. "What's he doing? Right now?"

"Who?" Alanar asked. "Oh, you mean Virrik?"

"Yes," Othi said. "I mean, is he doing anything when you're not thinking about him?"

Alanar frowned. "I...I don't know. I never..." His frown deepened. "He says he listens when I'm awake. He sleeps when I sleep. Except...sometimes he's awake when I'm asleep. And...Virrik, absolutely not! You are not allowed!"

"If he's saying he might take a grab at me when you're asleep, tell him he has to ask first, and let me know it's him asking." He glanced at Del, still asleep in his arms. "And tell him that Del is absolutely off limits."

Alanar looked startled. "You'd...you'd be fine with him doing that?" He shook his head. "No. I'm not fine with that. He might have your permission, but he won't have mine. Not to use my body. Every time he's done it, he's done it without my leave. If he did that...and...he used my body to have sex with you, without my permission, without me even knowing...how is that not rape?" The entire coach went silent, until Alanar snorted. "He's sputtering. And swearing that he'd never do that to me. But he's already done it. He's taken over my body twice without my leave, so how can I trust that he won't do it again? And I won't even remember it?"

"Oh, fuck," Owyn breathed. "Allie—"

"I've been thinking about this, off and on, since this morning. Since he..." Alanar paused. Then he sighed. "Since he stole my body between one word and the next, and I never noticed. Since he hurt you." He turned away, facing the side of the coach. "Maybe I need to sleep alone for a while. I can't protect you from him. I can't stop him if he wants to take over." He shifted again, his right hand closing around the pledge bracelet on his left wrist, and Owyn felt his heart stop.

"No!" he blurted, loud enough that Del jerked in his arms. "No, you are not taking that off. You are not giving that back."

Alanar looked startled. "I..."

"No," Owyn repeated. "And you're not sleeping alone, either. I promised you forever. No matter what. And I'm not letting him change that."

Del blinked, looking confused. "*What happened? Why are you upset?*"

"Sorry for waking you. Virrik is being...well, a problem," Owyn answered. "He's upset Alanar—"

"*Which upset you,*" Del finished. He nodded, slipping from Owyn's lap to sit on the floor of the coach. "*What did Virrik do?*"

Owyn translated, and Alanar sighed. "Proven that he can't be trusted where you and Owyn are concerned," he answered. "If I'm asleep, he can take over my body, and he's making jokes about taking advantage of that."

"*That's not good. What can be done to stop him?*" Del signed

"I don't know," Aven answered. "Alanar, is there anything that you can do about Virrik? Or anything that we can do to keep him from doing anything while you sleep?"

Alanar frowned. "I...maybe I should talk to Grandmother Meris. Maybe there's something she can teach me to keep him from being able to...to push me aside. And...I'll talk to Jehan." He rubbed his face. "If I drug myself to sleep, neither of us will move until morning." He snorted. "And he's sputtering again. He doesn't like that idea."

"Which means it's a good one?" Othi asked.

"Maybe." Alanar closed his eyes. "If I can find something that will knock me out that I won't end up addicted to, or that won't kill me by accident? Maybe."

"Allie—"

"I'll talk to Jehan," Alanar said. "Owyn, I'm not taking a chance on getting it wrong. I'm not taking a chance that I might hurt you, or Del." He raised his left hand. "And I'm not taking this off."

———⟨❀⟩———

THE COACH ROCKED AS it came to a stop, and Aven peered out the window into the dusk. "I think we're here."

"Good," Aria said. "I need to stretch."

"I need to do more than stretch," Treesi added. "Let's get out."

The door next to her opened as she finished speaking, and Memfis looked inside at them. "Come on out," he said. "The camp is ready, and there's food."

They all piled out of the coach, and Aria stepped away from the others, spreading her wings wide as she stretched. Aven leaned against the side of the coach and watched her.

"How do you feel?" Memfis asked.

"I hurt," Aven admitted. "But that's no surprise. I'm stiff, which is a surprise. I'm not used to sitting for so long. Where's Gathi?"

"Over by the fire, with Meris and Afansa." Memfis lowered his voice. "What happened earlier? Jehan said there was something in Owyn's saddle blanket?"

Aven nodded. "I don't remember what he called it. Owyn said it looked like one of Ami and Zia's counting stars. But it was sharp."

"A caltrop?" Memfis whistled. "Where did that come from?"

"What did Karse say? Have you asked him?"

"No," Memfis answered. "I haven't seen him." He gestured toward the camp — there was one large tent, and a myriad of smaller ones. "The large tent is yours, Aria, and your Companions."

Aria joined them, taking Aven's hand. "How are we sleeping tonight? Will it be like the trip from Forge to Terraces, where we slept on the ground?"

"No, there are beds," Memfis said. "Three of them in the tent, so you all have room if you want to spread out." He gestured again, and they started walking toward the tents.

"We'll catch you up," Owyn called. "I'm taking Allie for a walk."

"Don't be too long. It'll be dark soon," Memfis called back. He led them toward the fire, passing guards as they hurried around from place to place. "So, why did they move the camp?" Memfis asked. "I know they did, but not why, and I haven't been able to nail Steward down to ask him."

"Because the other camp site was where Owyn and Alanar were attacked by Teva," Aria answered, her voice low. "Owyn thought that if we camped there, he would not sleep. So I asked if the camp could be moved."

Memfis smiled. "Thank you. Now come and sit."

Aven brought Aria to sit down near Jehan and Aleia, then reached out and touched his mother on the shoulder. She looked up at him, clearly surprised.

"Maybe we can talk in the morning, Ama?" he asked. "Before we leave?"

She smiled. "I'd like that."

He leaned down and kissed her cheek, then slowly lowered himself to sit in one of the tripod camp chairs.

"Are you going to be able to get up?" Aria asked. "I can't get out of these by myself."

"I might have to ask Othi for help," Aven said with a laugh. He turned toward his parents. "What did Karse find?"

"You mean, besides a wolf puppy who has exceptional lungs?" Jehan asked. "I don't know. He took the boys off to take care of the puppy, and they'll be back soon."

"Talking about us?" Karse called. He came closer to the fire and dropped to sit on the ground, with Copper on one side of him and Danir on the other. He settled the puppy into his lap and looked down at it. "I'm going to try Howl on some chewed meat. See how he does. If he doesn't take to it, we can make up some of that gruel again."

"Howl?" Aria repeated. "Is that his name?"

"That's what he did, I'm told," Karse said. "Until I picked him up when we got here."

"He's loud," Danir answered. "He really wanted the Captain, the entire time we were coming here. If he wasn't asleep or eating, he was howling."

"So his name is Howl," Karse finished. He looked down and smiled. "Trey is going to love him."

Aven turned as footsteps came closer, smiling as Owyn, Alanar and Del joined them. Del went over to sit down next to Karse, while Owyn brought Alanar to Jehan.

"Senior Healer?" Alanar said. "Could we talk before we eat? I have questions."

Jehan frowned. "Of course. All of us, or just you and me?"

Alanar looked thoughtful, then turned to Owyn. "Do you mind?"

"No, you go talk. I want to talk to Karse," Owyn answered. He stretched up to kiss Alanar, then went to sit down. "How's the puppy?"

"A champion howler," Karse answered. "He made everyone's ears ring in the coach this afternoon."

Owyn chuckled. "Well, he was missing you," he said. "So, did you find who hurt Freckles?"

Karse nodded. He didn't answer immediately — a servant started handing out bowls. Aven took his and watched as Karse picked out a piece of meat, chewed it, then spat it out and offered it to the puppy. "Yeah, that's the way," he murmured. "Chew on that. That's good stuff." He smiled and turned to Owyn. "I think so. But he ran for it, it looks like. I know you talked to Keelan. You know Wren, don't you?"

"Yeah, I've known him since I was on the streets, and before he was one of your men in Forge," Owyn said. "He's lousy at cards."

"Yeah, him. He and Keelan said that when you ordered Freckles saddled, one of the grooms brought him out ready to go. That's the last time they saw that groom. Or anyone else saw him. I'm guessing he ran off when we found the caltrop." He picked another piece of meat out of his stew, chewed it, and offered it to the puppy. Then he took a mouthful of his own. "I thought we checked everyone when Hilah turned traitor. But maybe this was a new groom?"

"Could be," Steward said. "What was his name?"

"Merk," Karse answered.

Steward frowned and closed his eyes. Then he nodded. "He's been in the Palace a week or two," he said slowly. "So possibly."

"Well, we'll keep an eye on the other new servants and grooms," Aleia said. "And we'll take care."

"That's pretty much all we can do." Karse handed Del one of his gloves. "Here. I can see you're dying to play with him."

ALANAR WALKED NEXT to Jehan until Jehan couldn't hear the voices around the fire anymore. Then he stopped, clasping his hands behind his back. Alanar's heart rate was quick, his face pale.

He was clearly terrified of something.

"What's on your mind, son?" Jehan asked.

Alanar smiled. "It's not what's on my mind. It's who is in my mind. Virrik is...a problem." He took a deep breath. "He's taken over my body twice. Once I think we told you about? I was asleep. But this morning...he did it while I was awake. Between one word and the next, and I never noticed. I didn't realize anything was wrong until Owyn was yelling at me. And the only reason anyone else noticed was that my voice changed."

Jehan took a deep breath. This wasn't what he was expecting. "Changed how?" he asked.

"When Virrik talks through me, he has a Water accent. Othi heard it this morning. He said I sounded right. That's when Owyn realized, and that's when Virrik let me go." He stopped. "Jehan, I can't control him and I can't stop him. And I'm scared he might do something to hurt Owyn or Del when I'm asleep, and I'll never know until it's too late. And I can't think of anything I can take to drug myself to sleep that won't leave me raving or dead. Help me. Please."

Jehan took another deep breath, trying to stay calm. "Alanar, if I wanted to talk to Virrik directly, could I?"

Alanar blinked. "I...I don't know? Maybe. I can..." He stopped. Shook his head. And when he spoke again, he had a rolling Water accent. "Yes, you could."

Jehan folded his arms over his chest. "You're a presumptuous little fuck, aren't you? Did Alanar say you could take over?"

Virrik grinned. "You wanted to talk to me. And I thought the word was arrogant. That's what Risha called me."

"No, arrogance goes with ability. You might have been arrogant once. Now? You've got no ability on your own." Jehan shook his head. "Virrik, you are not allowed to hurt them. Any of them."

"Fine. I'll leave them alone. I'm just...Senior Healer, I didn't ask for this!" Virrik snapped. "I didn't ask to be shoved into Alanar's head. I don't know how I am, or why I am, or if it was your boy that fucked something up and now the Mother will never find me." He frowned. Then he shook his head. "That was unfair. He did his best. He tried. I know he tried. I'm grateful that he tried. I am. I could have been lost forever. But...I just...I don't know how or why I'm trapped inside Alanar's head. I don't know if I'm being punished, and if I am, I don't know why. All I know is that when he's the one in front, I can't see. I can't feel. I can't...he's not insane, Senior Healer, but I might end up that way. I'm trapped and alone, and he doesn't always hear me."

Jehan frowned slightly. "So what do you propose, Healer Virrik?"

Virrik frowned. "I...maybe I get an hour?" he offered. "One hour, when I can be the one to talk, to listen. To touch. That's what I miss most. Touching."

"And in return, you will leave Owyn alone. You'll leave Del alone—"

"I haven't touched Del," Virrik protested. "And I won't. I know he isn't interested. Although he is interesting. I'd like to know him better." He smiled slightly. "All right. Everyone is off limits. What do I do if they ask? If Owyn or Treesi asks me during that hour?"

"You say no," Jehan answered. "Because it's not your body, and you don't have Alanar's permission." He studied the man in front of him, the stubborn, sullen look that had no place on the familiar face. "Now, before you give control of the body back to Alanar, I have one thing to remind you of."

Virrik cocked his head to the side. "Which is what?"

"I've lived as Water for the past twenty-five years," Jehan said, stepping closer and pitching his voice low. "I know their laws. And I know the penalties for rape. Do not, for a single minute, think that I will not carry out those penalties if you overstep yourself. Am I clear?"

"But—"

"I will tell Alanar what I just told you," Jehan said. "But do not think that just because you're in his body that you get to abuse the privilege. Am I understood?"

Virrik nodded. Then he staggered, and when he spoke again, his accent was gone. "I...I can try, Senior Healer."

"Does it hit you that hard all the time?" Jehan asked. Alanar's head shot up.

"He did it again?"

"He heard me ask if I could talk to him. He took it as an excuse," Jehan answered. "I apologize."

Alanar's heart rate shot up again. "What do I do?" he demanded. "How do I stop him? I can't keep doing this! I can't!"

"Breathe, Alanar," Jehan said. "And we're going to talk. Because I talked to him. And I think he'll behave himself now." He slung his arm over Alanar's shoulders. "It will be all right, Alanar. I'll take care of you."

Alanar nodded. "Jehan?"

"I'm not locking you away in the green levels, Alanar. You're not insane." Jehan hugged him slightly. "Virrik says so."

"He did?" Alanar turned toward Jehan. "What else did he say?"

"Come on and eat, and we'll talk. I'm assuming you want Owyn as part of the conversation?"

"Yes, please. And the others. I want everyone to know."

"Then let's go talk to them."

Chapter Fifteen

Owyn sat on the ground, leaning against Alanar's legs, his empty bowl in his lap. Jehan sat across from him. The others were there, but for the moment, Owyn was ignoring them.

"So...Virrik wants an hour a day? So he can feel things again," he said slowly. "And...he promises to keep his hands to himself and not take over when it's not his time or without permission?"

Jehan nodded. "That's the deal. Alanar sets the time, and if Virrik violates the terms, then I will personally make certain that he can't take over Alanar's body while he sleeps. Without resorting to narcotics or sleeping brews." He took a deep breath. "And...I warned Virrik. I told Alanar, and now I'm telling you all." He paused and looked around. "I know what the penalties are among the Water tribe for rape—"

"Fa!" Aven gasped. "You wouldn't...not to Alanar!"

"He would," Alanar said, his voice flat. "And I've told him that if Virrik hurts any of you, he's allowed to do whatever he needs to do to keep it from happening again." He reached out and ran his fingers through Owyn's hair. "You're too important to me. If Vir ever really loved me, then he won't try to hurt you, because doing so would hurt me."

"What are the penalties?" Aria asked. "I haven't reached that part of my reading yet."

For a long moment, the only sounds were the wind, the crackling of the fire, and the soft buzz of conversations around the camp. Aria's brows rose.

"Is it that dire a punishment?" she murmured.

Aven coughed and nodded. "Yes. I...yes."

"And you would allow this?" Aria said. "Alanar, you would allow this?"

Alanar snorted. "I'm insisting on it. When Jehan told me that he'd warned Virrik? I told him that if Virrik actually used my body to hurt anyone, that I wanted him to do it."

"Are you going to tell me what it is?" Owyn asked. "Because I haven't gotten that far in my reading yet either."

"Castration."

Othi's voice was quiet, and more solemn than Owyn had ever remembered him sounding. When everyone turned to stare at him, he looked down.

"Neera had to order it done," he added. "After Grandmother and our mother died. It was before Aunt Aleia got back to us. Just before. I think Neera told her. I don't know." Absently, he reached for Treesi, she slipped her hand into his and leaned against his side. "We don't have a lot of troublemakers out in the deep. There's no time for that nonsense. But when we have them..." He paused. Frowned. "He thought Neera wouldn't do it. He thought she wasn't strong enough to be Clan Mother. I think that he was going to challenge her." He shrugged. "He was wrong."

Owyn stared at him. "Castration. You're serious?"

Othi nodded slowly. "It's a public punishment, and Neera held the knife. It's done in front of the entire tribe, and if they survive it, if they don't bleed out, they're cast out of their family canoe. Their tattoos are scarred off. They're no one, and they have nothing." He sniffed. "I don't think there's a man on the water over the age of thirteen who doesn't know in their bones that no means no."

Owyn turned so that he was looking up at Alanar. "And...you're fine with this. You're insisting on this."

Alanar nodded. "And Virrik knows it. He knows the penalties because Jehan reminded him. He knows what will happen to me if he hurts any of you. If he even tries to hurt any of you." He reached out, and Owyn took his hand. "Wyn, he loved me. He wouldn't do that to me. I'm sure of that."

Owyn nodded, squeezing Alanar's fingers. "I just...you trust him a lot more than I do, love."

"He's also been told that even if one of you invites him, he's to refuse," Jehan added. "Because Alanar won't have been able to consent. So remember that."

"We'll all keep watch on him," Aven said. "Mouse, if you don't want to be with him when he's Virrik, I'm sure Othi and I can keep him busy."

"Just don't let him eat sea oak," Alanar said, laughing. "I'll taste it for days."

Owyn let go of Alanar's hand and stood up, dusting sandy dirt from his trousers. He looked around. "Are we done here?" he asked.

"I think we are," Jehan answered. "I should go check on the puppy. And we should all get some sleep. It'll be an early morning tomorrow, and a long day."

Owyn nodded and reached out to take Alanar's hand again. "We'll meet you over at the tent. The big one is all of us, right?"

"That's right," Aria said. "Have you eaten enough, Owyn?"

Owyn considered the question, then nodded. "I think so. I haven't been as...ravenous as I was before I retested. Granna said something resettled. So I was out of balance before, and now I'm not. Now, if you'll excuse me, I want my husband to myself for a bit."

He tugged Alanar to his feet, and they walked away from the others, hearing them laughing as they walked away.

"Where are we going?" Alanar asked.

"Not too far. Just...I want some privacy." Owyn looked up at the sky, at the stars. The moon was rising, casting a silver-water light over the ground. "There's salt water around here. I smell it."

"We're not close enough for Aven and Othi to swim, though," Alanar said. "I don't think."

"We'll be in Shadow Cove tomorrow, and they'll be able to swim there." Owyn stopped and turned so that he was facing Alanar. "Allie...I don't like that you're doing this. You know what you're doing here? You're giving him the knife and asking him to hurt you. That don't sit right with me."

Alanar nodded. "I know. I just...I loved him, Wyn. I still love him. And I trust him not to hurt me. He knows that if he tries it, I'll pay the price. I can't think he wants that."

"Is he listening?" Owyn asked. "Can he hear me?"

Alanar cocked his head to the side. Then he nodded. "He's listening. He's listening now, anyway. And he just asked if he can come out and talk to you."

"He asked?" Owyn repeated. "That's new. I...no. I want to talk to you. I want you with me right now. Not him. He can just listen. I don't want you getting hurt, Allie. Not when I can't hurt him back for doing something that hurts you."

Alanar chuckled. "Telling him that you'll break both his arms if he hurts you or Del doesn't mean much when they're my arms, does it?"

"No, because I won't hurt you. And he knows it. And I think he's counting on it." Owyn frowned. "He's counting on us not hurting you, and he thinks he can get away with all sorts of shit because of it."

"Which is why I gave Jehan permission," Alanar said. "And I expect you to honor that, no matter what."

Owyn growled. "I know. And I will. But I don't have to like it." He stepped closer, slid his arms around Alanar. "I wanted privacy for another reason. But there's not a lot we can do out here without telling everyone what we're doing."

"I can be quiet if you can be quiet," Alanar murmured. Then he laughed. "Virrik is saying 'yes, please.' I think he wants to watch."

Owyn burst out laughing. "How is he going to do that? How can he watch?"

Alanar frowned. "I..." Then he shook his head and let go of Owyn, stepping away. "Well, fuck. Nice try, Virrik."

"What does that mean?" Owyn asked

"It means that I think we're not going to do anything for a while." He took a deep breath and sighed, wrapping his arms around his chest. "I'm not taking the chance on him trying to cheat, and neither of us noticing because we both fall asleep after."

Owyn stared at him for a moment, then stammered, "I thought you said you trusted him."

"I thought I did," Alanar said. He sighed again. "Let's go see the puppy, and visit with Grandmother. I want to see if she knows anything. Then...maybe tomorrow I'll ride with you."

"You'll do what now?" Owyn took Alanar's hand and started back toward the fire. "I...Allie, you didn't want to wear boots."

Alanar smiled slightly. "If I can't tell where I am, then neither can he. I'm willing to hobble myself if it will keep other people safe." He frowned. "Except for that coat. We're not doing that again."

Owyn nodded. "I won't let them do that to you again. And I won't do that to you. Let's go talk to Granna."

There were fewer people around the fire when they reached it. Memfis was sitting on the ground, his back to a log, and a cup in his hand. He smiled up at Owyn as they came closer.

"How are you two tonight?" Memfis asked.

"Fine," Owyn answered. "Is Granna still awake?"

Memfis frowned. "She should still be awake, but she's busy at the moment. She went off to tell the boys a bedtime story." He turned and gestured with his cup. "The third tent, over there. The boys are bunking down with Karse and Howl." He looked at them. "What's wrong?"

Alanar took a deep breath. "Wyn, maybe he knows."

"We can ask," Owyn said. He helped Alanar sit down with Memfis, then pointed to the cup. "Is that tea?"

"Redberry and spice. The kettle is by the fire," Memfis answered.

"Allie?"

"Yes, please."

Owyn poured two cups full of tea, and carried them back to Alanar. Once he was sitting, he nudged Alanar's arm. "All right. I'm not sure what we're asking, so go ahead."

Alanar nodded. "You know about Virrik, right?"

"That you think you hear him still? Yes."

Owyn blinked. "That sounds like you don't believe that Virrik is actually in there. In Allie's head."

Memfis shook his head. "I don't know, Mouse. You know how Smoke Dancers can get. I've known a lot of people who have heard voices—"

"In this case, it's more than hearing voices," Alanar interrupted. "He's taken over, three times now. When he does, my voice changes. I have a Water accent. And he doesn't know things that I know." He turned toward Owyn. "He didn't know anything about who Owyn was before I knew him. I know because Owyn told me. But we never talked about it after he came back, and Virrik didn't know. And he took over and he said something..." He frowned. "I still don't know why didn't you knock me on my arse. I deserved it."

"Well, first, it wasn't you that did it, love," Owyn said. "I just didn't know it at first. And honestly, knocking you on your arse isn't something I'd do. Aven might take a swing at you if he gets mad enough. I walk away."

"You were about to walk away this morning until Othi made us all realize that it wasn't me," Alanar said, nodding. He turned back to Memfis. "If you don't believe me, then I don't think there's a point in asking you to help me."

Memfis' brows rose. "Oh? Why is that?"

"I'm trying to find a way to keep the man in my head from taking control of my body," Alanar answered. "If you don't think he's really there, then what are you going to tell me to do?"

Owyn turned when he heard footsteps, and smiled as Del dropped down to sit next to him, pressing against his side. Behind him were Jehan and Meris.

"Granna's here, Allie," he said. "And Del."

Alanar smiled and held his hand out. Del reached out and caught it, lacing his fingers into Alanar's and resting his head on Owyn's shoulder.

"Were you waiting for me, my darlings?" Meris asked. "I'm not going to be awake much longer, I'm afraid."

"Grandmother, have you ever heard of anyone else having someone else in their head?" Alanar asked. "Not...not insane. Not hearing voices. Having a dead man move into their body?"

Meris sat down next to Memfis and took the cup of tea that Jehan poured for her. "I don't remember anything in the lore. But there is a great deal of lore, and not as much room in my memories. I may not be remembering it. Why?"

Alanar sighed and sagged against Owyn. "Because Virrik has taken over my body three times without my knowledge or consent, and it's terrifying me. I don't know he's doing it until it's done, and

I can't control it." He closed his eyes and sighed. "I'm scared that he's going to hurt Owyn, or Del, and I won't be able to stop him."

Meris looked thoughtful. "And...would he have done such a thing when he was alive? Would he have hurt someone the way you're afraid he will do now that he's dead?"

"Grandmother, I don't know!" Alanar sounded completely distraught, and Owyn put his arm around him to try and offer some small comfort.

Meris nodded. "And...have you spoken to him?"

"I did," Jehan said. "An hour or so ago." He sat down next to the fire, cradling his own cup in his hands. "We've come to an agreement, and he knows the penalties of violating that agreement."

Alanar frowned. "He's asking if he can speak," he said slowly.

"Asking is good," Owyn murmured.

Alanar nodded. Then he shuddered and sat up straighter. "If you want to move, Owyn, I will understand," he said, and the Water accent was back. Owyn started to shift, then tightened his arm around his husband's body.

"I think...I think you need this," he said.

To his shock, Virrik whimpered. "That's the problem!" he moaned. "Please, I'm trapped in here. Is there some way to get me out of Alanar's head so I can move on? I...I'm dead. I'm supposed to go on to the Mother. But I'm here instead!" He swallowed and turned to Owyn. "Thank you. I...I appreciate you being willing to even do this much." He frowned. "Who's holding my...his hand. Is it you? I can't tell."

"That's Del," Owyn answered.

Virrik smiled, and gently tugged his hand out of Del's. He closed his eyes. "Owyn, you should sit up. And move away. Because as...as touch starved as I am right now? I don't even trust me. And Alanar is right. I won't hurt him. I just...I didn't think it all the way through. He's right. He's right, and I was wrong, and I'm sorry." He frowned again. "And when I have my hour tomorrow, will you tell me what I said wrong this morning? And explain it?"

"We'll talk tomorrow," Owyn said. "Now, Granna, is there an answer? Because I need to get my husband to bed."

"I'm afraid I don't have any answers to these questions," Meris said gently. "It's beyond me. Perhaps when we reach the Temple, there will be answers."

"Aria suggested something like that," Owyn said. "If there's a priest there, they might be able to help."

Virrik nodded. "All right. I...I can be patient. And I think Alanar and I can figure out how to balance this." He swallowed. "I'm going back. Good night."

He shivered again. Then he laughed. "I heard all of that!" Alanar said, turning toward Owyn. "Wyn, I..."

Owyn leaned in close and kissed Alanar. "We'll make it work, Allie," he whispered. "I think he's really sorry. And we'll make it work so you both get what you need, until we get the answers we need."

"*If you tell me what to do, I'll help, too,*" Del whispered in Owyn's mind. Owyn turned and nodded, but didn't translate. Instead, he unwound himself from the others and got to his feet.

"We all need to sleep. Allie, finish your tea," he said. "Granna, thank you."

Meris shook her head. "Thank me when I've done something to deserve it." She looked at Memfis. "Out of curiosity, do you know anything? Your reading is more recent than mine."

"Memfis doesn't think it's real," Alanar said.

"You convinced, Mem?" Owyn asked. Memfis opened his mouth, then closed it again.

"Mouse, I've never seen anything like this. This was nothing like the Smoke Dancers who heard voices—" He shook his head. "I'm sorry, Alanar. And no, I don't know anything either."

Alanar nodded. "Then we'll keep going, and we'll figure things out." He got to his feet and held his hand out to Owyn. "Bedtime?"

"Bedtime," Owyn agreed. "Then, you can ride with me tomorrow. We'll dig your boots out, and we'll see if Meadowfoam was one of the horses that they brought."

"*Alanar can ride Lady, if he wants,*" Del offered.

"Or Del offered his Lady, if you want," Owyn added.

"But then he can't ride with us," Alanar protested. "I...we'll figure it out in the morning."

"And I'll be the one saddling the horses in the morning," Owyn added. "Right. Bedtime. Good night."

"OTHI, WHERE ARE WE going?" Treesi asked.

"I can smell the sea," Othi answered. "I wanted to see it before we went to sleep. And maybe swim, if we can get to the water." He looked at her and smiled. "I can teach you to swim."

Treesi smiled. "I'd like that. Can you teach me not to be seasick?"

Othi chuckled. "I don't think that can be taught. I...wait." He stopped, holding Treesi back. "Oh. We're not swimming tonight." He walked ahead, and looked down over the edge of the cliff. "That's a good distance down. I didn't realize we were so high up."

Treesi joined him, looking down at the white-capped waves far below them. "That's a bit far to dive, isn't it?"

"And I wouldn't," Othi said. "Not without knowing what was down there. That's a fast way to break your neck. And even if I did know, it doesn't look like there's a way to get back up here."

"It's much too far to jump," Treesi agreed. "I have a question."

"Let's head back." Othi turned back toward the camp. "What's the question?"

"When you jumped up to the ship, when we were just getting to the Palace, Aven said that you were showing off," Treesi said. "That it was a courting display. Was that what you were doing? Showing off? For me?"

Even in the pale moonlight, she could see Othi's face color. "He told you that?" he stammered. "I...yeah. Yes, I was showing off." He looked at her, clearly embarrassed. "You...you don't mind, do you? I keep forgetting that you don't do things like we do."

"I don't mind. It was impressive," Treesi said. She stepped closer, feeling the heat from body. She rested her hands on his waist. "It shows off the strength of your hips, Aven said?"

His heart rate sped up, and his breathing quickened. "I..."

"Show me?"

Chapter Sixteen

A ven woke up to the sound of birdsong, and for a moment couldn't remember where he was. This wasn't Aria's room. Then he heard Karse shouting, and remembered – the Progress. They were a day out from the Palace, and on their way to Terraces. They'd be in Shadow Cove tonight, and he'd be able to swim. But if he wanted to be able to move today, he needed to get up and stretch so he could dance.

And he needed to talk to his mother.

Gently, he slipped out of the bed, kissing Aria's cheek as she mumbled something and settled back into sleep. He stretched, reached for his trousers, then stopped. The bed closest to him had a tangle of bodies — Owyn, Alanar and Del. But the third bed was empty, and didn't look as if it had been slept in at all.

Had Othi and Treesi not come in last night? Where were they?

Clearly, not in here. And he wasn't going to find them if he stayed in here. He put on his trousers, looked around once more, then slung the harness for his hook swords over his shoulder. He picked up his walking stick and his boots, and walked out into the morning. Guards were hurrying this way and that, striking tents and working around a fire. He saw Gathi, sitting with Afansa and Meris near the fire, and headed toward them.

"Good morning," Afansa said as he reached them.

"Good morning." Aven sat down next to Gathi, setting his swords on the ground. "Have any of you seen Othi or Treesi? They weren't in the tent this morning."

Meris chuckled and pointed with her spoon. "They're sitting over there, completely wrapped up in each other. I honestly don't think that either of them slept."

"They might have," Afansa murmured. "Between bouts."

"Afansa," Meris chided. "Be nice."

"That was nice!" Afansa protested. "I'm jealous."

"Between..." Aven repeated, then snorted. "Oh." He grinned and shook his head. "Well, they can sleep in the coach."

"Are you going to practice?" Gathi asked. "May I come watch?"

"Not this morning," Aven answered. "I need to talk to my mother. Is she awake?" A hand settled on his shoulder, and he turned and looked up at Aleia. He laughed. "I should ask for Risha's head on a pike next, shouldn't I? It'll just appear."

Aleia chuckled. "Are you going to practice?"

"Once I put my boots on, yes," Aven answered. "I was going to ask if you wanted to join me."

"Breakfast first?"

Aven shook his head. "After. Once the others are awake."

Aleia nodded and came around to stand in front of him, watching as he dusted off his feet and pulled his boots on. "Do you always practice in boots?"

"About half the time. I've noticed that wearing boots changes my balance a little, and I need to be able to fight with or without them." He stood up and picked up his swords. "I haven't seen much of this place in the daylight. Where would be a good spot?"

Aleia looked around, then pointed. "I thought I saw Skela going over that way. I think he was going to warm up before getting Del. Let's go see."

Aven followed her as she started walking, not saying anything. She slowed to fall in next to him.

"Ven—"

"I know you're sorry," he said softly. "I just want to know why." He glanced at her to see that she was looking at him. "Why did you give up on me? You had no idea what happened while you were gone. You still don't know all the details, unless Fa told you."

"Your father did tell me everything. I didn't listen, and I almost lost both of you because of it. He barely talked to me at all until after he caught back up with us." She looked back over her shoulder. "Treesi is going to make a very good mind-healer."

Aven frowned. "I...I don't think I know what that is."

"Neither did she," Aleia said. "Ask your father. He'll explain it better than I will. Suffice it to say, it's a branch of healing that Risha couldn't do— "

"So she didn't teach us." Aven nodded. "I keep tripping over the holes in my education. And it doesn't help that Fa thinks that the Mother shoved me into a deeper pool of healing than I should have had."

"Your father didn't mention that," Aleia said, sounding shocked. "What does that mean?"

"It means that when Fa evaluated me out on the deep, I was a level two healer, with potential to be a level three. But now? I'm a level five. A natural five, Alanar calls it. And Fa says he can't explain it, because training won't hone a gift that much. He thinks the Mother shoved me into the deeper pool because I needed it to save Owyn's life." He took a deep breath. "Maybe if we'd gotten there in time, I could have saved Evarra, too."

"That's when you hurt yourself again."

Aven nodded. "I did something to my hip on the ride. By the time we got there, I couldn't even put weight on it. This is...well..." He shrugged. "Better is relative."

"Speaking of better, your healing isn't the only thing that's gotten better," Aleia said. "If I hadn't seen it myself, I wouldn't have believed how well you fight. You've gotten much better than the last time we sparred on the canoe."

Aven snorted. "That's from necessity. I've had people trying to kill me and everyone I love for months now. I may never be what I was, but I need to be able to fight. I need to be able to protect them."

"I'm serious, Ven," Aleia said. "Yesterday was the first time I've seen you fight since you last sparred with me. You didn't fight when you came back to the deep, and you didn't dance. To be honest, with as much pain as you were in, I didn't think you still could." She stopped, and Aven turned to face her. "I thought your father was humoring you. To make the sting easier to bear. I should have known he would never do that."

"So you didn't think I could...and then you thought Fa was lying to me?" Aven shook his head and started walking again. "Ama, did you stop...I don't know...thinking? At all?"

"Apparently? Yes," Aleia said. "I was completely, horribly wrong, and I am sorry. I should have trusted you both. And before you ask, I don't know why I didn't."

Aven nodded. "Thank you."

They walked in silence for a few minutes before Aleia spoke again. "Did your father tell you what he found when he examined you yesterday?"

"Alanar did. Rough spot in the bone, wearing away at the soft tissue." Aven nodded. "They'll put it to rights once we get to Terraces, he says. Then I'll be able to work back up to where I was before the nightmare ride. There's Skela."

They stopped out of range. Skela had found a level piece of ground, and was working with the falling stars. Aleia nudged Aven's arm.

"He thinks you should learn this," she said. "And your father does, too."

"I've been watching Del, and I want to try it. But Skela says I shouldn't until Del moves on to the smooth stars. He only has one set of practice, and Del needs them." He looked at his mother. "You should learn them," he added. "Someone needs to know, so they can teach. Someone other than Del."

Aleia nodded slowly. "I'll speak to Skela. See if he wants an old woman as a student."

"Ama, you're not old."

Aleia smiled. "I'm not young either."

Skela turned, saw them, and let the stars slow until they dangled from his hands. "Good morning!"

"Good morning, Skela," Aleia called. "What do you think? A good morning to dance?"

"A fine morning to dance, and I will watch," Skela answered. "Is my Del awake yet?"

"He wasn't when I left the tent," Aven answered. "He'll probably be up soon, though."

"If he is not, there will be no time to practice before we leave," Skela said. He gestured. "This is a good place. No rocks underfoot, and no holes. It's not as nice as the dancing floor in the Palace, but it is good."

Aven unslung the harness from his shoulder and unhooked his swords. He looked down at them, then at his mother. "Did I ever really show these to you, Ama?"

"I've seen them," she answered. "I haven't handled them." She took the blade he offered her, stepped away, and took a practice swing. "It's heavier than I like."

"It's balanced for my hand," Aven said. "Memfis made them for me." He grinned. "Twenty years ago, he said."

She looked startled. "What?"

"He made these for me twenty years ago. He made Owyn's smoke blades, and Aria's arm crossbow. And her javelins. And he hid them all under his anvil for twenty years, until we left to go to Meris' house." He took his sword back. "When we get far enough south, do you want to swim down and see if we can find your blades?"

Aleia shook her head. "We won't find them. Not with the volcano. There's enough molten rock and debris in those waters that we'd never find them. No, they've gone back to the Mother. Or back to Abin, who first bore them."

Aven frowned. "Then what are you using to practice? Do you have blades anymore?"

Aleia shook her head. "I have a set, but they're not the same. They don't feel like part of my arm the way the lost ones did. I should have brought them, but..." She shook her head again, then grimaced. "I'm being childish."

"A bit," Skela murmured. "If the blade is all you have to defend, then what matter how it feels in your hand? You use it." He gestured to Aven. "Go ahead and start."

Aven nodded and walked away from them, making sure there was twice as much room between them as he could reach with a long lunge. Not that he was lunging much now — he'd end up on his face. Once he was far enough, he set himself, took a deep breath, and started the slow sequence that were the opening movements of the basic forms, the moves that began every wardance he'd ever learned, that he'd ever seen. Looking at them with a healer's eyes, he knew that they were designed to warm the body and stretch the muscles. Knowing that had helped him adjust how he did them so that he wouldn't fall over or hurt himself before he really began.

The end of the first forms, flowing into the beginning of the second forms. These were faster, more explosive. Closer to fighting than dancing, even with the adaptations that he'd made to compensate. Clearly, the changes worked, and worked well — he'd beaten Othi. But being helpless to defend Aria from Hilah still gnawed at him. It wasn't going to happen again. He would protect his loved ones, from whoever or whatever threatened them.

Moving faster, moving into the third forms, the advanced forms. Strain in the hip, but not pain. Not yet, so he kept moving, kept pushing, trying not to wonder why he wasn't in pain yet. If he didn't think about it, maybe it wouldn't happen this time. Then he turned, striking out at an imaginary opponent on his left, and felt the stabbing pain up and down his left side.

Enough.

Too much, maybe.

He slowed, lowering his blades, and took a deep breath. And, to his surprise, heard applause from behind him. He turned to see that he had an audience — standing beside his mother and Skela were Steward, Del, and Owyn.

"I hadn't realized just how good you are with those," Steward said. "I never get out to see you practice."

"I'm not that good—"

Owyn laughed out loud. "And he's modest, too."

"Mouse!"

"Ven, he's right," Aleia said. "You're better than you think you are. And your grandmother would have been furious—"

"Was she ever not furious where I was concerned?" Aven asked as he limped back to join them. "It's not as bad as it was yesterday. Alanar must have gotten something to settle. I'll ask him and Fa to see."

Aleia smiled. "If she'd ever seen you dance the way you just did, or fight the way you did yesterday, she'd have had to admit that you were easily the best in our canoe. Possibly in the tribe."

"Or she'd have swallowed a spine-fish backwards," Aven countered.

"Or she'd have swallowed a spine-fish backwards," Aleia repeated, nodding her agreement. "Rather than admit it? Yes, she might have. But her pride would have meant that she'd have allowed you to dance in the festivals."

Aven shook his head. "I wasn't that good then," he said. "You beat me every time we sparred." He frowned. "Could you beat me now?"

Aleia tipped her head to one side, considering the question. "Honestly? I don't think so." She smiled. "Once you get that leg taken care of properly, we'll see."

He grinned. "Something to look forward to."

"Aven," Owyn said slowly. "I have a question. Actually, maybe Skela is the right person to ask."

"Ask the question," Skela said. "Then I must have Del practice. We have to leave soon, I think?"

"The tents are being struck, and the advance party will leave as soon as they're packed. We'll be leaving...an hour, more or less?" Steward answered. "That's why I came down with Del and Owyn. To let you know."

"Thank you," Aven said. "Owyn, what's the question?"

Owyn folded his arms over his chest. "Water has hook swords and falling stars. Fire has smoke blades and whip chain. And they're all really kind of similar with how they're used. I mean...Aven, you let me use your swords to dance when we were out on the Floating City. The moves are sort of the same, and it called the visions the same as my blades."

Aven nodded. "And...?"

"And which came first?" Owyn asked. "Either one of them inspired the others, or there was something else that came before all the others." He looked at Skela. "Any ideas?"

Skela laughed. "I've raised this question myself. And I have no answer for it. I know that Fire whip chain is similar our Water falling stars, but if they came from the same source?" He shrugged. "I am not that old." He looked at Owyn. "And I have been told that you fight with this whip chain. Will you show me?"

"Yeah, I can show you. Now?" Owyn looked around. "There's enough room. And then you can work with Del. I haven't seen what he's doing yet with the falling stars."

"Please," Skela said.

Owyn nodded and walked out to where Aven had been, taking his chain from the pouch at his waist. "If I fall down...well, just let me be. It means there's something I need to know."

"No visions today, Owyn," Aven called. "We don't have the time."

"Like I have any say in them showing up," Owyn called back. He shook the chain out and draped it over his shoulders. "Aven, you know what to do if I do go down."

Aven nodded. "Go ahead." He settled his swords back into their harness and slipped it onto his back, watching as Owyn snapped the chain out and started to move.

Aleia hummed softly. "He's very good, too."

"I've lost count of the number of people he's killed with that, because he was protecting one of us," Aven answered. "Upwards of eight, I think. Aria calls him her Warrior."

"And you're the Heart," Aleia said.

"Is the Warrior a role?" Aven asked. "Like the Heart?"

"It may very well be, going forward," Aleia said. "I don't know that the role was ever needed before. If that's the case, then why are you so worried about protecting them? Warrior is not your role."

"I don't think any of us are taking just one role," Aven answered. "I don't think any of us can afford to be so narrow. Not with the burden put on us." He turned back to watch Owyn. "I'm the Heart, and sometimes I'm the Warrior. Owyn is the Warrior, but sometimes he's the Heart. And sometimes Treesi is the Heart."

"Treesi will make an excellent mind-healer," Aleia said. "He's very good, isn't he? I've read about whip chains. I've never seen one before. Skela, what do you think?"

"It is very much like falling star. Yet different. I think there is something to our common question. They sprang from the same source. What that source was?" Skela shrugged. "Who can say?" He looked at Aven. "How many kills did you say?"

"At least eight?"

Skela snorted. "And he has no tattoos why? He needs his warrior marks!"

"Skela, he's Fire—" Aleia started.

"And Earth," Aven added.

"He doesn't have to have his warrior marks." Aleia finished.

Del tapped Aven's arm, and signed, "*Othi said the same thing. Remember? And Neera adopted him into the canoe, just like she did me. He needs the family mark and the warrior marks. There just wasn't time.*"

Aven nodded. "We'll ask Owyn if he wants them. Neera did offer, and Othi can do it if he has the right tools. He knows how. But it has to be Owyn's choice."

"My choice for what?" Owyn called. He slowed the whip chain down and let it wrap around his body as he stopped moving, then gathered it up as he walked toward them. "What am I choosing?"

"If you want your family mark and your warrior marks," Aleia answered. "Neera welcomed you into the canoe. You're entitled to them."

Owyn nodded as he tucked the whip chain back into the pouch. "I haven't had time to really think about it. Well...I mean...I have...but...I haven't. You know?"

Aven nodded. "I understand. And you have time. Now, Skela, are you and Del going to practice?"

"Yes," Skela said. "And then I want to discuss this theory of yours, Owyn, on the common ancestor among our weapons."

Chapter Seventeen

Owyn rolled his shoulders, then tipped his head from one side to the other. The day had been quiet, the ride peaceful enough that even Alanar had enjoyed it. They'd ridden alongside the coach for a time, then rode up to the front of the caravan to spend time with Karse and Steward.

"It's been months since we last were at Shadow Cove," Alanar said. "How do you think they're doing?"

"I'm sure they're all right," Owyn answered. "The headman there was a good man, remember?"

"Barsis was his name, wasn't it?"

Owyn nodded, then laughed. "Yeah. Barsis. I wonder if they rebuilt the guest house by now?"

"We won't be using it," Steward pointed out. "We'll be camping outside the village, so we don't put a strain on their resources."

Owyn nodded again. "I remember you saying that," he said.

"How's Freckles been today?" Karse asked.

"He's fine," Owyn answered. "I mean, I think he's fine. And Jehan said he wasn't hurt anymore before we started."

"And you saddled him yourself," Karse added. "I saw you do it."

"Yeah. No one gets to touch him or Meadowfoam. No one but me." He reached down and stroked Freckles' neck. "Not letting anyone hurt him. Him and me, we've been through too much together."

"I feel much the same way about Alabaster," Steward said. He looked around, then frowned. "Karse, is that one of our men?"

Karse nodded. "Yeah, that's one of the guard." He raised his voice. "Terent, what's the word?"

"The word is stop! Don't go to Shadow Cove!" Terent shouted back. "Plague!"

Karse swore, and raised one fist; Owyn turned to see the coaches and riders all coming to a stop. "Plague?" Karse shouted, and started to ride toward the guard. Terent raised his crossbow.

"Don't, Captain!" he shouted. "The baggage carts, they're all right off the road, at the crossroads near Shadow. They're guarded. We left men there. You take them and go. We'll..." He shook his head. "We'll be all right."

"Terent, report!" Karse snapped. "What happened?"

The guard lowered his crossbow. "We reached the campsite, and while the baggage was offloaded, some of us went down to the village to tell them that we were there, that the Progress was coming. None of us saw plague markers on the trail. Not even sure if there were any. I was last in the line, and the headman, he told me I should come warn you off, then go right back." He looked down at his horse, then back up. "We'll cordon off the town, make sure there aren't any more mistakes like the one we made."

"You'll go back and tell Barsis that the healers are coming is what you'll do!" Owyn shouted back. "Plague...what kind of plague?"

"Symptoms, Terent!" Alanar added. "What are we looking at?"

Terent stared at them for a moment, then stammered, "Fever. Cough. A deep cough. Chills and sweats. Rash...or maybe hives. Not sure. They're all red in the face. And the headman says that before they die, they swell up—"

"Mountain fever," Alanar breathed. "It's mountain fever. How the fuck did they get mountain fever? There haven't been any cases in years!"

"Terent," Karse shouted. "You go back and you tell them that the healers are coming. Understand?"

"Yes, Captain. But—"

"That's an order!" He turned. "Right. We need to rearrange the coaches. I want all the healers in one, so that they can get down to Shadow—"

"I don't think we can get a coach down that road," Owyn interrupted.

"We're going to try," Karse snapped. "All their supplies, everything into that coach. Move!" He turned back to face down the road. "Terent, go back. Tell them that we're got healers coming, and they're going to be fine."

Terent nodded slowly. "I...be careful, Captain." He turned his horse and started back toward Shadow Cove. Karse watched him for a moment, then rode back down the line, shouting orders. Owyn and Alanar followed him, and Owyn dismounted outside the Heir's coach, helping Alanar down.

"Let's get the boots off," he said. "You need to be able to move."

Alanar nodded and sat down, letting Owyn tug his left boot off. "I'm trying to remember everything I've ever read about mountain fever," he said. "And my mind is racing." He stopped and frowned. "Virrik remembers more than I do. He says he'll help."

"Good." Owyn tugged off Alanar's other boot, and looked up to see Treesi and Aven. Aven looked worried.

"Mountain fever?" he said. "That's what Karse said."

"How is that possible?" Treesi asked. "There hasn't been a case of mountain fever this far west in twenty years."

"Thirty," Jehan corrected as he reached them. "And I want to know the answer to that question, too. All right, you three. This is going to be ugly work. We're taking Gathi with us."

"I'm coming with you, too," Steward said as he joined them. "I've had mountain fever. I can't catch it again. Isn't that right?"

Jehan looked at Steward and nodded. "That's right. I was hoping you'd stay with Aria, though."

"I will be fine," Aria said. "I'll have Owyn and Del, and Aleia and Othi with me. And Karse. Take Steward, and help them."

Jehan nodded. "Right. Except you won't have Owyn. Owyn, I want you to ride on."

"To where?" Owyn asked.

"Terraces. As fast as you can get there. We're going to need more help." He frowned. "And Serenity, on the way. Tell Danzi to send canoes to Terraces. That will get Mother and any other healers back here faster than going overland. Then..." He took a deep breath. "Wait for us there."

"No," Owyn blurted. "I am not waiting for you there. Not with Allie off healing himself into getting sick again like the last time."

"I'll be more careful this time," Alanar protested as he got to his feet. He handed his socks to Owyn. "I won't do that again."

"We won't let him do that again," Aven added. "Mouse, will you trust me with your husband? To take care of him?"

Owyn met his eyes and nodded. "I trust you. And I trust him to take care of you." He looked around. "I'll need supplies, and I'll need them now. I need to get on the road."

"Wait," Othi said. "Uncle, would it be faster if I went to Terraces? I know the way. It'll be faster if I swim than it will be for Owyn to ride, won't it?"

Owyn looked over at him. "Even at Freckles' best speed, I won't get to Terraces before sometime late tomorrow. We're coming on to nightfall. How soon would you be able to get to Terraces?"

Othi looked at Aven. "Help? I'm not a navigator. Not on land, anyway."

Aven looked up at the sky, then looked to the western horizon. "We're in the part of the coast that curves inland. It's longer to go by road than by water. If we can get Othi down to the water, I think he can be in Terraces by dawn. Maybe even by moonset."

"He'll need to stop in Serenity Bay for the canoes," Owyn added. "Ummm...Danzi don't know him, I don't think."

"She knows me," Aleia said. "I'll go with Othi. We'll be back when we're back. Owyn, you stay with Aria. Del, help him."

"I don't need that much looking after," Aria protested. Aleia smiled.

"Othi, be careful," Treesi said.

"You be careful, too." He leaned down to kiss her. "I'm just swimming. You're going to be saving people. You be careful." He turned to Aleia. "Aunt, where do we need to go?"

"Come with us in the coach," Jehan said. "There's a place near the water before we reach Shadow. We need to get moving. Alanar, Treesi, Aven, Gathi, you all get in the coach. Othi, you, too. Leia, ride double with me."

"It'll be faster than saddling a horse for me," she agreed.

Jehan nodded and turned. "Is the coach ready?"

"Ready!" Karse shouted.

"Then let's go!"

ONCE THE COACH AND the riders were gone, the rest of the Progress set out once more, heading for the campsite. Owyn sat on Aria's left in the coach, and Del on her right. Each of them had one of her hands.

"They'll be fine," Meris said. She was sitting across from them with Memfis and Skela. "Jehan knows exactly what to do."

"He literally wrote the book on what to do," Memfis added absently. He stared out the window, drumming his fingers against his leg.

"What is it, Fa?" Owyn asked. "Something's bothering you?"

"I heard Jehan and Treesi, before they left. There hasn't been a case of mountain fever this far west in thirty years. And the epidemic that went through the Palace came in with a trader from the mountains. How did a coastal village get infected?" He turned to look at them. "Who brought it there? And when? Mountain fever spreads fast. It had to be recent."

"We're not going to get those answers until the healers are finished," Aria said. "We'll find out when they come back."

Del sighed, and Owyn looked across Aria at him. "What?"

"*It's too convenient?*" Del answered. "*They just happened to end up with mountain fever as we started the Progress, and this is our first stop?*"

Owyn frowned as he relayed Del's word to the others. "The guard said that he didn't see the plague markers when they went down to Shadow Cove. He wasn't sure there were any."

Memfis growled softly. "I'm not sure I like this line of thinking, Mouse."

"Me, either," Owyn admitted. "Del, when we get to camp, maybe we'll walk over to the trailhead and see about those markers..."

"You'll do no such thing!" Meris scolded. "By the time we get there, the guards who are there will have placed proper markers, and you'll be staying away from them until the healers say the town is clear."

"How bad is mountain fever?" Aria asked.

"Bad," Memfis answered. "Very bad. When it went through the Palace, Tirine wanted to close us away to keep us safe. She actually did order us to our rooms, but Jehan snuck out and went to work with the healers. And we went to work helping him." He shook his head. "I'm amazed that none of us caught it, but we were very lucky. And very careful. Jehan insisted that we all wear scarves over our mouths and noses when we went into the sick rooms. He had a theory that it was airborne. He was right." He took a deep breath. "The thing they don't tell you about being in a room full of people who are dying? There's a smell. I'll never forget it. It smells like bread baking. But sour. Like there's something wrong with it. And you could smell it through the scarves." He paused, then shook his head. "It was months before I could be in the same room as fresh baked bread without feeling sick."

Owyn shivered and looked out the window. "I see the camp," he said. "And...do you smell smoke?"

Del frowned and nodded. "*I smell it. It smells strange.*"

Memfis sniffed. Then he groaned. "They're burning the bodies. Mother hold them all."

FROM THE MOMENT THE healers got out of the coach in Shadow Cove, they were in motion. Jehan took the worst cases, the ones who were swollen and gasping for air. Steward stayed with him, a scarf covering his face, carrying basins and towels and doing whatever he could.

Alanar, Aven, and Treesi triaged the rest of those suffering, moving from makeshift bed to makeshift bed, seeing who needed to be put into immediate healing trances, and who could be settled with steam tents and tea and broth. Once they had been sorted, Aven and Alanar went back through the ones in trance, while Treesi worked with those who weren't as serious, and Gathi made those remaining comfortable while they waited to be treated.

"Healer Aven?"

Aven looked up from his patient, seeing the dark figure of a man standing over him. He had a lantern in one hand, and a bowl in the other. It was dark. When had it gotten so dark?

"Yes?" Aven said. "How late is it?" He looked up at the stars, then shook his head, blinking. "I can't tell. Mother, I must be tired. How late is it?"

"Moon set about an hour ago. Dawn in...three hours, maybe? Here." The man handed him the bowl. "Fish stew. Been keeping it warm for a few hours. Didn't look like you were going to stop, though, so I'm stopping you. I'm Barsis. I'm the headman here." He looked around. "You've done...you've done amazing things here, Healer."

Aven sat down and raised the scarf that covered his mouth and nose, sipping the salty fish broth. "We're not done yet," he said.

"No, there's still a job of work to be done, but we have a chance now," Barsis replied. "And we'd not have had any chance if it hadn't been for you." He nodded. "Healer Alanar is talking to himself. He do that a lot?"

Aven chuckled. "You get used to it. Where's my fa?"

"Asleep, last I looked. The one helping him made him lay down. That one...is that...but it can't be?"

"He's Steward," Aven answered. "And we'll explain it all when you meet the Heir. Whenever that happens. But trust me when I say that he's true to her, completely and totally."

Barsis nodded. "That's good enough for me, Waterborn. And I'm looking forward to meeting her. How's Owyn?"

"Probably not sleeping and pulling his hair out, with Alanar here without him."

Barsis laughed. Then he coughed, a deep wet-sounding cough that left him gasping. "Oh..."

Aven smiled behind his scarf and set aside his bowl. "Have a seat, Headman. Let's take a look at you."

THE CANOES ARRIVED from Terraces with the dawn, and Jehan met them on the beach.

"Well?" Pirit demanded.

"Good to see you, too, Mother," Jehan answered.

"Jhansri..."

"No one has any idea where it came from. There's no vector that anyone can figure out. Barsis realized what they had when the first person started swelling around the throat, and he locked the entire town down. No one went for help, because he was afraid it would spread. No one entered, no one left, until the Palace Guard arrived yesterday to announce the Progress. And they didn't leave, except for one who came back to warn us off, and he never came close enough to spread it." Jehan looked back up at the quiet houses. "It's been five days since the initial outbreak. Fifteen dead. Have there been any other cases on the coast?"

"None that have reached out to us, no. Danzi says it's been unusually quiet in Serenity. No vector?" Pirit repeated. "That...that's hard to believe. A small village like this? No stranger, no traders?"

"Barsis says no," Jehan looked around again. "I think we've contained the worst of it, and once we're rested, we'll be able to help you and your trainees finish off the last of it." He turned and pointed. "Mild cases are in those two houses there. More serious ones are in trance, and those are in the three houses down at the end of the beach. They're being monitored."

Pirit nodded. "And where are your healers?"

Jehan smiled. "The last I saw them? Asleep on the beach." He gestured, a tired wave of one arm, and fell in next to his mother as they walked up the beach. "We've got a new healer in training for you, Mother. Steady as a rock through all of this. Stubborn as a bull seal, too. Her name is Gathi." He grinned. "We found her when she accidentally almost killed your grandson."

Pirit's brows rose. "I'm looking forward to this story. And to meeting her. Now, where's the Heir?"

"There's a campsite outside of town." Jehan looked back at the canoes. "Where's my wife? And Othi?"

"They stayed behind in Terraces," Pirit answered. "Under protest. Quite strenuous protest, I might add. The young man, he's paired with someone?"

"With Treesi, and it's still new," Jehan answered. "They're still figuring their course."

"Healer Treesi?" Pirit sounded shocked. "Paired with someone? And...she's the Earthborn Companion."

"And Aria gave her blessing," Jehan said.

"So that means that the Heir's personal circle is...how many now?"

"Seven," Jehan answered. "And they all seem to work exceptionally well together."

"They're going to have to," Pirit said with a snort. "Right. Let's get to work. I..."

"Mother, before you go in, I need to explain something to you," Jehan said. "Walk with me."

"Isn't that what we're doing?" Pirit asked.

Jehan chuckled. "Very funny. There's going to be a familiar man in there. He's not who you think. His name is Steward—"

"I don't know anyone named Steward." Pirit stopped.

"You do," Jehan said. "But he's not the person you'll think he is." He paused. "The person you'll think he is was stripped of his name, and his deeds and his punishment recorded as an example to anyone who might think to follow his example."

Pirit blinked. She looked over her shoulder, then back at Jehan. "He's...really?" She smiled. "I'd wondered how Aria was going to do

it. How she was going to keep from having to have him executed."
She nodded. "And he's sworn himself to her?"

"Completely," Jehan answered. "I'm fairly certain he'd die for
her at this point. And they've all of them decided he's their adopted
uncle."

Pirit nodded. Then she smiled. "Now, tell me. How exactly did
this new healer in training try to kill my grandson?"

AVEN HEARD VOICES, but only distantly. He was warm, and
the sand was comfortable.

Sand?

He opened his eyes and remembered Shadow Cove. Working
through the night saving lives. That's why he was still so tired. Why
all of them were so tired — Treesi was curled up next to him,
her head on his shoulder. Alanar was on her other side, sprawled
out over the sand. And Gathi was on Alanar's far side, her cheek
pillowed on one of his outstretched arms.

Aven closed his eyes again. If he could get a little more sleep,
he'd be ready to get back to work...

"Now, tell me. How exactly did this new healer in training try
to kill my grandson?"

He opened his eyes again and looked around to see the people
walking toward the houses that had been dedicated to the sick.
One was his father. The other was his grandmother.

Time to wake up and go back to work.

"Treesi," he said softly. "Pirit is here."

She yawned and mumbled, "Pirit?" Then she blinked and sat
up. "Othi? Is Othi here?"

"I haven't seen him," Aven answered. "Come on. Stand up and
I'll brush the sand off you."

They both got to their feet and moved away from Alanar and Gathi, taking turns brushing sand off their clothes and bodies before going up the beach to where Jehan and Pirit were waiting. Pirit folded her arms over her chest as they approached.

"You both look like you need several days' worth of sleep."

"I agree with that assessment," Aven answered. He kissed his grandmother on the cheek, then looked around. "Where are Ama and Othi?"

"In Terraces," Pirit answered. "That young man has never lived on land before...what? Two months ago? Three? If he came into contact with someone with mountain fever...well, we knew fifty years ago that it hits Water harder than the other tribes. Possibly because they're isolated from other land-based ailments."

Aven nodded. "Before we leave, we'll have to check each other and make sure that none of us are carrying it."

"That's a question I want answered," Pirit said. "Who was the carrier? Mountain fever doesn't just appear. It's carried in the breath and the saliva of someone who is infected. How did it get here?"

Aven looked at his father. "What did Barsis say? I was busy."

"The fevers started five days ago, but Barsis says there haven't been any traders or travelers in the past ten days. By land or by sea." He frowned. "I...oh."

"What?" Pirit asked. "Jehan, what are you thinking?"

"No travelers. No traders. But we never asked about bodies." He turned, looking around. "Where's Barsis?"

"Probably asleep," Aven answered. "He started the cough and fever last night. Fa, what are you thinking?"

"I'm not entirely sure," Jehan answered. "Go wake up Alanar and Gathi. I'm going to find Barsis."

Chapter Eighteen

B arsis was at the communal cookfire, sitting with a bowl in his hands, talking to a woman who looked to Aven to be about the headman's age, or maybe a little younger. Barsis saw the healers coming toward him, and smiled.

"Good morning, Healers," he called. "Sit. Eat. There's porridge, and some of the fish stew from last night." He gestured to the woman. "This is my sister, Rhalien. If you need anything and you can't find me, go to her." He looked at them and frowned. "There's one more of you than there was yesterday. I'm certain I didn't see this lady last night. And I thought I saw healers in gray over by the sick houses not long ago, but you're all here."

"Headman, this is my mother, Healer Pirit," Jehan said.

"Acting Senior Healer, while my son attends the Heir," Pirit added. "The canoes arrived from Terraces not long ago. You must have seen my trainees."

"Canoes?" Barsis blanched. "But—"

"We knew before we left Terraces it was mountain fever," Pirit said. "We brought no Waterborn."

"And I'm already here," Aven added, sitting down and taking the bowl that Rhalien offered him. "Thank you."

"You..." Barsis turned and stared at him. "I didn't notice. You shouldn't be here!"

"He's my son, Headman," Jehan said. "He's a full healer. And I'm keeping a close watch on him."

"We'll have to check each other very carefully before we leave," Alanar added. "So we don't carry anything back to the Progress."

Aven nodded and looked around. "Is Steward awake?"

"And babyminding," Rhalien answered. "He took every child too young to help down the beach so they could make noise without disturbing anyone." She pointed. "The last I saw them, they were playing Drop the Bell."

Gathi, Treesi and Alanar all laughed, and Aven looked at them. "What's Drop the Bell?"

"Children's game," Alanar answered. "Lots of noise, lots of running. Everyone sits in a circle, facing in. One person walks around the outside of the circle with a bell sewn to a piece of cloth, or a ribbon. They drop the bell behind someone, and that person has to grab the bell, and chase the person who dropped it around the outside of the circle. If they catch them before they sit down in the empty spot, they get to drop the bell the next time while the other person goes and sits in the middle of the circle. If they don't catch them, then they sit in the middle of the circle, and the first person goes again."

"And Steward is off playing with them?" Jehan shook his head. "He's a big child sometimes. Right. Barsis, while we eat, I have questions for you."

Barsis nodded, and reached out to pick up the kettle. "Tea? Makes questions easier."

Jehan took one of the cups, and a bowl from Rhalien, sitting down next to Aven. Alanar sat down on Aven's other side, and Aven immediately felt the pain in his hip start to ease.

"Stop that," he murmured. "We have other people to heal. I'm fine."

"You ache, and I can feel it," Alanar grumbled.

"Honestly? I hadn't noticed. I'm getting good at ignoring it when it's not stabbing me." Aven took an offered cup from Rhalien and sipped the tea, then laughed. She'd added salt. "Thank you!"

"My pleasure, Healer." Rhalien said, and gave another cup to Alanar.

"Barsis, you told us that there were no travelers or traders," Jehan said. "What about bodies?"

"Bodies?" Barsis repeated. "You mean floaters? I...what was it, Rha? Ten days?"

"About that, yes," Rhalien answered. "Two floaters. Waterborn. Poor things."

Aven looked at his father, who nodded slowly. "And...?"

"And we had to keep the children away," Barsis admitted. "Not sure what killed them, but..." He paused. Then he looked at Aven and he paled. "Oh...You're the Waterborn Companion. I...now I remember. Owyn told me about you. About...he told Ketti, about her boy, told us all what that monster of a healer woman tried to do to you. I...the ones we found were done..."

"Risha did to them what she tried to do to me?" Aven said softly. "And...but that makes no sense. If she gave them mountain fever while she had them, she was risking killing her entire crew. And...can you even give mountain fever to a dead man?"

"They may not have been dead when she infected them," Pirit said. "But she was still risking her crew. And how...how could she have done to them what she did to Aven?" She rested her hand on Aven's shoulder. "She's not been to Terraces. I know. We sealed that section, and I posted guards to keep anyone from coming up from the docks."

"I'm not sure it matters now, since she's not on the water anymore," Jehan said. "But...Barsis, how long would you have said they were dead?"

Barsis frowned, draining his cup. "When we found them? A week or more. And with the currents here, they came from the north—"

"Oh, fuck," Alanar breathed. "She murdered them, and she made them into weapons. They weren't meant to reach there. They were meant for the Palace, and the harbor. And the whole blasted Water tribe!" He shook his head. "Counting on the currents...the wrong eddy at the right time saved hundreds of lives."

"Sounds more like the right eddy," Gathi said. "So what do we do about it? Are there more of them out there?" Everyone turned to stare at her, and she looked startled. "Well, you don't think she hinged this entire plan on two bodies, do you?"

"We need to get a message to Neera," Jehan breathed. "Danzi—"

"No, we can't send Danzi," Pirit said. "One woman, alone in a canoe, to the Palace? If Risha has any allies on the waves, she'd never make it." She frowned. "She took the canoe off-shore, to stay away from the fever. We can send her back to Terraces. Then Aleia and Othi can go north and warn the others. Underwater, no one will see them."

Jehan nodded. "That makes sense. Once we're done here." He turned back to Barsis. "What happened to them? What did you do with the bodies?"

"We didn't know they were carrying," Barsis answered. "So we sent them back to the deep." He gestured toward the water. "There's a place, out past the reef there. We can reach it from a skiff, and the Water folk who used to come to trade said that it was a good spot. Two of my men took the bodies out and did what was needful for them."

"And them?" Treesi asked. "Where are they?"

Barsis grimaced. "Dead. The first two to die. By the time they died, we knew what we were dealing with, so we burned their bodies like we were taught."

Jehan set his empty bowl down. "So that's our vector. And we'll get the Water tribe warned. For now, enough talking, Healers. We have work to do."

"Do I get to do real work today?" Gathi asked. "Or am I still just carrying things?"

"At this stage of your training, carrying is work," Alanar said. "Along with watching. Come with me, Gathi. Let's go find something for you to carry."

OWYN SAT NEAR THE FIRE and yawned, keeping his eyes on the road. Their camp was set up near the crossroads where his guide had left him when he'd left Shadow Cove for the first time. Gan, that had been his name. Owyn wondered if he was still alive. He yawned, blinked hard, and kept watching the road that led down to Shadow Cove.

It had remained stubbornly empty all night.

Another yawn, and he blinked again as he sipped the strong-enough-to-fight-back tea that the guards had given to him. He didn't have to watch the road. He knew that it was too early to hear anything yet. He knew that staring wouldn't make news come any faster. But he was almost certain that if he turned away from his post, if he went back to the tent to try and sleep, he'd miss something important. So he sat and watched.

"*You never came to bed.*"

Owyn looked up to see that Del had come soundlessly up behind him. "I'm going to put a bell on you," Owyn said. "And I couldn't sleep, so I came out here. Wasn't fair to you or Aria for me to toss and turn and keep you up all night."

"It's too soon to know anything."

"I know." Owyn turned to put his back to the fire and to the road, and really looked at Del. "You didn't sleep either, did you? And where's Aria?"

"She's still asleep. And no, I didn't sleep well at all. Is that black kettle tea?"

"Yeah, that's what they called it." Owyn turned back to the fire and used a rag to pick up the hot kettle, filling a cup. He handed it to Del. "Careful, now. It's hot, and it'll curl your teeth. We could have used that in the forge to strip metal." He stared as Del took a long swallow. "Del!"

"I like black kettle tea. I haven't had it in ages."

"You've had this before? And you like it?" Owyn laughed. "Every time I think I know you, you surprise me again. Where did you pick up a taste for rust remover?"

Del laughed and sat down next to Owyn, pressing his arm against Owyn's. *"Out here. I wouldn't stay at the Palace without Fa when he had to travel, so I had to learn to keep up with him when he rode out with the guard. That's how I learned to ride a knee-trained horse. I learned how to track and hunt, how to dress what I caught, and how to cook it over a fire. I can make camp in almost any weather, too. I trusted the guard — they were safe. And they were interesting. Because I was interested, they taught me. Some of them thought it was funny, because they didn't think I'd ever be able to use what they were teaching me."*

Owyn nodded. "Some of that, I want you to teach me. I'm still not sure what I'm doing out here most of the time." He tipped his head back. "And the sky still looks too big out here."

"It was bigger when we were on the canoes."

Owyn nodded. "It was bigger out on the canoes. But this is still pretty big when you grew up in alleys and streets, and the sky was what you saw between buildings." He frowned. "I wonder what it looks like now."

"*What?*"

"Forge. I mean, I know it's gone. I know the Smoking Mountain blew up. But I wonder what the city looks like." Owyn shrugged. "If there's even still a city. When we get far enough south, I think I want to go see."

Del nodded, sipping his tea. "*When you go, I'll go with you. I've never seen a volcano.*" He laughed again when Owyn looked at him. "*I know. I've been in Forge. I've seen the mountain. But it wasn't doing anything. Now...it's not the mountain I knew. I want to see the difference.*"

Owyn nodded and looked over his shoulder at the road, then turned back to see Karse and the boys come out of one of the other tents. Karse led them over to the fire and sat down, putting the wolf puppy down on the ground.

"No word yet," Karse said. "Wasn't expecting to hear anything, really. What's for breakfast?"

"There's porridge, and it should be ready," Owyn answered. "Couple of the guards went off to hunt, so we'll have fresh meat tonight. They decided it weren't a good idea to go try and fish."

Karse nodded. "They're right. Until we know more about what's down at Shadow, we stay away from the water. Wren!" Owyn turned to see the guard coming toward them. "Did you set the plague markers?"

"Just over the rise, Captain," Wren answered. "Can't see them from here, but if you go further down the trail, they're nice and clear." He came over and sat down across from Owyn and Del, and Owyn turned in his seat to face him. "How long do you think it will be before we hear anything?"

"Later today, I expect," Karse answered. "Or tomorrow. Shadow isn't a big place, I'm told. Owyn? You've been there?"

"Little town," Owyn agreed. "I dunno, maybe a dozen or fifteen houses? Forty, fifty people?" He shrugged and refilled his cup. "Nice place, and the headman is a good man."

"I've no doubt," Karse said. "Right. Wren, once everyone is fed, let's send some runners out, see what's around here. We're supposed to be out here to meet people, right? Let's see if there are people to meet."

"Yes, Captain," Wren said. "Who's cooking this morning?"

"From the smell of that pot? No one," a woman said from behind Owyn. Zarai the midwife came past him, peered at the pot, then picked up the long-handled spoon and stirred the porridge. "Oh, this is a right mess. And you expect the Heir to eat this?" She shook her head. "I'll be putting this to rights, then."

"Do you need any help?" Owyn asked. "I cook. I'm just not really any good outside a kitchen. But I'll help if you tell me what you need me to do."

Zarai looked at him and smiled. "And it's a distraction while we wait?"

Owyn grinned. "Yeah, that, too."

He spent the rest of the morning helping Zarai, learning to cook over an open fire, and serving breakfast to the others. Afansa joined them, teasing Owyn gently, and he found himself relaxing. When he looked up, Del was gone.

"He went off with Skela," Afansa said. "Skela said something about practicing?"

"Oh, falling star practice," Owyn said with a nod. He looked around at who else had come to eat. Memfis and Meris. Zarai, still at the fire. Karse was watching the boys play with Howl. "Has Aria come out and I missed her?"

"No, I haven't seen her." Afansa pushed her hair back with her wrist. "Why don't you go see where she is, and I'll start the washing up? You can help me when you come back." She smiled. "If you come back before I'm done, that is."

"I'll be back to help," Owyn said, and trotted off to the big tent. The flaps were closed, and he slipped inside as quietly as he could. He could see Aria, lying on her side in the middle of the big bed, curled up with her wings folded in close to her body. But something didn't look right. He stepped closer, and heard a muffled sob.

"Aria?" he whispered, moving to the bed. She curled tighter around herself in response, and Owyn crawled across the bed to her. He ran his hand up her arm, gently moving her until she was in his arms, sobbing against his chest. "I've got you," he whispered into her hair. "I've got you. I'm here." He held her tightly, rocking gently as he rubbed her naked back underneath her wings, trying to think of what might have upset Aria to the point of tears.

By the time her breathing finally slowed, Owyn thought he might know. "Nightmare?" She nodded, her cheek sliding against his shirt. He hugged her more tightly. "It's all right. It's over. It's daylight, and you're fine. It wasn't real."

"It might be real," she whispered, her voice strained.

"It wasn't real. We don't dream our visions, sweetheart, we dance them." Owyn picked up a corner of the blanket and used it to wipe Aria's cheek. "Want to tell me?"

"They aren't coming back," she whispered. "They're going to die down there, and we'll never see them again."

Owyn couldn't help it; he shuddered. "None of that," he whispered. "They're coming back. The best healers in the entire world are down there, with the man who wrote the book on how to cure mountain fever. They'll be back, and they'll be fine."

She looked up at him. "You promise?"

He forced himself to smile. "If I have to go down there and get them myself."

She smiled. Then she slid her arms around him. "Lay down."

"What?"

"You didn't sleep last night. You never came in. So lay down." She pushed him backwards, until he was laying on the bed. She curled up next to him, her head on his shoulder, her wing covering them both. He took a deep breath and let it out slowly.

"I didn't come in because I didn't want to keep you awake," he said, staring at the canvas roof. "I knew I wasn't going to sleep."

"Because you were worried?"

Owyn nodded. "Yeah. Because Allie pushes until he can't go anymore, then keeps going. The last time we were here together, it's when he started getting sick. And I'm not down there to take care of him—"

"Aven will take care of him," Aria said. She raised her head. "And you're here to take care of me," she added.

Then she kissed him.

Chapter Nineteen

For a moment, Owyn was too shocked to do anything. Then she shifted, running her hand up his chest, up his throat, into his hair. Surprise vanished, as did any kind of thinking at all; he pulled her closer, helping her to shift until she was straddling him, tugging at his shirt until she could run her hands underneath, her fingers warm against his skin. He ran his hands up her sides, and she moaned against his mouth. He groaned, hearing his heart hammering in his ears, and struggled to sit up. For a moment, she resisted, and he laughed.

"Too many clothes," he murmured. "I have too many clothes."

She laughed, a low laugh the likes of which Owyn didn't remember hearing from her, and let him sit up. He tugged his shirt off over his head and was about to toss it aside when he heard someone behind him, calling his name from outside the tent. He froze, then wrapped the shirt around Aria as a guard burst into the tent.

"Fireborn, I—" He stopped. His jaw dropped, and his eyes widened. "I...oh. Uh...I'm sorry." He turned his back. "I'm sorry. But...there's been a messenger."

"What?" Owyn and Aria spoke at the same time. Owyn looked at her, and she nodded.

"Go," she said. "I'll come out in a moment." She kissed him quickly. "This can wait."

Owyn looked back over his shoulder. "Go out. I'll be there in a moment."

The guard didn't look at them; he left the tent and closed the flap with the same gravity as if it was a solid door. Owyn turned back to look at Aria.

"I'm sorry," he whispered. "I..."

"There's nothing to be sorry about," she said. "I...shall we continue this later?"

Owyn grinned and kissed her. "I'd like that. Let me up, and I'll go out and keep them busy until you're dressed." He helped her to shift off his legs, and got off the bed, adjusting his trousers. She handed him his shirt, and he pulled it back on, letting it hang loose. The hem hung just long enough to hide his arousal.

"Are you going to be all right?" he asked.

Aria got up from the bed and moved closer to him. "It was just a dream," she said. "Just a bad dream. You're right. And you chased it away." She glanced at the closed tent flap. "Now go see what they have to say. I'll be out shortly."

Owyn nodded and left the tent, slipping out to see the guard waiting for him. "I know you. You're one of Karse's men from Forge, right? Lyka? You were still new when I left."

"Yes, Fireborn. And...I'm sorry." The guard glanced at the tent and whispered. "I didn't think...well, I'm sorry, Fireborn."

"Apology accepted," Owyn said. "You can call me Owyn, Lyka. Now, where's the messenger?"

The guard gestured toward the road. "Over the rise. He didn't come past the markers, but he asked for you. Said it was a message from Healer Alanar."

Owyn nodded. "Right. I'll go see. Just a minute." He turned back the tent. "Aria, it's me," he called as he ducked back inside. "There's a messenger waiting out by the plague markers. You go get something to eat, and I'll go see what the message is."

Aria nodded. "Go on. Hurry back."

Owyn hurried out to where Lyka waited for him. "Right. Show me where?"

Lyka gestured. "This way. They sent a child. Maybe the same age as Copper. He said he had to hurry back, so we shouldn't tarry."

Owyn followed the guard toward the road and away from the camp. He could see Del and Skela on the other side of camp, working with the falling stars. There were people milling around, taking care of the camp and the horses. Afansa was bent over the porridge pot, and Owyn felt a pang of guilt — he was supposed to be helping her to clean up. But he needed to find out what the messenger wanted first.

"The messenger say anything else?" he asked.

"Just that he was carrying a message from Healer Alanar, and to fetch you." Lyka picked up his pace, and Owyn matched it until they were both jogging along the road. They crested the rise, and Owyn could see the bright red flags of the plague markers on either side of the empty road. He slowed to a walk.

"Where's the messenger?" he asked.

Lyka frowned and shook his head. "Not sure." He looked around, then pointed at the trail that led down to the coast road. "Maybe he went over there?"

"He had a message to deliver," Owyn pointed out. "What would he be doing going running off down a washed-out trail?"

"It's washed out?" Lyka looked alarmed. "Would he have known that?"

"Considering I'm the one who told them that the trail was washed out, back when I was here in the spring? I think so." Owyn looked around. "Why would he have gone down there?"

"Maybe he saw something?" Lyka started toward the trail. "Rabbit or something. You know what it's like to be that young—"

"Not really, no," Owyn muttered as he followed Lyka. He looked around as they walked down the trail, trying to see where the messenger had gone. Then he whistled, the shrill sound bouncing off the rocks and making Lyka jump.

"Maybe...he went back?" Owyn suggested. "Maybe I took too long, and he went back down to Shadow."

Lyka turned in a circle. "Maybe—"

He jerked, his eyes widening, and he and Owyn both stared at the crossbow bolt that had suddenly appeared in the center of his chest. He crumpled, and Owyn tried to catch him as he fell, knowing it was futile.

Something hit him in the back, sending him tumbling as he dropped Lyka's still body. He came to rest on his side, and realized what had happened. He'd been shot. Animal instinct took over, and on hands and knees he scrambled off the trail and into the rocks before getting to his feet and staggering into a lurching run. His chest hurt. Breathing hurt. Pain made every step torturous, and he could feel the blood running down his back. How bad was it?

Bad enough. He needed a healer.

But first, he needed to hide.

A rivulet of water splashed down over the rocks, and he waded into it, following it back uphill. The water would hide his blood trail, and hopefully, they'd go downhill, thinking he'd taken the easier route. Now to get under cover...there! A narrow crevice in the rock...that he'd never fit into with an arrow sticking out of his back. He kept moving, feeling horribly exposed, expecting another shot at any moment.

But nothing came. Had they given up?

A shadow, off to the left of the water, and he splashed out of the stream and headed toward it. A low hollow under the rock, like a ledge...and it angled back, out of sight of the stream. Hopefully, out of sight of anyone looking for him. He squirmed in the only way he could — on his side, wiping the blood trail away with his shirt sleeves, until he was laying as far back as he could go. It wasn't perfect, but maybe it would help hide him until whoever was hunting him gave up, and he could get out and get back to camp. Or until someone found him.

How long would he have to wait?

Would anyone come looking for him?

Was this what it had been like for Evarra?

He moaned softly, and covered his mouth with his hand. No, this wasn't his place to die. He'd survive. He knew he'd survive. He just had to wait.

Then he coughed, and his fingers came away wet with blood.

ARIA WALKED OUT TO the fire and looked around. She didn't see Owyn. He must not have gotten back yet. Karse was sitting near the fire, playing with the puppy. Howl had a rag in his mouth, and was growling and shaking it as Karse tugged on the other end.

"How is he this morning?" she asked, coming up behind Karse.

"He's full of fire, this one," Karse answered. "He's going to be a handful. Took to eating from a dish like he'd been doing it forever. And he already knows his name." He grinned. "Howl!"

The puppy's ears perked up, and he dropped the rag and barked at Karse. Karse laughed and shook the rag again; Howl pounced on it.

"Good morning!"

Aria smiled as Memfis and Meris came toward her. "Good morning," she said, and hugged her great-grandmother.

"Aria, have you seen Owyn?" Meris asked. "I've been doing some reading, and I wanted to discuss it with him."

"There was a messenger from Shadow Cove," Aria answered. "From Alanar. A guard came to find Owyn, and they went to see what the message was."

"What?" Karse looked up as he dropped the rag. "When was this? No one told me there was a messenger!"

Aria blinked. "It was a guard who came after him. It seemed very important." She paused, feeling her face warming. "He didn't wait to ask permission to enter."

"He...oh," Karse coughed. "I'll talk to him about that. Which one was it?"

Aria shook his head. "I don't think I know his name. I think he was fairly new to the Palace. I heard Owyn say he was one of your men from Forge, though."

"New to the Palace, and one of mine..." Karse frowned. "Lyka. Must be Lyka. He didn't say anything to me about a messenger. Where?"

"By the plague markers," Aria answered. "Owyn said he was going to go see what the message was, then come back."

Karse nodded. He stood up and dusted off his trousers, then nodded toward the puppy, who was happily shredding the rag. "Keep an eye on him, will you? I'll be back." He started walking toward the road. Memfis frowned, then trotted after him.

Aria watched them, then turned to see that Del had come up next to her. He was dusty and sweaty, and wearing a wide grin.

"Why are you so happy?" Aria asked.

Del pulled his tablet out of his carrybag. "*I ran through the exercises with the practice stars without hitting myself once. Skela says that if I keep that up, he'll start me on the smooth stars.*" He looked around, then scrawled, "*What's happened?*"

"I'm not certain," Aria said. "There was a guard who came and got Owyn. He told us there was a messenger, but Karse knew nothing of it. They've gone to see..." She turned toward the road, and her voice trailed off. Karse and Memfis were running back toward the camp. As they got closer, Karse raised his voice.

"Guards, form ranks!" he roared, and guards came running toward him. Aria stared, then went to Karse's side.

"What is it?" she asked. "What's wrong?"

Karse glanced at her, then at Meris. Then he turned to Memfis. "Mem, tell them? I need to get my men out."

Memfis nodded and offered Aria his hand. She let him lead her away from the fire, where Karse was barking orders. Meris and Del followed, until they were standing outside the Heir's tent.

"There wasn't a messenger," Memfis said slowly. "There was no sign of anyone being on that track beyond the markers. There's a second trail, and we followed it. And we found Lyka. He's dead. And there's a blood trail." He looked back toward the fire. "Karse is taking his men back out to see if they can find Owyn."

"A blood trail?" Aria repeated. "What killed Lyka?" Memfis didn't answer, and she gripped his arm more tightly. "Memfis, what killed Lyka?"

"Crossbow, right through the heart," Memfis answered. "He was probably dead before he hit the ground. And...a blood trail...my boy is out there, and he's hurt."

"And we don't have a healer in camp," Meris breathed. "They're all down at the town." She looked around. "I'll tell Zarai that she'll need to be ready."

"She's not a healer—" Memfis said weakly.

"She's the best we have, until the healers get back," Meris replied.

Del signed something, his hands moving too fast for Aria to read. Then he turned and ran.

"Del!" Aria shouted after him. "Where are you going?" She followed him around the tent, saw him heading for the horses. "What is he doing?"

"Del!" Memfis shouted from behind Aria. "Del, what are you...you can't!"

A moment later, Del rode past them and disappeared down the road toward Shadow Cove. Aria stared for a moment, her heart hammering in her chest.

All of her Companions were gone. She was alone.

And she needed to do something.

She licked her lips and turned to Memfis. "Can you find Owyn?" she asked.

"I...the guards—"

"Owyn is hurt," Aria interrupted. "He must be hurt badly, or he'd have come back to camp. He would not have gone off to hide. Someone is out there, and we have to find him first. And we do not have time to waste." She looked up at Memfis. "Can you dance to find him?"

For a moment, Memfis just stared at her. Then he swallowed and stammered, "I...I haven't...I don't know if I can..."

"You still haven't tried?" Meris asked. "Memfis—"

"How am I supposed to dance?" Memfis demanded. "I can't hold my blades!"

"Owyn dances with a whip chain," Karse said as he came over to join them. "That's how he found Evarra. You going to look the same way?"

Memfis looked as if he wanted to either faint or cry. "I don't know if I can," he repeated.

"Then you'd better be finding out," Karse said. "Because knowing where to look may mean the difference between bringing back a Companion or a corpse."

"I didn't bring my blades," Memfis protested.

"Owyn's blades are in the tent," Aria said. "I will bring one to you." She went around to the tent flaps, going inside. Their baggage was along one wall of the tent, and she picked up one of Owyn's smoke blades and carried it back out to Memfis.

"Memfis, if I could do this, I would," Meris said softly. "But I haven't danced a vision in ten years or more. And Aria isn't trained. If we're going to find him, it has to be you."

Memfis took the blade from Aria, holding it as if it were the snake that had cost him his other arm, and he moaned softly, a sound that could also have been a sob.

"I'm not going to let my son die out there," he said softly. "I need a place to dance."

"Del and Skela were practicing over there," Karse said. He pointed. "That large rock, see it? They were just past that."

Memfis nodded and started walking, and Aria followed him. She heard quick footsteps a moment later, then Karse fell in alongside her.

"Lady Meris is going to talk with Zarai, and make sure that things are ready when we bring him back. There will be a tent set aside for him and whichever healer Del comes back with."

"You saw him?"

"Kind of hard not to," Karse said. "Where did he learn to ride like that?"

"I don't know," Aria answered. "Karse, this is twice in two days that someone has tried to kill Owyn. Who?"

"No fucking idea, and I don't like it," Karse spat. "We need to figure this out, and fast. But first, we need to find him." He looked back at the guards. "I'm going to send out scouts, see if we can find anything before Memfis does."

"Do that," Aria said. "And have them bring Lyka back."

Karse nodded and turned, running back to his men. Aria followed Memfis to the rock. He stopped there, the smoke blade dangling in his hand.

"I don't think this is going to work," he said softly.

"If you don't think it will work, then it will not work," Aria replied. "And it has to work. You have to find him." She frowned, trying to remember a beach, and lessons in stillness. "You have to clear your mind. And breathe. And...and listen without hearing."

Memfis glanced at her, and she saw the amusement in his eyes. "You remember all that?"

"If I'd learned more of it then, I might be able to do this now," Aria said. "I cannot."

"And I...I can. I have to." Memfis swallowed. He closed his eyes, then nodded and walked away from the rock. "Stay there. This will either work...or it won't."

"Owyn would say that was true of everything," Aria called after him.

Memfis nodded. "He'd be right," he called over his shoulder. He stopped walking, and Aria watched him as he took a deep breath. A second breath. A third one. Then he started moving.

Memfis' dancing wasn't anything like Owyn's. Memfis seemed more tentative, more deliberate in his movements. At least at first. The more he moved, the more confident he grew, and the more fluid his movements became...until he stopped. He looked at Aria, shook his head, then closed his eyes and started over. Three breaths, and he began to dance once more.

"What happened?" Karse asked softly from behind Aria. "Why did he stop?"

"I think he is still learning his footing," Aria answered, looking at Karse. "You heard him say that he has not danced since he lost his arm. It's changed his balance. He told me once that balance was important."

Karse nodded. "I've only ever seen Owyn dance. And when I saw him, it was with a whip chain. It wasn't this...slow."

"When Owyn dances with his blades, it is slower. But much more...energy?" Aria shrugged. "I'm not sure how to explain it." She looked back at Memfis. "I hope this works."

Memfis stumbled, then fell to his knees, dropping the smoke blade as he caught himself. Karse immediately burst into a run, only to stop when Memfis looked up and waved him off.

"Up," Memfis said, his voice sounding slurred and far off. "Up the down, find the hole and the hole will find him."

Chapter Twenty

Del slowed Lady as they reached the village, and he threw himself from her back before she'd come to a stop. He hit the ground and almost fell — it had been years since he'd last ridden bareback, and his legs were cramping. He gathered himself and looked around.

"You there!" a man shouted. "Where did you come from? Didn't you see the markers? He came closer as Del turned to face him, stopping well out of reach. "You need to go, boy," he said. "We have mountain fever here."

Del nodded. "*I came from the Heir's camp,*" he signed. "*We need a healer now.*"

The man's eyes widened. "Water signs? And...the look on your face. You need something, badly." He looked closer, and touched his own throat. "That's the Air Gem. You're the Air Companion."

Del nodded.

"Right. I'm the Headman here. My name is Barsis. And you sign too fast for me to follow. Stay here. I'll find the Senior Healer. Or someone." He turned, looking around. "I...Healer Pirit!"

"Barsis, what is it?" Pirit called. Then she saw Del. "Del? What are you doing here? What's wrong?"

"*Owyn was attacked,*" Del signed. "*We need a healer back at camp now.*"

Pirit blinked. "Where's your tablet, Del? I can't follow Water signs anymore. I've forgotten too much. Barsis?"

"He goes too fast for me," Barsis admitted.

Del rolled his eyes and reached for his carrybag, only to find it empty. Where was his tablet? Had he left it back in camp? He stared down at the empty bag for a moment, then swallowed and looked at Pirit. No choice. Not if he wanted to save Owyn.

"Weh...weh...ned...hep..." he stammered. Pirit's eyes widened.

"Well," she breathed. She stepped closer, resting her hands on Del's shoulders. "Deep breath, lad," she said gently. "Think about what you need to say. Take your time."

Del swallowed again. "Nuh...nuh...time..." He forced the sounds out. "Wuh...Wyn...urt."

Pirit nodded. "Well done. Barsis, go find my son, and Healer Alanar. I need to be cleared so I can go back to the camp." She looked at him. "And not a word of how you found out. Understand?"

"No, but there's no time for me to understand," Barsis answered, and took off at a run. Pirit smiled and turned her full attention on Del.

"Has anyone been working with you on speaking exercises?" she asked. "Or have you taught yourself how to speak again?"

Del shook his head and tapped his chest, feeling himself starting to shake. He closed his eyes, trying to stop the wave of panic by sheer force of will, and gasped in surprise when Pirit pulled him into a tight embrace. The shock was enough to dispel the darkness that was threatening to wash Del away.

"You did fine," she murmured. "You did wonderfully. It's all right. You're safe." She drew back and met his eyes. "I'm going to assume this is a secret? Since no one ever mentioned speaking exercises to me before you left, and you're quite advanced for someone I've been told has been mute for years. You've been working on this alone?" Del nodded. "Then I'll keep your secret. And I'll have some books for you when you get to Terraces, and we can discuss other exercises. But we'll do that later." She stepped back and turned, and Del saw Jehan and Alanar hurrying toward them. Behind them, looking almost frightened, was Steward.

"Mother, what does Barsis mean you're back going to camp?" Jehan demanded.

"Something's happened to Owyn?" Alanar added. "What happened?"

Del started signing, and Jehan translated, "*Owyn went out with one of the guards. The guard said there was a messenger from Alanar, Aria told us. But Karse said he never heard about a messenger, and he went after them. He found the guard's body and he can't find Owyn. But he said there was a blood trail. We'll need a healer for when we find him.*"

"I'm going," Pirit said. "I haven't done nearly as much as you all have. I'm the best choice. I just need you to clear me so that I don't carry anything back to camp."

"I'm going with you," Alanar said immediately.

"He came on horseback," Jehan said. "And...bareback. Can you ride without a saddle, Alanar?"

Alanar paled. "I can barely ride with a saddle," he admitted. "But..."

"Alanar, I need you to trust me with your husband," Pirit said.

"But—"

"I will not let him die without you there," Pirit added. Then she frowned. "That came out wrong. I'm not going to let him die at all."

Alanar looked stricken. "Pirit, I..." Then he shook his head. "No, we don't have time for me to argue. You have to go. We'll be back as soon as we can."

Pirit held out her hands. "Then clear me, so I can go."

Jehan took one hand, and Alanar fumbled for the other. Barsis came over to Del.

"You'd best get your horse ready while they're working," he said. "Do you need a leg up?"

Del nodded. Then he whistled to Lady, who perked her ears up and came to him. He scratched her forehead, then stroked her neck and moved alongside her. Barsis followed him, then crouched and offered his cupped hands, boosting Del into the air so that he could swing himself onto Lady's back.

"Del." Steward came to stand at Lady's shoulder. "You came down here alone. That's...I'm so proud of you."

Del felt his face growing warm, and ducked his head. "*I did what I needed to do.*"

"And you did it without hesitation, and without panicking," Steward said.

"Panic?" Barsis said. "This one? He rode bareback down that trail, fast enough that I didn't know how he was going to stop. And he came into a plague town, without batting an eye." He snorted. "I'd be wondering if this one felt any fear at all, ever."

Steward looked at Barsis, then up at Del. Del bit his lip and raised his hands. "*I did what I needed to do,*" he repeated, signing slowly so Barsis could follow.

"I'm ready," Pirit said. "And...Mother of us all, I can't even remember when I last rode bareback. Del, don't let me fall."

Barsis helped her to mount behind Del, and she held him tightly around his chest. He glanced back at her and arched a brow. She smiled.

"I'm fine," she said. "I have done this before. It's just been an age. Let's go."

Del nodded. He waved to the others, then urged Lady back toward the trail.

———— ❧ ————

KARSE LOOKED AT HIS search party, such as it was. Afansa had insisted on helping, as had Skela. Zarai was seeing to Memfis, who had passed out cold after his cryptic message. She had told them that he'd be fine, and that she and Meris would be ready for when the search parties brought Owyn back.

He had to bring Owyn back. If anything happened to Owyn, Trey would never forgive him.

When they finally found Trey. Which he wasn't sure they'd be able to do without Owyn.

He shook his head and forced himself to focus. He'd sent out other groups of guards already, but this was the team that was going with him — a woman, an old man, two boys, and a wolf puppy who had cried and howled and refused to stay with Aria. He looked down at the carrybag on his hip, and the puppy who looked up at him and yawned.

"You know, Aria had some nice treats for you," he murmured. "And she'd have played with you and scratched your belly." Howl yawned again, and Karse reached down and ruffled his ears. "Fine. You want me." He looked around again. "Right, are we ready?"

"Where are we going?" Copper asked. "I mean...we're good finders, Dan and me. We found the room—"

"And got trapped in it, yeah?" Karse countered. "This time, I want you to be extra careful. There's someone out there shooting, and we won't have a healer here until Del brings one back."

Danir looked at Copper, and they both nodded. "We'll be careful," Danir said. "We want to help Owyn."

"Then let's go." Karse led them out of the camp and down the road to where the trail split off. Wren was waiting for him there.

"We've searched all up and down the trail," he said. "And we followed the blood trail. There's a stream, and it looks like he might have gone into it to hide his tracks. Nothing on the far side that we can find."

Karse nodded. "Right. Well, we've got new eyes, and ones that are closer to the ground. We'll see what else we can see."

Wren nodded and fell in next to him. "Captain, how can we be sure they didn't take him?" he asked.

"Because the Smoke Dancer said he's here," Karse answered. Wren looked startled.

"Smoke Dancer?" He looked back up the trail. "You mean Lady Meris?"

"No," Karse answered. "Memfis. You were out here already. He danced, and he caught something."

"Up the down," Afansa said. "And something about a hole finding a hole. Did that make sense?"

"It'll make sense when we find Owyn," Karse answered. "This is about where Lyka was, isn't it?"

"Yeah, and the stream is that way." Wren pointed, and they started walking. Karse gestured, and the boys moved off to his sides, both of them studying the ground. Wren watched them, then looked at Karse.

"When did we start a junior guard?" he murmured, and Karse snorted.

"What color was Owyn wearing today?" Skela called. "What are we looking for?"

Karse frowned. He'd seen Owyn at the fire this morning. What color shirt...? "Green, I think," he answered. "Might have been blue. That in-between color that could go either way?"

Skela nodded. "I know what you mean. We call that shallow blue."

"Because the water isn't as deep where the sea is that color?" Copper asked.

"Just so," Skela answered, laughing. "Just so."

They heard the water before they saw it. They stopped on the rocks next to the rivulet, and Karse looked to see guards milling around on either side of the stream.

"You looked upstream?"

"And down," Wren answered. "We didn't go too far upstream. It gets pretty steep up that way, and I didn't think that someone who was hurt would get far."

"Memfis said up the down," Copper said, and pointed. "The water is coming down—"

"So we go up." Karse started up the slope, and the boys ran on ahead. "How far did you go?" he called over his shoulder.

"I'll come with you, show you where." Wren trotted up next to him. "It gets steep, and there's no cover, so we figured he didn't come this way and went to start searching downstream." He pointed. "There. See that broken rock? That's where it gets harder, and that's where we stopped. There's a waterfall up past it."

Karse nodded and picked up his pace, reaching the broken rock and climbing up onto it. From the top, he could see all the way down to where the guards were searching, and when he turned, he could see the rocks higher up, the camp, and the trail down to Shadow Cove.

"Wren, take a team up there," he said, pointing to the high rocks. "The shot had to have come from there. See what you can see." Wren nodded and headed down the slope, shouting to the men. Karse climbed down and leaned against the rock. "Up the down, Memfis said. We're up. Now what?"

Something at his hip squirmed, and Karse looked down to see an empty bag, and the flash of a puppy's tail as Howl jumped off the far side of the rock.

"This isn't the time for 'chase the pup,' Howl!" Karse shouted, scrambling after the puppy. His voice bounced back at him off the rocks, distorted just enough that when he heard it, he realized what he'd misheard when Memfis gave them his cryptic prophecy.

And the hole will find him.

But Memfis had sounded the closest to drunk Karse had heard from him in years. He'd slurred his words badly. Which meant he didn't say hole.

He'd said *Howl*!

"Copper! Danir! Follow Howl!" he shouted, and ran up the slope after the puppy. Howl barked, galloping up the rocks faster than Karse would have expected. He clearly thought this was a new game, and his happy barking echoed and mixed with the shouts of the boys as they raced past Karse. The steep slope forced Karse to slow down, but Howl kept going, and disappeared around a large pile of rocks. Copper followed, then Danir. Then Danir reappeared.

"Captain," he called. "I think we found blood."

Karse cursed softly and started to run, nearly slipping on loose rocks as he came around the pile to where Danir was standing. The boy pointed, and Karse went to one knee and looked closer at the rusty trail.

"Good eye," he said. "It is." He stood up and raised his voice. "Owyn! Owyn, can you hear me?"

"Captain!"

It was Copper. Karse ran towards the sound of his voice, and nearly tripped over the boy, who was stretched out on the ground, looking intently at something. Karse crouched, and saw the low cave under the rocks.

"Captain, Howl's in there," he said. "And I think Owyn is, too."

Karse nodded, fighting back a sudden, sick memory of a hollow under a rock shaped like a turtle shell. He took the carrybag off his shoulder and dropped it to the ground. "Right. Go and find the guards. I'll try and get them out."

"You're not going to fit," Copper said. "Dan, you go for the guards. Tell them we found him. I'm going to help the Captain."

"If Owyn fit in there, so can I." Karse said. He looked up as Afansa came around the rock, passing Danir as he ran off for the guards. "I think we found them."

Afansa knelt, then looked at Karse. "I heard Copper. He's right. You won't fit. I'll go in. I'm smaller than you. You can pull me out."

"Fancy!"

Both of her brows rose, and she regarded Karse with cool surprise. "I don't remember telling you that my man used to call me that. And I don't remember telling you that you could. And we don't have time to argue. Move over."

Karse shifted, moving out of the way, and Afansa shoved her hair down the back of her shirt and started to crawl into the cave. Her voice echoed as she called back. "It opens up a bit once you're in. And it turns...Karse, he's here."

"Call Howl," Karse murmured to Copper, hearing soft words from inside the cave, but not what Afansa was saying. "Let's have him out, so we don't have to worry about him."

Copper nodded and knelt by the edge of the cave. "Howl!" he called. "Come out, Howl. Come here."

The wolf puppy trotted out of the cave, his tail and ears both held high, the very image of a proud hunter. Karse laughed, and reached out to scoop the puppy up in his arms; Howl squirmed and licked his face.

"You did a good job, Howl," Karse said. "Good boy. Now, stay with Copper." He passed the pup to Copper, and looked at the boy. "Go back to the rocks by the water, where Howl got away from me. You and Danir wait for us there."

"Yes, Captain," Copper said, and carried the puppy away. Karse stretched out and looked into the darkness.

"Afansa?" he called.

"He's alive, but I can smell blood," Afansa called back. "I can't really see, but touching him, there's an arrow in his back. I think his lung is pierced. His breathing is terrible, and his pulse is weak." She paused. "I don't know how we're going to get him out. I'm not sure how he got in here."

Karse swallowed. They were going to have to do to Owyn what he and Owyn had done to Evarra. And he was going to have to hope for a different outcome. "Right. I can reach your feet. Can you grab him?"

"I've got his shirt."

"Good. I'm going to start pulling you out slowly. Keep him as still as you can, and tell me if you need me to stop." He reached out and grabbed her ankles, starting to pull, then stopping and shifting backwards so that he could bring them further out.

"I think he's waking up," Afansa called. "Wait a moment. Owyn, can you hear me? Owyn, it's Afansa. You're safe. We're going to get you back to camp." She tapped one foot. "We're ready."

Karse grabbed her ankles again and started pulling, and heard a low, pain-filled moan.

"It's all right, Owyn," Afansa said. "We have to get you out. It's all right."

Karse stopped to shift, to reset himself. Afansa's legs were out of the cave to her thighs, and he could see Owyn.

"Owyn, can you hear me?" he called. "We're getting you out. You're going to be all right. You hear me?" He grabbed Afansa's legs again and started pulling once more, hearing running feet and kicked rocks. He glanced to the side, saw Wren. "We need a litter!" he snapped.

"He's alive in there?" Wren gasped. "How?"

Karse looked up. "Our Owyn is stubborn as fuck, that's how. Now go get a litter."

Wren nodded. "Yes, Captain." He turned and ran back down the slope, shouting, and Karse turned back to bringing Afansa and Owyn out. He pulled again, and heard another moan, followed by whimpering.

"I know, Owyn," he called. "It hurts like fuck. I know. But this isn't your place to die. You know this isn't your place to die." He let go of Afansa's ankles and crawled into the space, wincing as the low rocks scraped his back through his shirt. He could see Owyn's eyes were open, but he wasn't sure that he was seeing anything. There was blood on his face, around his mouth. "Oh, fuck. You're right. Pierced lung. He's coughing blood." He looked to the side to see Afansa was looking at him.

"Karse, why would someone be trying to kill Owyn?" she whispered.

Karse shook his head. "I don't know. Right now, I'm more interested in making sure they fail." He reached out and grabbed Owyn's shirt, pulling, inching his way back out into the air, until he could sit up, until he could lay Owyn out on his belly and look at the wound. He whistled. "That's too fucking close," he said. "Not even a handspan." He looked up as Wren came running back with several other guards. "Got a litter?"

"We have a cloak," Wren said. "It's not the best, but it's faster, and on this terrain, it'll be easier to keep him level."

Karse nodded, reaching out and touching Owyn's cheek, running his fingers down to feel for his pulse. As Afansa said, it was weak, but it was there.

This wasn't going to end the way it had at Turtle Rock.

Trey would never forgive him if it did.

"Let's get him back to camp."

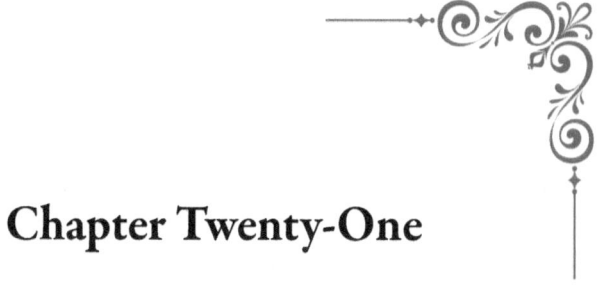

Chapter Twenty-One

It seemed to take hours longer to get back to camp from Shadow Cove than it had taken Del to get there. Part of that, he knew, was the steep slope — he couldn't make the same headlong ride he'd made going down to the village. And the rest was that Lady was carrying two, and Del was almost certain that Pirit had never ridden bareback before, no matter what she said. The way she clung to him, her shifts in balance, her tension, all added up to more bravado than experience.

But the ride was over, so it didn't matter anymore. He slowed Lady to a stop as they reached the camp, and he whistled, high and shrill. The first person who came to see was Wren, and he gaped at them for a moment before he came running to meet them.

"You made it!" he gasped. "In time, too." He pointed. "That tent, there. Zarai is with him, and Aria. He's...not doing well."

"Then you'd better help me down, Guardsman," Pirit said. Wren nodded, and reached up to help lift her down to the ground. He steadied her for a moment, then she looked up at Del and nodded. "You did well, Del," she said. She looked at Wren. "That tent?"

"Yes, Healer."

Pirit hurried off to the tent, and Wren looked up at Del. "Need any help?" he asked. Del shook his head and slid from Lady's back, leading her at a slow walk toward the picket line and the other horses. He'd get her settled and brushed down. Check her hooves for rocks. Give her a good feeding.

Try to distract himself from what was happening in the tent.

He managed to lose himself in caring for his horse, so someone calling his name was almost a shock. He looked up from his brushing to see Karse coming toward him. He raised his brows and held one hand up. Karse laughed.

"I know better than to bring a wolf into the picket. Howl is with the boys," he called. "You finished?"

Del nodded. He ran his hand down Lady's neck, then walked over to a basket and dropped the brush into it. He looked down at his empty bag and frowned, spreading his hands wide. Karse frowned.

"Where's your tablet?" he asked.

"*I lost it,*" Del signed slowly. "*Maybe it's here. Or it fell out on the road.*"

Karse frowned slightly. "Lost it? Did I get that right?" When Del nodded, he snorted. "That's annoying. But we'll manage."

Del nodded again, and fell in next to Karse as they walked back across camp.

"Memfis is a mess," Karse said. "He danced to find Owyn, and now he's completely off his arse on visions. Drunk without a drop in him. At least, that's how Meris explained it. She has him off sleeping it off, and she told me that she won't let him near Owyn until he's sobered up." He looked over at the tent. "You brought Pirit. That...he'll be fine. I know he'll be fine now. Thank you."

Del gestured toward the tent. Karse shook his head.

"Actually, I want you to walk with me for a minute. I wanted to talk to you." Karse looked around. "Come on." He started walking, and Del followed him, out of camp and out into the fields. They walked a good distance away before Karse stopped, looking back the way they'd come.

"Del, someone's trying to kill Owyn," he said softly.

Del blinked and gestured for Karse to keep going. Karse smiled.

"Hurry up, hm?" he asked. "Right. Look, yesterday it was the caltrop in his saddle blanket. Today, well...a quarrel in the back isn't any kind of accident. Someone was trying to kill him. And they failed—"

"*So they'll try again,*" Del signed.

"They'll try again," Karse said with a nod. "Which I think is what you just said. And...Del, you love him, don't you?" Del nodded. "Good. Then I want you to watch his back. You're his new bodyguard."

Del stared at him for a moment, then started to laugh. He stopped when Karse shook his head.

"*Me?*" he signed. "*But—*"

"Don't tell me you can't," Karse interrupted. "Because I know you can. You're learning how to fight, and you have an edge. No one thinks you can. You don't look like the killer you are. Which makes you perfect." He folded his arms over his chest. "You're looking at me like I have six heads. Skela thinks you can. Trey knew you could."

"*Don't talk about him like he's dead,*" Del signed.

Karse frowned. Then he paled and closed his eyes. "I didn't realize I did," he said softly. "Look. If anything happens to Owyn, Trey will never forgive me. I can't be with him all the time. I can't put a guard on him because I have no idea who is doing this. It clearly wasn't the groom we thought planted the caltrop yesterday. If we're going to keep him safe, we need to put someone with him we can trust, and who no one will suspect of being a guard."

Del frowned slightly. "*You want me there so we can draw out whoever this is?*" he signed, and Karse sighed.

"You went too fast for me," he admitted. "I'm not that good yet. Del, I want you at his back because I know you can. I know I can trust you. And I'll be having a similar conversation with Aven when he gets back here, so don't think I'm singling you out." He smiled slightly. "Much. People coming at Owyn are going to look at Aven and Othi and miss you entirely. Which is an advantage."

Del nodded slowly. The idea made him feel a little ill. But he'd killed to protect Aria and Aven. He'd kill to protect Owyn, too. And Karse knew that.

He nodded again. *"Just be ready to pick me up afterward,"* he signed slowly.

"Pick you up afterward?" Karse asked. "Absolutely. Come on. Let's head back and see if there's any word from Pirit yet."

ARIA SAT WITH HER HANDS clasped in front of her, on a chair set near the head of the narrow bed where Owyn lay, silent and still and so horrifyingly pale. Pirit had told her that she was not allowed to touch Owyn at all while she was working. A simple instruction that was so much harder than it sounded. Just hours ago he'd been in her arms, and now she couldn't even touch him.

Pirit knelt on the other side of the bed, one hand flat on Owyn's back, the other on the back of his neck. She'd been working in stages, the better to conserve her strength, and she'd explained each step before she'd started. In the first stage, she'd pulled the quarrel free and healed the hole in Owyn's lung. Now, she was working on clearing blood from his lungs, and on making sure the lung didn't collapse. It was, she'd said, the hardest part, and she could not be interrupted. So Afansa stood outside the tent, and Aria kept her hands to herself.

Pirit took a deep breath and sat back on her heels. "You can touch him now," she croaked.

Immediately, Aria reached out and ran her fingers through Owyn's hair, over his cool skin. "He's cold."

"He'll be cold," Pirit said. "He's lost a lot of blood. He'll be weak, more easily tired. At least, until his body replaces the blood he's lost." She wiped one hand over her face. "One more push and I'll be done, I think. That was...Aria, I'm not sure how he survived this."

"It wasn't the right place," Aria said.

Pirit nodded. "Smoke Dancers know their end. I'd forgotten that."

"How did you even know that?" Aria asked.

Pirit smiled. "Pillow talk, my dear. Now, once I get something to drink, I'll get started on the last session. Is there tea?"

Aria looked over at the small table and the empty water jug. She raised her voice. "Afansa?"

Afansa looked into the tent, clearly worried. "My Heir? Is he—"

"He'll be fine, Afansa," Pirit said. "However, I feel like the great salt plains. Is there tea?"

Afansa smiled, her shoulders slumping. "Yes. Yes, I'll bring tea in a moment. Thank you." She stepped away, and Aria heard voices from outside the tent. A moment later, Karse looked in.

"Afansa says he's fine?" he asked in a low voice. "I've got Del with me."

"You can come in, but only for a moment," Pirit said. "He'll live. He'll be weak for a few days, and I expect that will annoy him to no end."

"We'll make sure to point out that his choices are weak or dead, and that's no choice at all." Karse stepped into the tent, and Del followed him. He came straight to the bed, kneeling at Aria's feet, and leaning over Owyn to kiss his cheek. Then he looked up and raised his hands.

"*I lost my tablet.*"

"You didn't," Aria said. "You dropped it near the picket when you went for Pirit. One of the grooms brought it to me, and it's in our tent."

Del took her hand, kissing her palm. Then he looked at Pirit. She arched a brow, and he shook his head. She nodded and sat down on the ground.

"There's one more healing pass to make," she said. "I still have to heal the damage to the muscles of Owyn's back, and make sure that there's no infection or poison left behind. It's not nearly as intensive as the other two. It won't take me as long, nor will it take as much out of me. But I'll need to rest after this, and we'll need someone here to watch him while I sleep."

"*I will,*" Del signed.

"You just made a nightmare ride," Karse pointed out. "You should rest, too. You can't watch him if you fall asleep."

Del made a face. Then he frowned. He pointed at Aria, then Pirit, then himself. Then he pointed at Karse and arched a brow. Karse smiled.

"Good. You're thinking like a guard. Who do we trust?"

"What?" Aria asked. "Karse, what do you mean?"

He nodded toward the bed. "This weren't no accident, Aria. Someone killed one of my men, and tried to kill Owyn. Someone tried to kill him for the second time in two days. Which means—"

"Someone is following us?" Aria breathed.

"Or they're with us already, and we just don't know it." Karse folded his arms over his chest. "So, who do I trust? The healers. The Companions, old and new. Steward. My men, the ones who served under me in Forge. Fancy—"

"I still didn't give you permission to call me that, " Afansa said as she came into the tent. She set a teapot down on the table, poured a cup, and passed it to Pirit. "And how did you know that? I never told you. I don't think I told anyone."

Karse looked down, and Aria saw a faint flush of crimson rising over his collar. "I...ah...I been calling you that in my head for weeks now. Didn't know someone else did before me." He looked up and grinned. "He had good taste, your man. You're a good woman, Afansa. And I'll try to remember not to call you that out loud."

Afansa smiled slightly. "Or once your man comes back, we can discuss when you can call me that."

Karse turned bright red, and Pirit laughed. "Make your hay on your own time, children. Not when I'm working. Who's staying to watch while I sleep?"

"I will," Afansa said. "Lady Meris said I was to help however I could. This is something I can do. I'll just fetch my book so I can practice my reading while I stay."

Pirit nodded. "You do that." She finished her tea, then knelt up again and raised her hands. "All right. Last push. The pair of you, let him go and let me work."

ARIA WALKED OUT OF the tent and into the air, wrapping her arms around her chest and closing her eyes, pulling her wings in tight to her back. The final push of healing had gone well. Owyn would sleep until morning, Pirit said. But he'd be fine. And he and Alanar would have coordinating quarrel scars.

"How is he?" Aria opened her eyes to see a guard standing nearby. He nodded toward the tent. "Owyn. How is he?"

"He'll be fine," she answered. "Del brought the healer back in time." She tried to remember the guard's name, then shook her head. "I'm sorry. I should know your name, but I can't remember it."

"Nah, I'm forgettable," he said with a grin. "I'm Wren. I'm one of Karse's men, from Forge."

"Oh?" Aria studied him. "I don't think we met, either time I was in Forge."

"Well, I wasn't there when the mountain blew. Karse sent a bunch of us out when it got dangerous, guarding the evacuees. Once we got them to their new settlement, we headed north. Had no place else to go. Then we heard Terraces was the place to be. So we headed there. We got there...I dunno. A day or two after you left?" He grimaced. "It was me, Leesam, and Lyka to start with. Leesam stayed behind in Terraces. He liked it there. Wanted to settle down. Lyka decided to come with me, and we headed north to the Palace and joined the Guard there. Not sure how I'm going to tell Lee. Lyka was like his little brother."

"Leesam?" Aria repeated. "I remember him. He was there the night we saved Owyn from Fandor—"

"I'm sorry?" Wren gasped. "What?"

"You don't know?" Aria asked. She smiled. "Oh, that's why I don't remember you from the first time I was in Forge. You weren't there that night."

"Wasn't...oh!" Wren gasped. Then he laughed. "Oh, I know what you're talking about. Lee and Trey, they told me! No, I was...well, I was on punishment duty. So I missed all of it."

"What's punishment duty?" Aria asked. She gestured toward the fire, and Wren fell in next to her as they walked.

"Punishment duty? Well, that's what happens when you break the rules. And Captain Karse was stricter than most." He paused. "More strict?"

"You sound like Owyn," Aria said, looking back over her shoulder at the tent.

"He'll really be fine?" Wren asked. "He really survived that? I saw him when they pulled him out. He should have been dead."

"Pulled him out?" Aria sat down next to the fire, and Wren straddled the log so that he could face her.

"He'd wedged himself into a hole in the rock. Small enough that someday it might grow up to be a cave. It was higher up the slope than we thought he'd be able to go, with the blood trail we found, and I don't think any of us would have thought to look in there if we had gone that high up the slope."

Aria stared at him for a moment. "My Owyn? In a cave?"

"Yeah." Wren frowned. "Why is that grabbing you?"

"He must have been either terrified or desperate. Or both," Aria answered. "Owyn doesn't like small spaces." She shook her head. "So finding him in one surprises me."

"Didn't know that about him," Wren said. He waved, and Aria looked over her shoulder to see a guard wave back. "Now, you asked about punishment duty." He grinned. "When everyone else was seeing action, I was pushing the idiot stick." He laughed. "A broom, My Heir. I was on stable duty."

Aria nodded. "So...what did you do?"

"What, that I was on punishment?" Wren shrugged and grinned. "Gambling on duty. Karse caught me. He made me give it all back. And I was winning, too! That never happens!"

Aria shook her head, laughing. Then she smiled. "Wren, do you play Gambit?"

He looked puzzled. "Doesn't everyone?"

"I don't," Aria said. "I never learned. Steward was going to teach me, but we never had the time."

Wren nodded slowly. "And...we've got nothing but time until the healers come back," he said. "I've got a board. Should I go get it?"

"If you're not currently on duty," Aria answered. "I'm not certain what punishment duty we have out here. We're nowhere near a stable, and I do not think we have an idiot stick." She paused. "That I know of."

Wren stared at her for a moment, then burst out laughing.

"I'll go get my board." He stood up and walked away, still laughing. Aria smiled, and tipped her head back, closing her eyes and feeling the tension around her wings loosen.

Owyn would be fine.

By this time tomorrow, Pirit said that she thought the other healers would be back. They would all be together again. She'd make her first official visit on this Progress, and they'd continue on.

They'd find whoever it was who was trying to kill her Fire.

Everything would be fine.

"Aria?"

She turned, smiling up at Karse. "Have I thanked you yet?" she asked. "I've forgotten."

Karse sat down next to her. "You don't have to thank me," he said. "Owyn is my friend. But you're welcome." He took a deep breath, then leaned forward to ruffle the ears of the puppy currently chewing on his boot. "We need to talk."

Aria looked at him. "I agree. Captain, who do you think is trying to kill my Fire?" she asked, keeping her voice low. "Is it Risha, do you think? I cannot imagine why, but I also can't imagine who else would."

Karse studied her, then nodded. "Yeah, that's exactly what we needed to talk about. And no, I don't know who. I don't think it's Risha. I think we found all her folk. It's someone else. You said it yourself earlier. They're either following us...or they're part of the Progress." He turned. "I talked to Del. He's going to stay close to Owyn. I'm going to talk to Aven, too. And Othi. We'll make sure Owyn is guarded. And we'll find out who's trying this."

Aria nodded. "Is it possible this is an attack on Memfis?"

Karse frowned. "Attacking him through his son? Maybe. Aria, I don't know enough to answer that." He took a deep breath. "Right now, we'll keep an eye on him. We'll keep him safe. And when we find whoever it is...well, we'll keep them alive long enough to answer."

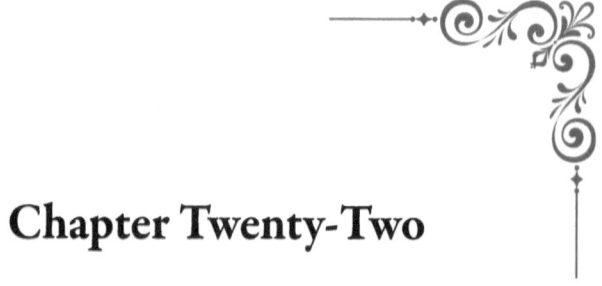

Chapter Twenty-Two

B irdsong. Owyn heard birdsong. He opened his eyes, expecting to see stone, dirt and the mouth of a cave from the inside. Instead, there was canvas and sunlight, and he was lying face down on a cot.

"Welcome back."

Owyn turned his head, seeing the inside of a small tent, and..."Pirit? Where did you come from?"

She leaned forward in her chair, smiling. "Shadow Cove," she answered. She shifted off the chair to kneel next to the cot and rested her hand on his shoulder; a wave of warmth washed over him, and he sighed. "Your Del is quite the remarkable man. He came down to Shadow to find a healer for you."

"Del did what?"

Pirit shifted to sit on the ground. "He rode bareback down to Shadow Cove. Alone, and without his tablet. He brought me back here to save your life."

Owyn closed his eyes, basking in the warmth of her healing. "How bad was it?"

"You're lucky they found you when they did," Pirit said. "And now you and your husband have matching scars." She tapped his back. "Yours is here."

Owyn snorted. "And I feel like I have no bones."

"You lost a lot of blood," Pirit said. "You'll be weak for a few days." She got up off the floor. "Now, if I help you roll over, do you feel like entertaining?"

Owyn smiled. "How long is the line outside the tent?"

Pirit chuckled. "Long enough, lad. Come on. Easy over."

Once Owyn was on his back, with pillows propping him up into a mostly-sitting position, he looked around again. "How long has it been? Is Allie back yet?"

"He should be back today, most likely," Pirit said. "And it all happened yesterday."

"Is that all?" Owyn laughed. "And I thought this Progress was going to be boring until we left Terraces!"

Pirit shook her head. "I don't think you could find boring anywhere on this Progress if you had a map that read 'This way to boring.'" She went to the tent flap and opened it, and looked out. "He's awake." She stepped back, and Memfis came into the tent, moving to kneel next to the bed.

"Fa—" Owyn didn't have time to finish anything he was going to say; Memfis threw his arm around him and hugged him tightly.

"Mouse," Memfis murmured. "Mother of us all, I was so scared."

"It wasn't my time, Mem," Owyn said. "I knew someone would find me." He frowned. "Not sure how they did, though. I hid..." He paused. "Fa, I know how to keep from panicking at small spaces now. Be running for your life. No problem with spaces when you're running for your life."

Memfis sat back on his heels. "Mouse...I danced. I caught the vision that helped Karse find you."

"You...you *danced*?" Owyn laughed. "Fa, that's wonderful!"

Memfis looked down. "I...borrowed one of your blades to do it—"

Owyn stared at his adoptive father. "You honestly think I'm going to be upset that you borrowed a blade to save my life? Mem, really?"

Memfis smiled slightly. "Meris said that's what you'd say." He nodded toward the tent flap. "She's outside, with Afansa. So are Aria and Del. And Karse and that pup of his, and the boys. To hear the boys tell it, it was the puppy who really found you."

"Well, then I owe Howl...something." Owyn frowned. "What do you get a wolf puppy to say thanks for saving your life?"

Memfis smiled and stood up, going to the tent flap and holding it open. Aria came into the tent, her wings pulled in close. Del was behind her, and he had his hands clasped behind his back. Meris came in next, and she came straight to the bed.

"Oh, Owyn," she murmured, and leaned down to kiss him. "Honestly, the trouble you get into!"

"It weren't my fault, Granna!" Owyn protested. "Not my idea to have someone trying to kill me!" He looked around until he saw Karse, who had Howl tucked until the crook of his arm. "Do you know who it is? And why?"

Karse shook his head. "Not yet. I was hoping you might have a better idea of someone who wants you dead. Anyone?"

Owyn frowned. "I can't even imagine. The only person I know for sure wanted me dead, I killed him first." He cocked his head to the side. "Wait. Nope. Two people wanted me dead. I killed one before he killed me. And...the other one sort of killed me, but I got better and Melody ate him."

Karse looked shocked. "Melody? Aven's water-cat Melody? Ate...oh. You mean Teva?"

"Yeah. And yeah. That's what Othi told me." Owyn shifted — his back itched. "So, no. I can't think of anyone who'd want to kill me. 'Cept Risha, maybe." He frowned, then shook his head. "Hey, let me have Howl, will you? I owe him."

Karse laughed. "He just found your hole. Afansa and I, we pulled you out." He put the puppy down on Owyn's legs. Owyn pushed himself up to sit upright so he could scoop Howl up. The pup wriggled and whined, then licked his chin, and Owyn laughed and scratched his ears.

"You're a good boy, Howl," he murmured. "Thanks. I owe you." He set the puppy down and looked around. "I owe you, too, Karse. You and Afansa and...who else?"

"Our boys," Afansa said. "They helped find you, too."

Owyn smiled. "Then I owe all of you. Not sure what I'm going to do—"

"You found us," Danir said. "Back in the Palace. So we're even."

Copper nodded. "Yeah. You came looking for us when we were lost and trapped. You're our friend. We weren't leaving you out there."

Owyn smiled. Then he yawned, and started laughing. "I just woke up!"

"You need to eat something, and sleep some more," Pirit said. "All right. Everyone out, except for Aria and Del." She herded everyone out of the tent, then stepped outside herself, leaving Aria and Del behind. Del looked at Aria, and gestured — *you first*. She smiled and returned the gesture — *no, you*.

"You can both sit," Owyn said. "And I really, really want you both to be holding me right now."

"*Is there room for both of us?*" Del asked softly in his mind.

"Let's find out."

A moment later, Del was on his right, and Aria on his left, and they both had their arms around him. Owyn sagged, letting out a shaky breath.

"They killed Lyka," he whispered. "So that they could kill me. I don't...why? Who wants me dead?"

"Karse says that when we find out, we will leave them alive long enough to ask them," Aria said into his hair. "And we will find them."

"*And we'll keep you safe*," Del added. "*Karse told me that I'm to stay with you.*"

"Karse says...why?" Owyn asked. "I mean...Othi I can understand. I'm going to need a guard of some kind. Why you?"

"What is this?" Aria asked, and Owyn repeated what Del said. Aria looked thoughtful. Then she smiled. "I see. Karse will probably have Othi guard you as well. Because everyone will see Othi. But no one will see Del, who is much more dangerous." She reached across and rested her hand on Del's leg. "Aren't you, my Air?"

Del grinned and nodded, and his arms around Owyn tightened. Owyn heard him swallow, then a whispered word, the clearest he'd ever heard from Del: "Mine."

Aria pulled back slightly. "Del? Was that you?"

Del glanced at Owyn. "*Will you tell her? It will be faster. Pirit knows now, too. I dropped my tablet when I went down to Shadow, and she doesn't sign.*"

Owyn nodded. "Aria...this is just between us. You, me, Del and Allie. And Pirit. She knows. But...yeah, Del has a voice. He can talk a little. Not clearly, and it takes him a minute. Allie is going to work with him, but he didn't want anyone to know."

"*Pirit is going to show me some things when we get to Terraces,*" Del said. "*She says she's impressed how much I've done without any teaching.*" He blushed slightly as Owyn translated.

"Does your father know?" Aria asked. Del shook his head.

"No one else knows," Owyn added. "Del told us...well, because it's the only way that he can talk to Allie when I'm not around. And it upsets Allie, so...yeah, we try not to do it much."

Aria sat back a little, no doubt so that she could see both of them. "Upsets him why?" she asked. Then she looked thoughtful. "Oh. Is this how Del was distracting Alanar?"

Del laughed, and it made the entire bed shake and creak. Owyn looked down. "Maybe having the three of us on here isn't a good idea," he said. "And...yeah. And it upsets Allie because it upsets Del."

Del shifted to sit on the ground next to the bed. "*It's hard,*" he signed. "*It's hard and it's scary. And I know I sound like an idiot when I do it. Talking is hard when your brain doesn't work right. And mine doesn't. I know that. I have to think about the right sounds, and how to make them, and it takes time, and—*"

Owyn reached out and caught one of Del's hands. "You're not an idiot. Your brain works just fine. And you have a perfectly good voice, through your fingers. Or...well, through my head." He tugged Del's hand up and kissed his fingers. "We will work on it, but only if you really want to. You know Alanar says he doesn't want you hurting yourself for him."

Del nodded. He knelt up and kissed Owyn on the cheek, then signed, "*You're supposed to sleep.*"

"And eat," Aria added. "Del, would you go and see what there is for him to eat? And you can fetch your tablet while you're out."

Del smiled and got up. He walked around the bed to kiss Aria, then waved and left the tent. Owyn waited until he was gone, then turned to Aria so that he could apologize for not telling her. He never had the chance — she leaned forward and kissed him. He turned, pulling her into his arms, falling into her kiss...until he broke it by yawning. He stared at her, trying to remember what words were, until she started giggling. He fell back onto the pillows, laughing with her.

"I have the worst timing, don't I?" he asked when he could breathe again.

"Perhaps the next time I should sneak up on you," Aria suggested. "Someplace with a door that locks so that we cannot be interrupted?"

Owyn grinned. "Your room in Terraces has a lock, don't it?"

"Are you going to be strong enough for that?" she asked, resting her hand on his chest. "Owyn, Pirit said you'd be weak for days because of the blood you've lost."

Owyn nodded. "Yeah, I believe it. I feel it. I told her it feels like I have no bones. But...you know...you could always make sure I'm not overexerting myself." He grinned. "I dunno...tie me to the bed?"

Her smile made it feel like what blood he had left was on fire. "Oh? And would that help?"

Owyn shrugged one shoulder, and winced at an odd pull in his back. "Well, you'd be doing all the work—"

"Something hurts?" Aria interrupted. "I saw your face. What hurts?"

'Not...not really hurts. Just pulls." He shrugged again, and felt the same tugging. "Yeah, something pulling in the muscle."

"I'll get Pirit." Aria said. She slowly stood up.

"Aria, I'm fine," Owyn protested. She ignored him, just like he expected her to. She went to the tent flap and opened it, then had to step out of the way of Del, who was coming in with a tray. He arched a brow at Aria.

"I was going to get Pirit," Aria said. "There is something wrong—"

"It's not wrong!"

She looked at him. "Did it do that before?"

Owyn frowned. "No."

"Then it is wrong." Aria turned back to Del. "There is something wrong in Owyn's back, and I want Pirit to look. See that he eats, and I'll be back."

Del lowered his head slightly and looked at her, and even if Owyn couldn't hear Del's thoughts, he could tell what the man was thinking. Aria could, too.

"I will eat when I come back with Pirit."

Del nodded, and brought the tray to the chair, setting it down. He helped Owyn to sit up again, rearranging pillows to support his back, then handed him a bowl.

"*What's wrong in your back?*" Del asked as he sat down on the ground with his own bowl.

"I shrugged, and something pulled," Owyn answered. He stirred the porridge in the bowl, then took a bite. "It felt weird. It didn't hurt, but it didn't feel good, either."

Del nodded and started on his own bowl. "*Then Pirit should look at it. It might be something to do with your older scars.*"

Owyn fought the urge to shrug again. "You know, I hadn't realized just how often I do that," he grumbled.

"Do what?" Pirit asked as she came back into the tent. "Oh, good. You're eating. What is it?"

"I shrugged and something pulled in my back," Owyn answered. "Del thinks it might be something about my older scars."

"It's possible," Pirit said as she came over to the bed and rested her hand on Owyn's shoulder, and warmth spread down his back. "I may have healed some of the tissue in ways that it shouldn't have been joined. Let me see...ah...yes. Yes, there it is." She looked over at Del. "You've read the medical texts in the library at the Palace, haven't you? Is that how you knew about adhesions?"

Del smiled. "*Owyn, tell her I read everything I can put my hands on, will you? But I don't have any practical healing. Just theory.*"

"Del says that he reads everything, but he's never actually tried putting someone back together," Owyn relayed.

"Well, then I'll have a word with my son and grandson. We should be able to turn Del into a competent healing assistant with little trouble." She straightened, and the warmth ebbed and faded away. "If you want that kind of training, I mean?"

Del looked thoughtful, then shrugged.

"Think on it," Pirit suggested. "There's no rush. Now, you eat that, Owyn. And then you need to get some sleep. And...what is that?" She went to the tent flap and opened it, standing with Aria to look outside. Owyn could hear loud voices and laughter, and he realized what it must be.

"The healers are back?" he asked. "You said today, maybe. Is that them?"

Pirit nodded and looked at him. "The healers are back."

Owyn put his bowl aside and lifted the blanket. "Trousers. I need trousers. Del—"

"*Why do you need trousers?*" Del interrupted. Owyn looked up to see that Del was signing as well.

"I'm going out to meet them," Owyn said. "I need to show Allie I'm fine."

"*You're not fine,*" Del insisted, his mental voice sounding as stubborn as Owyn had ever heard. And even across the tent, he could hear Del's fingers snapping as he signed. "*You're not going anywhere.*"

"Del, I don't want him to come in here with me flat on my back like a fucking invalid!"

Del arched a brow, and raised his hands again. "*So you'd rather have him come in here to find you flat on your face like a fucking idiot?*" He shook his hands out, then signed. "*Stay in bed, Owyn. I'll go get him.*" He paused, and didn't sign when he added, "*Don't move, or I'll tie you to the bed and you won't like it.*" He turned, bowed slightly to Aria, and left the tent. Aria looked at Owyn, and he could tell she was trying not to laugh.

"You understood all of that?" Owyn asked.

"Some of it," Aria admitted. "When Del forgets to be afraid, he's quite impressive." She looked out the tent. "Oh, they look tired. And I don't see Jehan."

"That's odd," Pirit said. "I'll go and see. Owyn, eat that. It will turn into plaster if you don't eat it." She left, and Aria came over to sit at the foot of the bed.

"Eat your porridge," she said gently. "You need to eat." She looked over her shoulder. "What did Del say to you, at the end? After he said he would go get Alanar? The look on your face...he said something."

Owyn chuckled. "He told me that if I got up, he'd tie me to the bed and I wouldn't like it."

Aria smiled. "I wonder how he'd manage that?" She looked around, then back at Owyn. "I know how I'd do it."

Owyn looked at her. "Do I want to know?"

"Will it keep you from getting out of bed?" Aria asked in response. She grinned. "I would tie you to the bed, and go sit over there." She pointed across the tent. "With a book."

Owyn blinked. He stirred his porridge and took another bite. Then he nodded. "That...would do it," he admitted. "So. I'll stay in the bed. And when I'm feeling better, then we'll ignore the book?"

Aria nodded. "We'll definitely ignore the book."

DEL WALKED ACROSS THE camp to the coach, seeing Aven leaning on his stick, with one arm around Treesi. Gathi stood with Alanar, and there were three people in gray that he didn't recognize. Healers-in-training, he guessed.

"Where's Jehan?" Pirit called as she caught up with Del. Aven turned at the sound of her voice.

"Grandmother," he said. "He stayed in the village to keep an eye on the last two patients. Steward stayed with him because it was too tight in the coach with seven of us. Fa cleared us all before we left, and said you should do the same when we got here."

Pirit nodded. "And now tell me why you're in pain. You were fine when I left."

Aven sighed. "We hit a rock on the way back up the trail. I bounced wrong. It aches, and I'm tired enough that it's worse than usual. I'll go get some sleep, but I want to see Aria and Owyn first." He looked past them. "Where is he? And how is he?"

"Those were my questions," Alanar said. "Pirit?"

Pirit nodded. "He'll be fine. He lost a lot of blood, so he'll be weak for a few days. But there should be no lingering damage, and the scar is minimal. And coordinates with yours." She looked at Del, then held her hand out to Alanar. "Give me your hand. Let me clear you before Owyn decides that he really wants to see what Del looks like when he gets angry."

Alanar laughed. "What? Del? Angry?" He cocked his head. "Del, are you here?"

Del raised his hands. "*Aven, tell him I ordered Owyn to stay in bed? And once he's clear, I'll take him to Owyn.*"

Aven translated, then added, "And I want you to teach me how to get Owyn to listen. Because he doesn't listen to me. Ever."

Del smiled and glanced at Pirit. "*I'll tell you later.*"

Chapter Twenty-Three

Once Pirit had cleared all the healers as being free from mountain fever, and had sent Gathi and the other trainees off to their beds, Del led Alanar into the tent, stopping when Alanar did. He looked up to see Alanar turning his head.

"I haven't been in here before," he said. "Where am I going?"

"I'm over here," Owyn said. He was sitting up in the bed, his empty bowl on the floor. Aria used her foot to push the bowl under the bed, then stood up. Del nodded and led Alanar to the bed. Alanar sat down and held his hand out. The moment Owyn took his husband's hand, he was pulled into Alanar's arms.

"Wyn," he breathed. "What am I going to do with you?"

"I'm fine." Owyn's voice was muffled against Alanar's chest. Del started to turn when someone tapped on his shoulder. He looked to see Aven, who nodded toward the tent flap. Del followed him, Aria and Treesi out.

"We'll let them have some privacy," Aven said. He sighed and leaned on his walking stick. "I want to see him, then I need to sleep."

"How was it?" Aria asked. "In the village?"

Aven glanced at Treesi, who sighed. "Hard," she said. "It was hard."

Aven nodded, then reached out and tugged Treesi into a one-armed embrace. "We didn't stop unless we fell over, and we slept on the beach last night and the night before because it was too much trouble to find a bed."

"I'm not sure I'm ever going to get all the sand out of my hair," Treesi added. "But I was too tired to care. I'm still too tired to care. But we saved a lot of lives."

Aven nodded. "We did," he agreed. "And hopefully, we'll have saved more."

Del frowned. "*I don't understand,*" he signed. "*They're all cured now, aren't they?*"

Aven looked surprised. "Grandmother hasn't talked to you yet?" he asked.

"She's been with Owyn since she got here," Aria answered. "There hasn't been time for her to tell me anything. Why?"

Aven took a deep breath and let go of Treesi so he could rub his hand over his face. "I should find Grandmother. And we'll need to interrupt Owyn and Alanar. We should all discuss this—"

"And now you are worrying me," Aria interrupted.

Aven turned to look at her. "Honestly? You should be worried. Let me find— "

"*I'll go,*" Del signed. "*Go in and sit.*"

Aven nodded and held his hand out to Aria. She smiled and moved closer, ignoring his hand so that she could embrace him. He put his arm around her and sighed.

"I missed you," he murmured. "It wasn't safe down there for you, but I missed you."

"I missed you, too," Aria answered. "All of you. Now come in and sit before you fall down."

Del walked away, looking around. Where was...ah. There. Pirit was sitting near the fire with Meris, and it looked as if Del was going to have to interrupt her breakfast. He took his tablet from his bag and wrote down his message, then walked over to the fire. Meris saw him coming and smiled.

"Del," she said. "Come and sit, lad."

Del smiled and shook his head, offering the tablet. Meris took it, read it, then handed it to Pirit. "He's here for you."

Pirit took the tablet, then looked up at Del. "Aven wants me to explain...oh. Oh, I know what he means. Let me finish this, and I'll be right there." She handed the tablet back, and made a shooing gesture with one hand. "Go on. I'll be there as soon as I eat."

Del smiled and turned to walk back to the tent. People were taking the coach horses out to the picket, and healing supplies were being offloaded from the coach. There were guards having some kind of weapon practice, while Karse barked orders and Howl just barked. The boys were there, as well, dueling with sticks. It all seemed completely normal — they might as well be back at the Palace.

Except that it wasn't normal, and it was only likely to get worse. He stopped and looked up at the bright, blue sky, shivered, and headed for the tent.

ARIA SAT UP AND STARED at Pirit, then stammered, "Risha did this?" She looked at Aven, and he nodded.

"We think so, yes," he answered, taking her hand.

"The only vector were the bodies that they found," Pirit answered. "Bodies that were...well, Risha put her signature on them. She's still trying to break the cycle of the change." She paused. "I still don't know how she took captives, but we sent Aleia and Othi to Neera to warn the canoes in the Palace harbor. They'll watch for other bodies, and avoid them."

"And they'll need to send word out to the deep," Owyn added. He sounded sleepy, and looked only half-awake, resting against Alanar's chest. "To the old folks and the children, and the rest of the canoes that didn't come inland." He paused. "Oh, fuck...how...how old were the bodies? The ones that carried the fever? Were they really old? Or...or really young?"

"Owyn, you don't think..." Aven started to say. He stopped. Frowned. Then he swore, "Fuck. You're right. You have to be right. If she'd moved on the canoes in the harbor, we'd have known. If anyone had vanished from those canoes, we'd have known that, too."

"It could have been the northern tribes," Del signed. *"Skela's canoes. They didn't come into harbor. They range too far north."*

Aven nodded. "And we're fairly certain she's hunted Skela's canoes before," he added. "But she's not on the water anymore. They're safe...if there are any of them left."

"Oh, don't say that where Skela can hear you," Treesi murmured. "Pirit, how long do you think it will take Aleia and Othi to get to the harbor, and get back to Terraces?"

Pirit shook her head. "I've no idea. I don't know how fast they swim."

Aven considered it, thinking about how fast his mother swam, and how fast Othi was. "They left two days ago to go to Terraces. They left Terraces...when, Grandmother?"

"Danzi left me at Shadow and went back yesterday morning. So I assume they left Terraces yesterday morning."

Aven nodded, closing his eyes. "If they left yesterday, they'll be in the harbor already. A day to rest before they head back...they'll probably be waiting for us in Terraces."

"So soon?" Pirit asked. "I hadn't realized your folk were that fast."

"It's not a long distance," Aven said. "And it's straight. Not like the road and the coast that's curved. It would be faster in a canoe. We can make it from Terraces to the Palace in a couple of hours with a good wind."

Pirit nodded. "You remind me that I need to get my trainees back to Terraces. We can't wait to leave with you, and I doubt you have room for us. Did Danzi bring the canoe back?"

"She hadn't when we left," Alanar answered. "But she might be there tomorrow when we go back."

"Ah, so the Progress is going to progress?" Pirit nodded. "Good."

"Steward says that we're to go down to Shadow Cove tomorrow to meet the village, while the camp is struck and the advance carts go on to Serenity Bay," Treesi said. "Then we'll follow them and camp outside Serenity tomorrow. We'll be in Terraces the day after. I'll go and tell Memfis that when we're done here." She smiled. "Do you really think Othi will be there when we get there?"

"I wouldn't be surprised," Aven answered. "Especially if he decides to take his canoe back to Terraces." He paused to take a deep breath, then looked at Owyn. "He's asleep, isn't he? He feels asleep."

Alanar chuckled. "Yes. Has been for a few minutes now."

"Then we'll let you rest with him." Aria said. "Aven, you wanted to sleep?"

"Please," Aven said. He stood up and stretched, then held his hand out to Aria. Treesi fell in next to Aria, and they started toward the tent flap.

"Del, are you coming?" Treesi asked.

Aven looked back to see Del shake his head. He sat down on the ground next to the bed. Alanar gently eased Owyn down and stretched out on his side next to him. Del looked at them, then back at Aven. *"I'm going to stay and guard."*

Aven blinked. "Did...did I understand you correctly?" he stammered. "You're going to guard?"

Del made a face at him. *"Yes, guard. Go get some sleep. You've forgotten your healer manners."*

Aven winced. "I did. I'm sorry. But what—"

"I will explain," Aria said, and tugged him out of the tent. Treesi and Pirit followed them.

"Let me go tell Memfis, so he can start ordering people around," Treesi said. "I'll meet you at our tent."

"Aven, that was very nearly my level of rude," Pirit murmured. "I am impressed. You're not usually that callous."

"I'm not usually this tired, either," Aven grumbled. "I'll apologize properly when I'm awake. He knows I don't mean to be hurtful. He put me to bed often enough when we were out on the deep. I was...well, I was in enough pain then that I was worse."

"I'd be interested in seeing you worse," Pirit murmured. "If only for the novelty of it."

"Really?" Aven shook his head. "No, you wouldn't. Ama threatened to scrub my mouth out with sand."

Pirit laughed. "It must have been really impressive, then. So I understand now why Del didn't give you the dressing down you deserved. Go get some sleep. Treesi, I'll walk with you." She and Treesi walked away, and Aria tugged on Aven's hand.

"Come with me. I'm putting you to bed."

"Are you coming to bed with me?" Aven asked, letting her lead him to the tent.

"I will lay with you until you sleep," Aria answered. She hugged his arm as they walked. "I missed you."

"Did you sleep last night?" Aven asked. "Did Del keep you company?"

"I think neither of us slept well. We were both worried about Owyn, for all that Pirit said he would be fine." She looked around. "When we're inside, I'll explain. But I must keep my voice down."

"If you're worried about being overheard, then here is better," Aven said. He stopped walking and looked around. "We can see all around, and there's no one near enough to listen. Or to read lips, I don't think."

Aria nodded. She looked around, then stepped close to Aven, putting her arms around him. In a quiet voice, she said, "Karse has asked Del to guard, because no one will suspect him of doing so. He'll be talking to you when you wake up, and to Othi when we see him. You will be the visible guards. Del will be the one no one sees, and therefore the most dangerous."

Aven slid his arms around Aria, feeling the curve of her belly against him. "I like that," he murmured. "It's very devious. And Del agreed to this?"

"Owyn said it himself. Del will kill to protect the people he loves. We both saw him do it." Aria tipped her head back and smiled. "May I have a kiss?"

Aven smiled in response and leaned down to kiss her, breathing in her scent of sun-and-wind. He stayed with his forehead against hers, breathing with her, until he couldn't contain the yawn building in his chest. She giggled, and they stepped away from each other and entered the tent; inside, Aven yawned again, letting go of Aria's hand so he could stretch.

"You need to sleep," Aria said. "Have you eaten?"

"We ate before we left Shadow, and I'll eat again when I wake up." He tugged his shirt over his head and draped it over the foot of the bed. Then he unwrapped his kilt and laid it aside. When he looked at Aria, she was watching him, a small smile on her face.

"I know you need to sleep..." she murmured, and Aven grinned.

"Later?" he asked. "Maybe?"

"Later," she agreed. "Maybe."

Aven got into bed, pulling the light blanket up to his waist. Aria laid down next to him, resting her head on his shoulder. Aven rested his hand on the curve of her belly, and felt the baby move. He smiled, turning to kiss Aria's forehead.

"I love you," he murmured.

"I love you, too. Now sleep."

ARIA MOVED OFF THE bed as carefully as she could. Aven was deeply asleep, as was Treesi, who had come in shortly after she and Aven had laid down. Thankfully, neither of them stirred when she shook the bed getting to her feet. She watched them breathe for a moment, then went to collect the bag that held the writing desk that Steward had given to her before they left. If she was meeting with the first official village of her Progress tomorrow, then she had enough time to review her notes on what exactly she needed to do.

She stepped out into the sunlight and looked around, then headed for the fire.

"Aria."

She turned and smiled at Memfis, who had just come out of his tent. "How are you feeling?"

"Good," he answered. "You're going to need a camp table for that? Or do you have the stand?"

"There's a stand?" Aria looked down at the bag. "I didn't know there was a stand."

"If that's Milon's writing desk, there's a stand."

"This was my father's?" Aria looked down at the bag. "Steward didn't tell me."

"He probably meant to, but with the ninety-and-one other things that needed to happen to get us on the road, it probably slipped his mind. I'll see if I can find the stand," Memfis said. "And until I do, we'll have a table set up for you. Just tell me where."

"Near the fire will be nice. And if there is some tea, that would be lovely."

"Zarai has taken over the fire and, I think, the cooking." Memfis fell in next to her as she started walking. "So there is probably some tea. And possibly something to eat. Skela was looking for Del. Have you seen him?"

"He was with Owyn and Alanar when I left him," Aria answered. "In the little tent."

Memfis nodded. "I'll tell Skela that he's busy."

Aria looked up at him. "How was it, to dance again?"

Memfis whistled softly. "It was...like coming home," he answered. "I didn't think I'd ever be able to again. I didn't think I could."

"Your arm being gone doesn't take away your ability."

Memfis waggled his hand. "Maybe so, maybe no. It's never been done before. And now we know that it doesn't take my ability, but it does take my balance. I'll need to practice." He tipped his head back, then ran his hand over his short crop of more-silver-than-black hair.

"Have you decided if you're going to let it grow?" Aria asked.

"Not yet," Memfis answered. "Lady Meris told me that she told Owyn I used to wear twists. I hadn't thought about having my hair that long in years."

"I cannot picture you with long hair. And what are twists?"

"Let me have a table set up for you, then I'll tell you." He left Aria at the fire and went off to talk to one of the guards. The guard ran off, and came back a few minutes later with a roll of...something. Something that unrolled to reveal four legs — when it was set up, it was a low, surprisingly steady table. The guard moved it so that it was near one of the logs they'd been using as seats.

"That's a marvelous design," Aria said as she sat down and took the writing desk out of the bag. She set it down on the table, running her hands over the smooth, warm wood. "This was my father's?"

Memfis sat down next to her and nodded. "That was Milon's. Meris gave it to him when he left Forge after he was chosen as Heir. I think it was her way of telling him to write to her."

Aria smiled and looked down at the desk. "I will have to ask her if he did."

"He did," Memfis said. "And knowing Lady Meris? She saved every letter."

"I did save every letter," Meris said from behind them. "And they're all back at the Palace. They were the first thing I put into my bags when I was getting ready to leave. I will show them to you when we get home." She sat down on Aria's other side and laughed. "Listen to me. I'm thinking of the Palace as home again."

Aria smiled and ran her hand over the desk again, taking out her pages of notes. "Grandmother? Memfis? Will you tell me about my father?" She looked at her great-grandmother, then at Memfis. "I never feel like I know enough. And reading his journals, it's helped. But it's also made it worse. I should have known him." She looked back at the desk, her vision blurring, as the tears welled up, falling to spot the paper on the desk. Memfis put his arm around her shoulders and hugged her to his side.

"I know," he murmured, his voice sounding thick and strained. "You should have. We should have watched you grow up. Take your first steps. Your first flight...which came first?"

Aria chuckled, wiping her face with her fingers. "My mother said I flew before I walked," she said. "But every mother in the flock says that. I don't know, really."

"Every mother in the flock might say that because it's true," Meris said. "I imagine that if we asked Steward, he would say the same about Del." She paused. Then she frowned. "Oh...but Steward wouldn't know that, would he? Never mind that. That was a horrible idea."

"That...must be interesting. And disturbing," Aria said. "Steward has no past. No blood family. He has us. We've adopted him, and call him Uncle. And Del calls him Father. But, there's no real connection to his history, to the Mother. Not anymore. I took that away." She paused. "I didn't think this through, did I?"

"You did what you needed to do in order to save his life," Meris said, resting her hand on Aria's arm. "I think Steward is at no greater disadvantage than Owyn, really. Owyn had no connection to his past for most of his life. It's only in the past year he's found that."

"But Steward will never have that," Aria pointed out. "He'll never have that connection again."

"Aria, you're forgetting something," Memfis said. "You saved his life, yes. But this was also his punishment. To atone for what he did, he had to give up everything that he was. And I honestly think he's happier for it."

Aria frowned, looking down at the page. At the marks of her tears, drying in the sunlight.

"Aven told me once that the Water tribe says that the Mother records the good we've done in ink, but the wrongs we've done are written in water," she said. "His entire past was written in water, and the page has dried. It's time for him to write his new page."

"In ink?" Memfis asked.

"In ink."

Chapter Twenty-Four

A ria went over her notes with Memfis and Meris, asking questions until she was clear on what she would need to do when the Progress arrived in Shadow Cove. Karse came and joined them, sitting on the ground at Lady Meris' feet as Howl crawled into his lap and curled up to sleep.

"So it sounds like the plan is that I escort you and the Companions, and the healers down to the village tomorrow, and once the visit is done, we head out to Serenity?" he said, absently stroking the puppy. "We taking all three coaches? Or are we sending folks who don't need to be down there ahead?"

Aria looked around at the people. "I think...just who needs to be there," she said. "I do not want to stress the village. Not after what they've been through."

Karse nodded. "I'll send the boys with the third coach, then."

"It might do them good to play," Meris suggested. "If you think it will be safe? And they'll be able to keep Howl for you while we ride."

"I thought I'd try him in the saddlebag, but we can do that on the way to Serenity." Karse looked down at the puppy, then up at Aria. "I didn't know that her man called her Fancy."

Aria blinked, then remembered Karse blushing when Afansa had chided him for calling her that. "Karse?"

"Look. I like her. She's a good woman. She got caught up in some bad things, but she's a good woman. And Trey liked her, once he got over her almost getting him killed." He looked down, and the color started to rise from his collar. "And before he went out, he asked me what I thought of her. If I thought of her. And...yeah, you can't be asked that question and not think about it." He grinned. "And I realized I had been thinking about it. About her. I was going to talk to Trey when he got back—" He stopped. "And now...yeah, I don't know what to do now. I don't know what he'd want me to do. I can't..." He took a deep breath. "Mem, will you walk with me? I think I need to talk this out."

Memfis nodded and stood up. "Let's go."

They walked away, and Aria sighed. "Once Owyn is stronger, I want to ask him to see if he can speak to my father. See if there's any hope he can offer to Karse."

Meris took Aria's hand, and pitched her voice low. "I spoke to him. When I tested Owyn. He touched Milon, and I spoke to him."

"Grandmother!" Aria gasped. "Isn't...isn't what happened in the test supposed to be a secret?"

"It is, but this is something you need to know. And something that we cannot tell Karse," Meris paused a moment. "Milon said—"

"That they'd taken Trey away," Aria finished, keeping her voice quiet. "I know. Owyn told us." She smiled at the shocked look on Meris' face. "Owyn will occasionally break the rules, when he feels it is necessary. I did not think you would."

Meris chuckled. "I thought it was necessary for you to know. Who else knows?"

"My Companions, and Alanar. Othi had already left when Owyn told us."

"Just your personal circle, then. Minus the one. And they're all to be trusted," Meris said. She nodded slowly. "I imagine I don't have to tell you not to share this?"

"Oh, of course not!" Aria answered. "Especially not where Karse can hear." She looked off in the direction where Karse and Memfis had gone. "I hope we're wrong."

"So do I."

"ARE WE TALKING OR CLIMBING mountains?" Memfis called.

"What's wrong with both?" Karse called back. "I think...yeah, this is right." He turned and looked back down the slope. "Can you make it?"

"I'm fine." Memfis stomped up the last bit of ragged trail and looked around. "What are we doing up here? We didn't need to come this far for privacy."

"No, we needed to come this far because I needed to see something, and I needed someone I can trust with me." He put Howl down and pointed over the edge of the ridge. "Look that way."

Memfis stepped closer to the edge and looked out. "What am I looking at?" he asked. "Wait...that's the road to Shadow Cove down there, isn't it?"

"Yes," Karse said. He stepped closer and pointed. "And that area there? That's where Lyka and Owyn were attacked. The shot came from up here."

Memfis stared at him for a moment, then looked around. "Are we looking for signs of who did it?"

"No," Karse answered. He studied the view for a moment, then pointed to a different place. "See that waterfall there? That feeds the stream that Owyn used to hide his trail. The rock there, the big, broken one, that's where Howl got away from me and ran off. And...that shadow there? Just around that is the overhang where we found Owyn."

Memfis frowned. "That...Karse, I don't understand. Whoever it was had a clear shot of him the entire time he was running."

Karse nodded. "You're right. They did. They could have killed him. They could have taken another shot. But they weren't up here. They shot Lyka, then shot Owyn. They killed Lyka, but they fucked up with Owyn. They realized that they didn't kill him, and they ran. I'm guessing they thought he was going to head back to camp instead of running off to hide." He looked around. "They ran off before they were caught. And I'm really afraid they ran right into camp."

"Karse, you think we have a traitor?" Memfis scowled. "One of the guards? Or one of the servants?"

"One of the guards is my guess. The servants, they probably wouldn't have access to the crossbows, or the skill to use one. The thing is that an even half dozen of these guards were my men from Forge. That's why I picked them for the Progress! I know them all. I trained them all. They were my pack." Karse paused, then added, "Lyka was one of mine. One of my pups."

"I remember him. Always a million questions when he came to the forge. He was a good boy."

Karse smiled. "He was a good boy. A good guard. He was the youngest of my pups. Came in...yeah, he was another of Fandor's cast-offs, come to think of it. Like Owyn and Trey, and a couple other of my men. Lyka didn't know a blasted thing about anything, but he was as eager to learn as Howl." He shook his head. "Burning his body? That hurt. I just don't know, Memfis. Someone murdered him, and is trying to murder Owyn, and I can't even imagine why."

"Do you think we missed one of Risha's people?"

Karse shook his head. "Considered it, but no. Not Risha, or her people. They wouldn't be going after Owyn. If it had been Aria or Aven? Or Del? Then I'd say maybe. But Owyn? No. She's not going to target him, or she'd have done it already. No, there's something else going on here. Keep an ear out, will you?" He paused, then hummed softly. "Maybe...see if Teva's name comes up. Maybe he had someone in the Palace? Someone who heard that Owyn killed him, and who's looking for revenge?"

Memfis nodded slowly. "Yeah, and we can ask Rhexa when we get to Terraces. There's been a lot of people going back and forth the past month."

"True. And we can ask Leesam. He's in Terraces," Karse said. "Do you remember Leesam?"

"I remember Lee. He was another good one. Used to borrow books from me. And he was with us the night we took down Fandor. He stayed in Terraces?"

"Wren and Lyka told me when they got to the Palace. They said that Leesam met someone on the road to Terraces, decided to settle down with her." Karse smiled. "I don't begrudge him that. And Rhexa needs good men to replace the ones who came north with us."

"She got one of your best," Memfis said.

Karse nodded. He went to the edge of the ridge and squatted, studying the terrain. He could hear Howl moving through the brush behind him, but he ignored the pup for the moment. "Crossbow, but we knew that. It wasn't a hard shot to make. Not from here. And whoever it was cleared out fast when Owyn went down. Had to have, or they'd have taken a second shot when Owyn ran off." He looked up at Memfis. "There wasn't anyone here when I sent men to look."

Memfis held his hand out, and helped Karse back to his feet. "You trust those men?"

Karse sighed. "Yesterday? I'd have said yes. Today? I don't know." He looked around. "Howl!" He heard rustling, and Howl appeared out of the brush, carrying something in his mouth. He trotted up to Karse, his tail wagging, and growled.

"Oh, is it playtime?" Karse asked. He leaned down, tugged at what Howl was holding, then realized what it was. "Give it up, Howl," he said. "Drop it." Howl growled and shook his head, so Karse growled back at him. The puppy dug in, tugging harder and pulling free from Karse. He shook his head hard, then dropped his prize and barked, wagging his tail.

"Fair enough," Karse agreed. "You win. Good boy. Now let me have it." He knelt down and gently wrestled with the puppy with one hand, picking up the now-battered leather glove with the other. He held it up for Memfis to see. "This is one of ours."

Memfis nodded. "I thought it might be. Do you think one of your men dropped it when they came up to find the archer?"

"Or they dropped it when they came up here to murder your son," Karse said. He stood up and looked around. "Let's go back."

"I thought you wanted to talk about Afansa," Memfis reminded him.

Karse reached down and picked up Howl. "I wanted a good reason to leave camp and check the site without setting Aria on edge or raising anyone's hackles." Karse started down the rocks, picking his way carefully and keeping an eye on Memfis. "I figured Aria wouldn't ask too many questions if she thought we were having a man-to-man talk. And anyone who might have been watching me? Well, they'll hear that I'm off with you talking about girls." He paused, waiting for Memfis to catch up. "Girl. Woman. Mem, she is a fine woman. And Trey did ask me what I thought of her. He likes her." He shrugged and put Howl down. "I like her. But I'm not doing anything until we have Trey back. Told Treesi the same thing."

"Treesi?" Memfis coughed. "Karse, she's young enough to be your daughter!"

"And she's a healer who saw that I was in pain, and who thought it would help me deal with my husband being who the fuck knows where and in what trouble." Karse shook his head. "I turned her down. And thanked her for the offer." He forced his shoulders to relax. "I'm sleeping alone until Trey comes home. And...how soon do you think Owyn will be strong enough to reach Milon?"

"Probably not until we're in Terraces," Memfis said.

Karse nodded. "I'll ask him once we're in Terraces. I need to know how he is. If he's alive. And I need for Owyn to tell Milon to let Trey know I love him, and we're coming."

"Trey knows that, Karse."

Karse looked at Memfis and nodded. "I know. But I need to say it anyway."

DEL SAT ON THE GROUND with his back against the bed, listening to the soft sound of breathing behind him, the louder sounds outside the tent. Wondering if he'd be able to tell if one of those outside sounds was someone he'd need to stop. Trey said he could. Skela and Karse did, too. Aria believed in his abilities. They all trusted him to keep Owyn and Alanar safe.

It would be a good thing if he could trust himself. If only Aven's doubt didn't add weight to his own doubts. Aven's reaction grated at him; he knew Aven got snappish when he was tired or in pain, but the sheer disbelief—

No. Aven knew full well what Del was capable of. He knew that Del had killed someone not even a month ago, in order to protect him and Aria. He was tired and in pain, and he'd probably grovel to apologize once he was awake.

A twig snapped, and Del moved, rolling onto his knees and snapping his arm down. The weight of a throwing spike landed in his palm. He set himself to throw...and nails scratched on the canvas by the tent flap. A moment later, Aven looked inside.

"Is anyone awake?" he called softly. Then he saw Del and smiled. "And here I thought breaking the stick was a good idea."

Del snorted and tucked the spike back into the sheath on his forearm. "*Idiot,*" he signed. "*I could have killed you.*"

Aven took a deep breath and clasped his hands behind his back. "I know, Del—"

"*I know you're sorry,*" Del signed. "*Sign, so you don't wake them up.*"

Aven nodded and came inside, sitting down in the chair next to the bed. He laid his walking stick down and started signing. "*I know you know. And I know you understand why I behaved so badly. But that doesn't mean I shouldn't apologize for doing it. You killed someone to save my life, Del. I shouldn't doubt you.*"

Del nodded and sat back down. "*I accept your apology.*"

"*Thank you.*" Aven laid his hands down, looking at the bed. "He looks better," he said softly.

"*Can you heal someone in your sleep?*" Del asked. "*Owyn's been looking better the entire time they've been asleep.*"

"*I don't know,*" Aven answered. "*When we see my father, we can ask him.*"

On the bed, Alanar shifted. He coughed softly, then raised his head. "Someone hurts."

"It's me," Aven answered. "I can leave if it's bothering you."

Alanar grimaced. "No, I'll work on it once I'm awake." He turned his head slightly. Then he smiled. "Del." Del turned and reached out, taking Alanar's hand. Alanar squeezed his fingers. "Barsis told us that you came all the way down to Shadow Cove alone. I'm proud of you."

Del felt his face grow warmer, and shifted so that he could kiss Alanar's hand. Alanar laughed softly and let his hand go. Del looked at Aven, started to raise his hands, then stopped. He trusted

Aven. And he could trust him with this. He closed his eyes, and opened his mouth.

"I..." he started to say. He stopped, frowned, then started again, "I...talk...to...Prit." He swallowed. "Drop...drop...my...tab...tablet. Sh...don...sign."

Aven blinked. "You're better than I remember. Have you been practicing?"

Del stared at him, and Alanar sat up. "You knew Del has a voice?" Alanar sputtered. Then he lowered his voice, "Fuck. I don't want to wake Owyn. How did you know?"

Aven looked stunned. "Del, I thought you knew!"

"*That you knew I have a voice?*" Del signed. "*No, I didn't! Before yesterday, the only people I thought knew were Owyn and Alanar. Now Pirit knows, and Aria. And I think you and Treesi should know, too. I was going to tell you. But how do you know?*"

Aven smiled and shook his head. "I've known for months you have a voice. Del, when you have really bad nightmares, you talk in your sleep."

Del blinked. If he talked in his sleep when he had nightmares...

"*My father* knows," he signed. "*He has to know.*"

"Knows what?" Owyn's voice was sleep-thick, but his color was good when he propped himself up on his elbow. "What does Steward know?"

"*Aven says that when I have nightmares, I talk in my sleep. He's known I have a voice since we first went to the deep.*" Del signed the words as he mentally said them, and Aven nodded.

"I think we were two days out from Serenity when you had the first nightmare. I've known since then."

"*If you know because of my nightmares, then my father has to know.*" Del paused and nodded slowly. "*And if he doesn't, then I'm going to tell him. No more secrets,*" he signed. "*I'll tell Treesi when I see her. And I'll tell my Fa when we see him tomorrow.*"

"Do you want one of us with you when you do?" Owyn asked. "Or all of us?"

Del looked at him and smiled, reaching out to take his hand. "All," he said.

"ARE YOU SURE YOU'RE feeling up to this?" Alanar asked.

"That's a funny question, coming from you," Owyn answered. He tugged the fresh shirt over his head and rolled his shoulders. "Am I feeling up to this?"

Aria chuckled, then blinked when Alanar cocked his head to the side. "Your back hurts?"

"It pulls, a little. Pirit tried to put it right." Owyn turned his head, then shrugged. "It's something about the old scars and the new scar not playing well together."

Alanar nodded. "I'll examine it later, see if I can get it to loosen."

"Owyn, you don't have to get up," Aria said. For the second or third time, she thought.

"That's the fourth time you've said that, and I keep telling you. I'm not spending another night in here away from everyone. I'm fine. I just need to build the blood back up. And that means I need to eat, and food is out there. Right?" He looked at Alanar. "Am I right?"

Alanar smiled. "You're right."

Aria stood up and went to the tent flap, looking out to see Del standing guard, a silent sentry. He looked over his shoulder and smiled at her, then signed, "*Is he ready?*"

"I think he is," Aria agreed. She looked back to the two men, and wasn't surprised to see that Alanar had pulled his husband into a tight embrace. She smiled and stepped out, letting the tent flap fall. "I don't think Alanar would let him out of the tent if he wasn't."

Del signed something, and Aria frowned. "Aven was going to ask what?"

Del pulled his tablet out of his carry-bag. "*If healers can heal in their sleep. Owyn woke up much better than he was when he and Alanar went to sleep.*"

Aria read the words, then looked back into the tent. "Alanar? Tell Virrik thank you."

Alanar looked up. "What?" he sputtered. "What am I...Virrik?" He looked distant for a moment. "I...yes. Thank you."

"What did he do?" Owyn asked.

"Worked on you while we were asleep. And he says he's sorry he missed the adhesion. We'll work on it later." He stepped back and held his hand out. "Let's go and eat."

Chapter Twenty-Five

They were up with the sun, eating a quick breakfast and dressing in their ritual finery so that the camp could be broken down and moved. Aven leaned against the side of the coach, then straightened so that he wouldn't rumple his kilt or his dark purple vest. He watched as things were carried out of the tents and loaded into carts, and as the pretty serving girl Steward had assigned to them for the trip brought a bundle to the coach and loaded it onto the top. She smiled at him as she jumped down.

"Changes of clothes," she said. "Figured you wouldn't want to be in the fancy clothes for the entire trip."

"I appreciate that," Aven said. "Thank you for taking care of us, Trista."

"My pleasure, Waterborn." Trista trotted off, passing Karse on her way.

"We'll camp tonight outside Serenity," Karse said, coming up to him. "Spend tomorrow with your aunt Danzi, and then go on to Terraces."

Aven nodded. "It'll be good to see Rhexa again. I wonder how many more refugees they've gotten since we left. Terraces is going to be crowded."

"We've had reports," Aria said as she came up to them. She wore long, loose white trousers and a white wrapped jacket with a long, flared skirt. "And most of the houses that Owyn and Marik had surveyed to be repaired or replaced are both finished and occupied." She pulled her wings in close and leaned against Aven's side, resting her head on his shoulder. "You should have read those."

"Should have, yes," Aven agreed. "Did I actually do it? I don't remember." He smiled as Aria laughed. "I probably did read them, but there's so much to know. Sometimes, it feels like my brain is full."

Karse laughed. "I remember that feeling from when I was in training myself. There are the others. We're ready to go?"

Aven straightened, fumbling for his walking stick as the others approached. Each of them wore the clothes that they'd worn when they'd taken their places in the Palace. They all looked wonderful; next to them, Pirit and the healers-in-training looked almost drab.

"Alanar has been telling me about his new talents," Pirit said as she walked up to him. "Sleep healing is something I think would be very useful to learn."

"I don't recommend it," Alanar added. "It is useful, but it's crowded." He snorted. "And Virrik doesn't recommend it, either. That whole dying-but-not-dying bit."

"I can see how that would be troublesome," Pirit agreed. "Right. We're in the other coach?" She looked around. "Gathi, you're with us. We'll see which of these delinquents of mine will be a good training partner for you."

"Grandmother, are these all the current trainees?" Aven asked. "You have more than I remember."

"We had survivors from other healing centers make their way in over the past month, once word got to them that there was still a healing center standing. There are four trainees who weren't ready to come with me, and I have two advanced trainees who stayed behind to keep an eye on patients," Pirit answered. "You remember Lidl and Tancis, don't you? They're both settling into their roles as senior trainees, and I'll probably recognize them as full healers by next spring. They're coming along very nicely."

"Tancis settled down?" Aven laughed. "Did he stop chasing Malani?"

"In a way," Pirit said. "They'll be married in the autumn."

"Malani? Married?" Treesi repeated. "That's...surprising."

"Marriage seems to be going around," Pirit said. "Alanar, you and Owyn started quite the marriage epidemic. Or made it fashionable. I'm not sure which."

"Who else got married?" Owyn asked.

"Marik told he was asking Esai to build a canoe with him," Pirit answered. "I'm assuming you knew that?"

Aria nodded. "We did."

"Garrity asked Evarra to marry him before they left—" Pirit's voice trailed off. "What? You've all...Mother of us all. Who died? Not both of them?"

"Evarra's dead, Grandmother," Aven said softly. "And Garrity...he took a blow to the head in the attack, and we barely saved his life. Now...well, his wits are wandering. We were going to tell you when we got to Terraces. Fa wanted to talk to you about him. Maybe send him to you and see if you could help him. Nothing we've tried has helped."

Pirit closed her eyes. "Mother hold her. Hold them both. When Destria comes again, I'll tell her to bring him. I'll see what I can do. It may not be much—"

"Just...don't lock him away in the green levels," Owyn said softly. "Don't hide him away and pretend he isn't a problem anymore."

Pirit looked startled. "What? Where did you get that idea?"

"Oh, we need to talk," Owyn breathed. "We have...a lot to talk about." He looked up at Alanar. "And we can't do it now, can we? We're not in the same coach."

Pirit frowned, then looked at the trainees. "Take Gathi to the other coach and give her an introduction. I haven't had the time to assess—"

"I tested Gathi in the Palace, to see if she had the gift," Alanar offered. "Based on that, I'd say she's a high two, with no training."

Pirit nodded. "Very good. We'll confirm that when we get to Terraces, but that gives me a good idea of where to begin. Locky, she'll be your training partner. Behave yourself. She isn't used to living with healers yet."

"Yes, Pirit." One of the young men in gray stepped forward. To Aven's eyes, he looked to be about Gathi's age. He smiled at Gathi. "Sit with me, Gathi. I'll answer anything you want to ask. And I think we'll get along just fine — I wasn't used to living with healers either when I started."

"How long have you lived with healers?" Gathi asked.

Locky grinned. "About a month now. I'm still not used to living with them, entirely. I came up from the Fire lands, so I had a lot to learn. We'll learn together."

She nodded. Then she glanced at Aven, and he straightened when he saw the look on her face.

"Aven?" she said, and her voice quivered. He opened his arms, and she ran into his embrace.

"It's fine, Gathi," he murmured as he hugged her. "It's a big step, but you're ready for it. And you can trust Locky. He's your training partner. You can trust your training partners completely." He squeezed her just a little tighter. "You're going to do just fine. Better than fine. You're going to do wonderfully. If you work as hard as I know you can, you'll be a full healer in no time."

"It's really happening, isn't it?" she whispered. "I...Aven, I don't know..."

"Now, wait a minute," Aven said. He stepped back slightly and waited until she looked up at him. "Where's my Gathi?" he asked her. "Where's the girl who marched up to the Palace gates with three babies and ordered the Usurper to give her a place? Where's my bold Gathi?"

"I..." She stopped and smiled. "That's me. And..." She paused. Then she nodded. "And you're right. If I didn't want this, I could have stayed in the Palace with the babies and just been a chambermaid the rest of my days. That's not what I want. This is what I want. I'm going to be a healer, like you." She drew herself up, then stepped closer, went on her toes and kissed Aven. "I'll see you in Terraces."

"I'M NOT SURE WHO WAS more surprised," Pirit said, looking at Aven as the coach started to move. "You, or Aria."

Aven laughed and looked at Aria. "I promise, I didn't know she was going to do that."

"I don't mind," Aria answered. "But she's a little young."

"Oh, I'll keep an eye on her," Pirit said. "And it didn't surprise me at all. A young healer? They often fixate on their first teacher. Many times, that's the first person who treats them as someone of value instead of an extra mouth to feed. Now, what was this about the green levels?"

Aven looked across the coach at Owyn, who was crowded onto the other bench with Alanar, Del and Treesi. "Owyn?"

Owyn nodded. "You know I died and came back. And...you know that I'm something more than just a Smoke Dancer, right?"

"Heart visions, if I remember correctly?" Pirit asked.

Owyn nodded again. "There's more. When I'm in the smoke, I've been able to talk to Milon. He's alive."

"What?" Pirit gasped.

"He's been alive the whole time," Owyn said. "He was hurt, in the attack on the Palace. The healers hid him, to protect him from the Usurper. But his injuries, they killed his legs. And when the healers figured out that he wasn't ever going to walk again, they gave up on him. And he went from being a patient to being a prisoner. For the entire time..." Owyn's voice trailed off. "And you knew. The look on your face. You knew he was in there."

"I knew he survived the attack. Agisti told me they hid him," Pirit said softly. "And before the seasons changed, they told me he'd died. I never told Jehan or Aleia. They were already in mourning, and Jehan was torturing himself because he thought he'd failed. I couldn't put him through that again. Either of them. Especially since Aleia wasn't having the easiest pregnancy...I worried that she'd lose the baby if she knew." She turned to Aria. "Aria, I had no idea—" She turned and held her hand out to Alanar. "Truth-read me. I swear to you, I had no idea!"

Alanar reached out, but Aria rested her hand on Pirit's arm. "I believe you," she said. "But tell us. Why would the healers have given up on him?"

Pirit frowned. "Tell me what you know."

"My father kept journals," Aria said. "We haven't finished reading them, and we didn't want to risk damaging them, so we have them locked away in the Palace. What we've read covers about ten years, I believe. They lied to him, and told him that all of his Companions were dead, save for my mother."

"They told him Meris died, too," Owyn added. "Probably to stop him from writing letters to her."

Aria nodded. "At first, he wrote that the healers told him that he'd walk again. Then he stopped saying anything about walking again. He mentions Anilis, but says nothing about Waran."

"When I talked to him the first time, he told me that he didn't have a name. And when I talked to him last, he told me that I wasn't the only one who died and came back." Owyn licked his lips and turned to Alanar. "I wonder...do you think he died twice? Once when they told Pirit he was dead, and then again when he had the ague that Nestor wrote about, the one that brought Ambaryl and Risha into the mess?"

"It...that might make sense," Alanar said slowly. "But I had a thought. Aria, you said he doesn't mention Waran?"

"No, he does not," Aria answered. "At least, not in what I've read so far. What are you thinking?"

"I'm wondering if it wasn't the healers that were the problem," Alanar said. "Maybe...it was Nestor?" He leaned forward, resting his elbows on his knees. "We focused on the Palace healers, but maybe it wasn't them? The Palace healers were Agisti, Anilis, Waran and Risha, right?"

Pirit nodded. "That's right. Agisti died. Anilis was assigned, but she refused to serve and refused to say why. And Waran...well, he was insufferable, and I needed to do something with the man."

"I think we know why Anilis refused to serve," Aven murmured. "When did Nestor become steward? Owyn, do you know? You and Alanar are the only ones of us who met the man."

Owyn frowned. "I...I don't think he told me. But Ankem was Steward during the attack. Remember his records? So Nestor became Steward after the attacks—"

"If I'm remembering correctly, Nestor is the one who requested a healer to replace Anilis," Pirit said.

Alanar nodded. "That explains it. The change in attitude wasn't because of the healers. It was because of Nestor. It was Nestor who thought Milon was broken."

"*The same way he and Ambaryl thought I was,*" Del signed.

"And they got Risha to go along with it, because they all believed the same thing. That different is wrong, and crippled means broken." Alanar shook his head. "I don't understand why Waran complied, though. It's such a violation of the healer's canon." He frowned. "Do you think perhaps he never saw Milon? That he didn't know?"

"We'll find out once we read the rest of the journals," Aria said.

Alanar nodded, tipping his head back and closing his eyes. His frown deepened. "Aria, I never spent a lot of time with my mother's flock, except for after the fire. And I remember my grandfather as being very kind to me. So is this...common? This attitude against women and those who are different?"

"No. At least, not among my flock. But Steward said that Nestor was wingless Air," Aria murmured. "I wonder if it might not be common among the wingless?"

"We'll find out when we get to the Solstice village, I suppose," Aven said.

Pirit looked thoughtful. "Explain to me what this has to do with the green levels?" she asked, looking at Owyn.

"When you put someone in the green levels, do they ever come out?" Owyn asked. "And when did that start, anyway? Jehan said there weren't any when he was in training."

"Ah. I see," Pirit breathed. She nodded. "Yes. The green levels are there only as a way to keep those who are a danger to themselves or to others safe until we know how to properly treat them. If we can help them, however they need to be helped, then yes, they are released. There's rarely anyone there for very long." He ran her finger down the bridge of her nose. "But I can see where you might have gotten the impression that the levels were something more sinister. Especially since I know what was done with mind-damaged people in Forge."

"You knew about that?" Owyn asked.

"And was appalled by it. We appealed to Tirine to change the laws so that they would be brought to Terraces for treatment, instead of being sent to their deaths, but it never happened." She paused, then continued. "If Garrity comes to me, then we'll assess him. We'll see if we can heal his mind. If we can't, then we'll find someplace where he can live and be safe and happy. The last time I helped treat a man with a serious brain injury, he never regained his full capabilities, but he lived another twenty years. He worked as a gardener afterward. An uncommonly good one, I might add. And, to answer your other question, there have always been green levels in Terraces, because the healing complex there specialized in mind-healing and in cases that required that level of care. Jehan was born at the main healing complex, and only left when he left as a Companion. When he came back to finish his training, he specialized in critical care. Not mind-healing. And when Jehan is focused on a goal, he's oblivious to anything outside that goal. I imagine the green levels were mentioned in his training, but he may not have remembered—"

"Because it had nothing to do with what he was studying," Aven finished. "That makes sense."

"Now, it may be harder to treat Garrity," Pirit added. "We don't currently have a healer who specializes in mind-healing."

"Aleia says I could," Treesi said quietly. "She compared me to someone named Miralis."

Pirit chuckled. "I hadn't thought of it, but you do have something of Mira about you. After the Progress, we'll sit down and explore the options." She looked out the coach window. "It will be good to get back to Terraces. I hope Danzi brought the canoe, or we'll be very crowded on the way back."

DEL HEARD A SHOUT FROM outside the coach. It sounded like a child, calling, "They're here!" And in response, a whoop went up on both sides of the road. Aria laughed, and Del looked out to see children running alongside the coach. He waved, then turned to face the others.

"We have a welcoming party."

Aven peered out the window on his side of the coach. "Some of the ones on this side are children we treated. They look good."

"Good," Alanar said, nodding. "We'll have to check on them before we leave again."

The coach slowed as it leveled, then came to a stop. The door opened, and Steward looked in at them. His clothes were rumpled and dirty, his hair tangled, and he needed to shave.

"Oh, you all look wonderful. And you all make me feel like an unmade bed," he said. "The village has been waiting for you. It's been feeling like they're all holding their breath."

Aria chuckled. "They must all be interesting shades of blue, then."

Steward laughed and stepped back, and Aven climbed out of the coach, turning to offer Aria his hand. She stepped out, followed by the others. Del came out before Pirit, and offered her his hand. She nodded her thanks as he handed her out, then went to stand with Alanar while the Companions arranged themselves around Aria.

Aria smiled at Aven as she took his hand, then turned to Steward. "Steward, if you'll present us?"

Steward looked down at himself. "I—"

"Uncle, you've been saving lives," Owyn murmured. "No one cares if you have soup on your shirt."

"I care," Steward grumbled. "It reflects poorly on my Heir." He ran his fingers through his hair, then stood up straight before bowing. "My Heir, if you will?"

Aria nodded, and he started walking. Del fell in on Treesi's left, glancing at Owyn on her other side.

"How are you feeling?" he thought. *"I forgot to ask you."*

Owyn smiled. "I'm a little tired," he murmured. "And Treesi is doing something about that right now. I'm all warm."

Treesi giggled. "I thought you wouldn't notice."

"I'll sleep on the way to Serenity," Owyn said. "Now, let's go meet people."

Steward led them toward the small group standing near the central firepit. He stopped and bowed, then raised his voice to say, "Headman Barsis, allow me to present you to the Heir to the Firstborn, Aria, daughter of Milon."

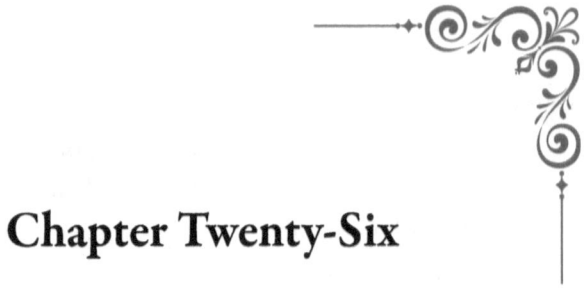

Chapter Twenty-Six

"**D**oes it bother anyone else that we're going the wrong direction?"

Del blinked sleep away and looked across the coach at Owyn. "*What?*"

Owyn looked up from the map that he was trying to study in the failing light. "We're going the wrong direction," he repeated, and tapped the paper that he'd spread out over his lap. "Risha is up here in the north somewhere. Trey and Milon are north, and we're getting further away from them by the minute. How are we supposed to find them and save them if we're going the wrong way?"

"We don't have much choice," Aven said. "We have to make the Progress and we have to go this way. It's part of the lore, Fa says. We have to go south first."

"But it was backwards the year they did it, he told us," Owyn pointed out. "When he was picked as Companion, Milon went north after they went out to the deep."

"Because there were floods. They had a reason to break tradition. And look how that turned out," Alanar said. "You know there are people who believe that Milon's Progress broke the tradition, and that's why things happened the way they did. We can't risk that. We have to do things properly, or the common folk will say Aria is cursed the same way her father was."

"Why do I have the feeling you only said that aloud because she's asleep?" Aven asked. He glanced at Aria, who had her head resting on his shoulder. "She is still asleep."

"I know. And you think that because you know me."

Owyn chuckled as he rolled the map up and put it under the seat. He stretched and put his arms around Alanar and Treesi. "It just bothers me that we are going in exactly the wrong direction. And we're already days behind, aren't we? How long before we get to Serenity Bay?"

Aven looked out the window, then shook his head. "I'm not sure. I haven't been this way by land, and it's getting dark."

Del looked out the window on his side and raised his hands. "*We'll be at the campsite soon.*"

Owyn nodded again. "You didn't have a chance to talk to your Fa today."

Del smiled. "*He didn't stand still the entire time we were in Shadow Cove. And he loved every minute of it. I don't think I've seen him this happy in years.*" He glanced out the window again. "*I'll tell him when we get to camp.*"

"And you still want all of us with you?" Alanar asked.

"Yes," Del answered aloud. Then he signed, "*It's getting easier. More comfortable. It's not as...scary, if that makes sense. But signing is still faster.*"

"It makes perfect sense. And everything gets easier when you practice," Owyn said. "But I think you're right. Signing is always going to be faster for you."

"It's just the way your brain works," Treesi agreed. "The same way mine reverses letters and directions."

Del nodded and looked back out the window. The road turned, and he could see torches and tents.

"*I see the camp,*" he signed, turning back to the others.

"Aria," Aven called her name softly. "You need to wake up. We're here."

"I'm awake," she murmured, and opened her eyes. She blinked and looked out the window. "I should not have slept so long. I won't sleep tonight." She turned to face Del. "I need to get used to hearing your voice," she added. "It's still new enough that hearing it woke me."

Del arched a brow. "*Should I apologize?*"

"No, you should not!" Aria answered with a laugh. Del laughed with her, reaching for her hand. He raised it to his laps and kissed her palm, then smiled as she cupped his cheek, her nails scratching gently over the stubble on his cheeks.

"Are you going to grow this out?" she asked. "Emulate Alanar? It would look good on you, I think."

"Oh, is Del scratchy?" Alanar asked.

"*I haven't thought about it,*" Del signed. "*I'm not sure I'd recognize myself in the mirror.*"

"If you do it, I'll do it," Owyn said. "We can be scruffy together." Del stared at him, and Owyn laughed. "Yes, I'm serious!"

"So, you're both going to grow beards?" Aven asked. He ran one hand over his face. "I can't join in the fun."

"It's not fun when you first start," Alanar said. "It can be itchy. But think of it this way. You're variety. Owyn has a beard, and you don't. It'll keep Aria from getting bored."

Aria blinked, looking startled. "I'm allowed to be bored?" she asked. She sounded incredulous, but her grin was pure mischief. "That's an option? Why did no one tell me I could be bored?"

They were still laughing when the coach stopped moving. Aven reached for the door, but it opened before he touched it.

"Sounds like you're having fun without me."

"Othi!" Treesi scrambled out of her seat and threw herself out of the coach. Othi caught her and held her off the ground while he kissed her, then set her on her feet. She clung to him and laughed. "I didn't think we'd see you before Terraces!"

"When Pirit got back to Terraces, she said you'd be stopping here tonight. So I came to meet you." He put his arm around Treesi and stepped back to let the others get out of the coach, smiling as he accepted a hug from Aven. Del was the last one to step out, and as he did, Othi nodded back the way they'd come. "So, how bad was it?"

Del snorted and looked at Owyn, who groaned and asked, "Who wants to tell him?"

Othi's eyes widened. "That sounds...not good."

"You could say that," Aven agreed. "Let's go get something to eat, and Owyn will tell you."

"I can't tell him all of it," Owyn protested. "I can't tell him what happened when I was trying not to bleed out—"

"What?" Othi turned to stare at them. "You're not joking, are you?"

"No," Aria answered. "We have something of a mystery. I think we'll ask Karse to explain the rest."

They walked over to the fire, where Memfis, Afansa and Meris were sitting. Meris smiled as they approached.

"And how was your first audience?" she asked. "I should have gone with you, to see you stand for your first audience on Progress."

"It was a lovely visit, Grandmother," Aria answered. "Headman Barsis is very nice. He showed us their village, and we met his people, and the children made a great deal of noise—"

"Children do that," Jehan said, coming to sit at Memfis' side. "A great deal of noise, and a great deal of joy. And after the past few days, we're not begrudging them any of it."

"We shared a meal, and then we left." Aria looked around. "Where is Steward?"

"Washing up," Memfis answered. "He said he was tired of feeling unkempt. We've got supper for you, so sit."

"Yes, sit, and Owyn gets to tell me how he almost bled out?" Othi said as he sat down next to Treesi. "What did I miss?"

"Someone is trying to kill me," Owyn answered, sitting down next to Alanar. Del sat down on Alanar's other side, taking the bowl that he was offered. "The morning after the healers all went down to Shadow Cove, a guard came and got me and told me there was a messenger. Only there weren't no messenger, and Lyka's dead now." He frowned. "Does that mean he was part of it? Or was he tricked?"

"Lyka?" Karse asked, leading Copper and Danir to the fire. As they sat down, Howl flopped at Owyn's feet and rolled onto his back to show his belly. "Pet that good boy, Owyn. He deserves it. And give him a bit of your meat. He's figured out how to chew it. I think Lyka was tricked. He had to have been tricked. He never could tell a lie."

"Lyka," Othi said. "About as tall as Owyn? Hair not really dark, and really short?"

Karse nodded. "You sparred with him a few times before you left."

Othi frowned. "He's dead? And...you were hurt. With no healers."

"Del came down to Shadow Cove and took Pirit back with him," Alanar said, turning to smile at Del. "Saved Owyn's life."

"So that's what you missed," Owyn said. "The important bits, anyway." He turned his attention to his bowl. "What is this? It's good. Spicy."

"It tastes like stone stew," Aria said. "It's not quite the way my mother made it, but it's very close."

"Stone stew?" Aven looked at the bowl. "What sort of stones are we eating?"

Aria laughed. "We're not! The stones are heated over the fire, and then the vegetables and meat and the stones are layered in a cooking pot, and you add water and seal the pot. The heat of the stones turns the water to steam, which cooks everything." She picked a piece of meat out with her fingers and ate it. "Where are the stones? And who made this?"

"They're cooling," Steward said. His hair was wet and slicked back, and his clothes were clean. He sat down with Memfis and took a bowl. "And Zarai did. I was surprised when we got here and I smelled it. I haven't had it in years."

"Zarai made this?" Aria looked at her bowl. "I didn't know she was Air!"

"I'm not, but my man was half-Air," Zarai said as she came back to the fire. "I was bringing a bowl to Skela. He's not used to being a coach all day, the poor thing. One of you healers needs to take a look at him when you're done."

"I'll go," Aven volunteered. "So what's special about the stones?"

In answer, Zarai offered him a bowl of black stones. Aven looked at them, then at her.

"What do I do?"

"Take it and rub it in your hands," Aria said. "The warmth and the fat are good for you." She reached out and took one, rolling it between her palms." She smiled. "My mother used to make this for my grandfather. He said the stones helped the pain in his joints."

"That makes sense," Jehan said. "The heat will definitely help swollen joints."

Del took a hot stone from the bowl when it was offered to him, sliding the slick surface over his palms, spreading the grease over his skin. It made his hands feel uncomfortable, somehow both slippery and sticky, and he grimaced and set the stone down in his empty bowl.

"I'm not sure I like the stone part. The stew part is very good, but the stones make my hands feel strange," he signed. *"Is there a towel?"*

From across the fire, he heard his father laugh. "You never did like getting your hands dirty," he said. He got up from his place and picked up another bowl, coming around to offer it to Del. Inside were gently-steaming towels. "Be careful. They're hot."

Del took one of the towels and wiped his hands clean. Then he looked around the fire. Everyone was here, except Aleia. All the people he loved. All the people he trusted. He smiled.

"Th...thank you."

When Del spoke, Steward had been turning away to offer the bowl of towels to Aria; he spun, his eyes wide, and dropped the bowl.

"Did I...did you..." he stammered. "Del? You...you spoke? You...you *can* speak?"

"Well, fuck me," Owyn murmured. "He *didn't* know."

Del stared, feeling as if his throat was closing, feeling panic starting to rise. He'd been so sure that his father knew, that he wasn't going to be in trouble for hiding this...

Alanar's arm encircled his shoulders, tightening. "It's all right," he murmured. "Del, he's just surprised."

"And delighted," Steward croaked. "No...that's not strong enough. Ecstatic!" He looked at the others. "How...how many of you knew?"

"I knew," Aria answered. "Most of us found out yesterday. I think Alanar and Owyn knew before any of us."

"No, Aven knew before we did," Owyn said. He reached across Alanar to take Del's hand. "But Del didn't know that. He didn't think anyone knew. And he didn't tell us he could until we realized that he can't talk to Alanar any other way when they're alone."

Del looked at Alanar, at Owyn. The only thing keeping him in place was Alanar's arm around him, Owyn's hand holding his.

And Owyn's hand holding his silenced his signs. He swallowed and nodded. "I..."

"Slowly, Del," Alanar murmured. "Take your time. No one is angry with you. No one is upset." He hugged Del a little tighter.

Del nodded. "Prit...say...says...shh..." He stopped. It was too much. He tugged his hand out of Owyn's. *"Pirit knows, because I dropped my tablet when I went for help, and she doesn't sign. She says she'll help me learn. And Alanar says he'll help, too. I can't talk fast, or clearly. There's something that doesn't work in my head."* He knocked his knuckles against his forehead. *"It makes me sound like the idiot that Ambaryl thought I was—"*

Steward closed his eyes and nodded. "Of course." He opened his eyes and looked at Del. "You're upset. I...did you think I'd be angry? Angry you kept this from me?"

Del nodded, lowering his hands. He turned and buried his face into Alanar's shoulder, not sure if he wanted to laugh or cry, feeling as if he'd run up the water stairs carrying a heavy weight. A hand settled on his shoulder, and he looked up to see his father standing over him, looking troubled.

"Walk with me?" Steward asked. Del swallowed. He fought the urge to look to Owyn and Alanar for help. He needed to do this alone. He nodded.

"Allie, let him go," Owyn said. "Del, do you want us to wait for you to go to bed?"

Del considered, then shook his head. *"I'll crawl in with you when I get back, if you're asleep."* He turned so that he could kiss Alanar's cheek, then stood up. He followed Steward away from the fire, and they walked side by side until they could no longer hear the voices behind them.

"Owyn seemed surprised that I didn't know," Steward said. "You thought I did?"

Del nodded, stopping so that he could turn to face his father. *"Aven knew because he says I talk in my sleep when I have nightmares. I thought that if I did that, then you had to know. So it was safe to tell you."*

Steward frowned. "Why wouldn't it be safe?"

Del shrugged one shoulder. *"I...before? Nothing was safe. Ever. There are still times when nothing is safe. But it's getting easier."*

"It has been, ever since you first met Aven," Steward said. "You've come so far in such a short time. And now...Del, I never thought I'd hear your voice again."

"It's not really a voice," Del signed. *"It's noise that almost sounds like words."* He held his hands up. *"These are my voice."*

Steward chuckled. "They're both your voice," he said. "You have a perfectly good voice."

"Owyn told me the same thing."

"Owyn is a very wise man for one so young," Steward said. "I will help you however I can. You know that?"

"I've always known that." Del grinned and lowered one hand, reaching for his father's hand with the other. Steward laughed and pulled him into a tight embrace.

"I'm enjoying seeing the man you're becoming, Del," he said. "Your mother would be so proud of you."

Del pulled back slightly. "Y...you...th...think...shhh..." He paused and sighed. *"Words that start in 'sh' are hard,"* he signed. *"You think she'd be proud?"*

Steward nodded. "I do." He draped his arm over Del's shoulders. "I wish I'd known Delandri. I wonder, sometimes, how much like him you are."

"I think I'm more like you," Del replied. *"I never knew him. You're the one I call Fa."* He looked up at his father. *"Let's go back. You're tired."*

"I'll definitely have no trouble sleeping tonight," Steward agreed. They started walking back toward the fire. "Del?"

Del turned to look at his father and arched a brow. Steward blushed, just barely visible in the growing darkness.

"I was wondering...if you would object..." He paused, licked his lips. "I think you know I've been corresponding with Rhexa? Would you object if I asked her if I could court her? Once the Progress is finished?" Steward smiled slightly. "I would ask her now, but it's not fair to her to ask when we'll be leaving almost immediately. And I know she can't just leave with us. So I thought that if I asked her for permission when we came back, she might say yes?" He looked at Del. "If you have no objections?"

Del smiled. "*No objections. I hope she says yes.*"

"So do I."

Chapter Twenty-Seven

"They're not all going to be this easy, are they?" Treesi asked as they walked back to the coach. She looked up at Othi, who was holding her hand as he walked next to her. "I mean...they know us here. Aven is related to some of them."

"And Shadow Cove, they knew us, too. I've been there, and they got to know Aven and Allie and Treesi when they were there for the fever," Owyn said. "So I doubt the rest will be like this. These are the easy ones. Terraces is going to be easy, too. These three? These are family visits, almost. After Terraces?" He sniffed. "Where are we going after Terraces? The maps aren't right anymore."

"The maps haven't been right in a long time," Steward said from behind them. "Rhexa told me that she's been sending scouts out to see the lay of the land and update the maps. While we're in Terraces, we'll redraw our map and plan the next leg of the Progress."

Treesi nodded, leaning into Othi's arm. "It will be good to be back in Terraces, if only for a little while." She paused. "You don't think they gave our house away, do you?"

"Our house?" Aria looked over her shoulder. "I would have no issue if they had someone move into that house. We weren't using it, and it makes no sense for them to keep a house empty in case we might visit. Not when there are people who need homes and beds."

Treesi nodded. "It makes sense, but where do you think we'll sleep? We can't go into the caves—"

"Thank you, no," Owyn said emphatically. "No caves."

"We'll find out tonight," Aven said. "It makes no sense to worry about it, and Aunt Rhexa won't let us sleep in the streets."

They climbed into the coach, arranging themselves to make room for Othi. Del stood outside the coach for a moment, then looked over his shoulder and frowned.

"You can sit with me, Del," Owyn said.

"No, you're still healing," Alanar said. "He can sit with me."

"*Or I can go ride in the other coach with my father,*" Del signed.

"Do you want to do that?" Treesi asked. "I mean, if you want to be with us, I can sit on Othi's lap."

Othi blinked. "I...yes, you can," he stammered, his face turning red.

Aria sighed. "Oh, stop that," she murmured. "Owyn, change places with Alanar?"

Owyn nodded and switched to sit next to Othi, while Alanar sat down next to Aria. She shifted closer to him, then looked past Aven. "There should be enough room for Del now, either on the end or between us."

Del grinned and got into the coach, squeezing between Aven and Aria. "*I like this seat,*" he signed.

"You don't mind being squashed?" Owyn asked. Del shook his head.

"*I like it. You know I like being squashed.*" He grinned at Aria. "*I think I have the best seat.*"

Outside the coach, Steward chuckled. "All right. Let's go. It's not that long a trip to Terraces." He closed the door and shouted up to the driver, and the coach started moving.

"We can talk now, can't we?" Othi asked, his voice quiet. "We're private?"

"Yes," Aria answered. "What is it?"

Othi nodded slowly, frowning slightly. Del wasn't certain if the frown made him look worried or angry. Maybe a little of both.

"Someone tried to kill Owyn," he said slowly. "Twice. In two days. That means it has to be someone traveling with us, doesn't it?"

Aria nodded. "So we believe, yes. And Karse will want to talk to you later about acting as a guard."

Othi nodded. "I can see that. Just me being with Owyn will make someone think twice."

"And will hide the fact that Del is also with Owyn," Aven added. "And he is possibly more dangerous than the pair of us."

Othi grinned. "Because no one thinks he could be. I like that. It's sneaky." He paused again, then asked, "What does it mean for the Progress when there's a traitor who is part of it?"

Aria frowned. "I'm not sure I understand the question?"

Del blinked. "*I do*," he signed. "*Owyn, would you translate?*"

"Yeah, go ahead."

Del kept signing, and Owyn translated his words. "*According to the lore, the success of the rule of a Firstborn is determined by their Progress. What Alanar said earlier, about us having to take the right route? That's part of it. But if the rule is determined by the Progress, what does it mean for Aria's rule if we have a traitor trying to kill Owyn at the start of it?*"

Othi nodded. "That's it. I mean...we can't go back, because the Progress has to finish once it starts. We can't take another route, because we have to take Axia's Way—"

"How do you even know this?" Aven interrupted.

Othi grinned and pointed at Alanar. "Virrik. He was like you. Half Earth, on his father's side."

"Virrik wants to come forward," Alanar said. "He hasn't had his hour in days, but we've been busy."

"Let him come, if he thinks it will help," Owyn said.

Alanar nodded. Then he blinked. "Thank you. I think I can offer some help. Mama used to bring Fa and me out to the deep, to spend time with her family," Virrik said in his rolling Water accent. "Fa was a storyteller—"

"He told some good ones, too," Othi said. "And he taught all of us the lore, that last year..." He stopped. "Virrik, I'm sorry. That last year, that was— "

"The year they died." Virrik frowned and shook his head. "Alanar is cross with me. I never told him about my parents. It...well, it hurt. To talk about. To think about. But you need to know all of it. So...now I'm telling it. We were on our way back to land, and there was a storm. Our canoe...there was a wave...a canoe-killer." He stopped. Swallowed. "I found my way back to my grandmother's canoes. I don't know how I did. And I waited for my parents to come back, but I never saw either of them again. Aunt Ketti took me in and raised me up, and she brought me to Shadow Cove when I started showing signs of having the gift. And it was Barsis' father who brought me to Terraces and the healing center there." He shrugged. "My father. Yes, he was a storyteller. An...ah...what did he call it? Oh. A Loremaster. And he told us that the reason things went badly was because Milon's Progress was wrong. That Milon didn't follow Axia's Way, and that's why things happened."

"And people believe that?" Aria asked. "That because we do not follow a certain route, then we will fail?" She frowned. "I do not like that. At all. Especially since there's no way for us to do it. We can't follow Axia's Way anymore. It goes to Forge, and there no longer is a Forge. It isn't there anymore."

"It's spindrift," Virrik said. "Complete spindrift."

"But the common folk, they believe the spindrift," Treesi countered. "Out east by the mountains? The people there hold to this kind of thing. They believe it. My parents believe it, and they're healers!"

"So according to the lore, what does it mean for the Progress if there's a traitor?" Othi asked.

"Nothing," Aven answered, his voice quiet. "It means nothing, because we're not letting anyone know." He looked around the coach. "We're not telling anyone we don't trust implicitly. And when we find the traitor, we deal with them. Quietly."

"Deal with it," Owyn repeated. "Deal with it how?"

Aven snorted. "There are four healers in this coach," he answered. "We can take care of it with no one the wiser, once we're sure of who it is."

"Aven!" Treesi sounded abnormally shrill, and absolutely horrified. "You are not—"

Aven held up one hand, and she fell silent. "Do you think that I wouldn't kill to protect any of you? All of you? I've done it. We've all done it. I don't think there's a person in this coach who hasn't killed someone to get us to this point."

"But..." Treesi frowned. "I know, but the canons—"

"I know," Aven said. He nodded slowly. "I know. But I also know that we can't risk the Progress being seen as a bad omen. We can't risk Aria's rule." He looked at Aria. "And we can't risk the chance that the lore might be right. That there might not be something to those tales."

"You actually believe the spindrift?" Virrik asked.

"Cousin, I don't know what to believe," Aven answered. He drummed his fingers on his leg. "Most of why we're here is because of the lore. The Prophecy of the Dove is lore. The Heir chooses their Companions because of the lore. And...really, we've all seen that the lore is right. The Diadem was in the box, until it wasn't. Then it was in the Temple when Yana got there, and was there again for Aria. The Fire gem was on Alanar's neck, until it wasn't. Then it was in Aria's pouch. That's all lore...and it's all real. We can't gamble that this part of the lore isn't real."

"Which means that no matter what the maps that Aunt Rhexa has tell us, we have to go to Forge," Aria said. "We have to follow Axia's Way."

Owyn reached underneath the coach seat and pulled out his map, unfurling it. Othi took one end and held it, looking curiously at what Owyn was doing.

"We're here, Othi," Owyn said. "About. That's Serenity Bay there. This is the road. Here's Terraces. And Forge...well, Forge was here." He tapped the map. "We're going to need to know how far the lava field extends, and how hot it still is. Aunt Rhexa will know, and then we can plan." He frowned down at the paper. "I wonder...does the lore say that we have to go to the city, or just the boundaries. And does the entire Progress have to go, or just the Heir and the Companions? Virrik?"

Virrik hummed softly. "Let me think...I...the histories of Axia's Journey says that she traveled south to the lands that forged Fire, and then walked in the shadow of the mountains until she reached the home of the children of Air."

Owyn nodded, looking back at the map. "Then...yeah, I think we can keep to Axia's Way, if that way is how the road used to run. Assuming that it's safe to go that way. If the entire Progress doesn't have to make that trip, if it's just us? Then we can go by horse—"

Aven groaned, and Owyn reached across and patted him on the knee. "Sorry. But it can't be helped. We can send the coaches on, and meet them later."

"Which separates us from the guard," Treesi said.

"We'll take Karse with us, and...I don't know. We'll talk to him about it." Owyn rolled up the map. "It might not even work. We won't know until we see what the scouts have found out. And we won't know that until we get to Terraces."

EVEN WITH HER EYES closed, Aria knew when they'd entered the tunnels that marked the end of their day of travel. She smiled.

"We're here," she murmured.

"Almost," Aven said. "A few minutes more."

She nodded. "And we'll be here for...how long? I forget."

"Steward said at least a week," Owyn answered. "But we're already a day or two behind, because of Shadow Cove. So I don't know. We might cut it short."

"*He won't,*" Del signed. "*Not if it means leaving Rhexa behind.*" He looked at Owyn and smiled. "*He asked if I'd mind.*"

"Asked if you'd..." Owyn burst out laughing. "He's going to ask her to marry him?"

Del nodded. "*Not immediately,*" he signed. "*He's going to ask if he can court her formally when we come back from the Progress. Because it's not fair to ask her now, when she can't come with us.*"

"Which gives him time to figure out if he's going to leave us," Owyn added. "Or figure out how to convince her to move north to the Palace. Which might take the entire Progress, because I don't think Auntie is going to want to leave Terraces."

"We'll swim those currents when it's time," Aven said. "For now? I'm tired. I'm more interested in where we're sleeping tonight." He shifted and winced. "Once this hip is better, I'll be able to ride again."

The coach slowed to a stop, and someone knocked on one of the doors. It opened, and a guard looked in. He looked familiar to Aria, but she wasn't sure why.

"Welcome back to Terraces, my Heir," he said, and Owyn laughed.

"I thought it was you!" he said. "Lee, how are you?" He looked around. "Aven, Aria, did you two meet Leesam back in Forge?"

"I did," Aria answered, remembering. "Wren told me that you stayed here."

Leesam smiled. "I'm honored you remember me, my Heir." He stepped back. "If you'll come with me? I'm to escort you through the tunnels."

He stepped back, and they all climbed out of the coach. Aria stepped away from the others and stretched, spreading her wings wide.

"I'm glad we'll be here for a few days," she said. "I'm tired of being in a coach all the time." She joined the others, seeing that Owyn was holding on to Alanar's hand tighter than seemed normal. "Leesam, if you'll bring us out?"

"This way, my Heir," he said, and started walking.

"How full is Terraces now?" Alanar asked. "You're still getting Forge refugees, aren't you?"

"Forge refugees and Forge criminals," Leesam answered. "There's a guard squadron in Terraces, and Administrator Rhexa says there's never been one before. Not officially, anyway. But the folks coming in have brought some of the bad habits they got into in Forge, and we're having to deal with them." He snorted. "I saw the Captain. Told him, and he's already ready to spit." He glanced at Owyn. "I didn't see Trey. Is he in the rear guard?"

Aria stopped walking. When the others stopped as well, Leesam looked at them and went ashen. "He's not...no!"

"No," Owyn answered. "But...fuck, Lee. His squad went out, and they were wiped out. He's alive. We know that. But he's been taken prisoner, and we can't go after him because it's the wrong direction for the Progress. But we've got...a way to keep an eye on them." He glanced at Aria, who nodded. "They don't know we're coming. But...we don't exactly know where they are. I've got it narrowed down—"

"What do you need?" Leesam asked. "How can I help?"

"I'll show you the map," Owyn answered. He looked over his shoulder. "Del, walk back with me? I'll get it now."

Del nodded, and the two of them walked back to the coach. When they came back, Owyn had the map tucked underneath his arm. "I should have brought it with me, anyway," he said as they started walking again. "I need to compare it to what you have."

Leesam nodded. "We'll do that. But not now. Administrator Rhexa is champing at the bit, waiting for you." He grinned. "It's funny, sort of. I've never seen her so rattled before today. But she knew you were coming."

"She's that bad?" Aven asked.

"I think she completely forgot how to spell," Leesam laughed. "And how many fingers makes five!"

Alanar laughed. "That's not possible!"

"It's true!" Leesam turned to walk backwards. "And...Healer Alanar, isn't it? You're Owyn's man? Rhexa told me about you. Nice to meet you."

Alanar nodded. "It's a pleasure to meet one of Wyn's friends."

Leesam grinned and turned back to face forward, leading them out into the air. The sun was setting out over the sea, casting long shadows as they walked down one of the spokes. Aria could see a crowd gathered in the open area outside the healing center.

"You really are crowded here now, aren't you?" Owyn murmured.

"And getting more crowded," Leesam answered. "Rhexa's planning on sending a group to resettle the town south of here. We're already sending folks east." He shrugged. "For right now? We're on top of each other."

"How have tempers been?" Owyn asked. "Fights?"

"Squabbles," Leesam answered. "And we've had some diceheads. Not sure where they're getting it. We can't find their source. Yet."

"Diceheads?" Alanar repeated. "What are those?"

"Drug addicts," Treesi answered. "Karse told me about it. They use a doctored form of paradise flower."

Leesam nodded. "It's pretty nasty." He took a deep breath. "But you're not here to worry about that. Everyone is waiting for you."

They kept walking toward the hub and the crowd, and Aria reached for Aven's hand.

"That is a lot of people," he murmured, and looked at her. "Are you all right?"

"It's not as many as were in the Hall that first morning," she answered. "I don't think. And we know many of them. I'm fine." She looked around. "Leesam, where are the others? The rest of the Progress?"

"The Senior Healer, the War-Leader, Fisher...no, sorry. Memfis, and Lady Meris, they're all waiting for you." Leesam paused. "And...my Heir, I was told that there's a person with you isn't who he looks like?"

"My Steward," Aria said. "He is not who you think he is. That one is gone, and his name forgotten. He shall be written into our history only as the Usurper. Did the news not reach Terraces?"

Leesam nodded. "It did, but I can't say I understood it. Rhexa said not to worry about it, and that we should trust you. And I do, but...yeah, it's strange. I used to see...the Usurper in Forge. I knew him on sight. And...yeah, that's not him. But he certainly resembles him!"

Aria chuckled. "We will introduce you. You'll like him. Now, let's get this done."

"There's Grandmother," Aven said. "And Aunt Rhexa."

Leesam nodded. He walked forward and bowed slightly. "Administrator? I've brought them."

Rhexa nodded, her smile as bright as the morning sun. "Thank you, Captain," she said. She stepped forward and bowed. "My Heir. Welcome back to Terraces."

Aria shook her head. "Aunt Rhexa, I don't want you to bow to me. Ever."

Rhexa straightened. "Just this once, you're going to have to put up with it. It's proper."

"I don't know about anyone else, but I don't want proper," Owyn blurted. "I want a hug!"

Laughter rippled through the crowd, and Rhexa grinned and walked over to Owyn, catching him in a tight embrace. "I've missed you," Aria heard her say. "All of you." She moved on to hug Alanar, then Del. Treesi was next, followed by Othi, who looked both surprised and delighted. Then Rhexa came back to Aria.

"Is it permitted to hug the Heir?" Rhexa asked, her eyes sparkling.

"It's insisted on," Aria answered, and opened her arms. Rhexa hugged her tightly, then stood back and looked at her.

"You look wonderful," she said. She turned to Aven, and arched a brow. "And you're uneven. That hip?"

"Has gotten worse," he answered. Then he grinned. "But I'm not breakable. Where's mine?"

Rhexa laughed and hugged him, then stepped back. "We've had to house people in Three Northwest. But we've made other arrangements for you and your Companions." She started to turn, but stopped when Aria touched her arm.

"Aunt Rhexa, you haven't met everyone, I don't think?" She looked around, and saw Steward, half hidden behind Memfis. No, he was hiding behind Memfis, and he looked nervous. She smiled at him. "I believe you have been corresponding with my Steward?"

Rhexa blinked. Then she smiled. "I have," she agreed. "But I haven't yet had the pleasure of meeting him. Is he here?"

Aria nodded. "Steward, attend."

Steward visibly drew himself up, and came out from behind the others. He walked over to Aria and bowed deeply. "My Heir," he said as he rose.

Aria smiled. "Administrator Rhexa, I'd like for you to meet my Steward. Who someday will tell me his name, so I can stop calling him by his title."

Steward grinned. "Steward is a perfectly adequate name," he answered. He bowed to Rhexa. "Administrator, it's a pleasure to finally meet you. I've greatly enjoyed your letters."

"As I've enjoyed yours," Rhexa said. She held her hand out to Steward, who took it, bowed over it, then kissed her fingers.

Rhexa blushed.

Chapter Twenty-Eight

"We needed the space." Rhexa sounded both apologetic and embarrassed by the admission as she led them away from the healing center. To Owyn's surprise, they didn't go down the stairs to the lower terraces. They went up.

"We understand, Auntie," Owyn said. "You can't let that many beds stay empty on the odd chance we might all come to visit at once. Not when there are people who need someplace to live." He looked up at the green levels. "But where are we going? The green levels?"

"Well, yes and no," Rhexa answered. "Back before everything, there were apartments up here. They were closed up, but after you left, we reopened them and renovated them. With all the new residents, we've had more than enough workers to do the job, and now the Heir's apartments are ready for you, whenever you want them. There are also apartments here for the Senior Healer and the entire complement of attending healers."

"Trainees?" Alanar asked.

"No, the trainees still live in the student quarters, along with the healers who are on duty. But everyone else is here, where we can have a little privacy." She smiled. "I moved up here a few weeks ago. Trinket seems to like the new apartments."

"You moved?" Alanar gasped. "You left your house? Rhexa, am I remembering wrong? I thought your house was your mother's house!"

"What?" Owyn turned to her. "Auntie!"

"Now stop that," Rhexa said. "I wasn't born here. You know that. Jaxia was an artist. She traveled quite a bit, and she spent time in a small village east of here. That's where she met my father, who was their healer. That's where I was born. Where your mother was born, Owyn. Mother left my father when I was fourteen, and she brought us back here, along with Ambaryl. Dyneh and Baryl and I were all old enough to be tested. Dyneh had the gift. I didn't, and Baryl didn't." She shrugged. "Mother and Dy and I lived further down Northwest when it was the three of us. When Dy moved into healer's quarters, and I...well, when I moved in with Ambaryl, Mother moved into Two Northwest. And I moved in with her when Ambaryl left me. I've been there ever since, but it's always been too much space for just me, and there was a lovely young family from a place called Tinker's Creek who needed just that much room." She smiled. "We did for them what you did for Del in Three Northwest — turned that big closet into a small bedroom. Just in time, too. She had her little girl about a week after they moved in. So don't you worry about me, Owyn. It was just a house." She reached out and took his hand. "Home is what's inside the house. Trinket and I are making a new home." She turned, taking Owyn with her as they walked toward buildings that Owyn didn't remember seeing when he and Marik worked on the survey last winter. He'd have remembered these — they were multistory buildings, built up against the cliffside.

"Auntie?" he murmured. "I don't remember surveying those."

"That's because you didn't survey up here. These have been here for years," Rhexa insisted. "But when Risha changed things so no one was allowed to be near the green levels, anyone who lived here moved down to the lower terraces, rather than deal with her guards. Not that there were many people living here. These were healer quarters, mostly. Since no one was using them, no one took care of them, and they were completely overgrown with ivy. No one has been in any of these buildings for years."

"Are you sure? You searched them all?" Steward asked.

"Searched, cleaned, rebuilt, repainted, and refurnished," Rhexa answered. "There wasn't anything inside but dust, mice and hunter spiders." She chuckled. "And Risha was terrified of hunter spiders."

Owyn laughed. "That might be useful to remember," he called. "Allie, we need to remember that!"

"I knew that already," Alanar answered. "All the healers knew that."

"And we knew what it sounded like when one got into the healing center," Treesi added.

"*How loud did she scream?*" Del whispered in Owyn's mind.

"Del wants to know how loud she screamed," Owyn asked.

"Loud enough to hear her outside the healing center and halfway to the spokes," Alanar answered.

"Which is silly, because hunter spiders are harmless," Treesi answered. "They're big and fuzzy and docile."

"Big, fuzzy spiders?" Aria repeated. "I...I'm not fond of spiders either. How big?"

"About the size of my palm," Treesi answered, and Aria paled.

"I never saw those when we were here before!"

"Because they like the dark," Rhexa answered. "They usually don't go down to the lower terraces, and when they come into the healing center, it's because they came up through the tunnels." She stopped walking. "Aria, if this is going to be a problem, I can put you all into apartments in the healing center."

Aria looked at Aven, then shook her head. "I don't know if it will be a problem."

"If they're that big, what do they eat?" Owyn asked. "They're not going to try and eat Trinket, are they?"

"Oh, they're horrible cowards," Rhexa said. "They eat worms, smaller insects, and tunnel snails if they're down in the tunnels where it's damp. Mice will eat them, given the chance."

Aria nodded again. "I will be fine, I think," she said. "If they're so afraid of me? I should not be afraid of them. Which house is ours?"

Rhexa gestured to the house at the end of the row. "This one. I hope you like it. Katrin and I put a lot of thought into making it just right." She opened the door and led them inside.

The front room was large and open, with low couches and tables that reminded Owyn a little of their front room in Three Northwest. There was a door off to the left, and a corridor right in front of them, through which Owyn could see a flight of stairs leading up.

"When we redesigned this house, we set this room up for entertaining," Rhexa said. "There's a dining room through that door—"

"And a kitchen?" Owyn interrupted.

"And a kitchen," Rhexa finished with a laugh. "The bedrooms are all upstairs, and the stairs are down that corridor. Which might not have been the smartest thing I've ever done. Aven, will you be able to manage stairs?"

"If I go slowly," Aven answered. "And Grandmother and Fa will work on this hip while we're here."

"That's good," Rhexa said. "Now, let me show you the upstairs, then there's food waiting in the healing center, in the large meeting room. Katrin and her staff have been cooking all day." She led them down the corridor, and Owyn caught a brief glimpse of the kitchen through a partially open door before they moved past it to the stairs.

Rhexa went up first, with Aria behind her. Aven followed Aria, climbing slowly, which meant that none of them could see what made Aria laugh out loud and exclaim, "Rhexa!"

"What?" Aven called. "What is it?"

"Nothing bad," Aria called back. "Come and see!"

Behind Aven, Owyn caught a whisper of his thoughts: "*Does she expect me to fly?*"

"I think she's just excited," Owyn whispered. "You know she doesn't mean any harm."

Aven looked over his shoulder, one brow raised. Then he grinned. "You heard me. I keep forgetting you can do that."

"I don't usually listen," Owyn admitted. "I mostly hear Del and Allie, and Allie doesn't make much sense because it's two voices at once." He looked up the stairs. "Want me to push?"

Aven laughed. "No, I do not want you to push!"

"How about support, then? It's wide enough." Owyn stepped up to stand next to Aven, and slid one arm around Aven's waist. "Lean on me. Let's go." They started back up the stairs, with Aven leaning heavily on Owyn's shoulder.

"Are you two all right up there?" Treesi called.

"We're fine," Owyn called back. "Just one step at a time."

There was no warning when Aven started laughing, and Owyn looked up at him curiously. Then he climbed up another step and could see the landing.

"No!" he gasped. "Wait a minute!" They climbed the last few stairs, and walked into their sitting room from the Palace. It was a smaller scale replica, but it was definitely supposed to be their sitting room. There were five doors off the room, each marked with the appropriate sigils.

Aven kissed Owyn's cheek, then limped over to join Aria. "Auntie, this...this is incredible!"

"Do you like it?" Rhexa asked. "We couldn't manage an exact match. The bathing room is downstairs, for example, and Aven's room doesn't have a salt water pool—"

"How did you know I have one?" Aven asked. He walked over to the door with the Water sigil and looked inside. "Rhexa, how did you manage this?"

"I had a lot of help," Rhexa admitted. "Or did you think all those letters back and forth between Steward and me were just flirting?"

Aria looked at Aven, then at Owyn. Behind them, someone snorted, which triggered the avalanche of laughter. Rhexa stared at them, then folded her arms over her chest.

"You thought...oh, for pity's sake!" She chuckled and shook her head.

"Auntie, seriously," Owyn sputtered. "You started us all off thinking it yourself!"

"How?" Rhexa asked.

"Your guest room," Owyn answered, wiping his eyes. "Remember? The one that you don't have?"

Rhexa frowned. "When did I say I had a...oh." She blushed. "I'd forgotten that. You all need to stop paying attention to my bedroom. Especially since that was someone else."

"True," Steward said from behind them. "Remember, Lady Rhexa and I have only just met." Owyn turned to see Steward's slow smile. "It would hardly be proper for me to stay in her guest room."

"Exactly," Rhexa said quickly. Too quickly, and when Owyn looked back at her, her face was flushed. "Now, this was a collaboration, and one that you helped with, Owyn."

"Me?" Owyn looked around. "Wait...Steward, that sketch you asked me for?"

"Steward, was this your idea?" Aria asked. "You knew that Three Northwest was going to be filled?"

Steward grinned. "I knew there was the possibility, yes," he admitted. "But the real seed of the idea came when Lady Rhexa—"

"Stop that. I'm not a lady!"

Steward continued as if he hadn't heard Rhexa. "— suggested that there should be proper apartments in Terraces for you all when you visited. Since you lived here for so long, she thought you'd want to come back and spend time when you could. And there's another building for the Firstborn."

"Which isn't quite finished yet, but will be when you come back after the Progress," Rhexa added.

"There aren't stairs in that one, are there?" Alanar asked. "That might be a problem."

Rhexa blinked. "Why?"

Owyn looked around, and Aria nodded. "Auntie, we've got a lot to tell you."

Rhexa immediately sobered. "You're going to eat first," she said. "We'll talk after. But first? Aria, go look in your room."

Aria looked around the sitting room, then went to the door marked with the Heir's sigil and opened it. "Mother of us all!" she breathed. "Oh, you all have to come see this!"

Owyn followed Aven to the door, hearing the others behind him. Aven burst out laughing, then backed out of the way so that Owyn could see in, and see the six-posted bed that took up most of the room.

"I've never seen a bed that big!" Owyn laughed. "Auntie—"

"I seem to remember someone saying that the big bed in Three Northwest wasn't quite big enough for everyone," Rhexa said. "So, I went to the carpenters and asked about a bed big enough for...I thought it was six, but it's it still?"

"We're at seven," Aven answered. "Othi asked Treesi to build a canoe."

"Really? Treesi?" Rhexa turned, looking for Treesi, then hurrying to hug the young healer. "Oh, I'm so happy for you!"

Treesi smiled. "Thank you. And this...thank you!" She turned. "Steward, do we have the room to have one of these in Aria's room at the Palace?"

Steward colored. "It was supposed to be a surprise for when we get back," he muttered. "They were supposed to start on it right after we left. And a matching cradle. So when we return, you all need to act surprised."

"By the time we get back, I think we'll all have forgotten," Alanar said. "So it will be a surprise." He turned, tipping his head to one side. "Wyn, I'll need to be led around for a day or so, until I know where the furniture is."

"Del or I can do that," Owyn said. He went to join his husband, and saw Del standing at the edge of the group. It was only then that he noticed that no one else had joined them. "Where are the others? Karse and Jehan and Mem and them?"

"Probably at the healing center by now," Rhexa answered. "Yours was the last coach to arrive. When the baggage carts got here, we moved all of your things into your rooms. When the others arrived...well, Aleia's been here, so she's been in the Senior Healer's apartments, and she took the others off when they got here, then they came back to meet you."

"Oh! If we're going off to dinner, do we need our fancy clothes?" Treesi asked. "Those are in our coach, aren't they?"

Othi nodded. "I saw them being loaded, while you were saying goodbye to Mother Danzi. I can go back for them, or we can send Trista."

"You won't need them tonight. The official welcome of the Heir is tomorrow," Rhexa said. "The dinner tonight is for family and friends. Which you have a lot of here." She looked around at them and smiled. "I missed you all so much."

Owyn grinned and went to his aunt, hugging her tightly. "We missed you, too. And...well, we'll talk after dinner."

DINNER WAS LOUD AND merry, and Del wasn't sure he'd ever been hugged or kissed quite so many times before. All the healing assistants and healers in training, Katrin and her assistants. People who did things in and around the healing center for Rhexa, who Del couldn't remember meeting, but who all called him by name and told him how happy they were to see him. It was daunting and overwhelming, and Del was happy when they finally took the stairs back up to the apartments.

"Who do you want to hear this discussion?" Aven asked Aria.

"Aunt Rhexa is, I think, the only one who does not know."

"No one else, then?" Aven looked around. "Not my parents, or Steward, or Karse?"

Aria tipped her head to the side, looking thoughtful. "I think our trusted ones. Jehan and Aleia. Memfis, Grandmother. Steward and Karse."

"Karse went to put the boys to sleep," Owyn called. "I can go see if he can come."

"Not by yourself you're not," Othi grumbled. "I'll go and collect people." He leaned down to kiss Treesi's cheek. "Mother Rhexa, which house?"

Rhexa pointed, watched Othi walk away, then turned to Owyn. "Why aren't you allowed to go off by yourself?" she asked softly.

"That's part of what we'll be telling you," Owyn answered, just as quietly. "Let's go inside."

They went into the Heir's house and sat down in the large sitting room. A few minutes later, someone knocked, and Jehan and Aleia came in.

"Othi said you wanted us?" Aleia asked.

"We're going to tell Rhexa what's been happening, and what we've learned," Aria answered. "We wanted you here for this."

A few minutes later, Memfis arrived with Meris on his arm. "Afansa is staying with the boys," he said. "Karse will be here in a moment. Steward was checking on Skela and Zarai, and Karse decided to wait for him. They'll be along as soon as he's done.

"Probably a wise move," Alanar said. "We haven't had a chance to officially announce the sentence. Or did you do it, Rhexa?"

"We spread the news when it arrived, but there have been newcomers since then, and some of them might not have heard. Probably best not to let him wander alone until we make it clear he's not who people think he might be."

Karse and Steward arrived a few minutes later, with Howl and Othi trailing behind them.

"I'm going to stand outside," Othi said. "Just in case." He stepped outside the door and closed it, and Del went to lean against the closed door. Karse smiled at him and nodded.

"Well, that reassures me not at all," Rhexa said. "What is happening?"

"Do you want bad, worse, or fuck all?" Owyn asked.

Rhexa's eyes widened. "Start at the bottom and work your way up to it."

Owyn nodded. "Work my way up, hm?"

"I cannot wait to see what order you put these in," Alanar said with a grin.

Owyn took Alanar's hand. "Bad. Risha has Trey. Worse. Someone is trying to kill me. Fuck all. Milon is alive. He's been alive all these years, and he's been prisoner in the Palace, right under the Usurper's nose. And now Risha has him, too." He looked at Alanar. "Match what you were thinking?"

"Actually, yes."

Rhexa stared at Owyn, looked around at the others, then turned back to him. "I...I don't know what to react to first. Milon is alive? And was a prisoner?"

"It appears it didn't start that way," Aria said. "They started out hiding him, to keep him safe from the Usurper. But it changed when they realized that he could no longer walk."

"Hence the problem with the stairs," Rhexa said softly. "We'll address that. And she has Trey now, too? How?"

"He went out following a lead on Risha, and his squad was wiped out. The only survivor other than Trey was Garrity, and he'll be coming here for treatment. He's...his wits are gone," Aven answered.

"And someone is trying to kill Owyn. Mother of us all, why?"

"No idea," Karse said. "But it isn't going to happen."

"It isn't Risha, is it?" Rhexa asked.

Karse shook his head. "I don't think so. She's got no reason to target him. But twice in two days—"

"Twice?" Aleia interrupted. "What did I miss?"

"Someone killed Lyka, just outside Shadow Cove, and tried to kill Owyn. But it was a bad shot."

"Bad only from their perspective," Owyn said. "I'm not complaining that it was a horrible shot."

"Aunt," Aria said quietly. "Not a word about this to anyone. We can't let anyone know that we have a traitor in the Progress—"

"Or bad things will happen." Rhexa nodded. "I understand. Are you sure it's someone in the Progress?"

Karse took something from his pouch and held it out. Del looked closer and saw it was a battered glove.

"Captain, where did you find that?" Aria asked.

"On top of the ridge over the road to Shadow Cove," Karse answered. "And I didn't tell you because I didn't have the secure space to do it." He turned the glove over in his hands. "It's from the

Palace uniform. It has the crest on it. Which means the traitor is one of the guard. I just don't know which one."

"But...." Owyn sat up straight. "But I know all of them! I've known some of them for years! Some of them were your men in Forge!"

Karse nodded. "I know." He sighed and leaned back in his chair, then grunted when Howl jumped into his lap. Rhexa smiled.

"I haven't met your friend yet," she said.

"This is Howl, and he's decided I'm a wolf pack leader in truth, and not just what the guards called me in Forge." Karse chuckled and steadied the puppy on his lap. "He's the one who found the glove. Also, he's the reason it has holes in it."

Aria laughed. Then she smiled. "Let him have it back," she said. "Let's see what happens when people see him carrying it around."

Karse studied her, then grinned. "See who makes a mistake?"

"Exactly."

Chapter Twenty-Nine

"I don't think Rhexa thought this through," Aven said as they gathered in the sitting room of the house the next morning. He was wearing his finery, as were the others. The ceremony to officially mark their visit to Terraces would begin when they arrived...on the lowest terrace.

"She had no way of knowing your hip was as bad as it is now," Alanar pointed out. "And there was no time to change the plans. We'll help you. You know we will."

"You're going to be at the back of the group with Othi," Aven said. "We set the precedent already. I'm in the front with Aria, Owyn has Del and Treesi behind us."

"So we can change it," Aria said as she moved to his side. "Have Treesi on your right so she can block the pain."

Aven nodded. "We may have to," he sighed. "We'll see how far I get on my own." He smiled and kissed Aria's forehead, then straightened the Diadem on her brow. "Are we ready?"

She nodded, and he held his hand out, palm down. She rested her hand on his, and they walked outside. Karse was waiting for them, with Danir and Copper and four of the guards. All of the guard were in dress uniforms, while the boys were dressed in page livery.

"You all look magnificent," Aria said.

"That's good," Karse grumbled. "I feel like this collar is strangling me. Wren, you and Tayki take the rear. Keelan, you and

Arco on the flanks. I've got point. Danir, you and Copper are in charge of keeping Howl from running off."

"He won't run off," Copper said. "He knows he's supposed to be with you. He'll be right next to you the entire way."

Karse nodded, and Aven could see him trying not to smile. "Then you two should be just behind me. Understand?"

Danir looked at Copper, then back at the two guards who had taken their positions. "Oh. We're the middle of the triangle legs. Copper, you're over there." He pointed, then he moved to stand behind Karse and to his left. "See?"

This time, Karse did grin. "Exactly. We'll make guards out of you two before we get back. Are we ready?"

"Just go slowly," Aven said. Karse nodded. He turned and started walking, and the procession followed him.

In the period when Aven had been a healer-in-training in Terraces, he had spent most of his waking hours in the healing center. In the month after he'd returned from the deep, he hadn't ventured outside a regular routine of going between their house at Three Northwest to the healing center.

He'd somehow managed to miss just how many stairs there were in Terraces. There were ramps around the edges of the terraces, normally for transporting goods. But the procession was supposed to travel down the four flights of stairs on the East road between the upper terraces and the healing center, go around the healing center, and continue down the West road to the lowest terrace, at the end of another three flights of stairs. And the road was lined on both sides with people, who clapped and cheered and waved and threw flowers. Aven forced a smile and leaned on his walking stick as they reached the bottom of the first flight of stairs down from the healing center.

"How much pain are you in?" Aria whispered, waving to the people on her side of the street.

"I don't think I ever realized how many stairs there were here," Aven whispered back. He turned to the side and nodded to the people there. He heard a shout behind him, and turned to see a child running toward them from Aria's side of the road. Karse stepped between Aria and the child, and the little girl stared up at him, then held up a flower. Karse chuckled and held out his hand.

"Come on, sweetheart," Aven heard him say, and he escorted the child to Aria, who took the drooping flower and tucked it into her hair. The girl laughed, darted in to hug Aria, then ran back to her red-faced mother. Karse smiled and turned to Aria.

"Shall we proceed?"

Aria laughed. "Whenever you're ready, Captain." She looked at Aven, and he leaned in to kiss her. A cheer went up around them, and Aven heard Owyn laughing behind them. Aven glanced back to see more children had gathered, and Owyn was kneeling with them, helping them to hand out flowers to Treesi and to Del.

"You're going to spoil all the children, aren't you?" Aria asked.

"Why not?" Owyn asked in response, looking up at her. "I never got spoiled. I have no idea what it's like. So why shouldn't I give our children what I never had?" He stood up and dusted off his knees, then shooed the children back to their parents before reaching over to do something to Del that made him laugh.

"*Are we going?*" Del signed. He grinned, and Aven saw the flower that Owyn had tucked behind his ear.

"Captain, shall we proceed?" Aria said, and they started walking again. Aven glanced at Aria, at the bright white flower against her dark hair, and almost forgot about the pain. She looked radiantly happy.

They continued down the rest of the stairs to the lowest terrace, where Aven could see a dais had been built. It faced the stairs, and there were five chairs on the dais, mirroring the arrangement in the Hall at the Palace.

"Just a bit more elaborate than Shadow or Serenity," he whispered.

"A bit, yes," Aria murmured. "But then, there are more people here, and they can do something like this. I can't think there will be anything more elaborate than this anywhere before the Solstice village."

"Oh, good."

He heard her laugh, and raised her hand to his lips before leading her to the dais and up the stairs to the central chair. He stepped back, bowed, and moved to the chair on her left, turning to see Owyn, Del and Treesi all bow. Del escorted Treesi to the chairs at Aria's right, while Owyn moved off to Aven's left. Aria looked to her right, then to her left.

"I am Aria, daughter of Milon and Liara. The Mother has chosen me as Heir to the Firstborn," she announced to the now-silent crowd

"Aven, son of Jehan and Aleia. I stand for the Water tribe."

Owyn's voice rang out. "Owyn Jaxis, son of Huris, Dyneh and Memfis. I speak for Fire."

"Treesi, daughter of Gisa and Elan. I am a healer, and I speak for the people of Earth."

Aven looked down the line of chairs and saw Del raise his hands. "Del," he translated the Water signs. "Son of Yana and Delandri. I am Air."

Aria looked to her left again, then her right. Then she sat down, spreading her wings to avoid the back of the chair. Once she was seated, the others took their seats.

The applause was deafening.

Aria smiled and held up her hand, waiting until the applause died away before asking, "Shall we begin?" She looked around, then nodded. "Rhexa, come forward, please."

Rhexa walked out of the crowd to stand in front of the dais. She bowed. "My Heir?"

"Rhexa, thank you. Please rise." Aria waited for Rhexa to straighten before asking, "You've been governing Terraces for how long?"

"A little over five years, I think," Rhexa answered.

Aria nodded. "And you've been doing so in the name of the Senior Healer this entire time, have you not?"

Rhexa looked mystified. "I have."

Aria looked at Aven, then past him. When Aven looked, Owyn was grinning from ear to ear. Aria smiled warmly, then turned back to Rhexa. "I realize that it has been tradition for the Chief Administrator to serve and support the Senior Healer. But times have changed, and the Senior Healer will be attending myself and my Companions while we are on Progress. And he will, I believe, be residing in the Palace after. I feel that having you act as a subordinate to the absent Senior Healer will hamper your abilities to properly care for the people of Terraces. I therefore formally recognize you, Rhexa, daughter of Jaxia, of the line of Mika, as Governor of Terraces. I empower you to hold and govern this city in my name, second to no one save the Firstborn. You may choose your councilors and your advisers as you see fit."

The crowd burst into cheers and applause. Rhexa stared at them, then gasped, "Really?" She turned and looked until she found Jehan in the crowd. "Senior Healer, did you know about this?"

Jehan shook his head as he walked toward her. "I had no idea. But it makes sense and I approve. You shouldn't be hampered in your duties." He turned to Aria. "My Heir, may I have the floor?"

"Senior Healer, of course you may," Aria answered. She glanced at Aven and arched a brow. Aven shook his head — he had no idea what his father was doing.

"My Heir, I'm claiming my right to name the healer who will succeed me as Senior Healer," Jehan answered, and Aven heard Owyn sputter.

"Are you?" Aria smiled. "Who, pray tell, do you name?"

"Well..." Jehan drawled. "Since you've claimed my son as your own, I name the son of my heart, Alanar, son of Dantris, to follow me as Senior Healer."

"You could have warned me!" Alanar called, coming forward. Laughter rippled through the crowd.

"Senior Healer," Aria announced. "I support and approve of this choice. I have every confidence in Alanar and his abilities as a healer." She smiled. "How he'll manage to be in two places at once, I'm not certain, but he and his husband, my Fire, will have time to answer that question." She nodded. "We acknowledge Alanar, son of Dantris, as heir to the title of Senior Healer. May that day be a long time coming."

"A very long time!" Alanar agreed.

Applause, which grew louder when Jehan stepped forward and embraced Alanar. Aven smiled, then turned to see Aria looking at him.

"Do you mind?" she whispered.

"I'm elated for him," Aven answered. "He deserves it."

Aria nodded. "Good." She faced forward. "Healer Pirit, come forward," she called.

Pirit came out of the crowd, taking Jehan and Alanar's place before the dais. She bowed slightly. "My Heir?" she asked as she straightened. One brow was quirked slightly, and Aven was amused to recognize the expression — he remembered seeing it as a child when he'd presented his father with a puzzle.

Aria nodded. "Pirit, you've served the Firstborn faithfully for a long time, have you not?"

"Since Tirine was Heir, my Heir," Pirit answered. "I served her, and I serve you." Her lips twitched. "I served your father, too, even through rumors of death."

Aven tried not to laugh as he looked sidelong at Aria. She was clearly biting her lip. On her other side, Del had ducked his chin, and Aven could see he, too, was trying not to laugh.

After a moment, Aria continued, "And I am asking you to continue to serve. While the Senior Healer attends the Progress, I request that you continue to serve and continue to teach. I would like for you to continue on as interim Senior Healer until such time as Senior Healer Jehan returns to Terraces."

Pirit snorted. "And that was a question that needed to be asked?" she said. "Of course I will!"

More applause and laughter, and Aria laughed with them. "I did have to ask, Healer Pirit. And I thank you," she said as the noise died away. "Now, attend, my people. There are things you must know. But first I should learn what you already know. Governor? What was announced here of the rulings made when we formally took our place in the Palace?"

Rhexa returned to the dais. "The sentence against the Usurper was announced, my Heir," she said. "And the sentence against the former Senior Healer Risha."

Aria nodded. "Very good. There have been no other rulings of impact. However, there has been a disturbing occurrence as we made our way here. Shadow Cove, to the north, was stricken with mountain fever. Our healers arrived in time to save them." She turned to look at Aven, who reached out and took her hand. "The headman of Shadow Cove told us that there were no travelers, no one from outside their community. The only possible source of the infection were two bodies that washed ashore. Bodies that bore the unmistakable marks of Risha's hand."

"She is no longer on the deep," Aven added. "Her ships were caught, and they were scuttled. She's gone to ground in the north, and we will find her."

Aria nodded. "But for now, be wary of any bodies that may come to shore. Do not approach them, or handle them in any way without a healer present." She looked out over the crowd. "I will not risk a single one of you to Risha's plots."

"Have the Water tribe been warned?" someone shouted.

"They have," Aleia called back, coming to stand with Rhexa. "I carried the news to the Clan Mother myself. Canoes were sent out onto the deep, to warn those who did not accompany us to serve the Heir. Water has done all that it can to protect our tribe. Now we warn the rest of the tribes."

"Thank you, War Leader," Aria said. "That is, I think, the last of the announcements that I have. Is there anyone who would speak with us? Who has questions, or concerns?"

"Who is that?" someone called. Aven saw someone he didn't recognize near the edge of the crowd. The young man was pointing at Steward.

Aria looked at Steward, then looked back at the people. "That is my Steward. Steward, attend."

Steward came forward. He bowed to Aria, then went to one knee in front of the dais. "My Heir."

Aria smiled, then looked over his head. "Steward has sworn himself to my service, and has proven himself to be loyal. He has become dear to myself and my Companions, and we consider him a part of our family." Her smile broadened, no doubt because of the blush creeping up Steward's throat. "He has...an unfortunate resemblance to one whose name has been forgotten."

"May I, my Heir?" Steward asked suddenly. Aria looked startled, then nodded. He rose, and turned to face the people.

"I know who you think I am. That one is gone, and his name is forgotten. And good riddance to him. He was...not evil. Not truly. But he was not a good man, either. He was...misguided, and blinded by his own misconceptions. I've read the records he left behind, and he did try. But trying to put the pieces back together doesn't count when your choices have left things irrevocably broken." He swallowed. "He was condemned, and he's gone. The Mother will never recognize him as Her own." He paused, then he looked back at Aria and smiled. "As for me? I have hopes that perhaps someday She'll see me, and know me. That I'll deserve Her gaze, and Her recognition. But until that day, I will serve my Heir, and I will serve my Firstborn, and I will serve the Companions who call me Uncle, and I will serve their children. And I am content with that lot." He held his arms out to the sides. "Does that answer the question?"

The young man stared, then stammered, "I...yes. Yes, it does." He came closer, moving out of the crowd and toward Steward, studying him. Aven tensed, saw Owyn lean forward slightly.

"My name is Kelin," he said. "I'm a tunnel guard. And I met him once. Before. I was the tunnel guard that brought him through, when he got here, dragging a half-dead man on a drawsledge—"

"Me," Memfis called. "That was me. He could have left me for dead. He didn't."

Kelin nodded. "I didn't even recognize him. I had no idea it was him. When my mates told me, you could have dropped me with a tap, I was that surprised." He frowned, clearly thinking about his words. "If someone like that...could change so much that he'd drag a man to safety over days and miles...then I think the Mother will have no trouble finding you when the time comes." He grinned. "A long, long time from now." He held one hand out. "It's a pleasure to meet you, Steward."

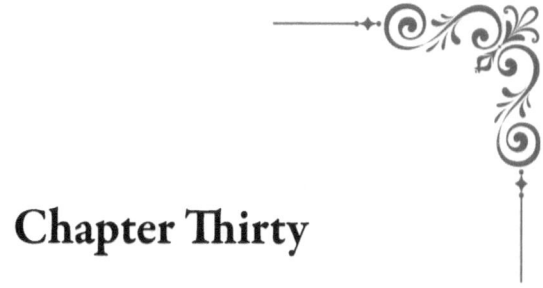

Chapter Thirty

There were more questions. How would things change? What was Aria going to do about the famines? About the drought? About the refugees?

"It's like this," a young woman said. "We're grateful to the Earth folk for taking us in, make no mistake. But we don't belong here. Our place is down around the Smoking Mountain. How do we go home? And when?"

"Aria, can I take this one?" Owyn asked, leaning forward in his chair.

"Please, my Fire," Aria answered.

Owyn smiled and stood up. "What's your name?" he asked the woman.

"Varity, Fireborn."

Owyn walked to the edge of the dais in front of Varity, and crouched down to put himself on her eye level. "Want to go home, hm?" he asked gently.

She blushed. "Yes, Fireborn."

Owyn sighed. "I know. I'd have liked to have seen Forge one more time before I died." A ripple of laughter, and he clearly heard Treesi groan from the other side of the dais. "Part of the problem of sending everyone home is that there's no home to go to anymore. And we don't know what's there. We're not sending anyone back south until we know it's safe. No one is going to die because we rushed to send you all back before we know what's there." He looked out at the crowd. "One of the things we'll be doing before we leave here is comparing our maps to the ones I know Admin...Governor Rhexa has been making." He looked around, saw Rhexa nodding, then looked back at Varity. "Then we're going to go south ourselves. And we'll see what we find. There will be a new Forge someday. I promise you that. But I can't tell you when. Not until I see what things look like around the Smoking..." He paused. "Auntie, is it still a mountain? Or is it a pile of rock that used to be a mountain?"

"It's a much shorter mountain," Rhexa answered, clearly amused. "Or so I'm told."

Owyn nodded. "Right. We need to see what it looks like around the Smoking Not-quite-a-mountain-anymore."

More laughter, and Varity smiled. "That makes sense. Forge won't be where it was, will it?"

"Probably not, no," Owyn answered, shaking his head. "But someday, maybe we'll be able to dig down to Forge that was, and find the things that survived." He held his hand out to her. "Is that a good enough answer?"

She took his hand and squeezed it. "It's a good answer. Thank you."

Owyn smiled. He raised her hand to his lips and kissed her fingers, then let her go and stood up. There was a smattering of applause as he turned back toward his chair. Then he heard a shout, and turned to see a man rushing out of the crowd toward the dais. Owyn realized what he'd shouted — *Death to the False Heir!* — just as he realized that the man had a raised knife. Aven lurched out of his chair, but he had only his cane...

The man jerked as a pair of throwing spikes blossomed in his chest. He stumbled back a step, then growled and started forward again, only to stop and fall backwards as a knife hit him. Owyn looked over to see Del standing in front of Aria. He lowered the throwing knife he had raised to throw and looked back over his shoulder.

"Captain, if you please?" Aria called.

Karse stalked forward, nodded toward the dais, then looked around. "Captain Leesam, this is your jurisdiction. Mind if I help?"

"Not at all, Captain," Leesam answered as he came forward. He bowed deeply to Aria. "My Heir, I apologize. We didn't even have a breath of warning there was anything like this in Terraces."

"Later, Lee," Karse growled. "Grovel later."

"Right." Leesam nodded, then looked at the dais. "I'll come by later to grovel, if that's all right?"

"I'm interested in what you find between now and then," Aria answered. "It might shorten your grovel."

Leesam bowed, then he and Karse picked the attacker up and took away; the crowd parted before them, as if they were afraid that being too close would incriminate them in the attempted assassination. Del stepped back toward his chair, but Aria stood where she was and looked out over the crowd.

"Is there anyone else who thinks I am false?" she asked. "Anyone who thinks that I am not the chosen of the Mother?" There was no answer, no sound except for the wind and the distant rush and fill of the waves on the rocks below. Aria waited, then nodded. "Governor, I would know if there are others," she added. "Who is this man? When did he come here, and who came with him?"

"I'll have all of that by evening," Rhexa said. "Aria, I'm so sorry. Lee is right — there wasn't even a hint of any kind of insurrection!"

Aria smiled. "I believe you, Auntie. I know you would not risk our lives. We've had enough of that. But the question must be asked, and it must be answered." She looked to her right, and smiled, holding her hand out to Del. "My Air."

Del smiled and sheathed his knife, reaching out to take her hand. He moved close to kiss her on the cheek. Then he kissed her lips and stepped back as Aven joined them.

"Aria?" Aven asked as Owyn and Treesi closed the circle around Aria.

"I'm fine, my Water," Aria said. "Surprised. I hadn't expected something like that here."

Aven nodded. "I think the ceremony is over," he said.

"No," Aria said. "Not like this. Go and sit." She looked at them all and smiled. "I am fine. Go back to your seats."

Aven growled softly, then looked surprised when Aria growled back. They stared at each other, then he laughed and leaned down to share breath with Aria.

"Yes, my Heir," he murmured.

"You only get to call me my Heir if you follow it with a kiss," Aria whispered back. Aven laughed again and kissed her.

"That true for all of us, my Heir?" Owyn asked. Aria giggled, and Aven stepped back and let Owyn take his place. There was heat in Aria's kiss, and a promise of things that they'd missed in the camp outside Shadow Cove.

"We have a real bed here," Owyn whispered to her.

"We do," she agreed. "And no interruptions?"

"From your mouth..." Owyn muttered, and let Treesi take his place. He went back to his chair, and stood there until Treesi surrendered her place to Del, who kissed Aria once more and returned to his seat. Aria looked out over the crowd, then sat down again, her Companions taking their seats a moment after.

"Now, are there any other questions?" Aria asked.

"My Heir?" A young woman came forward hesitantly. "Have you heard of the Seer?"

Aria looked stunned. "Yes. On the road here, we met a family who spoke of the Seer. They were sent west, they told us."

The young woman nodded. "Same as me, I conjure. There was a dozen of us, all girls. Our area, there was too many girls, not enough men. Seer said we'd find men to our liking if we came west to the hidden city. And if we came west, then we'd have a chance for a place of our own."

Rhexa walked over to join the young woman. "Tara is one of the group we'll be sending to repopulate Cliffside," she said. "I was hoping they could ride out with you when you left, but I thought we'd discuss it tomorrow."

"Cliffside was a good place," Aven said. "What little I saw of it, anyway. I was there once, on a market day."

"It was a good place," Treesi agreed. "I used to go to the market there every once in a while."

"Just watch out for snakes," Memfis muttered. "They're mean in Cliffside."

Owyn winced, and looked back at Tara and his aunt. Rhexa was looking at Tara, and her voice spiraled up as she asked, "There was something you didn't tell me?"

Tara nodded. "A message. He asked me to pass it on when I saw the Heir. I thought he was teasing. When was I going to see the Heir? But he's never wrong." She looked up at Aria. "He says he'll meet you when the crossroads come. I'm not sure what that means, but he's never wrong."

Aria nodded. "And where is that? When the crossroads come?"

"I don't know, my Heir. He's Wanderer stock. They never stay long in a place," Tara said. "I don't know where he's from. Where he was when he told me that? It was in Hanging Rock. But he went with us to Crystal Springs after, and then went south. He might be south still. I don't know. He don't stay in one place for long."

Aria nodded slowly, a distant look in her eyes. "Thank you, Tara. I look forward to meeting him."

"WANDERERS?" ARIA ASKED. They had returned to the house and changed, and were sitting in the large front room. For the moment, it was just Aria and her Companions, with Alanar and Othi, but she didn't expect that to last for long. "Who are the Wanderers? Why have I never heard of them before?"

"Because there aren't many of them, and they don't stay in one place," Treesi answered. She settled onto a couch with Othi and leaned into his side, smiling as he put his arm around her. "They migrate like birds, and you can't ever count them. They won't stand for that. They keep to themselves. I'm not sure how much is really known about them outside the mountains." She gestured with one hand. "They're usually east, usually in the foothills, but sometimes up higher in the mountains. We only ever had dealings with them when they needed a healer and didn't have one of their own."

"Who trains their healers?" Aven asked. He settled slowly onto a couch next to Aria, wincing. As he sat, Alanar groaned.

"If it's that bad, maybe we should start work on the reshaping now," he said. "I felt that."

"I think every healer on this level felt that," Treesi said. "And to answer the question, I know that there were Wanderer healers, but I'm not sure who trained them. My mother's mother was a Wanderer, I was told. But in the mountains, sometimes people claimed Wanderer blood even if they didn't really have it. It's something romantic."

"It sounds perfectly normal to me," Othi said. "Sounds like they move around the way the canoes do. Just...on land."

"Canoes on land?" Owyn asked as he came back into the front room. He'd insisted on exploring the kitchen when they'd returned to the house, and had a laden tray in his hands. "Tea and nibbles. There were baskets in the kitchen, and Katrin left a note. Everything was sealed, so it's safe." He set the tray down on a low table, and started pouring tea. "So, what's this about canoes on land?"

"Wanderers," Treesi answered. "Have you heard of them?"

"Stories," Owyn answered, handing a teacup to Aria. "And I've seen their carts. They're interesting — little houses on wheels." He handed another cup to Aven, then stopped. "I suppose they are canoes on land, if you look at it from the right angle."

"And with your eyes closed?" Othi asked. Owyn mock-scowled at him, then grinned.

"What nibble food, Wyn?" Alanar asked. "I'm hungry."

"Katrin's spiced tear-nuts. Cheese. That hard sausage you like. Twice-baked bread rounds with blackseeds. Apple compote."

"Yes, please. All of it."

Plates were filled, and were on their way to being empty before someone knocked on the door. Del was closest, so he went and unbarred it, letting in Steward, Rhexa, Memfis and Aleia.

"Come in," Aria said. "Sit. There is tea, and food. I hope you have some news to share?"

"Karse and Leesam will be along shortly," Rhexa said, sitting down on one of the single chairs. "Karse said he'll make an official report, but he didn't mind me telling you what we know. That man...His name is Lear, and he arrived alone. He told us that he came from Forge, and that he'd been a smith's apprentice. He was assigned a small house near the far end of North, and he worked with Persis. It turned out he wasn't really a smith's apprentice, and Persis turned him out before he hurt himself. He was reassigned to the stables." She frowned. "Lee says there were complaints about him shirking his duties. They've gone to search his house and see what else they can find."

"What's going to be done with him?" Owyn asked.

"He attempted to assassinate the Heir," Steward said. "Under Fire tribe law, that's life imprisonment in the mines. Which aren't there anymore. Earth tribe...Jehan, what are the Earth tribe laws on this? I can't remember."

Jehan sniffed. "You forgot? Really?" He closed his eyes for a moment, then shook his head. "Earth tribe has laws against murder and attempted murder, but nothing specifically against attempted assassination of the Heir. Apparently, it never occurred to us that someone would actually think of trying something like that."

"So what's the penalty for attempted murder?" Aria asked. When Jehan looked at her, she felt her face grow warm. "I'm still learning."

"That's fine," Jehan assured her. "You've been formally recognized as Heir for...what? Two months? You have a lot of education to catch up on. But this one, you should remember, because you just saw it recently. Banishment."

"Oh, right. That's what was done with that idiot who tried to kill Del!" Owyn said. "Do we really want to do that with this one? I mean...banishing him from Terraces means he could very well follow the Progress and try again."

"Which doesn't seem like a good idea at all," Aven agreed. "Are there any alternatives?"

Someone knocked, and Steward went to the door and opened it, letting Karse and Leesam in.

"Before anyone asks," Karse said. "Lady Meris has Howl and the boys, and she's taking them all to visit the children in the healing center. Rhexa, you told them?"

"I just finished," Rhexa said. "Did you find anything at Lear's home?"

"Paradise flower," Karse answered. "Based on how young the plants are, he must have carried the seeds in with him. They were growing behind the house—"

"I've told Pirit, and she'll bring them to the healer's garden," Leesam added.

Karse nodded. "There were full grown leaves soaking in tincture in vats in the house. We think he was getting the older plants in through the stables, but he's not talking."

"I can truth-tell him, if you want?" Alanar offered.

"I don't want," Karse answered. "I am not putting any of you near him. He's crackpot. Says there's no way Aria can be Heir. Says she's not real."

"He's one of Risha's?" Aven asked.

"Nah, it's weirder than that. I asked him what he meant by that, and he was more than happy to try and convince me. It's not because Aria is Air. It's because she's here. He's convinced that the Mother has turned on us, and that there's never going to be an Heir again. Never going to be a Firstborn again. He says that the Mother is gone, and we've all been abandoned, and that's why Forge is gone, and the reason for the famines, and everything that's gone wrong with the world right down to my sore feet. And, since the Mother is gone, Aria can't be the real Heir. See? Crackpot." He sat down next to Jehan. "Oh, and for the record, he didn't follow that other one either. Spat when we asked him that, on account that it was the Usurper's doing that the Mother abandoned us."

"That, I think, gives us an answer as to what to do with him, then," Aria said slowly. "Does it not, Senior Healer? If he is delusional, and a danger to others? Should he not be confined until he is well enough to be released?"

Jehan looked thoughtful, then nodded. "That seems the best course," he agreed. "I'll come and examine him, get a proper diagnosis. No...no, I'll ask my mother to do it. She's had more experience, and she's unbiased."

"Are any of us unbiased where Aria is concerned?" Leesam asked.

Karse snorted. "Truth." He rubbed his hand over his face. "I wonder if there are others out there like him?"

"Probably," Owyn answered. He leaned against Alanar's side, sighing as Alanar put his arm around him. "We just need to educate them. A lot."

"With a club, if necessary," Othi grumbled. "My grandmother used to say some folks need their heads knocked open to let the sense in."

"That's about the only thing Grandmother said that I'd agree with," Aven said. "Aria, how are you feeling?"

"Now that it's over? Tired," Aria answered. She leaned against him and fought the urge to yawn. "I wouldn't mind more tea. And then, perhaps, I'll go and lay down. What do we have next?"

"Nothing before tomorrow," Rhexa answered. "I thought you would want some peace and quiet after the ceremony. Tomorrow, I'll escort you down to the healing center, and you can meet the new healers-in-training and visit the children—"

"And read *The Stars Dance*," Owyn interrupted.

"And I think Katrin has a small something planned at her house," Rhexa added. "That's after midday."

"And tomorrow, I'm taking Aven for a day or two," Jehan added. "We're going to rebuild that hip. Alanar, I want to discuss this with you."

"Rebuild?" Aven repeated. "What do you mean rebuild?"

"It's your grandmother's idea, based on the brief examination she had of you at Shadow Cove. We'll examine you again in the morning to confirm her theory, but she thinks the best approach may be to put you into deep trance and shatter your hip so that we can rebuild it completely."

Aven coughed, and Aria felt him tense. "I...Fa? Is that...can you *do* that?"

"Of course we can do it," Jehan answered. "The question is will it work? And we won't know that until we try it." He shrugged. "It's a gamble. But if it pays off, you'll have two good legs again, and no pain in your change. If it doesn't? You won't be any worse off than you are now."

Aven shivered, and Aria looked up at him. He looked slightly green. "Aven, you don't have to do this," she whispered. "They can do something else. Something to better control the pain, or—"

"No," he said softly. "I...Aria, I need to be able to move. We're leaving the last safe place in a few days, and it wasn't even completely safe here! I didn't carry my swords today and I should have. But even if I had them, I wouldn't have been fast enough to stop that man. If it hadn't been for Del. Again." He paused, then swallowed. "I need to be able to move freely, and without pain. I need to be able to fight, and I need to be faster. Things are only going to get worse once we leave here. I have to be able to take care of you. Which means..." He straightened and looked at Jehan. "When?"

"I'll come get you at first light."

Chapter Thirty-One

Del woke the next morning to find the upstairs rooms empty. He pulled a robe on, picked up his tablet, and wandered down the stairs to look for the others. Had he slept so late that they'd all gone out without him? Maybe there was a note. He came down the corridor to find Aria in the front room, standing near the window and sipping a cup of tea. Del stopped and studied her for a moment. Normally, when Aria stood at a window, she stood in the center, as if she was going to step out and fly away. Today, she was off to the side, where no one could see her from outside. She looked over at him and smiled, then turned back to the window.

"Do not lecture," she said. "I am not a target if I stand this far over."

Oh. That explained it. Del grinned and scrawled, "*If I lecture, it'll either take all day or more paper than we have. Who lectured you?*"

Aria read the tablet, smiled, then answered, "Aven, before he left with the other healers. And Owyn, before he and Othi went off to get supplies so that Owyn can cook." She smiled. "I do not think Owyn heard Aven, but they said exactly the same things. They even paused to breathe in the same places. I was tempted to laugh, but Owyn wouldn't have understood and it would hurt him."

Del nodded and moved to stand next to her. When he looked out the window, he understood why she'd picked this spot, this window. She could see out, but there was no clear vantage point where someone could see her, and nowhere in range for an archer to have unimpeded aim without being seen. She looked at him, then laughed.

"Do you see why I chose to stand here?"

Del nodded. He wiped the tablet and wrote, "*You said Aven was gone. I missed him?*"

"Jehan came and got all the healers just at dawn," Aria answered. "Pirit was waiting for them at the healing center. Jehan said they would be working in teams, so that someone would still be available to work the rounds with the new healers."

"*Are they expecting it to take that long?*"

Aria nodded. "I think they are, yes. And I think they started so early so that Aven didn't have a chance to think too much about it. Not that he slept much last night."

Del grimaced. "*You should go back to bed.*"

"Now you're repeating what they said," Aria laughed. "I will take a nap later. For now, I am hungry, and Owyn wants to cook." She turned back to the window. "There they are."

Del nodded and went to the door, holding it open for Owyn and Othi, who were both carrying large baskets.

"Thank you," Othi said as he came in. "Owyn, where should I take this?"

"The kitchen is to the left," Owyn said, following Othi inside. "Good morning, Del."

"*Good morning,*" Del signed as he closed the door. Owyn wasn't looking at him, but he nodded to show he'd heard. "*Can I help with anything?*"

"I'll yell if I need you, but this morning, I'm teaching Othi to cook," Owyn said.

"I should learn," Othi added. "I just...cooking with fire? You know that's not something we do."

"And I think Treesi will appreciate that you're willing to do so," Aria said. Othi grinned.

"And breakfasts are easy," Owyn added. "We'll start there, and work our way up."

Del looked at the baskets. *"Do you have time to make bread?"*

Owyn shook his head. "No. We're not going to be here long enough for me to get a starter going. Katrin sent a few loaves of her seed bread, and maybe I'll get some beaten biscuits made for tomorrow. I don't think I'll be making more than breakfast for us." He looked at Del. "If you want to help, you should go get ready for the day. Go wash up, and meet us in the kitchen."

OTHI WATCHED AS DEL left the front room, then carried his basket into the kitchen. Owyn followed, wondering what was wrong. The big man was unusually silent.

"You can hear him, Treesi said," Othi said in a quiet voice. He put his basket down. "You can hear him in your head. How?"

Owyn put his basket next to Othi's. "I didn't realize you missed that. I thought you knew."

Othi shrugged. "I missed a lot when we were out on the deep hunting Risha's ships. So...how do you do it?" He took a jar out of the basket. "And where do these go?"

Owyn chuckled and took the jar. "Start handing me things. I'll tell you what they are and where they go. Then you can help me make something for us to eat." He looked at the jar, then set it on the counter. "This is porridge oats. We'll use this. And why I can hear Del? You know I'm a Smoke Dancer. You've seen me dance for visions." He waited until Othi nodded. "Well, apparently dying and coming back woke something else up in me, and I have what are called heart visions. I can hear people, and it's not just Del." He turned and took another jar from Othi, then nodded toward the basket. "Put the bread on the table. Let's see...I can hear Allie and Aven and Del and Trey and Treesi."

"You can't hear Aria?"

"We're working on that." Owyn put the jar in a cabinet. "We...well, last winter was hard on all of us. And she and I...we're still making things right between us."

"And when we do, Owyn will be able to hear me," Aria said from the doorway. "And when it is finally right, and we find that he still cannot hear me? It will not matter. Because I know he still loves me. And he knows that I still love him."

Owyn turned to face her. "How long have you been standing there?"

Aria smiled. "I came in after you told Othi to put the bread on the table. You had your back to me."

Owyn nodded. "I'll get the porridge started. Othi, there should be a jar of preserves in there. Katrin said she'd sent some. Cut some of the bread for Aria, will you?"

"I'm not entirely sure what you mean," Othi said, starting to take things out of the basket. "With anything. Can anyone do these heart vision things?"

"I don't think so," Owyn said. He held one hand over the stove, frowned, and picked up a towel to open the firebox. He laid another log in the box, then closed it up again. "I can't do it with everyone. Just the people I really love. Seems to be just people I love enough to sleep with. Which might be why I can't with Aria yet, since we haven't. But I can with Del, and we haven't either."

"You know I didn't need to know that, right?" Othi asked.

"Sorry. I never did learn what the difference is between far enough and way too far when it comes to talking about sex." Owyn turned to the pump, started to prime it. "Anyhow, Granna Meris isn't entirely sure why I can, and why it's...well, why it's just those people," he added as he filled a pot with water. He set the pot in place on top of the firebox, then turned to face them. "Look, I didn't ask to be strange—"

"Owyn, no one said you were strange!" Aria protested. "And I would not change a hair on your head. You are my Owyn, and I love you."

Othi cleared his throat, and Owyn and Aria both turned to look at him. He blushed. "Del knows what to do in here, doesn't he?" he asked.

"What, make breakfast?" Owyn asked. "Yeah, he knows how. Why...oh." He looked at Aria. "I...oh." He looked at Aria, found her studying him. Smiling. She held her hand out.

"I..." Owyn stammered. "I...ah...you have places to be. And you need to eat—" He looked at Othi, then bit his lip. He closed his eyes and heard only his own blood rushing in his ears.

That made the decision.

"Remind Del not to let it boil," he said, catching Aria's hand. "If it boils, it'll burn." He led her toward the door, hearing her laughter.

"I'll tell him," Othi called after them. And Owyn forgot about breakfast, forgot about the plans for the day, the worries of the Progress and who was trying to kill him. At this moment, his only thoughts were of getting up the stairs, and getting out of his clothes. Getting Aria out of her clothes. Getting them both into a bed, and he didn't much care whose bed it was. Whichever one was closest to the top of the stairs...

They were halfway up the stairs when Owyn heard the door open behind them, and heard Steward's voice, "Good morning!"

"In the kitchen," Othi called.

"I wanted to talk with Aria—"

Aria stopped. "I—"

Owyn met her eyes and shook his head. "You have a meeting," he hissed.

"I...oh, yes. I'm sorry, Steward. It will have to wait. I have a meeting."

Steward came to the foot of the stairs. "A meeting?"

Aria nodded. "A private meeting. I'll be free in...an hour?" She looked up at Owyn. "An hour?"

"Maybe," Owyn answered. "Maybe two. Depends on how many things we need to go over." He tugged her up a step. "And we might need to...revisit a few of them. Just to be certain. So we'll see you later."

Steward came to the bottom step and looked up at them, and puzzlement suddenly shifted to understanding. "Oh. Of course. I'll go and visit with Othi. Is Del around?"

"He's washing up," Othi said. "Then he's going to help me cook breakfast without burning it."

Steward turned to look at Othi. "Do you know how to cook?"

"No. Del is going to teach me," Othi answered. He laughed. "He doesn't know that yet, though."

"Right. Why don't I start teaching you?" Steward looked up at Owyn and Aria. "Have a good meeting."

Owyn coughed, feeling a tickle in his throat. It might have been a laugh, and if he started laughing now, he wasn't going to stop. So he turned and tugged Aria up the rest of the stairs and into the sitting room. The door closed, and she was in his arms. The fire that had been banked when they'd been interrupted in the tent outside Shadow Cove roared back to life, and Owyn had to force himself to think.

"Which room?" he asked against her lips. "Yours or mine?"

"Whichever is closer," she answered, starting to fumble with the buttons on his shirt.

"Right. Mine." Owyn swallowed, then stooped and scooped her up in his arms. She gasped, then giggled and twined her arms around his neck.

"I forget how strong you are," she whispered in his ear as he headed toward his door. Halfway there, he remembered something, and changed direction.

"Where are you going?" she asked.

"Your room. I want the big bed," Owyn answered. "I'm going to make you happy over every blasted inch of it. Twice."

She hummed. "Only twice?"

He groaned. "Woman, you're going to be the death of me." He had to wait for her to open the door, then he kicked it closed behind him and settled her onto the edge of the bed. She smiled up at him.

"Now what?" she asked.

He grinned at her and stripped his shirt off. "Now? I told you. Every blasted inch of the bed. When we're done, you're going to want that nap after all."

ARIA WASN'T THE ONLY one who wanted a nap.

And she wasn't the only one who'd been happy over every inch of the bed.

Twice.

Owyn drowsed, her warm weight covering him, her feathers brushing against his skin. The feeling made him smile; somewhere in the middle of everything, he'd used some of her shed feathers to tease her into a frenzy. Apparently none of the others had ever considered feathers as something to use in the bedroom, and it was a lesson she'd learned with enthusiasm, proving her mastery almost immediately.

He could feel her sleepy contentment, and was perfectly willing to let it lull him into sleep. But they had places to be and things to do. And he was hungry.

As if on cue, his stomach growled. Aria jumped at the sound, and raised her head to look at him. She looked surprised for a moment, then smiled.

"For a moment, I thought I'd dreamed it again," she murmured, and stretched up to kiss him. "Was that worth the waiting, my Owyn?"

"Was it worth..." Owyn repeated. He laughed. "Worth every minute of it. Now, you tell me. Again? You were dreaming about me? Did I live up to expectations?"

She rested her head on his chest. "Yes. And I think I didn't know enough to have the right expectations. You know more about what to do in bed than I do."

"I think I might have all of you beat there, and that includes Treesi and Alanar," Owyn said. He shifted, resting his hand on the small of her back. "Not as much with women as with men, but yeah, I know a bit more." He took a deep breath, let it out, feeling a distinct lack of tension that he hadn't realized he'd been holding on to.

"Can you hear me now, my Owyn?" Aria asked softly. "Are we whole?"

"I..." Owyn stopped. Frowned. He could feel her, the same way he could feel the others when they were feeling something strongly. He could feel her pleasure, and the sleepy satiation. Feel her curiosity, and her worry. But he couldn't hear words. "I...it's different. This is new. I'm feeling what you're feeling," he answered. "But I'm not hearing your thoughts. I wonder...you're the first one since I retested and since Granna said something settled. Maybe I'm not going to be able to?" He met her eyes, and saw reflected in them the disappointment he could feel radiating from her. "I'm sorry."

"You don't need to apologize. I meant what I said before," she said. "I love you. That hasn't changed." She paused, then smiled. "Owyn, I decided something."

He forced a smile. "When? Before the feathers or after?"

She giggled. "No, not today. Days ago. After we found you in Shadow Cove." She took his hand, brought it to rest on the curve of her belly. "I want my next baby to be yours."

Owyn's mind froze. He raised his head and stared at her, then felt the baby move under his hand. "I...really?" He swallowed. "A little baby Owyn? Wouldn't that be something?"

Aria smiled. "Can you imagine a baby Owyn with wings?"

Owyn blinked. "I...yeah, they might have those, wouldn't they? And they might be a Smoke Dancer!" He fell back into the bed. "How much trouble do you think he'll be? She'll be? Ummm...they'll be?"

Aria giggled and put her head back on his chest. "They'll be wonderful."

"Well, of course they'll be wonderful," Owyn scoffed, running his hand over her back. "They'll have you as a mother. They can't help but be wonderful."

Aria raised her head and smiled, then stretched out over him and kissed him. Owyn wrapped his arms around her and reveled in the warmth of her body, her slight weight pressing him into the mattress. He closed his eyes, considered sleep, then sighed.

"We should get up."

Aria groaned. "We should. Even though I would much rather have that nap now."

Owyn trailed his fingers up her spine. "Sleep? Or food?" he asked, and heard Aria's stomach rumble. "Well, that answers that. Let's get you fed."

They got up, hunting around the room until they found all of their scattered clothes. Then Owyn slipped out to his own room to wash up at the basin and dress. Aria was waiting for him in the little sitting room when he came out.

"Something smells odd," she said. "It does not smell like food."

Owyn sniffed. "That's not porridge. What did they do?" He led the way down to the stairs. The kitchen was empty, and the smell stronger. He wasn't sure what it actually was. And there were no pots on the stove.

"They're in here," Aria called. Owyn followed her voice down the corridor and into the dining room that he hadn't yet seen. Othi, Steward and Del were sitting at one end of the long table, not saying anything. Del had his head down on his clasped hands. Steward looked up as Owyn and Aria came in, then immediately looked down.

"Did you...ah...have a good meeting?" he asked, his face turning red.

Aria glanced at Owyn, then folded her arms. "It was very productive. But I am confused. What happened to breakfast? What are we smelling?"

"I...burned the porridge oats," Othi said. He shifted in his chair, making it creak alarmingly. "I didn't pay attention to what Del was telling me to do, and I thought I could fix it, and I put in...something." He looked at Del. "Del, what did I put in?"

Del raised his head, scowling at Othi as he lifted his hands. "*He threw a jar of wine-soaked cherries into the pot. And the wine caught fire. I don't even know how, but it did. And he grabbed the ash bucket because he thought it had water in it.*"

"It put the fire out!" Othi protested.

"*And it ruined the disaster!*" Del signed back, making Steward snort.

"We cleaned up," Steward said. "And the pot is soaking in the scullery—"

"We have one of those?" Owyn interrupted.

"And we boiled eggs, and brought the bread and preserves out here, away from the smell. There's still tea, but it's cold. I can make a fresh pot."

"That won't be necessary," Aria said, sitting down. "Cold tea is fine. Boiled eggs are fine. Othi, thank you for trying."

Othi looked down. "Can we...not mention this to Treesi?" he asked softly. "Del, I'm sorry. I should have listened to you."

Del snorted. Then he reached over to slap Othi on the back of the head.

"Del!" Steward gasped. To Owyn's surprise, Othi just laughed.

"No, he knows what he's doing. He learned that from Neera, who learned it from our grandmother. I said it last night, remember? Some people have no sense unless their heads are knocked open?" He looked over at Del and grinned. "I've got no sense, hm?"

"None," Del answered, his voice clear.

"Well, we'll work on it," Owyn said. "Now pass the bread. We're hungry."

Chapter Thirty-Two

"Othi needs a horse," Owyn said as he finished his tea. "And trousers, and boots. I can take him to the dispensary once we're done here."

Silence, as everyone turned to stare at him.

"A...a horse?" Othi stammered. "Owyn, I'm not sure—"

"I know we talked about this," Owyn interrupted. "We have to follow the set route of the Progress. Which means going to Forge, or as close as we can get. We can't do that in coaches, so we're going to have to go on horseback. Now, you don't have to go. You can stay with the coaches. But I thought you'd want to stay with Treesi. She has to make the trip."

Othi nodded slowly. "We did talk about this in the coach. I remember. I just...I don't know how to ride."

"We can teach you that," Steward said.

"Aven learned. You can ask him about it, when they're done with him." Owyn reached over and picked up another egg. "He learned early that it takes skill he don't have to sleep in the saddle."

Aria laughed. "I'd nearly forgotten that. He was all purple the next day."

"Not that it stopped him at all," Owyn said, nodding. He bit into his egg, chewed, and swallowed.

"Treesi couldn't do anything for him?" Steward asked.

"That was right before we met Treesi," Owyn answered. "A few days before. And then we were running for our lives from the guards that we thought were the Usurper's, and he almost got killed." He shook his head and finished his egg. "You know, it's weird. We were running for our lives, but it was...I dunno, simpler?"

"Less complicated," Aria agreed. "But that may have been because we had no idea how complicated things really were. There is peace in ignorance, after all."

Othi nodded slowly. "So...no chance of me staying ignorant, hm?" he asked. "And not learning to ride?"

"Not if you want to stay with Treesi," Owyn answered.

Othi nodded. "All right. What do I need to do?"

"You might be getting ahead of yourself, Owyn," Steward said. "A horse to carry Othi is going to need to be big. The sort of horse they use for hauling ore in the mines around Forge." He glanced at Del. "Remember Giant?"

Del grinned and signed, *"He was taller than you at the shoulder. He was huge!"*

Steward chuckled. "Sweet horse, but massive. You're going to need something broad-chested, and at least eighteen or nineteen span—"

"What's a span?" Othi interrupted.

Steward held his hand up. "On average, about from the base of your thumb across your palm," he answered, tracing across his hand. "My Alabaster is sixteen span, for reference."

"Maybe you should come with us," Owyn said. "You know horses. I don't really. They like me, but really, I just know donkeys and Freckles."

Steward nodded. "Then we can go and review the maps for the journey."

"And I'll stay with Aria," Del signed. *"When we go visit the children. One of us should be with her."*

"Well, then. That sounds like we've gone and made a plan. First, we go to the dispensary and get Othi measured for trousers and boots." Owyn leaned back in his chair and looked at Othi. "I don't think that Katrin will have anything already made that will fit you, so they'll have to make something. That'll take time. Good thing we're here for a few days. Then we'll go to the stables and see if they have a horse that's big enough to carry you. And once that's done, we'll hunt up Aunt Rhexa and see about the maps."

"Did I hear my name?" Rhexa came into the dining room. "Good morning. I knocked, but no one heard me. I'm here to get Aria so we can go to the healing center." She stopped, looking around. "What am I smelling?"

DEL WALKED NEXT TO Aria through the streets, looking at the people. At how many people there were. At how many faces he didn't know. Somehow, it wasn't as frightening as it would have been before they left.

"Aunt Rhexa, are all the houses filled?" Aria asked. "It seems as if there are twice as many people here as there were two months ago."

"Closer to three times as many, and yes. We're housing people in the caves now, and starting to send out groups to resettle some of the abandoned towns to the east. And there's a group that will be heading out with you when you leave to start resettling south."

"You mentioned that yesterday," Aria said. "Are there still refugees coming in?"

"Not as many as there were," Rhexa answered. She held open the door to the healing center and gestured for Aria to enter. "Maybe one or two every few days. I don't think we'll have the flood that we did again."

"*From your mouth to the Mother's ears,*" Del signed. Then he tugged out his tablet and wrote the words for Rhexa, who looked puzzled. She read his writing and nodded.

"Exactly," she said, and gestured to the healing assistant at the desk. "Aria, Del, you remember Malani?"

"It's only been two months," Aria protested. "Of course I remember Malani! And I'm told congratulations are in order?"

Malani came around the desk to welcome them, and burst into laughter when Aria hugged her. "Yes, thank you. I'll tell Tancis that you said so. He's on rounds. You might see him."

Aria nodded. "If we do, I will congratulate him as well." She turned to look around. "Rhexa, I don't think I remember the way to the children's ward."

"Malani, would you take Aria on? I'll catch up in a moment," Rhexa said. "I wanted to have a word with Del."

Del blinked and waited for Malani and Aria to disappear down the corridor, then turned to Rhexa and arched a brow. She smiled.

"I wanted to let you know that what we're doing after this is women only. So you'll have to trust me with Aria," Rhexa said in a low voice. She looked over her shoulder, then back to him. "Do you know what a baby welcoming feast is?"

Del grinned and nodded.

"Good. We didn't think Aria would have one, and she's so important to so many of us, we decided to give her one." Rhexa frowned. "Do they do baby welcoming feasts in the Air tribes? Do you know?"

Del shook his head, then wiped his tablet and wrote, "*I don't think it matters. We're here now. She'll love this. Thank you for thinking of it.*"

Rhexa linked her arm into his. "It's my pleasure. Now let's go catch them up."

Del swallowed, then looked around. He trusted Rhexa, but...not here. Not where someone he didn't know could hear. Instead, he let Rhexa lead him through the halls to catch up with

Malani and Aria. Aria looked quizzically at him as he fell in next to her, but smiled when he shook his head.

"Something to do with Steward?" she murmured. Del laughed and took her hand.

She'd find out.

"I'M SURPRISED THAT they'll be able to get boots made before we leave. Usually, that takes weeks," Steward said as they walked down the tunnels toward the stables. Owyn tried to ignore the tunnel. It wasn't working, and it was only worse when Steward asked, "Is the tunnel getting any easier for you?"

"Not so you'd notice," Owyn answered. He wiped the sweat off his face and looked around. "Steward, distract me. Where's everyone else? Mem and Granna and Mamaleia and Karse?"

"Karse and the guard are off drilling with Captain Leesam's guards, and the boys are with him," Steward answered. "Meris took Aleia, Afansa and Zarai off for...I'm not even sure. She told me it was something for women, and I wasn't equipped. I'm not sure where Memfis went off to. And Skela went to the healing center to see about something for old bones, he said."

"Is he sick?" Othi asked.

"I think it's just he's not used to this sort of travel," Steward answered. "If I thought he'd listen, I'd send him back to the Palace. He's far too old for this journey." He looked around as they reached the stable. "Meris is, too. But if I told her that, she'd rip my head off."

"Skela would, too," Othi said. "What do we do now that we're here?"

"We talk to the stable hands," Owyn answered. "Which...where are they?"

"Busy!" A familiar groom came hurrying out of one of the other tunnels. "Owyn! I was wondering if I'd see you. I just been with Freckles. He's looking good." He looked up at Othi. "Well. Didn't know they made people in ore-horse scale."

Othi grinned. "I'm Othi. Nice to meet you."

"Othi. Nice meeting you. I'm Teasil." He nodded. "So what can I help you with?"

"We need to teach Othi how to ride. Which means he needs a horse that can carry him."

Teasil whistled. "Makes sense. Ore-horse sized person needs an ore-horse for riding," he said.

"And...do you happen to have one?" Steward asked. "By the by, I'm Steward. We haven't met either."

Teasil frowned. Then he nodded. "Right. I remember. Yours is that pretty gray gelding, isn't it?"

Steward nodded. "That's Alabaster."

"Got a sweet eye, that one." Teasil nodded again. "Right. Wait here. Let me go bring the Mountain out." He turned and hurried back down the tunnel, and Owyn looked at Steward and Othi.

"Bring the Mountain out?" he repeated. "That is what he said, isn't it?"

Steward nodded. "It is. Owyn, if this gets to be too much for you, go back to the house. I can help Othi."

"No," Othi said. "He's not supposed to go off alone. He—" He stopped as Teasil emerged from the tunnel, leading a massive horse.

"Mother of us all!" Owyn breathed. "That...that's like the Othi of horses!"

"This is the Mountain," Teasil said. He reached up and ran his hand over the horse's neck. "He's a heavy ore-horse, and he came up here with the refugees from the mines east of Forge. He's sweet as anything, this boy."

"Is he saddle trained?" Steward asked, then shook his head. "Of course not. How could he be? Where would you find a saddle to fit him?"

"Now that's where you're wrong, Steward. He's trained to harness and saddle, like our horses are. And he has a saddle. We don't use it much, though." Teasil grinned. "We've had four, sometimes five littles on his back, taking them all out at once for a ride around the lower terrace. He's gentle as a lamb, and he loves the attention. And we've taken him out hauling supplies to the new settlements out east. Feet like iron, he's got, and he can haul a wagon all day." He looked fondly up at the horse. "Come here, Othi. Let me introduce you."

Othi walked slowly over to Teasil. "Does he understand me?"

Teasil shrugged. "I never really know. Horses are either really smart or really dumb. They can be taught to come when they're called, and to follow commands, but something out of place, or something new? That's a horse-eating monster. Even if it's just as simple as a saddle on a fence rail."

Othi snorted, and Mountain snorted back at him. Teasil chuckled.

"Now, Mountain here is a blue roan. Which is why we call him Mountain."

"Because he looks like rock?" Othi asked.

"Exactly. Now, come over here and talk to him. Let him get to know your voice. Introduce yourself."

Owyn went to stand by Steward as Othi reached out to stroke Mountain's neck and started talking to him in a low voice.

"The two of them together look...normal. He's the right size for that horse, and the horse is the right size for him," Steward murmured. "It's like they were made for each other."

"There's a lot of that going on," Owyn murmured back. "I wonder if the Mother is trying to help us along."

Steward snorted. "If She is, maybe She can shove Risha in our direction?"

Owyn chuckled, then straightened when Othi blurted out, "You want me to what?"

"Breathe into his nose. Let him get your scent," Teasil said. "Why?"

"Because that means something different to Water folk," Owyn answered. "Relax, Othi. You're not marrying the horse."

Othi arched a brow. "Treesi would have problems with me if I married the horse," he said, and turned back to Mountain. After a moment, Mountain snorted again and rubbed his nose against Othi's chest, making him laugh. "I think he likes me."

"I think so, too," Teasil agreed. "Up for a lesson? I'll get his saddle, and we can go down to the lowest terrace. And I can teach you how to take care of him on the road."

Othi looked thoughtful, stroking Mountain's nose. "I...I don't have trousers or boots or anything. Owyn says I need those to ride."

"We'll work around it," Teasil said. "Don't worry. I won't let you get hurt."

Othi nodded. "If I can." He looked back at Owyn and Steward. "Can I do that?"

"Do you want us to come with you?" Owyn asked. Othi frowned, then shook his head.

"No, you have other things to do." Othi looked back at Mountain and grinned. "I think I'm going to go make friends with my horse."

"HE'S RISKING TOES TRYING to ride without boots," Steward grumbled as he and Owyn walked back through the tunnels. Owyn felt his shoulders start to relax as they came out into the air. "And risking other things riding in a kilt."

"Are you going to be the one to tell him he can't?" Owyn asked. "When he's willing to try, and before he knows what happens when you fall off? Because he's going to fall off. We all fall off. Nah, Teasil will take care of him." He stopped. "Aunt Rhexa is going to be busy with Aria, so we're not going to have access to the maps. Unless she's got an assistant? Do you know?"

Steward looked at him. "Now why would I know?" he asked. "I've only just met her." He looked around, then lowered his voice. "So, was your meeting with Aria this morning productive?" he asked softly. "You can hear her now?"

Owyn took a deep breath and let it out through his nose. "No," he admitted. "I can feel her. But I can't hear her. Maybe...I dunno, maybe whatever happened when I was retested means I won't hear her. But it don't matter." He grinned. "And I'm fine with it. And so is she."

Steward nodded. "Well, that's all that matters, then." He looked around again. "So what do we do until we have access to the maps?"

Owyn considered, then decided that he had questions. "Come for a walk with me. I'll introduce you to Persis. Maybe we'll learn something."

"Why do I know that name?" Steward asked as they started walking again.

"You heard it yesterday. That man who attacked Aria, he was assigned to Persis, but wasn't really a smith like he claimed he was." Owyn led the way down northeast, following the sounds of a ringing hammer. Outside the forge, they stopped by the half doors to watch the smith at work. Persis glanced up once, then grinned.

"It's my favorite dead man! I heard you were back, Owyn. Didn't get out to the ceremony yesterday. Too busy."

"That's all right," Owyn said. "I understand a smith's work is never done."

"Truth," Persis said, looking down at his anvil. He raised what Owyn now saw was a long knife blade, frowned at it for a moment, then set it back down on the anvil. "I heard there was a ruckus, though."

"Old associate of yours, we're told?" Steward said. Persis looked at him, then at Owyn.

"Persis, this is Aria's Steward. And that's his name."

"Well, nice to meet you, Aria's Steward." Persis said. "And you mean Lear? That one wasn't anything of mine. I'd have kicked his arse from here back to the smoking rubble he crawled out of if Rhexa had let me. Lying piece of shit." He scowled, then folded his arms. "Heard there was a ruckus. It was him?"

"He attacked Aria," Steward answered. Persis coughed.

"And he's still alive?" he asked. "Owyn, were you asleep or something?"

"Unarmed," Owyn answered. "We didn't think anything would happen here. Not in Terraces. But Del is sneaky. And armed to the teeth."

Persis laughed. "That quiet boy? Really? He looks like he'd faint if you sneezed too hard."

"If you tried to sneeze on him? Maybe," Owyn said. "If you even thought about sneezing on Aria or one of the rest of us? You'd never finish the sneeze."

Persis looked thoughtful, then nodded. "Ah. Makes sense. So, you here to visit, work, or looking for something?"

"Little of each," Owyn answered. "If you have the time to talk?"

"Tell you what," Persis said. "Feel like getting your hands dirty?"

Owyn grinned. "The last time I got into a forge was the last time I helped you. I've been missing it. Yeah, I can get my hands dirty."

"Good. You help me out with these blades, I'll tell you everything I know about that liar Lear."

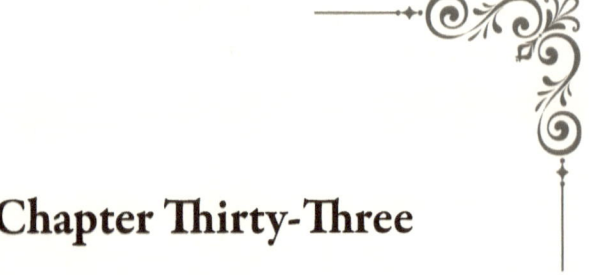

Chapter Thirty-Three

Treesi settled into a familiar overstuffed chair and sighed, closing her eyes.

"Tired?" Alanar asked.

"Completely," Treesi answered. "How long were we working?"

She heard the couch creak and complain as Alanar sat down. "A few hours, at least. I'm not sure. Pirit said that she'd have someone bring us something to eat, and that we should rest. I think we're sleeping here tonight."

"I suppose it makes sense," Treesi said, and opened her eyes. Alanar had stretched out on the couch, his long legs crossed at the ankle. "I'm tired enough to make wrong turns on a straight line."

Alanar chuckled, and she clearly heard the Water accent when he answered, "You always do that, Little Fish."

Treesi smiled. "It's been ages since anyone called me that. Virrik, did you ask?"

He laughed again. "Alanar was asleep by the time he was stretched out. I just wanted a minute with you, Little Fish. I've missed you." He smiled. "So you're building a canoe with my cousin? I wish you both well."

"Thank you," Treesi said. She shifted forward in her chair, leaning her elbows on her knees. "Virrik, have you figured out why you're in Allie's head?"

Virrik snorted. "I still have no idea. It's not where I'm supposed to be. And I can't say I like it much." He frowned. "Which is odd. I mean, I love him. And I love you. And I'm getting to love the rest of you. I wish I'd had the chance to know all of them before. But...I'm dead. I'm supposed to have gone back to the deep. I don't know why I'm here, especially since Owyn says that Aven sent me back to the deep before they even met Alanar." He shrugged. "It makes no sense. And I should stop. I'm overstepping my boundaries in a big way. I just wanted to tell you I'm happy for you, Trees."

Treesi nodded. "Thank you, Vir. I miss you."

Her only answer was a snore. Treesi smiled and tipped her head back, closing her eyes once more. Only to open them as someone tapped on the door.

"Come in," she called softly. To her surprise, Jehan walked in. He grinned at Treesi, and held the door for a familiar healer-in-training, who was carrying a tray.

"Gathi!" Treesi jumped up and took the tray, putting it down so that she could hug the young healer. "How are you? How are you liking your first few days?"

"I was dreadful sick on the canoe coming back here," Gathi answered. "I'm not good at sea, Healer Pirit says. And I'm ever so busy. I thought all of you were teasing me when you told me how much work I'd be doing. You weren't!"

"No, they weren't," Jehan said. "But you're not afraid of hard work."

"No, Senior Healer," Gathi said with a smile. "But I need to get back to it. If you'll excuse me? And say hello to Healer Alanar for me when he wakes up?"

"We will. Now off with you." Jehan closed the door behind her and turned to Treesi. "I thought you'd be asleep."

"I was going to, but I had a chat with Virrik—"

"Did he have permission?" Jehan asked, sitting down. He covered the bowls on the tray and started to fill a plate. He handed it to her, then looked at Alanar. "Wake him or let him sleep?"

"Let him sleep a little more," Treesi said. "And I don't think he did. He said Alanar was asleep as soon as he lay down. He wanted to congratulate me. Then he went away." She took the plate from Jehan. "He still has no idea why he's in Alanar's head, or how he got there."

Jehan nodded, fixing a plate for himself. He leaned back in his chair and started eating. "We'll sail that current when we get there," he said. "Right now? What did you think about the work we did today?"

Treesi considered the healing they'd done on Aven's hip. "Is that hip ever going to be as strong as it was? Reassembling the bone the way we did...it seems like it will be fragile."

Jehan nodded. "Good assessment. Mother says that she thinks it will strengthen, but that he might be old enough that it won't change much. His bones aren't as...malleable, I suppose. Not anymore. But he should be able to walk without pain. Ride, too, unless he pushes too hard. I'm not sure about running or fighting. We'll have to see. And we've still got work to do."

"Restoring the muscle and tendons, and the cushion between the bones," Alanar said without opening his eyes. His voice was back to normal. "Virrik's apologizing for taking a liberty. What did he do?"

"Congratulate me on building a canoe with his cousin. He's very pleased."

Alanar smiled. "That's all right, then," he said, and sat up. "What am I smelling?"

"I'll make a plate for you," Jehan said. "Your assessment?"

"On Aven's hip?" Alanar shook his head. "It's going better than I expected. How long will we be keeping him in trance?"

Jehan took a bite of bread, chewed and swallowed. "Mother has Tancis monitoring him and maintaining the trance while she rests. Once we're all rested and ready, she says we've got one more big push to work on the soft tissue, then we'll let him wake on his own. So he'll be out until tomorrow morning, I think."

Treesi nodded. "Aria's going to be worried. You know she will."

"Right now, Aria is distracted, and Rhexa is going to attempt to keep her that way," Jehan replied. "The women of Terraces are having a baby welcoming party for her. Aleia told me."

"Oh!" Treesi laughed. "Oh, that's lovely! I wish I could be in two places at once!" She sighed and looked down at her food, taking a bite. "Even though I'd fall asleep in the middle of the party."

"Eat that and go get some sleep," Jehan said. "Alanar, you do the same." He set down his empty plate and stood up. "I'm going to my office to sleep on the couch."

"You could stay here," Alanar said. "The third room is empty. That was Aven's room."

Jehan looked past Treesi, seemed to be considering it, then shook his head. "There's a hammock in there, isn't there?"

Treesi blinked. "It might have been moved out. But there was one."

Jehan grinned. "I'll go sleep on the couch. If I'm needed, they'll know to look for me in my office, and if I turn the wrong way on the couch, we won't have to put my bones back together. I'm not getting any younger."

OWYN LOOKED AROUND his room once more, then went back out and down the stairs to where Steward was waiting for him with a bundle under his arm. "I don't see them anywhere. I checked all the other rooms, and they're not there either."

Steward frowned. "Trista knows that your smoke blades should be put with your things. I can't imagine where they might have gone."

Owyn sighed. "Well, we're not going to find them here. I've got my whip chain. I can dance with that, and maybe catch a vision that way. Let's go down to the lowest terrace. Maybe we'll see Othi."

They left the house, and started walking down the spoke toward the healing center.

"Leesam wasn't happy that we went and found out more than he did," Owyn said. "Why would that bother him?"

"Because it means he's not doing the job he should be doing," Steward answered. "He should have gone and talked to Persis yesterday, not waited until you went and did it for him."

Owyn nodded. "Think they'll find anything else? I mean, Persis said there were people he didn't know who came looking for Lear after he stopped working the forge."

Steward shook his head. "Probably to do with the paradise flower Karse and Leesam found. I doubt anyone will be able to find them. But Leesam knows now that he needs to keep a closer eye. He'll do better. Rhexa needs him to do better."

Owyn glanced at Steward. "I'm changing the subject, since it's just you and me. You asked a nosy question. My turn. Are you going to ask my aunt for something more than letters?"

Steward smiled. "Having you all call me uncle means I keep forgetting Rhexa really is your aunt. And...if she'll have me. But not until the Progress is done. My responsibilities are to Aria." He looked around. "And then we need to figure out a thing or two. She's governor now. And...well, I'm the Palace steward. We neither of us can be in two places at once. I don't know if we'll be able to move past that hurdle."

"Well, you won't know until you ask her. And I'm all for you asking her." Owyn grinned. "Get to call you Uncle for real."

Steward burst out laughing. "You're putting the cart so far before the horse they might as well not even be on the same street."

"Maybe. Or maybe not." Owyn looked around as they turned to skirt the healing center. "Is that Del up there? Who is he with?"

"It is, and it looks like Skela." Steward whistled, the sound piercing enough that Owyn winced. Del waved, and he and Skela came to meet them.

"Good morning, Twiceborn," Skela said. "I was coming to find you. Your father asks forgiveness, because he could not find you to ask permission."

Owyn blinked. "Asks...oh, is that where my blades went?"

Skela nodded. "He is on the lowest terrace, learning to dance again. I went with him, to see how he did it. It's very like our sword dancing."

"Skela, you didn't leave him alone, did you?" Steward asked. "If he catches a vision—"

Skela laughed. "He is well attended by two young men and a wolf. One of whom has decided he wishes to be a Smoke Dancer when he is grown."

Owyn closed his eyes and shook his head. "No," he said. "No, that's too silly. But with the way things have been going with us, I'm not entirely sure you're not talking about the wolf." As the older men laughed, he shook his head again. "Let's go make sure my fa isn't getting himself in trouble."

"*Where's Othi?*" Del asked.

"Making friends with his horse," Owyn answered. "The horse is named Mountain, and he is one. Feet like dinner plates."

Del whistled. "*An ore-horse?*" he signed. "*Here?*"

"You'll see him when we go down to the lowest terrace," Steward said. "The stableman took Othi down to teach him to ride."

They started walking, and Del looked back the way they'd come. "*I don't like leaving Aria alone,*" he murmured in Owyn's mind. "*She's got all the women with her, though.*"

"Is Aleia with her?" Owyn asked.

"*Yes. Oh.*" Del looked at him and smiled. "*She doesn't need another guard, does she?*"

"Skela, you were in the healing center," Steward said. "Any word on Aven?"

"I saw Jehan," Skela said. "He said that they have more work to do, but the work that they have done is promising. They were going to rest before they continued."

Owyn nodded. "I hope it works," he said. "I never did get to see Aven dance before." He frowned. "There were a lot of things we said we were going to do, but we never did. I still haven't heard either of them sing."

Del smiled. "*I haven't heard that, either. We haven't really had time to sing. Maybe we should just have some time for us, once Aven is out of the healing center and before we leave.*"

Owyn nodded. "I like that. We'll arrange it."

Del reached out and took Owyn's hand. "*I never asked. Can you hear her now?*"

"Not yet, no," Owyn said, keeping his voice low. "Not sure why. I need to talk to Granna. But before we do that, I want to dance and check in on Milon. I haven't since we left the Palace, and the last time, I lost him because he was upset."

"Milon?" Steward asked. "Why was he upset?"

"Because they told him that Granna was dead," Owyn answered. "And she was there with me when I reached him. She touched his mind, talked to him. He had no idea that Granna was still alive. I should have checked on him, but...well..."

"Nearly dying does make it harder to dance," Steward pointed out, and Owyn laughed.

"Yeah. That."

They continued walking, following the same track that they'd taken the day before. Today, there weren't as many people, but there were still the remains of flowers and paper streamers in the streets. And people nodded and smiled, and waved to them as they passed.

"It's weird, having everyone know us, and I don't know a single one of them," Owyn muttered. "I keep trying to remember the names of people I know I haven't met yet, because they all know me."

"At least they're not screaming and running," Steward said softly. "Or trying to kill you."

"I'm not going to ask about the first one. And I'm really glad of the second," Owyn said. He trotted down the last few stairs to the lowest terrace and looked around. "Where would Othi and Teasil be, do you think? And where's Mem?"

"Memfis is this way," Skela said. "And perhaps we should wait to find the others after you do what is needful."

"*Owyn, did you bring food?*" Del asked, signing quickly. "*You're supposed to eat after dancing.*"

Steward hefted the bundle he'd been carrying. "Bread and soft cheese, and some apples. I promise, I'll take care of him."

Del grinned and nodded, and they followed Skela through the paths that were far more manicured than Owyn remembered from his first time in the lowest terrace. There were people walking around, and he noticed several pairs meandering arm in arm down by the railing that overlooked the sea. He grinned and nudged Del's arm.

"That's nice," he said, nodding toward them. "We should do that. You, me and Allie."

"*It's romantic,*" Del said, nodding. "*I think Allie would like it. And then we can have a picnic. Just us? Or all of us?*"

"Is it romantic?" Owyn asked. "I don't have a lot of experience with romance."

"It appears to be what courting young ones do here," Skela said. "I imagine none of them actually notice the view of the water. They're too busy looking at the view of their other."

"Then we'll definitely come down here," Owyn said. "The whole lot of us." He turned back to look across the terrace, and saw familiar movement. Memfis, dancing with one of the smoke blades, with a rapt audience of two. He was moving far more slowly than Owyn was used to seeing, and he stopped when he saw them coming across the grass.

"I was wondering when you'd come find me," he called, lowering the blade he held. "I'm sorry for taking them without asking, Mouse—"

Owyn shook his head. "It's fine, Mem. The only reason I even noticed is that I wanted them. So when you're done, it's my turn." He cocked his head to the side. "How'd you keep the vision from coming?"

"He was telling us what he was doing," Copper answered.

"And telling us all the names of all the moves," Danir added. "And he said we could try, when we were bigger, because the blades are too long and too heavy for us right now."

"We could have done it now, if we could have found sticks," Copper finished. "But there aren't any, so we can't." He looked around, then whistled. "Howl!" They heard barking, then Howl burst out of the underbrush and ran over to flop in Copper's lap. Copper laughed. "You're all over prickles! And I just picked them all off you!"

"He likes the attention," Steward said, coming over to crouch next to the boys so he could pet the puppy. "Memfis, you should sit."

"I'm going to," Memfis said. He brought the single blade to Owyn, then nodded to the ground next to Danir. "The other one is over there. You hunting visions?"

"Checking on Milon," Owyn answered. "It's been a few days, and I don't like this not knowing." He picked up the second blade, and walked away from the others, turning around to see that they had all sat down around the boys. He grinned.

"All right. I'll be back when I'm back," he called. He took a deep breath. A second. A third. He started moving, closing his eyes and waiting for the vision to rise to meet him.

When it did, it was with the force of a tidal wave. He couldn't see. He couldn't breathe. He was flat on his back, hearing wordless screaming. He recognized Trey's voice.

"*Milon!*" Owyn gasped. "*Can you hear me? What the fuck is happening?*"

He felt a surge of panic, and something bit against his wrists. He heard laughter.

Risha's laughter.

"That's enough for now," she said, and Owyn felt a rush of cool air as something moved away from his face. No, from Milon's face. "We'll resume the experiments tomorrow."

Footsteps, moving away. A door closed. Someone was crying.

Trey. Trey was crying.

"*Milon?*"

"*Owyn...go back,*" Milon answered, his mental voice weak. "*Go back, and don't come again.*"

"*What's happening? What's going on? What experiments?*" Owyn tried to figure out what he was feeling from Milon. Ropes? Or...or chains? He was bound, somehow. Something that hurt when he fought it. And Trey..."*What's wrong with Trey?*"

No answer. Instead, he felt a gentle push. "*Go back, Owyn. I don't want you in this. I don't want you to share this.*"

"*Milon, we're coming,*" Owyn said, pushing back. "*We'll find you. We'll stop her.*"

"I don't know if you'll find us in time, Owyn. She's killing us. Killing us both. I don't know how much time we have left." Milon paused, and Owyn heard chains rattling. Then a soft touch on his face, and a low moan.

Was that...Trey?

"Milon, what did she do to Trey?" Owyn asked. *"Please. He's my friend. What's happened to him? What did she do?"*

"He put himself between Risha and me. He tried to protect me. He failed. They took him away. And she broke him." Another push. Harder, and Owyn felt himself slipping. *"Don't come again, Owyn. Tell them I am dead. By the time you reach us, I will be."*

Chapter Thirty-Four

"Breathe," Steward said gently. His hand was heavy on Owyn's back. "Deep breaths. Memfis, he's fine."

"Mouse?" Memfis sounded worried. No, he sounded scared.

"I'm fine, Fa. Just...shaken." Owyn forced a smile. "You look like how I feel."

"What happened?" Steward asked. He moved his hand, then handed Owyn a piece of bread with a smear of soft cheese on it. "Eat this. Then tell us what happened."

"You didn't bring your book?" Memfis asked.

"Wasn't a point," Owyn answered, and took a bite. "I don't see anything when I talk to Milon," he added, mumbling around a mouthful of bread and cheese. He swallowed, then met Memfis' eyes. "Fa...I really don't want to tell you. Really."

Memfis stared at him, then breathed, "Fuck." He closed his eyes. "What is she doing, Owyn? What is she doing to my Milon?"

Owyn turned to the two boys sitting nearby, staring at him. "You two, go take a walk. This isn't for you to hear."

Copper opened his mouth, looking like he wanted to argue. Danir just grabbed his arm and dragged him to his feet. "Do you want us to come back?" he asked.

"Go find Othi. He's having riding lessons somewhere down here," Steward said. "We were going to go look for him when we were done. See if you can find him, then come back."

Danir nodded and pulled Copper away from the group. Owyn looked up at Steward. "Thanks." He turned back to Memfis. "She's...Milon won't tell me what she did to Trey, except that she broke him. But Risha...she's torturing Milon. Experiments, she said. I heard her." He paused, then let it out. "Mem, he told me not to come back, and to tell you all he was dead. Because he don't expect to survive long enough for us to find him. He don't expect him or Trey to live that long."

Memfis went very still, then stepped back; his legs went out from under him and he sat down hard on the ground. For a moment, Owyn was sure that his father was going to faint. Then Memfis shook his head. He stood up slowly, and held out his hand.

"Give me one of the blades." His voice was like nothing Owyn had ever heard from him before. No inflection or emotion. It was quiet. Flat.

Terrifying.

"Fa, what are you thinking?" Owyn asked.

"I need to see," Memfis answered. "I need to see this for myself." He stepped closer, his hand still out. "Give me a blade."

Owyn nodded slowly, and held out one of his blades. "Fa, I don't know if you can reach him the way I can."

"I know that I can't," Memfis replied. "I just need to see. I need to see him." He took the blade and turned to walk away.

"Don't go too far," Steward called after him.

Memfis didn't respond. He walked a short distance away and stood with his back to them. Owyn watched his shoulders lower, watched him breathe. Once. Twice. Thrice. Then he started to move.

"I..." Owyn breathed. "I haven't seen him dance. Not since...not since he came back." He looked at Steward. "And you never saw him dance before. Or did you?"

Steward didn't look at Owyn. "I never did. But I'm told he danced for the Usurper, once. Why?"

"He looks different." Owyn looked back at Memfis. "He looks unbalanced. He always taught me that you needed to be balanced to dance."

"He found you, dancing like this," Steward said.

Owyn nodded. Memfis stopped. He took three more breaths, then started moving again. Owyn slowly got to his feet, suddenly worried. Something didn't feel right...

Memfis fell backward, his arm flailing, the blade flying off to land in the grass. He twisted, rolling up onto his knees, folding over them before rising up to howl in wordless anguish at the skies.

"Mem!" Owyn took off running, but Steward was somehow faster. The older man dropped to his knees next to Memfis, grabbing him by the arm.

"Memfis!" Steward shook Memfis until he looked at them. "What did you see?"

Memfis blinked at him. "Nothing," he growled, and pulled his arm free. "She pushed me out. She won't let me see." He staggered to his feet and looked around. "Where's the blade? I need to try again."

"Mem, if the Mother pushed you out, you know you're not going to see anything," Owyn said. "You taught me that."

"I need to try again," Memfis repeated. "I need to see. I need to know." He looked up at the sky and shouted, "Let me see! Let me see him!"

Owyn walked over to pick up the blade. He carried it back to Memfis, holding it in both hands. "Fa. You told me that we can't force visions. That we have to let them come when and how they come. You taught me that. If you try again, you're going to hurt yourself."

Memfis met his eyes, and held out his hand. "So be it."

Steward caught his breath. "Memfis—"

"No," Owyn interrupted. He looked back at Steward and shook his head. "No, this is something that needs doing." He nodded back to where Del stood with Skela. "Go wait with them."

Steward nodded slowly. "Memfis, try not to hurt yourself?" he said.

"No promises," Memfis answered. Then his lips twitched slightly into something that might resemble a smile in poor light. "Thank you, my friend."

Steward blinked. Then he smiled. "Well, that was unexpected," he murmured. "Right. I'll be out of the way." He turned and walked back to Del and Skela.

Owyn held the blade out of Memfis, but didn't immediately let go of it. "If She pushes you out again," he said. "Then you're done. Understood?"

Memfis tugged on the blade, then scowled at Owyn and nodded. "Understood, Mouse." He took a deep breath and nodded again. "Thank you."

Owyn took a step back, then another, watching as Memfis set his feet, as he took his first deep breath. He knew what was going to happen.

And, just as Owyn expected, as Memfis began to take his third breath, he grunted and fell, sprawling his length over the grass. He looked up, startled.

"The fuck just happened?" he demanded.

Owyn snorted and went over to offer Memfis his hand. "She said no. She meant it." He helped Memfis up. "She did it to me, before Allie and I went north."

"So...when you handed me the blade, you knew?" Memfis asked. He brushed his hand down the front of his shirt. "And you didn't warn me?"

"Remember how I wouldn't listen to you, and you used to let me get myself into all sorts of fuck-ups, so that I'd learn for myself?" Owyn asked. He stooped and picked up his blade. "Same thing."

Memfis snorted. "So you're using my own tricks against me?"

"Hey," Owyn protested. "That's not fair. I just...learned from the best." He grinned. "You know you get to teach my children the same things, right? Grandfa Mem?"

"Grandfa?" Memfis' brows rose. "Is there something you need to tell me? Or is this your way of telling me?"

"No!" Owyn laughed. "No, not yet. But you'll be..." He stopped and frowned, counting. "Not sure. Somewhere in the first ten people we tell when it does happen."

Memfis barked with laughter. "Fair enough." He took a deep breath and blew it out. "You'll look for him again?"

"What, did you think that when he told me not to come back, I was actually going to listen?" Owyn asked. "Do you even know me?"

He heard laughter from behind him, then arms slipped around his waist. He turned to see Del, who rested his chin on Owyn's shoulder.

"*Shall we go find the boys?*" Del asked. "*And...what's that noise?*"

"What noise?" Owyn turned, stepped out of Del's arms and looking around. "No, wait. I...no...no, I don't hear it. I...I *feel* it." He dropped to one knee, resting his hand on the ground.

Which might have been all that saved him from being thrown to the ground when the terrace underneath him shivered like a fly-stung horse. Del and Memfis both toppled, and Owyn heard Steward swearing, heard screaming, and the distant, high-pitched howl of a young wolf. Then it stopped, and things went still.

Steward groaned and picked himself up, helping Skela to his feet. "That was..." He started to say. Then he stopped and looked around. "A tremor," he breathed. "Aria."

It took a moment for Owyn to understand the single word and all that it implied. Then it did, and he went cold.

"Aria," he murmured. "Or...or Treesi or Aven. Del, where's Aria?"

"*I know where she is,*" Del answered. He snapped his arms down, and twin spikes appeared in his hands. "*I'll go to Aria. You go to Treesi.*" He turned and ran, toward the stairs.

"Fa, find the boys and Othi!" Owyn shouted over his shoulder as he scooped up his blades and ran after Del.

"RHEXA, THIS WAS LOVELY," Aria said as they left Katrin's house. "You didn't have to do this."

"We wanted to, Aria," Rhexa slipped her arm into Aria's. "You're one of us, and you mean so much to so many of us. We wanted to show that to you, and celebrate the little one." She smiled. "Did Aven tell you if this is a boy or a girl?"

"I asked him not to," Aria answered. "I didn't want to know. Now...I want to know but he won't tell me." She smiled as Rhexa laughed. "I think all of my healers know. But none of them will tell me. I'll find out in a few months."

"Well, they'll be very much loved," Rhexa said. "And I can't wait to meet them. I'll walk you back to the house." She turned. "Why don't you all come back with us? I'll make some tea."

Aria looked over her shoulder to see Aleia, Meris, Afansa and Zarai had come out of Katrin's house. Meris smiled. "Tea would be lovely. I don't think I could eat another bite, but tea would be just right." She walked up to take Aria's other hand. "And perhaps you should rest?"

"I feel fine, Grandmother," Aria said. Then she looked around. "Do you feel that?"

"Feel what?" Rhexa asked. Before Aria could answer, the ground dipped and swelled underneath her feet. She flared her wings wide to keep her balance, twisting to grab onto her grandmother to try and keep her from falling. She heard glass breaking, something cracking, and shouts and screams of alarm. Then people started to pour out of houses, heading for the open air.

"Come with me!" Rhexa called, taking Aria's arm again. "This way! Into the open, away from the cliff-face." She tugged gently, leading Aria and Meris away, toward the healing center. Aria looked back to see that Afansa had Zarai's left arm, and Aleia had her right.

"Another tremor?" Aria looked around. "Where are my Companions?"

"I...I don't know," Rhexa stammered. "Aria, what is it?"

Aria looked at the healing center. "Aven and Treesi are there. I need to find them." She turned to Rhexa. "Aven was almost killed, and we had the storm. Owyn died, only for a moment, but the Smoking Mountain erupted. What just happened?"

"Mother of us all," Rhexa breathed. "I...come on. Let's find them."

They made their way through the crowd of people, and Aria tried to keep calm, tried to smile and reassure the frightened people around her that things were fine. That they were safe. That it was only a tremor. Nothing more.

Then she heard a still-unfamiliar voice shout, "Ar-ya!" She turned and saw Del, running through the crowd. He stopped, breathing hard as he looked her up and down.

"I'm fine," she said quickly. He nodded, tucking his throwing spikes back into his sleeves. Then he started signing, only to stop when Aria held up her hand. "Your tablet, please? I can't translate."

Del dug his tablet out of his carrybag. *"Owyn has gone to the healing center to see about Aven and Treesi."*

"That's where we were going," Rhexa said. "Del, I'm not imagining that? You spoke?"

Del blushed slightly and nodded. He wiped his tablet and wrote, "*I can, but not well. I was going to tell you, but in private.*" He looked around and his blush deepened.

"But needs must," Meris said. "And you make yourself perfectly understandable when you have something to say, however you say it."

Del smiled and wiped the tablet off, putting it back into his back. He held his arm out to Aria, and they started walking again. Aria hugged his arm tightly. He was fine. Owyn was fine. What about Treesi and Aven?

They came around the healing center building, and saw Owyn pacing back and forth. He turned, saw them, and ran toward them. "Aria!"

"I'm fine," Aria repeated. "What's happening?"

"Everyone is out of the building," Owyn answered. "Jehan has them all checking on the patients, who are all over there." He pointed. "Aven is with the other patients. He's still in trance, and Tancis is with him, keeping him that way."

"Why not let him wake?" Meris asked.

"I asked that," Owyn said. "And it's because they're not done yet. If they let him come out of trance, he'll wake up and be in pain, and he'll want to help and that will undo all their work. So they're keeping him asleep." He turned and looked at the building. "I don't understand. We're all fine. But that tremor...why?"

"It could have been natural," Rhexa said. "I mean...couldn't it?"

Aria nodded, seeing Othi coming through the crowd. She waved, but he'd already seen her.

"There you are," he said. "Where's Treesi?"

"With the other healers, seeing to the patients," Aria said. "Owyn says she's fine. We're all fine."

Othi arched a brow. "Then what just happened?" he asked, keeping his voice low. "That wasn't a normal tremor. Not if it came alone. They come in schools, like fish. Big one and a lot of little ones." He frowned. "At least, that's what they do underwater. Is it different up here?"

"It isn't," Aleia said from behind Aria. Aria turned to look at her, and she smiled "Afansa is with Zarai," she said. "Zarai is a little shaken. She's never felt a tremor before. When I see Pirit, I'll ask her to speak to Zarai."

Aria nodded. "Thank you. And what do you mean, tremors don't come alone?"

Othi looked at Aleia, then scratched his chin. "How can I explain it?" he muttered. "I...I know. When you drop a pebble into a container of water, what happens?"

"Ripples," Owyn answered.

"And when they hit the edge of the container?" Othi asked him. Owyn frowned.

"They bounce back," he answered.

Othi nodded. "Right. And how hard they bounce back and how many times, that depends on how hard the wave was in the first place. Understand?" He waited for Aria to nod. "Tremors are like that. They shake. And they keep shaking until things finally calm down. They don't just shake once. There should be lots of little ones that come after."

"That's a nice description, Othi," Aleia said. "He's right. A single wave? That's not a natural tremor."

"It's a message," Owyn breathed. "Oh, fuck me. We're all fine. We're all safe." He looked around and lowered his voice. "Milon isn't. I...I think I need to go dance again."

"Again?" Aria and Aleia both spoke at once. Aria looked at her, then continued. "You danced already? You spoke to him?"

"Not here," Owyn said, keeping his voice low. "Not talking about this in public. But yeah, I did. And yeah, it's bad."

Aria swallowed around the lump in her throat, the happiness caused by the celebration evaporating like mist. "Let's go find the others," she said. Then she looked around. "Then we should make ourselves seen. Speak to the people. Help them to understand that this was frightening and nothing more."

"We'll set up places for people to sleep outside in the parks, if they don't want to spend the night inside," Rhexa said. "Thankfully, it's still good weather for it." She looked around. "I need to get that started. Aria, if you'll excuse me?"

"Auntie, do you want help?" Owyn asked.

"I...no. You attend to your Heir," Rhexa said. Then she smiled. "If Steward comes back, send him to me?"

Owyn grinned. "I'll bring him to you when I see him."

Rhexa smiled, then hurried away. Aria looked around again.

"Where did you say Aven was?" she asked. Owyn offered her his arm.

"This way, my Heir," he said. She took his arm, and he led her through the crowd. They kept a slow pace, and Aria had to fight her impatience. She wanted to push through the people, see that Aven was safe with her own eyes. But she wasn't sure what that would do to people who were already frightened. So she went slowly, stopping to share a word, a smile, a touch. A crying child grabbed onto Aria's skirts and wailed until Owyn picked her up.

"Hey, now. It's all right. You're safe now. I've got you. What's your name?" he asked, wiping tears from the girl's face with his sleeve.

"Hesha," the little girl sniffled. She looked at Aria with wide, ember eyes. "I know you. You're the Heir." She looked at Owyn. "Are you her Earth?"

"Me? Nah. I'm her Fire."

She nodded. "I'm Fire, too," she said. She looked around. "We came here from Tinker's Creek because the mountain was on fire. But I don't know where anything is here. Or where Mama and Fa and Tovi are."

"It's all right, Hesha," he crooned. "Let's find your parents, yeah?" He glanced at Aria and grinned. "Cover your ears. I'm gonna get loud."

Hesha's eyes widened, and she clapped her hands over her ears. Once Aria had done the same, Owyn took a deep breath.

"We've got some lost parents here!" he bellowed. "Hesha's parents wandered off! Anyone seem them?" He took another breath, and Aria lowered her hands to hear Hesha giggle.

"They're not lost!" she protested. "I'm lost!"

"Nah, you're not lost. We know where you are," Owyn told her, making her laugh again. "We don't know where they are. So they're the lost ones." He looked around again. "Othi, you're taller. See anyone looking frantic?"

"I see a lot of people looking frantic," Othi answered. "And...yeah, a couple heading this way." He waved. "Hey! You our lost parents?"

"Hesha?"

At the sound of the woman's voice, Hesha twisted in Owyn's arms. "Mama!"

A woman pushed through the crowd, followed by a man carrying a baby. "Hesha!" the woman gasped. "Sweetheart, you shouldn't run off like that!" She blinked, and clearly realized who was holding her daughter, and who was standing with him. "My Heir. Fireborn. I—"

"Don't you dare apologize," Owyn interrupted.

"Mama, I wasn't lost," Hesha added. "We knew where I was. We didn't know where you and Fa and Tovi were. That means you were lost. Right?" She looked at Owyn, who grinned.

"Exactly right," Owyn agreed, putting her down. "Now, go hold on to your mother's hand and make sure she don't get lost again. That's your job."

Hesha nodded. Then she frowned and looked up at Owyn. "Whose job is it to make sure Fa doesn't get lost?"

"Your mother's," Owyn answered, and the woman laughed.

"Thank you," she said. "I'm Sanna. My man is Orvis, and the baby is Tovi."

"It's nice to meet you all. And...I'm curious. Hesha said you were from Tinker's Creek," Aria said. "Are you by chance the family that moved into Two Northwest?"

"No, my sister and her family are in Two Northwest," Sanna said. "I was helping them with the baby, and that's when Hesha slipped off. How did you know?" She looked at Owyn. "Oh! You're Rhexa's nephew! She told me about you."

Owyn nodded. "Yes, that's me."

Sanna laughed. "You're going to make an excellent father someday." She stooped and picked Hesha up. "We're camping outside tonight, sweetheart. In the park by the house."

"Like when we came here?" Hesha asked. "Will there be spiders?"

"No spiders," Orvis said. "I already checked." He smiled, shifting the baby to his other shoulder. "When we were on our way here, we set camp one night, and didn't see that the tent was on a stilt spider nest. Thankfully, they don't bite."

Aria shuddered. "Go and check again, just to be certain," she said. Hesha laughed.

"Mama, the Heir don't like spiders neither!"

"You have that in common, then," Sanna said. "We'll let them get on with what they were doing." She smiled. "Thank you. For everything."

Aria smiled and watched them as they made their way back through the crowd. Then she looked at Owyn. "She's right."

"About what?" Owyn asked, offering his arm again.

"You're going to make an excellent father." Aria hugged his arm. "Where did you learn that? From Memfis?"

"Not sure," Owyn said slowly. "I mean...I don't know a lot about children. I told Marik that, when he told me he wanted me to talk with Copper. But...I dunno. I didn't want her to cry anymore. I wanted her not to be lost. Because I remember what it was like when I was that little and lost, and no one came looking for me." He shrugged. "That I knew about, anyway. And I didn't want her to feel like that. No one, no child should ever feel like that." He looked at Aria. "You've got a funny smile on your face. What did I say?"

"I didn't realize I was smiling," Aria said. "Owyn, I do love you. You're going to be wonderful with our children."

He grinned. "That implies more than one."

"Did I ever say I wanted to stop with one?"

Chapter Thirty-Five

Treesi made one more pass through the rows of stretchers, checking the makeshift canopies that shaded the patients from the sun, then headed back to where the other healers were sitting. Or, in the case of Tancis, lying — the younger healer had been relieved of his duty watching over Aven, and was asleep underneath a tree. Pirit now sat on the ground next to Aven's stretcher, one hand resting lightly on his arm. Alanar sat on Aven's other side, not touching him.

"When can we take them back inside?" Treesi said as she reached the others.

Jehan was sitting with his back against the tree. He straightened and turned to face her; she could see the fatigue in his face. She suspected that he'd been shaken out of a sound sleep the same way she and Alanar had been.

"Once we're sure it's over," he answered. "And once the building is inspected. Probably not until nightfall." He looked around. "I imagine there will be people sleeping outside tonight. I hope it doesn't rain."

Treesi nodded, then jumped when she heard someone shouting. "Was that Owyn?"

Alanar sat up straight. "It was. Someone's lost?" He scrambled to his feet. "What's happening?"

"I can't see," Treesi answered.

"I see Othi," Jehan added, coming to stand with Treesi. "He doesn't seem upset."

"Can we go to them?" Alanar asked. Treesi took his hand, feeling his heart racing.

"Allie?" she whispered. "What is it?"

"The last time the ground shook was when Owyn died," he whispered back, and Treesi shuddered.

"Do you think something happened?" she asked. "It can't have. We're all safe."

"It's likely something to do with the Smoking Mountain," Jehan said, coming to stand with them. For a moment, Treesi wondered if he'd heard what she and Alanar had been saying. Then she realized that people were listening and that Jehan's voice was pitched to carry. "Once we've got our own settled, we'll send riders south to see."

Alanar nodded. "That's fine. Can we go to Owyn now?"

"They're coming this way," Jehan said.

A moment later, Othi led the way through the crowd. He grinned when he saw them.

"Sorry we kept you waiting," he said. "Lost parents."

"Lost *parents*?" Treesi repeated. Then she immediately forgot the question when Aria came through the crowd behind Othi, holding on to Owyn's arm.

"I am fine," Aria said quickly. "Owyn is being overprotective. As is Del." She looked back to where Del was escorting Meris. "We're all fine. Just shaken." She turned to Owyn, leaning in to kiss his cheek. "Go see to your husband."

"Was just about to," Owyn answered, and left her side to embrace Alanar. "I'm fine, Allie. I'm here."

"The last time, you weren't fine," Alanar replied, and Treesi heard the shiver in his voice. She moved away to give them some privacy, and found herself engulfed in Othi's arms.

"I'm fine, too," she said, resting against his chest. "But you don't have to let go."

"Good. I wasn't going to," Othi murmured. "Treesi, this wasn't—"

"Othi," Jehan interrupted. "Where's Aleia?"

Othi tensed, and his arms around Treesi loosened. "She was with us, but maybe she went back for Mother Zarai and Afansa. She said Mother Zarai was shaken up, and she wanted to have Mother Pirit speak to her."

"I don't see them," Jehan said, and Treesi turned in Othi's arms to see him looking out over the crowd. And she saw, behind him, the small group surrounding Pirit.

"They're behind you," she said. "They must have come around through the crowd."

Jehan turned and laughed. "I missed them entirely." He looked back around. "I don't see Steward. Or Memfis."

"They were on the lowest Terrace when the ground shook," Owyn called. "The boys were, too. Matter of fact, they were supposed to be looking for Othi. Othi, did you see them? And what happened to Mountain?"

"Teasil took him back to the stables. Said I should come find you lot," Othi answered. "I didn't see the boys." He turned and looked out over the people, then shook his head. "I should go look for them. They're little. They'll be frightened."

"I'll go with you," Owyn called. "Now that we know everyone is all right. You all stay here, and stay together." He kissed Alanar again. "I'll be back, love."

"Be careful," Alanar said. "There might be another tremor."

Owyn nodded and came toward Treesi and Othi. "Trees, stay with Aria, will you?" he asked softly. "I dunno...get her settled over with Aven?"

"I'll take care of her," Treesi assured him. "You go find the boys."

"And Steward. And Mem. And...whoever else might be down there." He frowned. "Skela was down there. Del, you coming or staying?" He paused, then nodded. "Thank you."

"What did he say?" Othi asked. "I didn't see what he signed."

"He didn't," Owyn said. "That was private. You have to let go of Treesi now."

Othi laughed. "That's no fun," he grumbled.

Treesi grinned and wrapped her arms as far around him as she could. "Pay a forfeit."

Othi looked surprised. Then he smiled, and arched a brow. "Or?"

"Or..." Treesi stopped, unable to think of a single thing. She made a face at him, and stuck out her tongue. "Or...something. I'll think of something!"

"Trees, you need to plan your threats out better," Owyn said with a laugh.

"I'm horrible at threatening people," Treesi replied, and tipped her head back. "Forfeit?"

"Threaten to stop smiling at me," Othi said. "That will work." He leaned down and ran his fingers through her hair before he kissed her, deep enough and intense enough that the ground could have shaken to pieces and Treesi would never have noticed. She whimpered softly as he stood up straight. "More when I get back."

"Is that a promise?" Treesi asked.

He smiled. "Definitely a promise."

"SO WHAT DID DEL TELL you?" Othi asked.

"That he'd stay with Allie and keep him from fretting while I'm down here," Owyn answered. "Othi, can I ask you a question?"

Othi nodded. "Of course. Hey, how do we know we're not missing them? If they go to the healing center along another street?"

"This is the street we went down to get to the lowest terrace," Owyn answered. "I'm hoping that they'll come back up this way. And...are you only with Treesi?"

Othi looked startled. "What?"

"Well." Owyn drew the word out. "Allie is married to me. But he's not only with me. And I'm not only with him—"

"Because you're a Companion."

"And he's a Healer," Owyn said with a nod. "Right. And Treesi can't only be with you, because she's a Healer and a Companion. So the question is, are you only going to be with her? If one of us invites you..."

"I haven't thought about it," Othi answered, quickly enough that Owyn was sure he'd given it a lot of thought already.

"Not sure how you'd answer, hm?" Owyn asked softly. "I didn't mean to make you uncomfortable, Othi. I'm just..." He grinned. "I'm curious."

Othi's dark skin turned dusky. "You're curious...about me? Why? I mean...you've got Alanar...and...and Aven...and...well...do you have Del?"

"Not like that, no. And why wouldn't I be curious?" Owyn looked up at him. "I like you. You're a friend. You've really turned the head of someone I love a lot. So...yeah, I'm curious. And I'm sure the others are, too."

"The others?" Othi repeated. "I...you don't think Aven...?"

Owyn shrugged. "We haven't talked about it. But Aven? His compass points straight at Aria. Occasionally at me and Treesi. Once in a while at Alanar. So I don't know if he's thinking of you as anything other than his baby cousin who's bigger than he is."

Othi laughed out loud. "Been a long time since anyone called me the baby. Look, Owyn...can I think about this?"

"Of course you can," Owyn said. He trotted down the last few stairs to the lowest Terrace, then turned to look back at Othi. "Take as long as you want."

"It'll be a while." Othi joined him at the bottom of the stairs, looking back and forth across the terrace. "Did Treesi tell you?"

"Tell me what?" Owyn pointed. "We were over there."

They started walking, and Othi let out a long breath. "When we get back from this Progress, I'm leaving. For a year. To apprentice to the hammer."

"You're going to do it?" Owyn grinned. "That's wonderful!"

"If I can find someone to take me on, as old as I am," Othi said. "And if I can get my warrior marks removed. I have to talk to Uncle Jehan. I keep forgetting."

"Yeah, it's not like it's been busy or anything." Owyn looked around. "Mem!" he called, raising his voice. "Steward!"

"Owyn!" Memfis shouted back. "This way! Over here!"

Owyn looked up at Othi. "That don't sound good." He started trotting in the direction the voice had come from, hearing Othi behind him. "Mem!"

"Over here!"

They followed the sound, and came around one of the arbors to find Memfis kneeling on the ground next to Skela. The older man was lying flat, and his face was ashen.

"What happened?" Othi demanded, dropping to the ground.

"After Owyn left, Steward went off to look for the boys, and we were going to go up to the healing center," Memfis answered. His voice sounded hoarse. "Skela said his chest hurt, and he fell...I've been shouting, but no one is left down here." He looked around. "Othi, pick him up. He needs a healer."

Othi scooped the old man up in his arms. He didn't wait for instruction, turning and hurrying toward the stairs that would take him back to the healing center. Owyn watched him go, then held his hand out to Memfis.

"Come on, Fa," he said. "You should get looked at, too."

"I'm fine," Memfis said. "I just..." He got to his feet. "I could have carried him. Before. Now...I might have killed him. Because I couldn't leave him, and I couldn't carry him."

Owyn swallowed. There really wasn't anything he could say in response. He put his hand on Memfis' back. "Come on, Fa. Let's go."

Memfis nodded and walked toward the steps. His movements were stiff, almost mechanical. "Is Aria safe?"

"Everyone is fine," Owyn answered. He glanced at Memfis, nodded, and for only the second time in his life, lied to his father. "I think it was the mountain again. Something that didn't quite settle the last time."

Memfis grunted, but didn't say anything else, and Owyn tried not to sigh in relief. He was pretty certain it hadn't been the mountain. He was pretty certain he knew what was really wrong. That something had happened to Milon. But he couldn't say that to his father. He didn't dare. Not with as fragile as Memfis felt right now.

He needed to get back down here to dance. Which meant getting his blades from Aven's stretcher where he'd left them, and slipping back down here without Memfis seeing him.

He just wasn't sure how.

"Steward went to look for Danir and Copper, you said?" Owyn asked. He looked over his shoulder. "If they're not there when we get to the healing center, I'll come back and look for them."

"They probably took another street," Memfis said. "They'll beat us there."

Memfis was right — Steward and the boys were waiting under the tree with Othi. The only healer Owyn could see was Pirit, still sitting next to Aven.

"Where's Skela?" Memfis asked.

"They took him into the tent," Othi answered. He nodded toward a canvas tent that hadn't been there when Owyn left the healing center. "They're working on him now. Aunt Aleia is with them. She promised Del that she'd look after Skela for him."

Owyn nodded and looked around. "Where's Howl?"

"Sleeping over by Healer Aven," Copper answered. He looked down at his feet. "That was a tremor? I've heard about them. Never felt one before. I don't like it."

"No one does, Copper," Steward said. "Everyone is safe?"

Owyn nodded. "We're all fine. Aven is still in healing trance. I...don't know where Del got to. He was with Allie when I left. And Aria was with Aven." He turned, looking around at the people milling about. The crowd parted, and he caught a glimpse of Del, Aria and Meris, sitting next to Aven's stretcher. Someone had found chairs for Meris and Aria, and Del was sitting at Aria's feet, looking worriedly at the tent. She had her hand on his shoulder, and was saying something that Owyn couldn't hear. It reminded Owyn of how they'd looked when he opened the door after Meris had tested him again...had it only been a few days before?

"You know, this trip feels like it's been ten years long already," he said. "We haven't even been away from the Palace ten days!"

Steward chuckled. "It does feel that way, doesn't it?" he said. "Now, I haven't seen Karse or Leesam yet."

"They might be with Rhexa," Owyn said, and remembered his conversation with his aunt. "And she was hoping you'd help her with organizing things so folks have places to sleep tonight."

Steward nodded. "I'll go and find her. Her office is...where?" He looked around.

"Go around the building to the left," Owyn said, and pointed. "I doubt she's in the building, though. If she's outside the building, she'll be outside her office."

Steward nodded. He looked at Memfis, then nodded again. "Come with me. You'll be a big help."

Memfis looked at him, then looked away. "I need to stay here. I need...no, I won't be a help. Not right now."

Othi put his hand on Memfis' shoulder. "It wasn't your fault," he said gently. Then he looked at Owyn. "Why don't you go take Steward to where he needs to be? And...maybe help him?" He jerked his head to the side. But not in the direction Owyn would be going. Instead, it was toward where Aria and Meris sat. Where Aven still slept, blissfully unaware.

Where Owyn had left his blades.

Owyn nodded. "Good idea. I'll be back when I'm back," he said. "Let me just go tell Aria where I am. Steward, you coming?"

He started off through the crowd, hearing Steward behind him. A moment later, the older man was next to him. "What was that?" he whispered.

"I need to go dance," Owyn said. "And Othi knows it. He was telling me to go get my blades."

"Dance? Again?" Steward frowned. Then he stopped and looked around. "Oh, Mother of us all. What do you think happened?"

"I don't know," Owyn whispered. "And we're not talking about it here. I'll tell you everything later. I just need...I need someone to come with me, to make sure I don't fall on my face after I dance." He frowned. "I can't take Del. Even if he wasn't worried about Skela, someone needs to stay with Aria."

"And you can't go alone," Steward added. "It's not safe. And even if it was safe, it's not safe."

Owyn snorted. "I understood that," he said. "Which...which of us is rubbing off on the other?" He looked around. "I...fuck. Who can I take?" He blinked. "Afansa. Where's she?"

"Afansa isn't much of a guard, Owyn," Steward said.

"Then I'll take a guard, too. Someone I know." He looked around. "There's Wren. I've known him since I was still on the streets. He used to slip me boiled sweets when he thought no one was looking."

Steward chuckled. "All right. I'll get Afansa. You go talk to Wren."

Owyn nodded and turned, trotting toward the guard. Wren saw him coming and waved.

"What's wrong?" he asked as Owyn got closer. "You've got a definite look of something wrong."

"You mean, besides the ground shaking like it got bit by a fly?"

Wren's eyes widened. "Big fucking fly," he muttered, and Owyn snorted.

"Yeah. I don't want to know how big," he replied. "No, I need someone to come down to the lowest terrace with me."

Wren looked puzzled, then nodded. "All right. Now?"

"I just need to get my blades," Owyn said. He headed back toward Aria, seeing Steward standing with Afansa. He nodded to Owyn, then bowed to Aria and left, heading in the direction that Owyn had originally told him to go.

"You're going to go dance again?" Aria asked softly as Owyn joined them and picked up his blades.

Owyn nodded. "Yeah, I have a bad feeling about all this. Wren and Afansa are coming with me, so you don't need to worry. I'll be back when I'm back."

Del looked up. "*Be careful,*" he said in Owyn's mind. "*I'll keep an eye on Alanar when he comes out.*"

"Would you mind if I came with you?" Meris asked. "This has...unsettled me."

Owyn smiled at his adoptive grandmother. "You never even have to ask, Granna." He took his blades in one hand, and held his other out to Meris. "Are you all right?"

"I'm fine," Meris answered as she stood up. "But poor Zarai took a fright, and needed to be seen to."

Owyn looked around, seeing Zarai sitting in another chair, her feet up on a box, and with a familiar girl with her. "Is she all right?"

"She's resting, and Gathi is taking good care of her," Meris assured him. "Now, shall we?"

They walked slowly back through empty streets down to the lowest terrace, and Owyn left Meris and Afansa sitting on a bench. He walked out into an open greenspace, and turned to see that Wren had followed him.

"What are you going to do?" Wren asked.

"Hunting visions," Owyn answered. "You know from smoke dancing, right?"

"I knew it was outlawed," Wren answered. "And that Lady Meris was one of the last."

"Yeah, that's not quite the truth," Owyn said with a grin. "Mem is a Smoke Dancer. So am I."

"You're joking!" Wren said with a laugh.

"Nope," Owyn grinned. He nodded back toward the bench. "Go stay with Granna and Afansa. I'll be done soon, I think."

Chapter Thirty-Six

O nce.
      Twice.

Thrice.

The vision grabbed Owyn by the throat and dragged him down, slamming him bodily into a hard, dirt floor and knocking the breath out of him. He wheezed, unable to move. This was not how his visions usually went!

He heard moaning, and it wasn't coming from him. He rolled onto his knees and sat up on his heels. Where was he?

Small room, low ceiling. A cellar? It smelled like a cellar — musty, earthy and damp. There was a small window that let in a little light, high up on one wall. It wasn't enough light to really see into the shadows, to see where the moaning was coming from. So he got to his feet and looked around again. There was a shape...there. That wasn't where the noise was coming from, and as Owyn moved closer, realized that the shape he was seeing was a man, lying flat on his back on a table. Bound to the table. It was hard to see his face, but the vague outline of his profile was so like Aria's that he knew who this had to be.

"Milon?" Owyn gasped. Then gaped as Milon jerked, turning his head slowly.

"I know that voice," he murmured, turning his head this way and that like a hound on the trail. Then he snorted. "Owyn. She got you. How could she have gotten to you? You're supposed to be south. You're supposed to be safe. I promised Trey that you were safe."

"You can hear me?" Owyn breathed. "I...Milon, I am south. I am safe. She didn't get me. I'm not here. I went hunting visions. I'm in Terraces. I...I think. This..." He reached out and touched Milon's arm, and there was enough light that he saw the shock on Milon's face.

"You are here? You...you projected?" he whispered. "I was taught it was possible, but not...there hasn't been a Smoke Dancer who could project in...in generations, and...and I *told* you not to come back!"

Owyn snorted. "You don't know me well, but here's the thing. I don't listen real good." He squeezed Milon's arm. "Where's Trey? And what's happening here? What's she doing to you?" He stood up. "Whatever it was...it made the ground shake at Terraces."

Milon frowned. "I...don't understand."

Owyn looked around. His eyes were adjusting to the dim light, and he could see the door. Hopefully, it would stay closed. "It's a long theory, but in a nutshell, if something happens to us, to one of Aria's Companions, bad things happen. The Smoking Mountain blew when I died for all of a minute. Today, the ground shook. We're all fine...but something happened to you when I contacted you before, and the ground shook right after."

Milon nodded slowly. "She pushes me...to the point that my heart will stop. It's not strong. Not anymore. Not since I was so sick. That was what happened. She brought me back again. Said she wasn't done with me."

"Oh, fuck," Owyn breathed. He heard the moan again and turned. "Is...is that Trey?"

"Don't," Milon said. "Leave him be. Don't...leave him alone, Owyn. She's hurt him. And you don't want to see." He turned his head suddenly. "She's coming. Go back."

"How?" Owyn looked around. "I don't know how I got here!"

Milon closed his eyes, and for a moment, Owyn was sure he could hear the man swearing under his breath.

"You weren't taught how to break a vision?" he asked. "Memfis...I'm going to wring your blasted neck...right. Close your eyes."

Owyn did as he was told. "Now what?"

"When you open them, open them in your real body. Now go!"

Owyn opened his eyes, then coughed as the air rushed back into his lungs. He rolled onto one side, wheezing, and felt his blade underneath his arm. Blinking, he looked around. Terraces. Wren was staring at him, a knife in his hand.

"You...you looked sort of dead..." Wren said slowly. "Were you dead?"

"Don't think so," Owyn wheezed again. "At least, not this time." He pushed up onto his knees. "I need to get back." He frowned. "Where are Granna and Afansa?"

"I sent them back," Wren said. "One of the boys came down and said that Memfis was looking for you. I sent them back as a diversion, so he wouldn't come down here looking for you."

Owyn nodded. "Help me up, will you?" he asked. "Where's my other blade?"

"Stay there a minute," Wren said. He sheathed his knife and walked past Owyn, coming back carrying the blade. "Got it. Let me get the other." He took both blades in one hand, then held his other out to Owyn. "You look like you've had a long night on Tannery after payday."

"Feel like it," Owyn replied as he took Wren's hand and got to his feet. His legs felt wobbly, and he swayed, feeling like he was out on the canoe in a high wind. Wren caught him before he tipped.

"You really are smashed," Wren chuckled. "I should take you to the drunk tank."

"I don't think they have a drunk tank here," Owyn muttered as they started walking toward the stairs. His legs felt as if they were two different lengths, and he grimaced and shook his head. "I need to eat something."

"You need to sleep this off," Wren replied.

"Nah, this isn't drunk. Well...it sort of is, but it isn't. Smoke Dancers need to eat after they dance. To re-anchor to the real world." Owyn shook his head again. "It's...I'll explain it all later."

"Fine with me," Wren said. "We'll get you back, get you fed, and...what did you see? Did you see something?"

Owyn nodded and grimaced again. "Yeah. I'll tell you once I eat. I've got to tell Aria and Fa first. These streets are long, aren't they?" He frowned. "Is the ground shaking again?"

Wren snorted. "No, my friend. That's all you." He laughed. "Haven't you ever been drunk before?"

Owyn laughed. "Of course I have! Alcohol, and sometimes whatever street drug was big when I was still whoring. Whatever the men who paid for me were willing to give. It helped." He shivered. "Can we not talk about that?" he asked. "Did you mean that?"

"Sorry, and did I mean what?"

Owyn smiled as they stumbled up a flight of stairs. "You called me your friend. Did you mean that?" He looked up at the taller guard. "I never had a lot of friends before. Trey...Trey was it, I think. You don't make friends when you're on the street."

"No friends?" Wren scoffed. "You've got the Heir and all the Companions, and Alanar and—"

"That's different," Owyn interrupted. "Aria and Aven and Treesi, they like me cause they have to like me. Allie...well, we were friends. Now he's my husband. Which is sorta different and sorta the same? I dunno. Never had one of those before either. Husband, I mean." Owyn looked down at his feet. There were still two of them. "Othi's a friend. Karse is a friend. Trey, but fuck if I know if I'll see him again. She's hurting him, Wren. Don't you tell Karse that."

"Not a word," Wren promised. "And yes, I meant it."

Owyn nodded. "Good. I like you. Always have." He grinned. "You used to slip me boiled sweets when you saw me, remember? Back when you were first training?"

"You remember that?" Wren shook his head. "I'd nearly forgotten."

"When you come up on the streets, and someone does something nice for you, with no strings attached? You remember." Owyn yawned. "I'm going to need to eat and sleep."

"We're almost there." Wren stopped. "And they've come looking."

Owyn looked up, and saw Othi coming toward them. There appeared to be one more of him than usual, and Owyn shook his head and blinked his eyes.

"Which one is the real one?" he whispered.

"Oh, fuck," Wren breathed. "Othi, he's seeing double. I think he needs to be off his feet."

"I just need to eat!" Owyn protested, as one of the Othis scooped him up. "I'm...well, I'm not fine. But I'm not sick."

"Not sick yet," Othi corrected. "Let's go make sure you don't get sick at all." He started walking, carrying Owyn as easily as if he was a child. It was interesting. Owyn couldn't remember ever being carried like this. But someone must have, before his parents died? Huris must have carried him like this, put him to bed. Or maybe Dyneh did, when he was still too small to remember. And she sang to him. He knew that.

He wished he remembered.

"HE'LL BE FINE," ARIA said, rubbing her hand over Del's shoulder. "Jehan will let us know soon."

Del tore his attention from the tent, tipped his head back and nodded, then looked back. Memfis was pacing in front of the tent, with Steward standing nearby, watching him. Memfis had snarled at Del the last time Del had gone to see if he needed anything. But Del understood. He was worried. They were both worried. But...Jehan was one of the best healers to ever live, Del was certain. Skela would be fine. This time...

"Ar-ya," he said softly. "He...shhh...go."

Aria frowned. "Do you mean Skela? Go where?"

Del nodded and tugged his tablet out. It was faster to write. "*He's too old for this trip,*" he wrote. "*He and Zarai should both go back to the Palace. We don't know what else we're going to face. It's not safe for us, let alone them.*"

Aria took the tablet and read it. Then she sighed. "You're right," she murmured. "As much as I hate to admit it, you're right. Aven won't like it. He wanted Zarai with us in case the baby came early."

Del took the tablet and wiped it. "*If something happens to Zarai, then he'll feel guilty for bringing her.*"

"He will," Aria agreed. She shifted in her chair, and Del frowned and arched a brow. She noticed, and laughed. "I am a little uncomfortable. This chair makes my back hurt. And I drank too much. Can we go inside for that long? Pirit?"

Pirit nodded without turning her attention from her grandson. "You should be fine to go back inside, so long as you don't linger. I'll see to your back when you come back."

Del stood up and offered his arm, and helped Aria out of the chair. She stretched and turned, and stopped to point. "That's Othi."

Del turned, and saw Othi coming toward them, with Owyn cradled in his arms. Next to Othi was one of the guards, carrying Owyn's smoke blades.

"Owyn!"

Memfis' voice rang out, and Del hear Aria swear softly. "I didn't think he was paying attention to anything other than the tent," she muttered. "Memfis, wait!"

Memfis didn't listen, leaving the tent at a run and pushing past people to get to Othi.

"He's fine," Othi said, his voice clear and soothing. "He needs to eat."

"He went and danced?" Memfis demanded. "Again?"

"Bring him here," Aria called, and stepped out of the way. Othi bent, and poured Owyn into the chair. Owyn grabbed on to the seat with both hands, looked up, and grinned at Aria.

"You look just like him," he said. "Your fa."

"What?" Memfis dropped to his knees in front of Owyn. "You saw him? You danced, and you actually *saw* him this time?" He looked around. "Get him some food! Where's Lady Meris? I..." He turned back to Owyn. "She was with you. She knew you were doing this. You could have killed yourself!"

Owyn shook his head, then closed his eyes. "Nah, I'm fine. Just need to eat."

Aria heard a commotion behind her, and turned to see Steward and Meris coming toward them, Meris' face lined with worry.

"What is it?" she asked as she reached Aria. "I heard Memfis shouting. Is Owyn all right?"

"He danced," Memfis growled. "Again. And you knew he was going to do it."

Meris raised her chin. "I did. And I agreed with his reasons."

"Which we are not discussing here," Aria added, keeping her voice low. "We will discuss what he saw in private." She looked at Memfis. "He acted on the will of his Heir, Memfis."

Memfis blinked. "I—" He swallowed, then nodded. "My Heir."

"Now, will you go and find something for him to eat?" Aria asked. "You know what he needs better than any of us, I think?"

Memfis nodded and turned, walking away. Othi arched a brow at Aria. She nodded, and he followed after Memfis. Once he was gone, she turned to Wren.

"Thank you, for being with him," she said. "I appreciate your help."

Wren smiled slightly. "My pleasure, my Heir. Besides, he's my friend."

Owyn tipped his head back. "Thank you."

Wren clapped him on the shoulder. "You feel better. I need to get off and find my captain, see what I'm supposed to be doing. I'll check on you later." He turned and walked off, and Owyn turned to look at Aria. She leaned down to kiss him, then cupped his cheek; he closed his eyes and sighed.

"Later. I get to tell you later," he murmured. "It's not good."

"I didn't expect that it would be," she answered softly. "Just tell me that he lives?"

Owyn nodded. "Yeah, he's alive."

Aria sighed softly. "Good."

Owyn nodded, then looked up at Meris. "Granna, what the..." He paused, then coughed before asking, "Granna, what's projecting?"

Meris paled. "What?"

"Projecting," Owyn repeated. "I..." He looked around. "Fuck, we're not talking about this now. Not in public. But Granna, I was there. I saw him. I was *there*, in that cellar, with Milon and Trey. At least...I think Trey was there. I didn't see him. But Milon heard me. And I touched him. I was really there."

Meris covered her mouth with her hand and nodded. "I...I should have expected this," she murmured as she took her hand away. "You're so sensitive, so open. I should...but there hasn't been a Smoke Dancer capable of projecting in generations!"

"Memfis is coming back," Aria warned. Meris nodded, and touched Owyn's shoulder.

"We'll discuss this once you've eaten. You and I and Memfis will have to have a long talk." She turned to face Memfis, who was carrying a basket in his hand. "What did you bring?"

"I haven't any idea," Memfis answered. "A woman named Sanna sent it. She gave it to Othi and said they were from Hesha. Who's Hesha?"

Owyn chuckled. "Little girl with lost parents. I'll tell you later. What is it?"

Memfis put the basket in Owyn's lap. "Here. Open it."

Owyn opened the basket and burst out laughing. "Pasties! When was the last time we had pasties, Mem?"

Memfis smiled slightly. "The last time we got them from Gwenet's shop. What...a few days before we went and found Aria and Aven? You never did get the knack of making the dough."

"I swear, there was something she wasn't telling me about that dough," Owyn grumbled as he pulled something that looked like bread out of the basket. "Aria, you should try these."

"You eat first, Owyn," Aria said. "Settle yourself. I'll try one when I come back." She held her hand out to Del, who took it and led her toward the healing center.

OWYN WATCHED AS ARIA and Del walked away, finishing his mouthful as they entered the healing center.

"Should they be going inside?" he asked, and took another bite. "These are really good."

"They'll be fine," Meris said. "How are you feeling?"

"Hollow," Owyn answered as he swallowed. He took a deep breath and closed his eyes, slowly taking another bite. As he finished, curiosity prevailed over caution. "Tell me more about projecting while I fill up."

"Projecting?" Memfis repeated. He sat down at Owyn's feet. "Why are you asking about that?"

Owyn looked around, made sure no one was close enough to hear him, then leaned forward and spoke in a low voice. "Because I did it. That's how I saw him. I was there. And he knew I was there." He smiled and took another bite. "He yelled at me for doing it. And told me how to get back. Why didn't you tell me about projecting?"

Memfis shifted, resting his elbow on his knee. "Because there hasn't been a Smoke Dancer strong enough to project since...Meris, it was Fantrada the Wise, wasn't it?"

"You remember your history," Meris said. She rested her hand on Owyn's shoulder, and he looked up at her.

"Granna, you can sit. I'll sit on the ground." He started to shift, but her hand tightened.

"If I sit in the chair, I'll fall asleep," she said. "Right now, I want to stand. Fantrada the Wise was...let me see..." She paused, her eyes narrowed. "Your...fifth grandmother? I think fifth."

"That means five greats in front of the grandmother part, don't it?" Owyn asked. "And...your line or Mem's?"

She chuckled. "Yours, my darling Owyn. Huris was of her line. Once we were settled in the Palace, I traced your bloodline in The Book of Silver."

Owyn stared at her. "Really? You did that? You didn't tell me!"

"I was going to, but it slipped my mind before we left," Meris sighed and shook her head. "Getting old...it's not always a blessing."

"The alternative isn't either," Memfis muttered, and looked over at the tent.

Owyn looked down at the basket in his lap, then held it out to Memfis. "Eat something, Fa."

Memfis shook his head. "I'm not—"

"Memfis, you haven't eaten in hours. Eat something," Steward growled. Memfis glared, but took a pasty and started eating. Owyn looked up at Steward.

"I forgot you were there," he admitted. "Want one? They're good." He offered the basket.

"I haven't had a good pasty in...I can't even think when," Steward said. "And...the shop you got them? Silversmith Lane?"

Memfis blinked. "You know it?"

"They were the best ones in Forge," Steward answered. He took a bite and smiled. "But these are better. So what is projecting? I've never heard of that. Part of the mysteries of the Smoke that I don't get to know?"

"It was, but I'm not sure if it benefits anyone to keep the mysteries secret, not when the result is uncontrolled projecting. This is something that Owyn should have known." She looked thoughtful. "A very strong Smoke Dancer can send their consciousness out and be in two places at once. Their physical body is where they were dancing. Their mind, and the thought-forms of their mind, are elsewhere, and can appear solid. That is projecting."

Steward nodded. "And...where was Owyn? When his body was here?"

"North," Owyn said softly. "With Milon." He looked around, saw Aria and Del coming back. "I'll tell you all everything when we're private. But it's not good."

Chapter Thirty-Seven

It was nearly dark before the healing center was deemed safe, and they started taking the patients back inside. Aria sat next to Aven's sleeping form and watched as attendants came, gently picked up stretchers, and left. By the time they came for Aven, the stars were coming out; Aria was about to get out of her chair and follow the attendants into the healing center when Rhexa came around the corner of the building. With her was Steward, who was carrying a lantern.

"I had your house checked," Rhexa said. "It's safe. Nothing broken, no cracks. You can go and get some sleep."

"What about you, Auntie?" Owyn asked. He was sitting on the ground at Aria's feet, his head resting on her right knee. Del was on her left, his head heavy on her leg. Aria was fairly certain that he was already asleep.

"I honestly don't know if I'll see my bed tonight," Rhexa admitted. "There's too much to do." She smiled up at Steward. "You're being a big help, you know."

"I'm pleased to be of service," Steward said. "Now, the healers are all staying the night in the healing center, as are Lady Meris and Afansa. Skela wanted to sleep in the water, so Othi and Aleia went with him. That means you have to make do with just these two, my Heir."

"...eard...t'at," Del muttered, making Steward laugh.

"Where's Mem?" Owyn asked.

"I put him to work," Rhexa answered. "While we're making the plans and organizing the inspection teams that will be going back out at dawn, he's arranging for tents and food to be brought to all the areas where people are camping. Although I fully expect to find him asleep on the table by the time we get back."

"It would be understandable, after the day we've had." Aria ran her fingers through Del's hair. "Let's go back to the house and get some sleep. We all need it. And Owyn, I want to know what happened."

"Now?" Owyn looked up at her. "You don't want to wait for everyone?"

"If you don't mind telling it twice, I'd like to know. Then you can tell everyone else tomorrow when we're all together."

Owyn nodded. He rolled onto his knees, stretched, then got to his feet and held his hands out — one to Del, the other to Aria. "All right. Let's go back. I'll make some tea. We'll talk, and then get some sleep. All in one bed?"

"Please?" Aria let him help her up, then held onto him as he tugged Del to his feet. To her surprise, he slipped one around her waist, and the other around Del's, pulling them both close.

"I'm sorry I worried you both," he murmured. "I didn't think it would hit me that hard. I haven't been as bad as I was. And thanks, for backing me up with Mem. For telling him you told me to. I appreciate you not letting him yell at me. Because...yeah, I kinda should have been yelled at. We're taught not to do things like that. It's dangerous."

"It was necessary," Aria countered. "And I want to know why it was necessary. Let's go back to the house."

"Here." Steward offered them the lantern. "You'll need this."

They walked slowly through the dark streets. Owyn let Aria and Del go so that they could walk without worrying about tripping over each other. Aria walked carefully, keeping an eye on the ground, her wings flared slightly for balance. It had the unfortunate effect that neither of her men could walk close to her, but she'd have them close soon enough. The stairs up to the terrace and the house were cracked in places, and uneven under her feet, and it seemed to be a much longer walk back to the house than it had been before.

"More damage than I thought there'd be," Owyn said. "Aria, are you doing all right?"

"I'm fine," Aria answered. "I am tired, though."

"We can wait until tomorrow—"

"I am not that tired, Owyn." Aria smiled when he looked at her. "I told you. I want to know."

Owyn nodded. At the top of the stairs, he held his hand out to her, and to Del, and they walked the rest of the way to the house together.

The house was dark, the air chilly, and Owyn groaned. "The stove is most likely cold. It'll take a while to heat up for tea."

"No tea," Del said. "Bed."

Owyn chuckled. "You heard him. Bed." He took the lantern from Del and led the way through the house and up the stairs. "Let me get a slip, and we'll get some lamps lit and maybe a fire lit. I've had enough sleeping cold as a kid to never want to do it again." He went to the sideboard and picked up a long slip, lighting a pair of lamps from the lantern. "I'll light another in the bedroom, and get the fire going. There's not going to be hot water to wash."

"We can bathe tomorrow once the boiler is fired," Aria said. "Right now? A quick wash, a long talk, and bed. In that order."

Owyn nodded. "Take one of the lamps, then. Go wash up, and I'll get the fire started. Then you can get warmed up while I wash." He headed into Aria's bedroom, and Aria turned to Del.

"I didn't ask you, and I should have," she said. "Do you want to share my bed tonight?"

Del smiled. He stepped closer, looked her up and down, then moved slightly to the side. She turned to watch him, and he gingerly reached up to cup her cheek before leaning close to kiss her on the lips. It was tentative, sweet and exploring, asking without words because how else would Del ask? He pulled back slightly, and even in the dim light of the lamp, Aria could see the crimson creeping up his throat, staining his cheeks.

"You've gotten very good at that," Aria said, smiling. His blush deepened.

"*I like kissing,*" he signed. "*Do you want to wash up first?*"

"I'll go get started, then you can join me, or you can take the bathing room if I finish before you come down." Aria leaned in close and kissed Del lightly on the lips. "If you want more practice, we can. Later."

Del nodded, then stepped away, picking up one of the lamps and handing it to her.

ONCE ARIA WAS GONE, Del bit his lip and looked around, then went to the bedroom door and looked inside. Owyn was kneeling in front of the little fireplace, building up a small blaze.

"*Owyn?*"

Owyn looked up. "You done washing up?"

"*Not yet.*" Del looked over his shoulder. Something felt strange in his chest. Tight. Uncomfortable. It wasn't physical, he didn't think. But..."*I kissed Aria.*"

Owyn shifted so he was sitting on the floor, looking up at Del. "Did you?" He grinned. "And?"

"*And she liked it,*" Del answered. "*And...and I liked it. And...now what do I do?*"

Owyn smiled. "Nothing you're not comfortable doing. And...well, do you want me in here? I can go to my room if you want to figure it out alone. Aria will help you."

Del coughed. "*I want you to stay!*" He saw Owyn wince, and shivered. "*Sorry.*"

"No, I'm sorry," Owyn said. He stood up, dusting off his trousers. "I didn't mean to make you uncomfortable. Del, what you do next is up to you. And you've been in bed with me and Allie. You know what comes next. But only if you want to. And only if you're ready." He rested his hands on Del's shoulders, rubbing them up and down his arms. "Del, you don't have to do anything you don't want to do. All you have to do is tell us to stop. And if you can't say the words, just think them and I'll hear you. You know I will."

Del nodded, then stepped into Owyn's embrace. Owyn's arms closed around him, warm and strong and comforting. "*I like kissing.*"

Owyn's laugh wrapped around Del like a warm blanket. "I know you like kissing. And you're getting really good at it. And it's fine if that's all you want. Now, why has this got you all twisted up? Because it didn't bother you this much when you were in bed with me and Allie."

Del frowned, then tipped his head back so he could look at Owyn. He was right. "*I don't know,*" Del admitted. "*I just...I'm not sure. You and Allie, you didn't want more from me than I was ready to give. And I don't know if I'm ready to give more. And I think Aria wants more. I just...I don't know if I can be more. More than I already am, I mean. At least, not yet.*"

Owyn nodded. "Right. I followed all that. Have you told her?"

Del shook his head. "*Not yet, no. I don't know how. I don't want her to feel bad—*"

"Is something wrong?"

Del turned to see Aria in the door. He swallowed, looked up at Owyn, then sighed. She arched a brow and came closer.

"Del?" she said slowly. "Did I do something wrong? Did I push?" She groaned. "I pushed, didn't I? I made you uncomfortable. I'm sorry!"

"Tell her she didn't do anything, Owyn?"

"Del say it wasn't anything you did," Owyn relayed. He let Del go, but kept one hand on his back. "Del's not sure how far he's ready to go yet," he said. "And he's worried he might hurt you trying to figure that out."

Aria let out a long breath and smiled softly. "Then I have been pushing. And I'm sorry, Del. Asking you if you wanted to explore things further...I didn't think." She made a face. "I seem to have that problem, don't I? I don't think things all the way through." She sighed. "Del—"

Del closed his eyes and swallowed. "Ahm...no...reh...ready," he said slowly. He gestured to his face. "Li...like...tis..." He paused. "Ah...ah..." He frowned, then growled and tugged his tablet out of his bag. *"I'll get there. Maybe. But I have to work on it. Like talking. And Pirit said I might not ever get there with talking. I might not ever get there with this."*

"Del," Owyn said slowly. "Allie said that there are some folks who just...don't, and that's normal for them. So there might not be a 'there' for you to get to. Not and still be...well...you."

Del shrugged, then wrote, *"Everyone has a 'there.' A place where they don't feel right going past. I won't know mine unless I try. I don't know where my limits are. Except I know I like kissing everyone. And I liked making you and Allie happy."* He shrugged again. *"But I don't know what else there is. I want to know. I want to see how far I can go before I stop liking things."*

"Then you set the pace, Del," Aria said. "And tell us if we're going too fast, or the wrong way. And don't worry about hurting me. I'm more worried that we might hurt you." She smiled. "I enjoy kissing you, too. And if that is all we ever do? Then that is all we do. Because you mean so much more to me than that. You are so much more to me than what we may or may not do in bed." She looked at the bed. "Speaking of the bed, I am tired. We're all tired. I do want to have this talk before we sleep. Go and get ready for bed."

Del laughed, feeling the discomfort in his chest easing. He nodded, set his tablet down on the bed, and smiled. Owyn nodded toward the door.

"Go on. I'll be down in a minute to wash up. Once I'm sure this fire is set right." He looked back at the fireplace. "Go on. I'll be along in a minute."

Del looked at Aria, who smiled. "Do you feel better?"

Del nodded. Then he grinned. *"Yes, I think so."* He looked around the room. *"You're right. We are all tired. It's been a long day. And you wanted to talk. I'll hurry."*

THEY SETTLED IN THE middle of the big bed, and Owyn wound a blanket around himself, and watched as Del and Aria both did the same.

"Owyn, what did you learn? How bad is it, truly?" Aria asked, tucking her wings in close as she pleated the blanket between her fingers.

"Real bad," Owyn answered. "Your father has a weak heart. He said it's been since he was so sick. Probably when he had the ague. And the ground shook because his heart stopped. Whatever Risha did to him, it made his heart stop. And then she brought him back. She told him that she's not done with him. But..." He frowned. There was something...he couldn't remember. He shook his head. "There's something...I can't think of what it is. But...yeah, it looks like if something happens to him, Adavar takes exception to it, just like with one of us." He shifted, tugging the blanket more tightly around his shoulders.

"*What about Trey?*" Del asked. Owyn sighed.

"I don't know," he answered, shaking his head. "It's not good, but I don't know. He...Milon told me that Risha hurt him. That Trey tried to put himself between Risha and Milon, and she hurt him. She broke him." He stopped. Frowned. "When I was there, I heard someone moaning. I think it was Trey. Milon...he told me to not look. And he told me not to come back. The first time I danced today, when I talked to him, he told me that he didn't think they'd survive long enough for us to find them."

Aria looked at him in horror. "He said that?"

Owyn nodded. "He said that. And...fuck, Aria, I don't know what to do about it. We can't stop the Progress. We can't go north. Not without endangering everything we've worked for. Which means...well, I think we all know what it means. So...yeah. That's what I saw." He shifted. "So...are you going to be able to sleep now that I've told you?"

Aria took a deep breath and shifted, looking away. "I...I need to think."

"How clearly are you going to think, as tired as you are?" Owyn asked. She glared at him, and he smiled. "Aria, I know you. I know me. We don't do our best thinking when we're tired." He held his hand out. "Come on. Let's get some sleep. We'll talk again once we wake up, and I'll tell the others, and we'll do what we need to do."

Aria sighed, and looked like she wanted to protest. Then she shook her head. "You're right," she grumbled. "How are we sleeping?"

They shifted and tugged blankets and arranged pillows, until they were curled around each other. Owyn was flat on his back, with Aria on his left shoulder, and Del on his right. He put his arms around them both, then chuckled.

"I'm not going to be able to get up and cook breakfast if we stay like this."

"I don't care," Aria mumbled. "I want to be held."

Owyn smiled and ran his hand up her back, feeling her feathers tickling his arm. "Try to sleep, love. You need it."

She grumbled at him, a soft, sleepy sound. Then she stretched up and kissed him before resettling on his shoulder. Owyn closed his eyes, hearing Del's sleepy, wordless mumble in his mind.

It was the last thing he remembered.

OWYN WOKE UP ON HIS side, curled around Del. He blinked and raised his head, but Aria wasn't in the bedroom. He shifted slowly, crawling out of the bed and looking out into the sitting room. No one there. He looked back at Del, still asleep, then sighed and went to pick up his trousers. He pulled them on and headed for the stairs, fastening the waist as he went down to the main floor.

"Aria?" he called softly as he reached the bottom of the stairs.

"I'm out here," she called back. He walked out to the front room and found her leaning against the wall next to the window. She was wrapped in a blanket, and looked as if she hadn't slept at all.

"How long have you been awake?" he asked as he joined her. "And—"

"No one can see me here. And there is no one out there this early." She looked at him and smiled. "I did sleep. But I woke and couldn't fall back to sleep. So I came down here to watch the sun rise."

Owyn snorted. "You can see through rock now? Sunrise is behind the mountain."

She smiled, which was what he was hoping she'd do. "I can see the sky change color from here."

Owyn nodded and put his arm around her, pulling her to his side. "Why don't you go tuck in with Del for a bit while I get breakfast made?" he suggested. "He's still asleep. Go see if you can get any more sleep and I'll come get you both when it's time to eat."

Aria leaned into him, and seemed to be about to object. Then she yawned. Her face colored slightly, and she smiled. "I think I might."

Owyn hugged her more tightly to his side. She turned and reached up, catching the back of his neck with one hand and pulling him into a kiss. He wrapped his arms around her, whimpering as her fingers tangled in his curls and pulled.

"You could come back to bed with me," she murmured against his lips. "We could go to your bed."

For a moment, Owyn was tempted. Then his stomach growled. He looked down, and he and Aria both started laughing.

"Or...not," she added. "I will go back to bed and try to sleep. And you'll make breakfast. And we'll get on with our day. Aven should be released from the healing center today."

"And people are going to want to see you," Owyn added. "The ones who didn't see you last night. They're going to want to know that you're safe, and that you're caring for them. So let me..." He stopped talking when he saw movement out the window. Who was awake this early?

"Owyn? What...oh!"

Owyn and Aria watched as Steward and Rhexa came up the stairs from the lower terrace. They were both still in the clothes they had worn the day before, looking rumpled, tired and dirty. They walked hand in hand, and as they reached the top of the stair, Steward stopped. Rhexa turned to face him, and he pulled her to him, leaning down to kiss her. Then they walked on, and neither seemed to notice Owyn and Aria watching them.

"Well," Owyn breathed. "I think...we're going to keep this between us, right?"

"I think we will, yes," Aria agreed. "And I am going back to bed."

"I'll come wake you for breakfast when it's ready." Owyn stepped back, and watched as Aria walked back toward the stairs. Then he headed for the kitchen. He'd fire the stove, then go down to the dispensary for supplies.

Chapter Thirty-Eight

They sat down to eat breakfast at the small table in the kitchen — Owyn set out a bowl of fluffy eggs, a platter of griddlecakes, sausages, and strong tea.

"It's too much food, Owyn," Aria protested.

"Nah," Owyn answered. "I'm starving, you've got a passenger, and Del can eat his own weight. We might have enough. Maybe."

He put down the teapot, then looked up when he heard someone calling, "Is anyone awake?"

"Jehan?" Owyn went to the kitchen door. "We're in the kitchen. There's breakfast, if you haven't eaten." He went to the cabinet and started taking out more plates. "Is anyone else with you?" he called over his shoulder.

"You could say that."

Owyn turned, nearly dropping the stack of plates. "Allie!"

Alanar stood in the doorway, leaning against the doorframe. He looked tired, and his clothes were dirty and had clearly been slept in. But he was smiling.

"We're all starving," he added. "So I hope you made a lot of whatever smells so good."

"All?" Aria asked, turning in her chair. "Who is included in that?"

Alanar grinned. "Me and Jehan, to start. Treesi, once Othi lets her go. Maybe Othi. I don't know if he ate yet." He turned slightly, and Aven stepped into the doorway. "And we found this stranger...." Alanar added, and Aven laughed.

"Aven!" Aria pushed her chair back, but never had the chance to stand; he was by her side in a heartbeat, helping her out of the chair and into his arms. Owyn stared at him.

"You're walking," he gasped. "You're not limping! Not at all!" He turned and looked at Jehan and Alanar. "What did you do?"

Jehan smiled. "Something we didn't think would work, to be honest," he answered. "And I'm not entirely sure why it did. But...basically, we crushed the bone and rebuilt it."

"And it shouldn't have worked," Owyn repeated. He looked at Aven. "Will it stay fixed?"

"We'll see?" Jehan shrugged. Then he yawned. "Is there tea?"

"Yes, and more food, and you can help us move everything to the dining room." Owyn looked at Aven again. "Once I get my turn."

Eventually, they moved to the dining room, and the food wasn't too cold by the time they all sat down to eat. Del and Aria sat on Aven's left, and Owyn and Treesi sat on his right. Jehan, Alanar and Othi sat across from them, and all three of them looked amused.

Owyn ate slowly, because he had to keep reminding himself to eat, and to stop touching Aven's arm, or his leg. Or looking at his relaxed smile.

"You know, I don't think I've seen you smile like that since the picnic," he blurted out.

Aven looked at him, clearly puzzled. Then he blinked. "The one we took in the park, before...before everything? Really?"

"That night, you were a mess of nerves, and you weren't relaxed. And then...well, after that, you were always hurting. Even when you were happy, you weren't. Because you hurt. You haven't smiled like this in..." Owyn paused, then continued. "In most of a year."

Aven refilled his teacup, spooned some salt into it, stirred it, and took a sip. "There were points, after I came back and Fa and Grandmother and everyone worked on this hip the first time. There were points where it almost didn't hurt. Now? It doesn't hurt. At all."

"And will it stay like this?" Aria asked. She looked across at Jehan. "Will you need to do this again?"

"Mother of us all, I hope not!" Jehan answered, and laughed. "That was...for some of it, I wasn't even sure what my mother was doing. I was just feeding her the power she needed to do it." He shook his head. "I know what I know about healing from book-learning. Mother is an intuitive healer. She just knows what needs to be done. Once she's done it, she can explain why. But I've never been sure that she knows what she's actually going to do until it's done."

Aven stopped with a spoonful of eggs half-raised. "You mean she was guessing?"

Jehan made a face. "No...but in so many words, I suppose yes. But I have also never known her to be wrong."

"*What about swimming?*" Del signed. "*Have you tried to change yet?*"

"Not yet," Aven said. "We came here first." He looked to his left, then to his right. "I needed to be here first."

"We're going down once we eat," Othi added. "Del, come with us. Skela wants to see you."

"How is he?" Aria asked.

"Better for having had a night's sleep in the deep," Othi answered. "But he's already told Aunt Aleia that when we leave, he's not going on. I think this scared him, so he's going back to the canoes." He frowned. "What will that mean for the lore?"

"So long as the Heir and the Companions continue on, the integrity of the Progress will be maintained," Jehan answered. He sighed and sipped his tea. "That, and following the right route."

"Fa, do you believe the lore about Axia's Way?" Aven asked.

"I didn't, when I was on Milon's Progress. Avoiding the flooded areas made sense." He paused. "Now...I've had it proven to me that the lore isn't just a story." He sighed again. "And I wonder if things might have been different if we'd just waited out the flood and gone the right way."

"There's no way for you to know that," Aria said. "And no way to know if things would have changed if you had. What's done is done, Jehan. Fretting over it won't change anything." She shifted in her chair, and leaned into Aven's arm. "I want to come down to the water with you. I want to see you swim."

Aven colored slightly. "Want to swim with me?"

Aria smiled. "I would like that. But perhaps not today. Today, I need to let people see me, see that the tremor yesterday was nothing of import. Then we need to talk. Owyn danced yesterday, and learned things."

Aven nodded slowly. "Council?"

"Council," Aria agreed. "Jehan, would you tell the others? I want nothing in writing. Not for this."

"When do you want us here?" Jehan asked. "And am I including people who aren't usually part of the Palace Council? The last time we had Council in Terraces, Rhexa and Pirit were here."

Aria looked thoughtful. "Yes," she said slowly. "I value their opinions."

Aven set his cup down. "Tremor," he repeated. "The ground shook again yesterday?"

"No one told you?" Owyn asked. He looked at Jehan. "Why didn't anyone tell him?"

"Mostly because once his eyes were open and we took the block off his nerves, he was kind of insistent on coming here," Jehan answered. "And wasn't about to stop to listen to what he'd missed. Or his aftercare, for that matter."

"Tremor first, aftercare after," Aven said quickly. "What did I miss?" He looked around the table. "Is everyone safe?"

"We are," Owyn said. "And...that's what we need to talk about."

Aven blinked. Then he swallowed. "Milon?"

"What?" Jehan gasped. "Owyn!"

"You're all going to know at the same time," Owyn said. "I'm not telling it sixteen times. I told Aria and Del last night, and I'll tell everyone else when we're all in the same room. Which...when, Aria?"

Aria closed her eyes and shook her head. "I'd like to have it done sooner rather than later. But I do have a responsibility. Midday?"

"I'll tell everyone to come here for midday," Jehan said. "Now. Aftercare. And I'm telling you all this because you all need to know." He pointed at Aven. "That hip may not hurt now, but Mother thinks it will be a problem as you get older. And you're going to have to be careful. The rebuilt bones don't seem to be as strong as they were. I'm not certain why, but the reformed bone is closer to what I'd expect in someone from Earth or Fire than from a Waterborn." He looked around the table. "You understand the difference?" he asked. "Not the healers. I know you know."

Owyn frowned and looked at Aria. "Water bones are heavier, aren't they? Denser?" he asked.

"Exactly," Jehan answered. "They have to be, in order for the tribe to survive in the deep water." He paused and looked at Aven, an odd expression on his face. "Although you do seem to have a special talent for breaking bones, now that I think of it. More than

I'm used to in Water, anyway. Probably my fault — the Earth blood in your veins."

"I don't think it's anyone's fault, Fa. And only one of those broken bones was my doing," Aven pointed out. "My arm, when I dove into the rock. That was me being stupid. The rest were things done to me."

"You dove into a rock?" Alanar asked.

"I was twelve," Aven answered. "And stupid. I knew better than to dive into waters I didn't know. I did it anyway."

"That's unlike you, my Water," Aria murmured.

"I was showing off." Aven grinned. "For a girl."

"Regardless of what happened when it wasn't your doing, I think the difference in your bones when compared to someone who is fully Water may have been what saved your life—"

"Unlikely," Alanar interrupted, his voice quiet. "It didn't save Virrik's life."

Jehan winced. "Alanar, I'm sorry. I'd forgotten. Virrik—"

"Virrik says that it's understandable, since you never actually met him. And he accepts your apology. As do I." Alanar smiled and shifted forward, resting his elbows on the table and lacing his fingers together. "Go on, then. What do we need to know? It sounds like more than regular protocol for broken bones or damaged muscles."

Jehan nodded, and Owyn fought the urge to laugh. He did laugh when Jehan gave him a sour look.

"It's a more intensive protocol based on the regular one," Jehan answered. He scowled at Owyn, then smiled. "The muscles are still healing, and they're still tender. They're not as strong as they were, and they'll need to be built back up, so they'll need to be worked carefully until they're stronger. Now as for the bones, we're just not sure how far that hip can be pushed. So Mother recommends incremental activity, taken very slowly." He smiled. "No getting back into the saddle and riding all day, even at a walk. When we leave here, I suggest no more than an hour a day for the first week, and we'll see how you fare. No pushing."

"I'll need to be able to do more than an hour by the time we reach Forge," Aven said. "Have there been any plans made?"

"We haven't had the time, or had you with us to make the plans," Aria answered. "The only discussion was what we talked about in the coach."

"Besides," Owyn added. "We don't have the updated maps yet. I'll do that today, if Aunt Rhexa is available. Del, you want to help me?"

Del cocked his head to the side, then signed, "*If I can. If Skela wants to see me, and spend time with me, then I should do that.*"

"How is Zarai?" Aria asked. "I didn't see her before we came back to the house. Nor did I see Grandmother. They had all gone to sleep before we left."

"Zarai was helping in the healing center this morning, and seems to be no worse for wear," Jehan answered. "Treesi, you saw Lady Meris, didn't you?"

"Briefly," Treesi answered. "She and Afansa were going to go see what help they could be to Rhexa. They left early."

"They probably won't find Auntie for a while," Owyn said, glancing at Aria. She arched a brow at him, and he remembered that he was supposed to keep what they'd seen to himself. "She said last night that she probably wasn't going to get any sleep. Hopefully, she's getting some now." He frowned. "I should go find Mem and see how he is. Auntie said she was putting him to work, too. And that she expected him to fall asleep over the table. I'm not even sure where that table is!"

"In the tent outside the healing center," Othi answered. "And yes, he was. I woke him up, because Skela told me to yell at him." He grinned. "I didn't yell. But I did tell him that Skela said he was being thick as whale blubber, and that none of yesterday was his fault."

Owyn blinked. "How thick is that?" he asked. "Whale blubber, I mean. And what is whale blubber?"

"It's a layer of fat," Aven answered. "On me, it's only an inch or two thick. On a whale? As thick as the length of your arm, from the wrist to the elbow."

"Or more," Othi added.

"Or more." Aven nodded. "It's to help keep warm. It's cold in the deep."

"And it has the added benefit of making you very warm and lovely to snuggle up to," Treesi said. Aven and Othi both looked at her, and she smiled. "Both. Both of you."

"She's not wrong," Aria murmured. "At least, so far as I know." She looked at Aven, who leaned close and rested his forehead against hers. Owyn nodded his agreement, and looked across the table to see that Othi was studying his griddlecakes with a fierce intensity. His face was bright red.

"Right," Owyn said. "We all have things we need to do. We should get on to doing them." He looked around. "Aria is going to tour the city and talk to the people. Aven, you going with her after you swim?"

"I can," Aven said. "It will do me good to walk a bit."

"Not too much," Jehan warned.

"Not too much." Aven smiled and leaned back in his chair. "We should all go down. And then all make the tour. We should stay together. It won't be seen as odd, and you can get the maps tomorrow, Owyn. Let Aunt Rhexa get people settled. Or sleep, depending on where she is at the moment."

Owyn nodded. "All right. Are we done eating? And if we are, who is helping me clean up?"

IN THE DAYLIGHT, THERE was more damage than Aria had thought. There were deep cracks in the pavement, shards of broken glass and pottery and splinters of wood littering the streets. And everywhere there were people — going in and out of buildings, bearing brooms and shovels and tools.

"Good morning, my Heir!" a young woman called from in front of a house.

"Good morning," Aria called back, and walked across the street. "Is there much damage?"

The woman looked back at the house. "Some things fell off of shelves. Some windows cracked because the frames twisted. But it looks like it's still solid enough. Not nearly as bad as it could have been." She smiled. "I'm Viara. It's nice to meet you."

"Viara, it's very nice to meet you," Aria said. "Please, call me Aria. I don't remember you from when we lived in Terraces."

"I came up here from Fire," Viara said. "I used to live in a place called Anvil Lake. My folks are all carpenters. House builders. Rhexa, she asked us to handle some of the inspections "

"Anvil Lake was a good sized town," Owyn said. "A few hours east of Forge."

Viara nodded. "Right. Have you been there?"

Owyn shook his head. "No. I never really spent much time outside Forge before we left to come here last year. I saw it on the maps, though. And we had traders from there who came to the forge to buy tools."

She smiled. "My father used to make that trip. There was one smith in particular that he liked. A man named Fisher—"

"Wait," Owyn blurted. "Are you Vastril's daughter? You look like him! I remember him. He's a good man. Did he make it out?"

"He did. He's around here somewhere." Viara looked at him. "You're too young to be Fisher!"

Owyn burst out laughing. "No! Fisher's my fa. Well, adopted. I'm Owyn."

Viara's eyes narrowed. "I...Fisher had a son named Owyn? I don't remember...oh." She blinked. Then she turned back to Aria. "We're about half done with the inspections. I think we'll be able to have people moved back in by tonight."

Aria nodded. She looked at Viara, then at Owyn. Owyn was wearing a no-expression face, and had turned to look down the street. He was giving a definite impression of ignoring the young woman. Who was now clearly ignoring Owyn. Aria cleared her throat.

"Is there something amiss?" she asked. "You seem to be taking exception to my Fire."

Viara sniffed. "Your Fire is a slave and a whore. I've heard about him—"

"My Fire is a smith, and a Smoke Dancer, and he is a wonderful man, and I will not hear otherwise," Aria interrupted. Someone touched her arm, and she turned to look. Owyn shook his head.

"Aria, it's—"

"You are not going to say it's all right. It is not all right." Aria looked at Viara, fighting to keep her temper in check. "You were chosen by the Mother to stand by my side. There is nothing else that people should need to know about you. There is nothing else that should matter. Certainly not stories, or rumors. You are here. You are mine."

"Aria." Owyn's voice was pitched low. "It's not worth fighting over."

"It is. Because you are worth fighting over," Aven said. He came around Aria and put his hands on Owyn's shoulders. "But some people aren't worth fighting with. Aria, let's go. Skela is waiting for us, and we have work to do."

Viara sniffed. "I should have known better than to expect manners from a fish."

Aria heard Aven's breath catch. She looked at her men, at the shocked looks on both their faces. Then she looked back at Viara. "And I should have thought that someone of Fire blood would know better than to play with it," she said. "Your behavior is an affront to the Mother who dreamed us all." She turned away. "My Water? My Fire? Shall we go?"

Aven nodded, putting his arm around Owyn's shoulders and steering him away, walking down the street toward the tunnel entrance that would take them down to the water. Aria hung back until she was certain they wouldn't hear her, then turned back to Viara. "I should pack if I were you."

"What?" Viara looked startled. "Why?"

Aria looked down the street, seeing that Del had brought Alanar after Aven and Owyn. Treesi and Othi both stood where they had been, but neither of them were looking at Aria or Viara. Aria nodded, then answered, "Because while Owyn is my Fire, he is also Governor Rhexa's nephew. How comfortable will things be here for you, I wonder, when she learns of this?" She turned and walked away, hearing Othi and Treesi fall in behind her as she passed them.

"They all like that in Fire lands?" Othi asked. "Going south is going to be so much fun if they are."

Chapter Thirty-Nine

Owyn took a deep breath, trying to force the tightness in his chest away by sheer force of will.

"I remember Vastril," he said. "I liked Vastril. I can't believe he thought that. And she..."

"Ignore her," Alanar said. He took Owyn's hand. "Her opinion means nothing. And you are so worth fighting for, Wyn." He snorted. "Virrik agrees. So you're outnumbered."

"But she's right," Owyn protested. "I was a slave and a whore. Is that what people will see when they look at Aria? That she has a slave and a whore for her Fire? That she couldn't find someone better?"

"That's what you were," Aven said. "It's not who you were. Or who you are. There is no one better than you are."

"Ven, no one is going to see that." Owyn stopped and turned to look up at Aven. "All they'll see is the street-whore, the freed slave—"

"No one?" Aven repeated. "Am I no one? Is Alanar?" He folded his arms over his chest. "Persis? Rhexa? My parents? Ah...let me think. Steward? Karse?" He paused. "Trey?"

Owyn swallowed. "I—"

"Owyn, there are closed-minded people everywhere," Alanar added. "You can't let their lack of vision blind you to how many other people love and respect you." He grinned. "And yes, I'm aware of the irony of the blind man saying all that."

Owyn couldn't help but smile. He walked over and wrapped his arms around Alanar, burying his face in his husband's chest.

"She don't even know me," he mumbled. "She feels like that, and she don't even know me."

"People do that," Alanar said. "Honestly, we all do that. We believe what we're taught. Remember Treesi and having to be thumped about subhumans? She learned. They'll learn. They'll all learn."

"Yeah, but Viara didn't want to learn." Owyn looked up. "She didn't want to know anything."

"Well, that's because she's an idiot," Aven said, and Owyn burst out laughing.

"You're insulting idiots," Othi said as he, Aria and Treesi joined them. "Just so you know."

"Once we find Rhexa, I want her to know about this so that she can do something," Aria said. "And I will have to do something."

Owyn blinked and looked at Aria, at the spread of her wings, and the look in her eyes.

"Aria, put your wings down," he said softly. "We're not telling Rhexa. And you're not doing anything."

"Owyn, she can't be allowed to keep spreading that poison—"

"And you can't tell people what to think, Aria!" Owyn countered. "You can't change minds by making laws. And punishing people for thinking things you don't like? What's that going to do?"

Aria looked stunned. "But...but she hurt you!"

Owyn shook his head. He let go of Alanar and went to Aria, taking her hands. "More surprised than hurt. I know her father, and he was never like that. But he was always there when Mem was, so maybe he just didn't say anything." He looked around at the others. "Look, I know none of you think like that. I know there are people who don't. But there are people who do, and I don't want to be the weak link in the chain."

Aria took a deep breath, and was about to speak when they heard someone shout, "Owyn! Owyn!"

Owyn jerked and turned, looking up the street to see a man coming toward them. Behind him, a sullen look on her face, was Varia.

"Vastril?" Owyn called. "Is that you?"

"It is." Vastril came closer and held his hand out. "Didn't get out to see the ceremony. Missed seeing you then. Now, look at you! You were a scrawny little alley cat when Fisher first took you in. Now look at this man!"

Owyn grinned and took his hand. "I'd forgotten you used to call me that."

"You looked it. All skin and bones and big eyes. Now...I believe my girl owes you all an apology." He looked over his shoulder at Varia, who looked down. "She didn't know I was in earshot. Didn't know I heard every word. And believe me when I say that we'll be having some words. I don't know where she got these ideas, but I'm not having it." He shook his head and gestured. "Varia, make it handsome."

Varia went ashen, but she stepped forward. She didn't look up. "I apologize," she said. "I...I was very rude. I said things I should not have said—"

"And got caught," Owyn interrupted. "Which is, I think, the only reason you're apologizing. You're not sorry you said it. You're sorry you got caught."

Varia looked up, her eyes wide, and Vastril chuckled.

"You hit that one solid, Owyn," he murmured. "You're right. She's not sorry."

Owyn shrugged. "You making her apologize won't change her mind. Laws made won't change minds. My aunt said that kind of thinking was a weed. You can pull it, but it just keeps coming back. No way to stop it, really." He looked at Varia. "I don't accept your apology. I know you don't mean it. You're not at all sorry. But I want you to think on something. The Mother dreamed all of us. Right?" He waited for Varia to nod. "She created all of us. The way we are. So who the fuck do you think you are, to judge the Mother's children and call them less? Or call them animals?"

Next to him, Aven coughed. "You're more angry about her calling me a fish, aren't you?"

Owyn nodded. "You are not a fish. You never were, and no one should judge you for that." He looked back at Varia. "I've learned a lot this past year. Learned that I'm more than the whore and slave I used to be. The Mother says I am, because she sent this to me." He reached up and touched the Fire gem at his throat. "And...you don't see that. I don't understand why. But I don't need to, either." He turned away from Varia. "My fa is around here somewhere. He'd enjoy seeing you. But...ah...Fisher isn't his real name."

Vastril's brows rose to disappear into his fringe of curly hair. "And what would his name be, truly?"

"Memfis," Aria answered. "Companion to my father, Milon."

Vastril stared at Aria. "Fisher...is Memfis? Truly?"

"Yes," Owyn said. "Oh, and Vastril, when you see him? Just so you know, he was bitten by a Widowmaker snake a few months back. And...they had to take his arm to save his life."

"Mother be merciful," Vastril breathed. "That isn't an easy choice to make, not for a smith of his skill."

"Lose the arm, or lose his life?" Alanar said. "That's not much of a choice."

Owyn took Alanar's hand. "Vastril, I want you to meet someone," he said. "This is my husband, Healer Alanar. Allie, this is Vastril."

Vastril smiled. "The Blind Healer. I've heard your name, sir. You'll be Senior Healer someday."

"Mother willing, that will be a long time from now," Alanar said with a laugh. "A pleasure to meet you."

"Likewise," Vastril said. "Now, Owyn, I'm not ever likely to be this close to the Heir and the Companions ever again. Introduce me proper?"

"SO, WILL IT BE LIKE this the entire time?" Othi asked as they walked back through the tunnels from the docks. "Not knowing if they're going to be for or against us?"

Aven nodded, taking a deep breath. His hip had an odd ache, a strange pull in the muscles, a weird stretch that hadn't been there before everything. It wasn't the tearing pain that had accompanied his change until only a few days ago. He could live with this. And the feeling as the water had embraced him, enveloped him? Welcomed him home?

He could definitely live with that.

Aven dragged his mind back to Othi's question. "You've been thinking about this since we went down?" he asked.

Othi shrugged one shoulder. "Deep water for deep thoughts. Things are more complicated on land, aren't they?"

"I've been saying that for a year," Aven grinned. He looked ahead of them. He could see Owyn in the lead, flanked by Alanar and Del. Behind them, closest to Aven and Othi, were Aria and Treesi. "It's worth it, though."

Othi nodded. "When you were down below, did you check on Skela? I saw you with him."

"I did," Aven answered. "And I think his decision to stay in Terraces until he can be taken back to the Palace and the tribe is a good one. It's the best for him."

"Do you think he'll still be alive when we get back?" Othi asked quietly. "Will we see him again?"

"I wish I could tell you that, Othi," Aven answered. "He's strong for such an old man, but...well, having his heart fail that way does damage to the body. And he's going back to the Palace, where there's no healer." He paused. "I wish he'd stay in Terraces, with my Grandmother, but then he wouldn't even have the tribe. He'd be alone."

"Yeah, there's no good choice there," Othi said. He sighed. "Things are too complicated. I don't like complicated. I like simple."

"We all like simple," Aven agreed. "But simple doesn't seem to like us."

"Truth!" Owyn called over his shoulder.

"You can hear me up there?" Aven called back.

"You're thinking really loudly," Owyn answered. "Which, since it's distracting? I'm not complaining. Is this tunnel longer than it was when we went down?"

"We're almost out," Aria said. "Look, there's the door."

They emerged from the tunnel into one of the small parks that were scattered throughout Terraces. Owyn slumped onto one of the covered benches and tipped his head back, taking a deep breath, then letting it all out in an explosive burst.

"We need to go," he said, his quiet voice barely carrying. "We need to get on the road."

"Owyn?" Aria sat down next to him. "Why? What is it?" She looked up as Aven and the others crowded around the bench. "I thought we'd have more time here."

"That's just it," Owyn said. He frowned. "I...I don't think this is a vision. It might be. Or it's just a feeling. But...we need to get moving." He paused. Frowned. "Father Adavar is losing patience.

That's what happened yesterday. We're running out of time to put things right."

"Father Adavar rolled in his sleep," Othi said. "That's what tremors are. Father Adavar rolling in his sleep."

"That's just it. Are we sure he's still asleep?" Owyn asked in response. "Or is he waking? And...what happens when he wakes all the way up and sees what's happening?"

Aria folded her hands over her stomach, drawing her wings in as she sat silently for a moment. Then she looked up.

"I want everyone in Council," she said, her voice firm. "Now. Owyn, come back to the house with me. Everyone else...collect who you can, bring them back to the house as soon as you can. If they cannot come immediately, tell them that we will proceed without them, and come back to the house." She stood up, and held her hand out to Owyn. "You look as if you're going to fall down. We'll go back, and you will eat something."

"Aria, I'm fine," Owyn protested. He stood up and swayed, and Del caught him before he fell.

"You're fine," Aven repeated, laughing. He rested his hand on Owyn's shoulder. "Are you sure you haven't been having heart visions again? You're unbalanced."

Owyn shrugged, closing his eyes. "I...maybe? Might explain why I'm feeling like this. Like we need to go now."

Aven nodded. "Del, Alanar, you go back with them. Allie, you stay with Aria and Owyn. Del, you can go find Steward, Rhexa and Karse after. And if you see Lady Meris, tell her, too. And Memfis." Del nodded and took Owyn's hand. Alanar took the other hand, and they started walking up the street toward the healing center. Aven looked around. "Treesi, you and Othi go after my fa and grandmother. I'm going back down for my mother."

OWYN SAT DOWN AT THE kitchen table and watched as Aria opened the firebox on the stove. "I can do that," he said.

"You can sit," Aria answered. She picked up the poker, stirred up the coals, and laid a fire. "How are you feeling?"

"Weird. I...I can't tell what this is. What I'm seeing but not seeing."

Alanar sat down across from him. "What do you want to eat?" he asked.

"Just...something quick. There's seed bread in the breadbox. And I think there's hard cheese. And nuts. There are nuts."

"I'll get them," Aria said. She filled a kettle and set it onto the cooktop, then went to the cabinets and started filling plates. As she put one down in front of Owyn, they heard Steward's voice.

"Owyn? Aria?"

"In the kitchen!" Aria called. A moment later, Steward came in, followed by Rhexa. Both of them were still wearing their clothes from the day before, and neither looked as though they had slept.

"What's happened?" Steward asked. "What's wrong?"

"Owyn's having a vision, we think. But it's stuck."

"Stuck?" Owyn looked at his husband, who shrugged.

"Do you have a better way to describe it?" he asked. "You're getting dribbles, nothing of any import other than feelings. It's stuck."

Owyn frowned. "You get to tell Mem that one," he said. "That's...that's an interesting way of looking at it."

"And you're sick again?" Rhexa asked. She rested her cool hand on his forehead. "Steward told me you were getting so sick—"

"He shouldn't have worried you!" Owyn protested.

"He very well should have!" Rhexa snapped back. "I was very close to getting on the ship and coming to take care of you!"

"Auntie..." Owyn smiled. "Thank you. That...that means a lot."

She kissed his forehead. "You're welcome. Now, hold out your hands."

Owyn did, and Rhexa reached into her skirt pocket and pulled out a small ball of flame-colored fur.

"Trinket!" Owyn laughed and ran his fingertip over the fire-mouse's fur. "How has she been?"

"Good company," Rhexa answered. "She's a marvelous sounding board when I have a problem that needs answering. I tell her all about it, and that helps me find the answer."

"She used to listen to me learning to read," Owyn said. "So she's good at that sort of thing." He picked up a nut from the plate that Aria had put in front of him, offering it to the mouse. "I'm glad she's taking care of you, Auntie."

"We take care of each other. And now, we're taking care of you."

"Del went on to wake Memfis, then he's going after Karse," Steward said. "What help can I be?"

"I'm making tea," Aria said. "We'll want that ready for when everyone gets here. Then, we will talk." She looked around. "We should go to the front room."

As they reached the front room and Owyn sat back down, there was a knock on the door. Del came in first, followed by Memfis, Meris and Afansa.

"What's wrong?" Memfis asked. "Karse is coming. He didn't think you wanted the boys in this meeting, so he's taking them to Leesam so they can drill with the guard. Del said that Owyn had another vision?"

"Part of one," Owyn answered. "Just the feelings. Allie says I have a vision that's stuck."

"That's an interesting way of describing it," Meris said. She sat next to Owyn, smiling when she saw the fire-mouse in his hand. "Is that Trinket?"

"Aunt Rhexa brought her over for a visit," Owyn said.

Meris held out her hand. Owyn slipped his free hand into hers, and closed his eyes. He heard the door open, but ignored the voices he heard, trying to concentrate on what he was feeling.

"Can you tell anything?" he asked.

"Not much," Meris said after a moment. "There's an impression...a taste...There's so much urgency."

"Yeah, that's it," Owyn agreed. He opened his eyes to a much more crowded room. Karse and Jehan and Aleia, Aven and Treesi and Othi. "It's...we need to go now. As soon as we can. We need to be back on the road."

"And you have no idea why?" Karse asked. "Not that I doubt you, Owyn. I know you too well for that. But a reason would be nice."

Owyn shook his head. "I don't know. Not yet. But...we're all here. Let me tell you what I saw yesterday."

The people shuffled around, taking seats, all of them looking at Owyn. He took a deep breath and let it out, then nodded.

"The tremor yesterday...wasn't just a tremor. It was a warning. Risha...she don't have anyone to hurt right now. She's lost her access to the Water tribes, and the Air folks she can reach, they don't have wings. She has no one to experiment on. So she's hurting Milon and Trey." Owyn heard his father moan softly, and didn't dare look. He couldn't. If he did, he wouldn't be able to finish. "Milon told me the first time I danced, before the tremor, that I wasn't to go back. That he wanted me to tell all of you that he was dead. And after the tremor, I went and danced again. And I projected, I was there. I was north, where she's hiding them. I saw Milon. Talked to him, and he told me what caused the tremor." He frowned. "Jehan, when someone gets the ague, really bad, it can damage their heart, can't it?"

Jehan stared at him, his face going pale. "I...yes. And Milon had the ague, badly enough that they brought in Risha. We know that from the journals."

Aven coughed. "Do you think she botched the healing?" he asked. "She must have."

"Either that, or she got there too late to fully heal him," Alanar added. "Or she just wasn't strong enough."

"Don't matter which," Owyn said, stopping the chatter before it overtook the room. "What matters is that Milon has a weak heart now. And what she's doing to him...yeah, he wouldn't tell me what. He just told me that it pushes him to the point where his heart will stop. And she brings him back so she can keep doing it." He looked around, saw the horror he had been feeling since the day before reflected on the faces around him. "And if she keeps doing it—"

"She'll reach a point where she can't bring him back," Memfis said softly. "Where are they?"

Owyn shook his head. "Don't know. I have a guess, based on how fast carts move, and the direction we think they went, but I couldn't see out when I was there. And... I don't think Milon can see. At all. It's always dark when I talk to him, but it weren't that dark when I was there. I... I don't know. And...." He stopped, but not soon enough.

"And what?" Karse demanded. "What about Trey?"

"I don't know," Owyn answered. "I asked...and Milon told me not to look for him. He...he said that Trey tried to put himself between him and Risha...and she broke him for it."

Karse went quiet. Still. He closed his eyes for a moment, then turned to Memfis. "So...we going north? We can stop at the Palace, get more men. We can find this bitch and end this in a month."

"What about the Progress?" Steward asked. "We can't stop the Progress, and we can't turn back."

"I'm not saying we have to stop, or turn back. I'm saying I go. Maybe Memfis goes with me. The Progress goes on—"

"Without your protection," Aven interrupted. "Going into Fire lands where there are people who don't even think Aria is human, and with someone trying to kill Owyn still hiding in plain sight. Are you going to turn away from your responsibility to the Heir?"

Karse snorted. "First, you're not the one to talk, Aven," he snapped. "How long were you gone again? Second, I had a responsibility to Trey before I ever had a responsibility to the Heir. He's my man. I can't just leave him, not knowing he's hurt and alone out there. You don't need me—"

Four voices spoke as one, as all the Smoke Dancers announced, "You are the Protector of Now. You are needed."

Owyn coughed and looked at the other Smoke Dancers. "I...the fuck was that?"

"That was exceedingly odd," Aria murmured. "I wasn't going to speak, but my voice had other ideas."

Karse looked at each of them in turn, stopping at Meris. "Lady Meris?"

"I think you've just been given your orders, Captain," Meris said. "By a higher authority than the Heir or the Firstborn." She swallowed. "Steward, is there something to drink?"

"I'll go fetch the tea," Steward answered. He left the room, and Rhexa followed him.

"So...I'm being given my marching orders," Karse said. "Can one of you please tell me he'll be at the end of this? That I'll have my Trey back?" He sank into a chair. "Give me that much hope?"

Owyn swallowed. "I could—"

"No." Aria turned toward him. "You are not going to make yourself sick again. Someone else can seek a vision on this. You're already making yourself ill."

"I just...why won't this come out?" Owyn shook his head. "I don't like feeling like this!" He looked up sharply. "Granna, will I be able to see other things? Or is this like a plug?"

"It'll pass," Memfis said. "Sometimes this happens with a big vision, one that you're not ready to see yet. You got it too soon. It'll pass." He paused, then turned to Karse. "Come with me to the lowest terrace. I'll dance," he said. "The Mother won't let me see Milon, but maybe I'll be able to see Trey."

"I rather think that you won't see much," Meris said. "This...this is feeling very much like the Prophecy of the Dove. I wonder how many other Smoke Dancers said those words?"

"If she doesn't show him anything, at least we'll have tried," Karse said. He stood back up. "So we go and Memfis dances. And maybe we learn something. Then what?"

"We leave," Aria said. "As soon as we can. We follow Axia's Way. We follow the lore. And we find them."

Don't miss out!

Visit the website below and you can sign up to receive emails whenever Elizabeth Schechter publishes a new book. There's no charge and no obligation.

https://books2read.com/r/B-A-KGBH-GAUBC

BOOKS 2 READ

Connecting independent readers to independent writers.

Also by Elizabeth Schechter

Heir to the Firstborn
Worlds Begin
Written in Water
Forged in Fire
Bones of Earth
Wings of Air
Visions in Smoke

Rebel Mage
Counsel of the Wicked
Haven's Fall
Where Home Lies

Swords of Charlemagne
Hidden Things
The Lady and the Sword
Ashes and Light
Table of Stone
Swords of Charlemagne: The Complete Series

Standalone
The Rape of Persephone
Fools Rush In
Her Captive
To Market
Infernal Machine
Chains of Light

Watch for more at elizabethschechterwrites.com.

About the Author

Elizabeth Schechter has been called one of the top erotica and alternative sexuality writers in the world. Her writing credits include the award-winning steampunk erotic romance *House of Sable Locks*, the Celtic fantasy *Princes of Air*, and the dystopian fantasy *Rebel Mage* trilogy. Her shorter work has appeared in anthologies edited by D.L King (*Carnal Machines*), Laura Antoniou (*No Safewords*), and Cecilia Tan (*Jingle Balls*; *Like a Prince*).

With *Written in Water*, the first in the *Heir to the Firstborn* series, Elizabeth is exploring new ground, with her first new adult romance that was written entirely in real time on Patreon.

She was born in New York at some point in the past. She is officially old enough to know better, but refuses to grow up. She lives in Central Florida with her husband and son.

Elizabeth can be found online at http://elizabethschechterwrites.com, or on Facebook at https://www.facebook.com/Elizabeth.A.Schechter. You can also find her on Patreon, at https://www.patreon.com/EASchechter.

Subscribe to Elizabeth's newsletter at https://www.subscribepage.com/k4u7k2

Read more at elizabethschechterwrites.com.

www.ingramcontent.com/pod-product-compliance
Lightning Source LLC
Chambersburg PA
CBHW020249030726
47499CB00001B/122